HUNT *for* YOU
Hide & Seek: Book 1
By Aimee Lynn

All characters appearing in this work are fictitious. Any resemblance to real persons, living or dead, is purely coincidental.

Hunt for You: Hide & Seek Series © 2024 Aimee Lynn

All rights reserved. No part of this book may be reproduced or transmitted in any form or by any means, electronic, mechanical, photocopying, recording, or otherwise, without prior written permission from the author. If you would like to use material from this book (other than for review purposes), write to authoraimeel@gmail.com.

First edition October 2024

Cover design by the author who owns copyright on the image. Do not use or reproduce without permission.

For Alan

*Thank you for loving my hot,
even in the presence of my crazy.*

IMPORTANT NOTE FROM THE AUTHOR:

This book contains graphic depictions of many violent and sexual situations in a *fictional* relationship.

It is not, in any way, intended to accurately represent practices that are commonly used in Dominant/submissive relationships in the real world. (First and foremost, Dominants generally don't go around agreeing—or wanting—to kill people.)

If you are new to Dom/sub relationships, or to primal play, please be aware: I have taken liberties with generally agreed practices to create a set up that suits my characters and their unique situations and backstories. What you find between these pages is *not* indicative of what might be found in real life.

If you live these lifestyles, please rest assured: Any deviations from real life common practices are not oversight, but intentional choices for this story.

Bridget is *not* a submissive, or a switch. She is a broken young woman with misguided ideas about how to take control of her own destiny. She has sought a very particular kind of experience, and thinks she found what she needs in Cain.

Cain's relationship with her is *not* representative even of the relationships his character has had with submissives in the past. Let alone a real-life primal Dom, or dominant behavior.

If you live these lifestyles, or know people who do, you will observe "gaps" in their story, especially around contracts/agreements and boundary setting. Those gaps are because they have not entered this relationship with the usual rules in place. Quite the opposite, Bridget's entire goal was to ensure there *were no rules.* I'll let you read to see how Cain is forced to deal with that (insert laughing emoji here.)

I hope you enjoy their story. I hope by the end you will understand why Bridget would request the arrangement that she has. And why Cain would agree to it. But regardless, I hope you will simply enjoy the story for what it is, and their interactions for what their characters bring, and not take it as intending to be instructional.

This is a story, not a textbook.

In fact, I'd strongly advise *against* following Bridget anywhere in real life. (I love her dearly, but my girl has some serious issues.)

With that said, I hope you'll sit back and enjoy reading it as much as I enjoyed writing it.

See you on the other side!

Aimee

1. Show Me in the Dark

~ *BRIDGET* ~

SYSTEM NOTE: CHAT ENCRYPTED END-TO-END. ENSURE ALL ACCOUNTS ARE LOGGED OFF BEFORE DISCONNECTING.

SleepingBeast: Why would you even consider this?

DeadGirlWalking: Long story short: Everyone in my family dies young. Cancer and heart attacks mostly. Somehow, I hit the genetic lottery, and got the genome markers for both.

DeadGirlWalking: I am almost thirty years old. My body is a literal ticking time-bomb. And my life is hell.

DeadGirlWalking: Let me rephrase that. My *non*-life is hell: No drinking. No drugs. No fatty foods. No elevated heart-rate (so, no sex, or any other form of extra-curricular fun. I can't even watch a scary movie). Apparently, if I do absolutely nothing, I will probably get to do it for a pretty long time. Except, maybe not. Maybe I'm sitting calmly in the café reading a very unexciting book when I twitch once and fall face-first into my frappucino.

DeadGirlWalking: I am *done* living in fear of what is inevitable. I need to feel alive again.

SleepingBeast: You think me murdering you is going to make you feel alive?

DeadGirlWalking: No, I think knowing that my day is coming soon will make life a lot more interesting until it does. And then when it finally does, I won't have to think about it anymore at all.

SleepingBeast: That's dark.

DeadGirlWalking: You're homicide-for-hire and you're calling *me* dark?

SleepingBeast: Touche.

SleepingBeast: Though, for the record, I'm not for hire. You won't pay me a cent. And I'm not homicidal. I classify my services as *assisted suicide adjacent.*

DeadGirlWalking: Did you hear that? It was my snort of skeptical derision. You get off on killing people. Pretty sure that makes you homicidal. Or is there another name for it if it's a kink?

DeadGirlWalking: Found it. Apparently you're a Erotophonophiliac (Erotophonophilian?) God, what a mouthful.

DeadGirlWalking: THAT'S WHAT SHE SAID.

SleepingBeast: Nope. I get off on the hunt.

DeadGirlWalking: Such a giver. But, let's be clear. I'm no sub. I'm in this for the hunt. I want to run for my life, and lose.

SleepingBeast: We're clear. I am a Dom. But I'm happy to provide additional services until it's my turn to die.

DeadGirlWalking: So, will you also be finding some dude on the dark web to knock you off when that time comes?

SleepingBeast: I expect to take my last breath gasping, laying in a pool of my own blood because the FBI finally caught up with me.

DeadGirlWalking: Suicide by cop?

SleepingBeast: More like government sanctioned murder.

DeadGirlWalking: Geez, and you call me dark.

SleepingBeast: No… I call you prey.

DeadGirlWalking: Holy shit. I just got goosebumps. So I guess that means we're doing this?

DeadGirlWalking: Beast?

SleepingBeast: Go back to your non-life, D. Sweet dreams.

DeadGirlWalking: Wait, are you coming for me or not? Because if you aren't, I need to find another whacko.

SleepingBeast: Goodnight D.

DeadGirlWalking: Just answer the question. Are you, or are you not, going to hunt me down to primal-fuck me, then kill me?

DeadGirlWalking: TELL ME.

DeadGirlWalking: Beast?

DeadGirlWalking: For fuck's sake.

DeadGirlWalking: This better be part of the game, otherwise I'm reporting you to the Manager. Call me a dark-web Karen.

DeadGirlWalking: Seriously, I need confirmation here. You said this could take weeks—months? I can't go through another Christmas alone because you got bashful. If you aren't coming I need to find someone else.

DeadGirlWalking: I'm doing this with you or without you. You get that, right?

DeadGirlWalking: Would you just answer the fucking question?

DeadGirlWalking: This brings a whole new meaning to "the strong, silent type."

DeadGirlWalking: Fucker. Or should it be *non*-fucker?

DeadGirlWalking: Just tell me.

DeadGirlWalking: Is this one of those moments when a guy thinks what he's doing is foreplay, but it's not? Because it's not. Just in case you were wondering. I'm being fucked right now. And not in the fun way.

DeadGirlWalking: Beast?

DeadGirlWalking: Fine. I guess I'll just wait and see. But I'm keeping my options open. If another dude shoots his shot (literally) and beats you to it, that's going to be your fault for not making your intentions clear.

DeadGirlWalking: Should have put a ring on it. Just sayin'.

SleepingBeast: Stop whining. We'll meet.

DeadGirlWalking: Thank God. How soon?

DeadGirlWalking: Growl once for "this week" and twice for "this calendar month."

SleepingBeast: Goodnight, D.

SleepingBeast: Sleep while you can.

DeadGirlWalking: Wait! Don't you need my address or number or something?

[SleepingBeast has left the chat.]

I pushed away from my desk, heart racing so fast I wondered if I was going to pass out. My vision was tunneling.

Holy shit, this was really happening.

Finally.

It was strange blinking back to my real life and my real body. Every time I was online I kind of got lost in the virtual world.

My psychiatrist called it *escapism*.

I called it relief from *existential crisis and the utter fucking tedium of this world.*

Tedium? Not for much longer. Not if Beast was really who I thought he was.

Unable to resist, I clicked through to the screenshots I'd kept of his response to my post in the definitely *not* government sanctioned forum called Weirdos Whackos and Freaks Playground.

I'd been ranting that night, drunk and despairing. The responses had mostly fallen into two categories: Those who were frantic to help me feel better, and those who hoped I would kill myself and were willing to incentivize me.

Not him, though.

He had been a man of few words, right from the start.

I know how to make you feel alive. Then a link.

That was it. I'd assumed he was some pervert hoping to find a desperate woman who'd fall into bed with anything that pretended to care. Or maybe he just wanted to find a woman period and it didn't matter what she thought about it.

I was open to either scenario.

His profile picture was a muscular guy, standing with his feet shoulder width apart and his hands at his sides, kinda clawed, like he was ready to fight, silhouetted by glowing flames.

I would have bet real money he was ex-military. Or he'd dedicated himself to some kind of organized training.

He was clearly aggressive. Strong. Probably abusive.

Hyper-intelligent. Extremely self-reliant. Definitely a loner. But decent social skills. All the better to lure in vulnerable women.

The only reason I'd clicked the link was because I didn't give two shits if he hacked me. I wanted to see if there were any clues to whether I was right.

I'd expected to find his amateur pornography—why did men always believe that all it took was a visual of them strangling their own purple-headed wonder worms to make a woman shiver?

I'd figured there was an outside chance he ran a sex club, or some other IRL experience he was selling to the kind of people who looked for things on the fringes. As in, me.

But the link only led to a profile page. That was my first surprise.

Cain.
Experienced primal dom.
Seeking real life prey.

I'd been immediately intrigued. And then I talked to him and got consumed. And then obsessed.

And then… eventually we got here.

Sighing as the adrenaline in my veins slowly faded, I closed all the windows on the screen and began to shut the computer down, but my hands were shaking so badly from the rush that I kept accidentally using the wrong key commands. I had to make myself slow down and focus. But when the laptop finally whirred to silence and I was left sitting in the silent blackness, I still didn't move away from the desk.

I could see the light-glare of the words from my screen across my retinas in the dark.

Seeking real life prey.

And he wasn't bluffing. I'd done my homework.

I had to take a deep breath to calm the new wave of flutters in my stomach. It took a moment to put a name to what I was feeling because it had been so long...

I was *giddy.*

Cain, AKA: SleepingBeast, a primal Dom, probable serial killer, and bona-fide *whacko* had taken my case. I was now officially *prey.* The game of cat and mouse was about to begin. I wouldn't know when, or how. But at some point soon, our paths would cross. He would make certain they did. And if he liked what he saw when he found me, that moment would spark a hunt that might last weeks, or even months.

He'd warned me that he would toy with me. That thought brought a whole new rush of adrenaline, and a hum between my thighs. I was counting on it.

I gave a weird, cackling laugh that sounded way too loud in my dark little closet of an office.

Cain was coming for me.

Life just got very, very interesting.

Thank God.

2. The Scent of You

~ BRIDGET ~

The next morning I woke up to the usual hollow emptiness in my chest—until I remembered what had happened the night before and adrenaline began to thread through my system, making me shiver.

I knew it was unlikely, but I couldn't resist logging on to the dark web forum *just in case* he'd messaged again, or was giving me some clue of when or how he might show up.

But of course, there was nothing.

Then I decided to check my email because I hadn't done that for a couple days, and it was time for my monthly payment.

I immediately regretted it.

FROM: Asshole (Jeremy Haines)
TO: Bridget
SUBJECT: You agreed to the rules

Ugh. I hovered the mouse over the email for a moment, considering opening it. But the truth was, I knew what it was about, and I didn't want to think about that yet.

Muttering a curse under my breath, I marked the email as "read" knowing he'd get a notification of that. It would hold him off for a time.

Jeremy was an asshole, but a fairly patient one. He believed in letting people think about stuff. If he thought I'd read it, he'd give me a couple days before he'd decide he needed to up the stakes. And by then I might feel differently.

Or I might be dead.

I giggled as my skin goosebumped and sparkled and my heart raced. But then I put Jeremy out of my mind, closed out my email, made sure my computer was logged out of everything before disconnecting the VPN and turning it all off.

Looking at that blank screen made my skin itch, so I slapped the lid of the laptop down and pushed out of the chair.

I'd go to the gym. Then at least I'd feel shaky from tiredness instead of anxiety.

I also smiled at the idea that Cain might already be coming after me. And when he found me at the gym he'd be pissed. *I thought you weren't supposed to raise your heartrate?*

Shouldn't and *wouldn't* were two different things.

Some things were worth the risk. Namely, my sanity.

I liked living on the edge.

So I dressed quickly, shoved my black hair up into a ponytail that, because it was cut in a blunt bob, was really just a sticky-uppy top-tie that made me look about six years old, but kept most of my hair off my neck, then jumped in the car, watching the rearview eagerly for any sign of a car following me as I drove the fifteen mile route to the only decent gym in the area.

A heavenly scent assaulted me the minute I walked into the actual gym, but there were already dozens of people there, and lots more than half of them were men. I considered taking a quick circuit of the room and seeing who'd picked the gorgeous cologne, maybe asking him what it was. But he'd think I was hitting on him, so I walked over to the weights praying that whoever he was, he'd walk past at some point and maybe he wouldn't be a dickhead. He smelled good enough to lick.

In today's world there wasn't enough licking outside of preschool in anyone's life, in my opinion.

Then I was at my first machine, and I had to pretend I was totally casual about messing with the hardware on my body. At least I could just slip my arms inside the big hoodie I wore and do it out of sight. Let them think I was messing with my bra straps or whatever.

As a concession to the doctors, and because they really wouldn't let me do *anything* if I didn't have some kind of observation, I wore a heart monitor while I worked out, or any time I thought I'd be walking more than a mile. Because my resting heartrate was sixty-five, I wasn't allowed to let my working heart rate exceed one hundred or the fucking monitor would start screaming louder than a church lady at an R-rated movie, and everyone at the gym would look at me.

It was a royal pain in my ass, because it meant that between sets on the weights I had to sit there like an idiot while it lowered—which inevitably invited *comments* from the gym monkeys who thought I was a princess who didn't want to break a sweat.

"You need a towel over there, sweetheart? I'd be happy to come wipe you down."

Fuck around and find out, douchebag.

"I'm good." I didn't even make eye-contact. There was no point. I might actually topple him off his too-high center of gravity with the force of my disdain.

When I'd done all my sets, I went to the bank of cardio machines and *almost* jumped on the stair-stepper. But that really would get my heart rate up too fast. And besides, those machines had their back to the room and the pitbull was still glancing my way once in a while. I didn't want him leering at my ass.

So I stepped up to my usual treadmill. But just as I was turning the machine on, I took a quick glance out the big window to the street three levels below in case there was any sign of a dark, probably homicidal maniac following me.

My heart rate jumped high enough for the monitor to give a faint beep when I saw a guy leaning in a doorway across the road, smoking a vape. He had hair as black as mine, shaved on the sides and long enough to fall into his eyes on top. He was pierced through every visible orifice and protrusion, and he was *strong*. Athletic and muscular without the ridiculous bulk of the body builders in here. *That* was a body that had been honed for moving and dominating, not just to impress the eye.

He was frowning at the doors into the gym and for a moment I stopped breathing and my heart rate jumped up another notch. But then another guy trotted up to him and they kissed briefly, then disappeared into the apartment building.

Oh well, maybe not.

My heart monitor gave one more warning beep before I snapped out of the thrill-trance, took two or three deep, controlled breaths, then turned on the machine and started a slow jog that I could sustain for an hour at a heart rate of ninety-five. I wouldn't though. Just five miles today. I needed to preserve *some* energy, just in case Cain really did show up.

My heart monitor peeped at me again, but I was smiling that time.

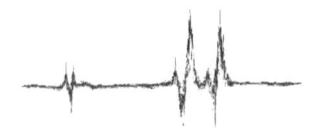

~ *CAIN* ~

She was more aware of her surroundings than I would have anticipated, but pretty soon it became clear why.

Every time she turned her back in this room, the fuckers that were supposed to be here working out, but had really come here to see and be seen, were following her with their eyes, murmuring to each other—slapping chests and snorting as they said things that I would cut their tongues out for actually speaking if I got the chance.

And yet, a part of me understood the allure. One particular part of my anatomy, understood a great deal. And that was *not* good.

I had learned years ago that any kind of emotional, or sexual attachment beyond the hunt itself not only complicated the game, but threatened *my* safety. It influenced my objectivity.

For that reason, I'd almost left the moment she walked in, turned my back and never contacted her again. Because the first time I clapped eyes on her it was like the air in the room shifted.

I'd positioned myself strategically behind a few weight machines so I could see her, but wouldn't be easily seen myself. I knew roughly what she looked like, but it still punched me in the solar plexus when she actually showed up.

I almost laughed at her raven-black hair sticking straight up on top of her head, like a five-year-old's. Especially since she'd hidden the rest of her trim body in a thick, black hoodie that would have been big enough for me—was it her boyfriend's? Did he know what she was doing? Who she was talking to at night while he slept?

Or maybe he was behind this?

The hair on the back of my neck stood up. Maybe it was something they did together? It wouldn't be the first couple I'd met that were into dark shit together. And she wouldn't be the first woman who pretended to be single and was actually looking for someone to help her make it a reality.

But as she strode into the gym with a little bag over her shoulder, swimming in that massive hoodie, her skin-tight shorts hugging only the top half of her tight thighs, my entire body went still and my heart began to thud against my ribs.

Despite the fact that she'd done everything she could to hide it—she was *stunning.* When she turned her head to look through the glass doors behind her, her eyes were so big and penetratingly bright, for a second I stopped breathing.

The handful of photos I'd seen online didn't do her justice *at all*. They were all from college, before she was really a woman.

Her hair was shorter and a lot more severe now. And her skin, while unblemished except for what appeared to be a scar on her forehead, looked *too* pale. Like she didn't get enough sun. Which was probably true, considering what she'd told me about her health issues. Yet, not only was she a member here at the gym, I'd found an old archive clipping from her childhood hometown in which the local newspaper showed her and a dozen other high school students who'd received belt promotions at their local Karate dojo over a decade ago.

She definitely moved like someone who knew her own body. But then, a lot of women did—especially when they knew men were going to be looking at them. It didn't necessarily mean she'd kept up with her training.

I was both fascinated, and frustrated.

Records of her had been easy to find after she was ten years old, which was about the age most people started leaving a trail online. But while I could dig up school records and sports teams and even what appeared to be a college degree earned online, it was like she had only existed in the most shallow ways.

No social media at all, not even old ones. Not even an old *Facebook* account that uneducated parents might have suggested and then monitored while she was in high school. Which was shocking in this day and age.

And no work history, which made zero sense.

It was like she'd dropped onto the planet at the age of ten, then disappeared again as soon as she got her degree, six or seven years ago. No birth certificate that I could find, definitely no marriages. She had to have a legal name and identity I was, as yet, unaware of.

That was okay. I liked a challenge. A lot.

And, of course, I was still working on the darker side of her online life. I knew there'd be a real harvest there. It was a helluva lot harder to pin down, though. I'd been stalking her profile in the dark web forum we shared since the day we *met*, but it didn't save history. Public chats only stayed visible for twenty-four hours, then were wiped. So except for our direct messages, and the homework I'd done following her in real time both online and in person, she was an enigma.

Fucking fascinating.

And that was a problem.

I felt the clench of arousal low in my belly when she sat down on the bench to do some curls and opened her knees, and my brain immediately conjured *everything* under those shorts.

Or tried to, at least. There were too many questions still unanswered.

My heart was beating faster, which it always did when I was stalking prey. But she shouldn't have affected me so deeply yet, because I hadn't actually decided whether to take her or not.

This was what I affectionately called the *interview* stage: Seeing whether she was realistic about what she wanted—and just how much she was lying to me. Because everyone lied some. The question was whether they did it to protect themselves from *everyone*, or just to misdirect me.

Was she a desperate woman looking for that heady rush that only danger could bring?

Or was she a manipulative bitch getting her kicks out of toying with a man online?

I didn't know yet. That wouldn't have been a problem—I was a patient man. But the way my soul sucked towards her the moment she showed up, and the resistance I now felt in my skin the second I started thinking about leaving, definitely was.

She was my *type*.

I couldn't decide if that would make this whole fucking game easier, or harder. And *that* was a problem. Because she wanted me to kill her.

I needed my head clear. I needed to be decisive. I needed to be in control of every step of this journey.

I didn't need to keep wondering what she looked like under that hoodie.

Nope.

Nope, nope, *nope.*

Shaking my head and taking hold of my balls—metaphorically—I let the weights I'd been using clank back to earth and pushed off the machine.

It was time to go. She wasn't right. Or rather, she was *too* right. I wasn't going to be able to disconnect from this one and that made the whole endeavor way too dangerous for *me.*

I'd already packed my stuff up and slung my backpack over my shoulder and was wiping my forehead with the little towel, looking for the route through the machines that would take me to the door without crossing her path, or being obvious about avoiding her, intending to go home, block her profile, and never speak with her again—even if that thought did give me a little pang. But as I was weaving between machines and drinking from my waterbottle, keeping my eyes off of her and my head slightly turned away, one of the gym bums who was here to build useless muscle for the sake of it, made a sly comment to her and her head jerked up.

It was reflex, when someone moved that quickly, to check and see where the danger came from.

"I'm good," was all she said. She didn't even look the guy in the eye. But that meant that her face was turned a little towards me and even though she didn't look at me either, I could see her clearly.

See the empty, hollow darkness behind those startling eyes.

I sucked in a breath and my step faltered. And right then I knew I was fucked. Because that was the moment I started planning how to intercept her in broad daylight without her seeing my face.

It was my favorite tease. And the way I introduced myself to prey whenever possible.

And I shouldn't have been planning that for her.

But damn... I *wanted* to see light behind those eyes. Even if it was only the spark of survival fear.

So I kept moving, and I left without looking back. But I didn't leave the property—just that room.

I had a plan in place for her before she finished her workout and trotted out to her car, looking over her shoulder and in every direction.

Looking for *me.*

I smiled.

Good girl.

3. See You Soon

~ *BRIDGET* ~

I dropped into the driver's seat in my car considering whether or not to stop for coffee on the way home when that heavenly smell washed over me and my entire body thrilled.

I gasped, tensing, beginning to turn just as a thick, man-hand whipped out from behind my seat and clapped over my mouth and pulled my head back against the headrest. I struggled for a second, kicking against the floor of the car, fingers clawing into that hand as I screamed behind it, but then that scent got stronger and warm, and a smooth cheek brushed my jaw at the same time a very deep, gravely male voice whispered.

"I told you I'd see you soon."

I froze, eyes wide, my breath tearing audibly in and out of my nose.

"Just breathe," he said, and I could *hear* the smile in his tone. But my pulse was so loud in my ears it made it hard to hear him.

I tried to take in every detail I could—the scent, the size of his hand over my mouth, the callouses on his palms, the unique timbre of his voice. My senses were heightened, but focus was impossible, my heart racing so fast I was glad I'd already taken the monitor off because the doctors would have *flipped.* Lights sparkled at the edge of my vision.

"*Relax, Bridget.* I'm not going to hurt you—I just wanted to introduce myself."

He knew my real name already?

I stopped trying to claw his hand off my face and after a few heaving breaths through my nose, made myself drop my hands to my lap, gripping the hem of the hoodie instead, but my heart was still going a mile a minute, and my panting was loud in the car.

I felt something brush the side of my head and realized he'd buried his nose in my hair and was inhaling deeply. I didn't know whether to blush or fistpump.

"Are you calm enough to remember what I'm about to tell you?" he rasped a minute later.

I nodded. My breath was still coming in deep pants and my hands had started to shake, but I was gripping the hoodie and praying he wouldn't notice that.

"Very good." He was still whispering, still keeping his voice in a gravel barely above the volume of my pulse so that his actual voice was masked. "We're going to have a few rules. Blink once to tell me you understand what I'm saying."

I blinked hard, squeezing my eyes shut for a second then opening them again to stare through the windshield at the blank, cinderblock wall of the gym, feeling both idiotic and *ecstatic* that I'd parked back here. But as he continued to speak, I couldn't help smiling behind his hand. The initial panic was quickly being replaced by a *rush* that was going to leave me shaking for hours, I was sure.

"First rule: No one knows the game we're playing. *No one.* Do you understand? The moment I learn that you've spoken to *anyone* about me—and I will find out, trust me—I'll disappear and you'll never hear from me again. Blink once if you understand."

I squeezed my eyes shut and opened them again, bolt upright in the chair, my feet planted hard on the floor.

"Second rule: Until the final hunt, either of us can stop this game at any time. I'll send you a message before the first hunt with a safeword that I'm assigning you. That word crosses your lips in my hearing—or on any communication we might have—just once, and you'll never see me again. Blink once if you understand."

I blinked again.

"See how easy this is? Third rule: Tomorrow I'm going to send you a list. Within 48 hours of receiving that, you'll visit a pharmacy or drugstore and pick up every item. Every single one—and in the quantities that I assign to each. Even if you have to visit more than one store. When you have all of it, you'll take a picture of all of it on your kitchen counter and post it as a unique post in the forum where we met. If you have skipped anything or don't have enough of something, you'll never seen me again. So don't post it until you have everything. Blink once if you understand."

I squeezed my eyes closed, my mind whirring with curiosity. When I opened them again it was just as he moved, turning his head to look out the passenger window to see if there was anyone who could see us. I realized then that I could make out a very faint reflection of him in the windshield. I locked eyes on it and tried desperately to memorize the details, but couldn't see much more than a strong, square jaw that was cleanshaven, full lips, and the tip of his nose because he was wearing a hoodie that shadowed most of his face.

When he turned back, he kept his chin low so I didn't see anything more. Disappointment fluttered in my stomach.

"Final rule," he growled. "You give *no* indication to anyone in your life that you know you're going to die. If you have legal or financial details to put in place, you do so casually—you're just being responsible. But you don't say goodbye. You don't give things away. And you don't breathe a word to anyone in your life that you wish to die, or that you plan to. Leave notes or instructions with a lawyer if you need to. If I hear even a *hint* that someone suspects what we're doing, I will disappear and you'll never see me again. Blink once if you understand."

I blinked again, my breath still coming in short, sharp puffs through my nose.

23

"Now… I told you that I knew how to make you feel alive. I wasn't lying. I'm not a liar. Remember that. It'll be important later. But for now, just know that I won't warn you when a new hunt begins. Between hunts you may go days, or even weeks without seeing or hearing anything from me. But just because *you* don't see *me* doesn't mean *I* don't see *you*. At times I might choose to leave you signs that I'm near, or I might not. But I *will always be near.* Whether you're aware of it or not. So don't get complacent and break the rules, or you won't see me again. Blink *twice* if you understand."

I did as he asked, my heart trilling in my chest.

"Good girl," he purred and a zing of need like I hadn't felt for years jolted behind my navel. He leaned closer again and I swallowed hard, inhaling that scent deeply, crystalizing it in my senses, knowing for as long as I lived I'd associate that smell with him.

There was a pause, and the clunk of the car door handle. My stomach dipped, but he didn't let me go even when he swung the door open and the cool morning air rushed in, taking some of his scent away and replacing it with the smell of warming cement.

He paused again, and I braced, expecting him to run and getting ready to turn and look as quickly as possible, see if I could catch a glimpse of his face. But he gave a low, disapproving growl like he knew what I was thinking.

"You won't see my face, Bridget. Ever. When we meet it will be darkness, and I'll wear a mask. And if it's the latter and you try to remove it, it will be the last thing you ever do… do you understand?"

I nodded quickly and he paused again, sinking down a hair behind me as if he might be about to leave, but then he froze.

"I almost forgot," he whispered. "As the hunt progresses it will get… aggressive. I don't expect you to submit. You can fight, you can resist, you can run—you can try to escape me any way you want. In fact, I encourage it. But our agreement involves no weapons. Everything that happens between us, happens organically. We use our bodies, and anything we find in the vicinity of wherever we meet. If I find you carrying a weapon, you'll never see me again. And if you bring a weapon against me, it will be the end. Do you agree?"

I swallowed hard and nodded under his hand.

For a moment, he was still and quiet, then his thumb moved to stroke my cheekbone.

"You're a very beautiful woman, Bridget. What a waste to take you from this world." Then his other hand snaked around the seat, his fingertips stroking down my throat, then along my collarbone as he audibly inhaled. His hand over my mouth loosened just a hair.

"This is your one and only chance to prove you'll play by the rules, Bridget. If you don't, you'll never see me again. I'm going to remove my hand from your mouth, and you're *not* going to scream. You're not going to move at all. You'll keep your eyes on that wall in front of you and answer my questions. Then, when I leave, you will give a slow count of thirty during which time you won't turn around to watch me go."

I waited for the instruction on whether to blink or nod, but then he gave a little rumble in his chest and suddenly the deathgrip he had on my face loosened, then his hand was gone. But he was still there, breathing in my ear.

I froze, my heart hammering.

"Very good girl," he whispered hoarsely.

My stomach thrummed. I swallowed and breathed through my mouth, gulping at the air, my heart pounding like it might actually break through my ribs.

"Now, answer my questions quietly, but quickly. Do you know the man who was leering at you in the gym today?"

I blinked. I wasn't sure what I'd expected, but that wasn't it. "No," I said quickly.

"Have you seen him there before, or spoken to him at all?"

"I've seen him, but we haven't spoken before. Except… like that."

He was silent for a second. He cleared his throat and I thought I heard a hint of his actual voice, but when he spoke again it was still in a whisper.

"Why do you want to die?"

I blinked. "I told you, I have—"

"There are plenty of people in this world who would happily take every day of health that was available to them There's something else in your life that makes you want to die. What is it?"

My heart rammed at my ribs. I gripped the hem of the hoodie tighter. "Life is... empty," I said. "Boring. Hollow. Whatever you want to call it. There's *nothing* here. What's the point?"

"A nihilist?" he asked, sounding a little amused, which pissed me off.

"My psychiatrist calls it fatalism, and says I confuse thrill with purpose."

He hesitated. "Do you want to die? Or do you want the thrill of being hunted?"

"It isn't a thrill if I can't actually die," I said without hesitation.

"That's not the question—"

"Yes, it is," I interrupted him, then blinked, wondering if that was breaking any rules. But he paused, so I swallowed and plowed on. "The only time I feel *alive* is when I feel like life might be taken from me. For real. You said that the first day. You said you knew that."

He grunted again. "So you'd give your life up in search of the ultimate thrill?"

"No," I said. "Giving my life up *is* the ultimate thrill."

He huffed. I couldn't tell if he was laughing or disapproving and I caught myself about to turn to measure his reaction. My heartrate hit the ceiling.

"Do you have any questions for me?" he finally asked, still whispering.

"Why do you do this?"

I waited. The car jiggled as if he'd shifted his weight like he was squirming in his seat. But still he didn't answer.

I licked my lips. "I'm not judging," I said. "I'm just curious. Is it just the... the Erotopho-whatever it was?"

"I am not *turned on* by death. Or by killing," he hissed.

I frowned. "Then why do you do this?"

He hesitated again, and every hair on the back of my neck stood up. It felt like my *skin* was listening for his answer.

And when it came, it was a low grunt—almost his natural voice, which was still rough and deep, but warmer than I'd expected.

"For exactly the same reason you do," he said finally. Then the car jiggled and eased up like a weight had been lifted.

Shit! He was leaving?

I sucked in a breath at the patter of quick footsteps on the cement outside, grabbed the arm of the car door, but remembered his rules and didn't turn around. I made myself keep my eyes forward and started counting slowly, breathlessly to myself, my pulse threatening to lift the top off my skull.

30… 29… 28…

The second I got to the count of one, I whipped my head around, but of course he was gone. My heart was pounding mercilessly and my head was beginning to ache with it. But I deflated immediately.

He was gone. And that delicious scent was fading because the back door was wide open, allowing the morning air and sun to pour in.

Cursing to myself, I clambered out of the car on shaky knees, slammed the back door closed, then looked over the car to search the parking lot.

But it was empty, the morning sun cutting an angled shadow from the building, slanting across the cement.

Just as empty as my chest suddenly felt as the adrenaline from his visit began to ease from my veins and all the strength went out of my legs so that I had to sit in the seat for a few minutes more before I could turn the car on and drive.

But at least when I did, I was smiling.

Because he was real. And he was here.

I could smell him on my hair.

4. Consequences

~ *CAIN* ~

Watching her leap out of her car looking for me, then slap the roof when she didn't find me made me grin.

It was less fun seeing her drop back into the driver's seat a few seconds later, like her knees had given out, and watch her sag over the steering wheel. Was she just resting, or had she had a medical episode?

She stayed in that position long enough that I was just beginning to consider breaking my own rules and making a second appearance to check on her, when she finally pulled her head up and, with slumped shoulders, turned the car on and reversed out of the parking spot.

I stayed low in the backseat of the truck I was using to watch her. It had an extended cab and tinted windows at the back. I could look out at her, but she couldn't see me as she drove past, shaking her head.

But even though she was frowning, I didn't miss the high spots of color in her cheeks.

And that made me smile again.

Good thing, since that little high would have to sustain me for quite some time, since it was *hours* after she left before that shrivel-dick finally lumbered out of the gym.

He was one of those meat-heads who wore bike shorts and tank tops that didn't even cover his nipples. So thick and 'roided out he probably couldn't touch his elbows in front of his face. Neck and thighs the size of tree-trunks, veins on his temples and forearms... He assumed that his sheer size and power out-weighed everything else. Literally. I was an inch taller and strong, but at least fifty pounds of pure muscle lighter. He'd dismiss me as a threat if we passed on the street.

Stupidly.

I slipped out of the truck, I tried not to draw his attention yet, just closed the door quietly and started to walk towards the gym doors, scanning the parking lot and nearby street for any potential threats and finding none. I kept my head down so he couldn't see my face, but eyes up, checking him out as we drew closer

There is a point at which the human body's bulk begins to outweigh its frame—a size at which a man's muscle volume exceeds what the rest of him is capable of moving efficiently, and so his size becomes a *disadvantage* against a skilled enemy. This dude was already twenty pounds past that threshhold, and if the weights I saw him lifting earlier were any measure, he was still gaining.

The excess weight made him walk in a rolling gait as he was forced to shift all that bulk. But that isn't what ruled him out as a threat. *That* was the fact that the dude was so unobservant, he didn't even notice me walking towards him.

"Hey," I said, keeping my head down over my phone so all he'd see was the top of my head.

He gave a lazy grin and tipped his chin up in greeting, which shifted his center of gravity and raised his line of sight just high enough for me to deliver a short, sharp right hook to his undefended belly—though it felt like punching a wall. My knuckles screamed as he pitched forward, his lungs emptying in a whoosh. Moving with his forward-and-down momentum, I gripped his wrist and twisted it behind him, wrenching his shoulder as I whipped his arm around and put a knee to his back so he dropped to the cement with enough force to break his knee-caps.

His cry of shocked pain was loud, but we were already below the level of the parked cars nearby, and I got down in his ear to warn him before he bellowed again and drew the attention of some do-gooding gym bunny who didn't know who they were dealing with.

"What the fu—"

I took the point of the quality, metal-barrelled ballpoint pen in my pocket and shoved it against the side of his neck so he felt the cold point and went utterly still.

"Shut up and listen, or I'll bleed you out right here before anyone even knows they need to hire a crane to move your pharmaceutically enhanced ass."

He spluttered, blinking, his cheek pressed hard against the cement.

I waited until his breath was hissing in and out between his teeth because he couldn't move without hurting himself, but all that testosterone was still screaming at him that he couldn't be taken down so easy. Sweat dripped from his temples and his face went red as he shook and growled with frustration—but one nudge with what he thought was a blade and he stopped fighting my grip that kept one meaty fist twisted up near his shoulder-blades.

Stupid fucker was so big he wouldn't even be able to undo the bra he must need for those D cups.

"You finished?" I asked a moment later when he gave another little roar, but he didn't try to get loose. I let the pen-tip dig deep in his skin and he began to whine.

"What the fuh… what the *fuck?* Who the fuck *are* you?"

"I'm six two and two-twenty and kicking your ass, that's who I am," I drawled. "But that's not important. Just wanted you to know so when you're thinking about this later you don't get to convince yourself I was some kind of Mack truck that ran you down. Now, tell me what you know about the girl."

He spluttered again, drops of spittle hitting the cement in front of his mashed cheek. "What girl?"

"Black hair, crazy eyes—you thought you were cute harrassing her a few hours ago."

"The fuck? I didn't even touch her—if she said I did—"

"She didn't have to. I watched you, shrivel-dick. You think those made-to-order muscles give you a right to scare the shit out of women?"

"What? I didn't scare any—"

Digging that pen a little deeper, I leaned down to whisper in his ear, running my nose against his sweaty temple. "You seem a little damp, sweetheart. Do you want a towel? I'd be happy to *wipe you down*."

His eyes bulged and he spluttered another excuse, but I was done toying with him.

"Now you know how it feels when a real man makes you helpless, maybe you want to rethink how you talk to the ladies who didn't even *look* at you?"

"I am not helpless—*argh!*"

He'd tried to wriggle loose, tried to ripple-flip me off his back. But I understood his anatomy better than he did. Something gave in his shoulder when I didn't let his hand move and he yelped like a dog, then went still, panting in pain.

Good.

Shoving the point of that pen actually into his skin, his entire body vibrated. "STOP! FUCK! WHAT IS—*STOP!*"

A door thudded somewhere and that was my cue.

Letting go of his limbs, I shoved the tip of the pen into his ear cavity, clamping his skull between that and the flat of my other palm.

"You move a fucking fingernail and I will shove this knife straight into your brain. All those muscles won't save you when you're pissing your anti-chafe shorts." I hissed.

He froze, still panting, and began to whimper. "What the fuh… wha—"

"Tell me you'll never talk to her again."

"I'll never t-talk to her again."

"Tell me if you're here and she comes in, you'll finish your set and you'll leave, and you won't even look at her."

"I won't! Fuck! I don't even care! It was just a—"

I pressed the point of that pen far enough into his ear that his body started to jiggle and despite my order he squirmed away from it, whimpering again. Then I hissed in his other ear.

"The next time you make a woman feel small, I'm not going to warn you. I'm just going to kill you. Do you understand?"

"YES!"

I shoved off him and ran hunched, between the two nearest cars, keeping my body below the level of the lines of parked cars, darting between vehicles and parking island trees until I reached the final row, then following it back along the side of the building until I could dart down a narrow alley between two nearby buildings. The moment I was in the shadows, I ripped the hoodie off, holding it with one hand as I slowed to a walk, slipping the pen into the pocket of my pants and strolling casually back around the block towards the parking lot by the gym.

By the time I reached it, there was a group of guys coming out of the doors, talking, bags slung over their shoulders, waterbottles in their hands. I slipped up behind them, walking just a couple feet from the last guy, pulling my phone out and keeping my head down like I was focused on that.

"Yo—you okay, bruh?" One of the men ahead of me called to the beefmeat in the parking lot.

Adrenaline shot through my veins. I made myself wait a beat before I looked up, fixing an expression of only mild interest on my face.

But my walnut-balls friend was stumbling to his car, waving them off with one hand while he struggled to open the door of his Jeep.

Of course it was a Jeep.

The guys ahead of me watched him until he got the door open, then obviously dismissed him as nothing, said their goodbyes, and split up.

I kept my face in my phone and split off when the rest of them spread out to their cars, walking to my truck with my hoodie in my hand.

I couldn't resist looking up when the Jeep rolled past, but the guy inside was hunched forward, hunted eyes scanning the lot ahead of him, gripping the steering wheel like it was the only thing keeping him tied to gravity. He didn't even see me walking between two cars as he drove too-fast down the line in the parking lot, his brake lights flaring red for a moment, then he squealed the tires pulling out into traffic.

I got into the truck and blew out a shaky breath.

Holy shit.

Holy shit.

We hadn't even started the hunt and I'd already broken almost every rule for myself. He'd almost seen my face—might have recognized me from inside the gym. They'd have security footage. If he asked, they might look at whoever was there…

It had to stop now. It *had* to. *I* had to stop.

No more interference in her life. Period.

No more hunt. She was all wrong for this. I couldn't stay separate. I was going to make mistakes. She was too big of a risk. I should have turned around this morning when I saw her walk into the gym, because I *knew.*

Except… Something about the way those guys had leered at her had twisted in my guts—especially when her eyes had been so dead and glazed when she answered him. Like she was dissociating.

I slammed my hands on the top of the steering wheel, started the car with my trembling fingers and tore out of there almost as fast as my 'roid-ridden friend had done, telling myself she wasn't worth the risk.

I wasn't even halfway home before I had convinced myself that I needed to check on her, keep tabs for a few days, make sure the guy didn't go after her.

I was still five miles from home when I had justified giving her at least the first hunt, since she clearly needed *something* in her life.

By the time I made it in the door, I already had the app on my phone open that monitored the tracker I'd put on her car and showed me *exactly* where she was. Safely at home, thank God.

As I got a glass of water and downed it, it took a minute to realize I was staring at that dot on a map and assessing her neighborhood again, weighing the thrill of venturing into her territory against the control of choosing my own ground.

And the hair on my arms was standing up, which was my body's way of saying, *let the hunt begin.*

Five minutes later, cock aching, and body thrumming because I was staring into the distance, remembering how she'd smelled, I wasn't even arguing with it anymore.

She was either going to be the best I'd ever had, or the death of me. And I found I kind of liked that idea.

Maybe she wasn't the only fatalist.

5. Self-Destruct

~ BRIDGET ~

I dreamed that his eyes were on me, watching from the shadows. But instead of feeling creepy, it felt like protection.

God, I'm a mess.

I logged onto the computer the second I got up, hurrying through the VPN and masking, humming with anticipation—only for every system in my body to slump when there were no messages from him.

Then it felt like I didn't want to move. Like my body had already burned through the fuel for the day and my blood was thick and running slow.

I checked my email because I was expecting a package, but only found another from Jeremy.

FROM: Asshole (Jeremy Haines)
TO: Bridget
SUBJECT: Stop playing games

What the fuck? Two days in a row?

The first niggle of uneasiness started in my chest. If Jeremy wasn't waiting for me to *think,* then something was going on that was going to spell trouble for me.

Once again, I sat there, staring at the email, biting my lip, the mouse hovering over it... but I shook my head and left it unread. Let him figure out that.

My message window pinged and my heart jolted with hope that it was Cain. But instead, there was an image of the insane purple monster puppet and a notification window.

SYSTEM NOTE: CHAT ENCRYPTED END-TO-END. ENSURE ALL ACCOUNTS ARE LOGGED OFF BEFORE DISCONNECTING.

PurplePeoplEater: You're up early.

DeadGirlWalking: That's my line. Since when do you rise with the sun?

PurplePeoplEater: Since I never went down with the dark.

DeadGirlWalking: Ooooo, new boyfriend keeping you awake?

PurplePeoplEater: No. New meds. New levels of insomnia. I'm bored and exhausted and procrastinating. Tell me your dreams.

DeadGirlWalking: I dreamed I had a normal day—gym, lunch, around the house—but every second there was a guy watching me. It was hot.

PurplePeoplEater: Sound stalkery.

DeadGirlWalking: Exactly.

PurplePeoplEater: You need therapy.

DeadGirlWalking: Already taken care of.

Shit. *Shit.*
I looked at the date on the corner of the screen.
Fuck.
How had an entire week passed already? I groaned and tucked my hair back behind my ears.

DeadGirlWalking: I gotta go.

PurplePeoplEater: Nature calls?

DeadGirlWalking: No, you pervert. I literally have therapy.

PurplePeoplEater: You're shitting me.

DeadGirlWalking: I wish. See you tonight.

PurplePeoplEater: No doubt. It's not like I sleep or anything.

I sent a GIF of an orange fluffy blob hugging a depressed looking purple fluffy blob, then logged out and went through the process of shutting everything down, my stomach dropping closer to my toes with every window that closed, or screen that disappeared.

When the computer had gone quiet, I reassured myself that I still had an hour to shower and brace. But it didn't work.

That hour went all too quickly.

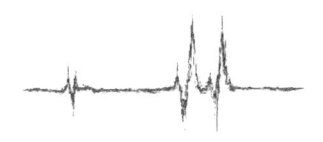

"Any progress on a visit to your father?" Gerald asked casually, keeping his eyes down on the papers in front of him so I was staring at the bald pate of his head.

"Going straight for third base," I drawled. "Bold. Can we even *pretend* you're going to buy me dinner first?"

He lifted his eyes to shoot me a look over the top of his glasses. "Deflection," he said, enunciating each syllable perfectly, because that's what Gerald did. He didn't need to say more. We'd had this conversation dozens of times.

I stopped pretending. "My father is dead."

"Your father is being housed in the State Penitentiary."

"No, the monster that inhabits the body that was once my father is in prison. My dad died when I was seven." He was the literal nightmare before Christmas.

Gerald pulled his glasses off and let them drop to the desk in front of him, rubbing his eyes and pinching his nose in frustration. "Bridget, we've talked about this. You cannot simply *decide* something is true. The man whose DNA is in your body is alive—and definitely *un*well, and has attempted to reach out to you several times. Whether you like it or not, he is your father. He might die. And this could be your last chance to speak with him before he does."

"I don't give two shits whether his body dies or not."

Gerald sat back in his chair, staring at me with open frustration. "I have been on this earth more than twice as long as you and I'm telling you, the day will come that you will wish you asked your questions and got your answers before he was gone and there was never another chance."

I sat forward, elbows on my knees and snarled through my teeth. "And I'm telling you just because *you* have daddy issues, doesn't mean you can project them onto me."

He shook his head and pointed at me. "Deflection. *Again.*"

I pointed at myself. "Fucks. Not given."

I saw the corners of his mouth tighten because he was trying not to smile and got a tiny little warm fizz in my chest.

Gerald wasn't bad when he wasn't fixating on trying to solve me like a puzzle. He had a great sense of humor and could be extremely clever and cutting in his commentary on the world. It was my goal before our sessions ended to make him laugh outright—and to not let him know when I thought he was funny. I might have stolen a few of his better, intelligent insults to use in jousts against the trolls online. I thought if we met outside a therapeutic setting, we could have been friends. Or something.

But he was a respected Psychiatrist, and thought he knew everything about me. And because it was his job, he thought he had me figured out.

He knew *nothing.*

"You aren't cute," he muttered, all hint of humor dying on the crags of his aging face.

"So, now we're listing traits we *don't* aspire to? Okay, cool. You aren't—"

"What happened this week? What are you so scared I'm going to notice that you don't want to talk about?" he asked quietly.

I froze, then cursed myself when the triumph flashed in his eyes. Trying to play it off, I rolled my eyes and shook my head, sitting back on the couch as an excuse to look away.

"God, you're like one of those irritating little dogs, yap yap yapping—"

"And you're panicking. What's going on?"

"Nothing's going on! My life is *boring."*

"You could get a job."

"Why? I don't need the money. Are you trying to tell me there's some greater human experience in being forced to bend over and take it from a dude whose only outlet for his masculine rage is to lord the power of the swipe-card over the drones in the office?"

"How about, so you could find a purpose beyond your own impotent rage? Something to contribute to outside your own misery?"

"I have a purpose."

"No, Bridget, you have an addiction to adrenaline caused by childhood trauma, erratic moods, and *probably* borderline anti-social personality disorder."

"I'm not anti-social. I'm anti-dicks."

"Oh, really? How many sexual partners have you had in the past month?"

I folded my arms and gave him a nasty grin. "Not *those* kinds of dicks, Gerald. But thank you for taking the cheap shot again. I'm keeping a log."

"And that, right there, is exactly why we're never going to get anywhere, Bridget. I am here to help you, to guide you, to offer insight and advice. I am not your combatant to be manipulated or... or forced into submission."

I raised one eyebrow. "Is that how you like it, Gerald? Do you want to be dominated?"

He gave me a very flat look.

I smiled. But my heart wasn't in it.

I kind of liked Gerald. He wasn't intimidated by me. He was the eighth "therapist" I'd had since I was emancipated at the age of sixteen, and the first one to have lasted more than a year since I hit legal adulthood and could tell the Powers That Be where to shove their ass-puckered, pearl-clutchers that called themselves professionals but got wheezy at the first mention of blood play.

God, if they only knew.

But they didn't. And neither did Gerald. But he got *enough.* He didn't treat me like fragile glass that was going to shatter at the slightest push. Of course, he was also a right royal pain in the ass, and not in the good way.

He'd dropped his face into his hands and was rubbing his eyes again, which was a little concerning. I *enjoyed* the combative nature of our exchanges. He wasn't going to pussy-out on me now, was he?

Then he dropped his hands to the desk and looked at me and his expression was grim.

"It was a joke," I muttered.

"I know," he snapped back. "But that's the problem, Bridget. *Two years* of this... war. Two years and I don't see you getting better and that's not because I haven't given you good advice."

I pouted. "Awwww, is the doctor wowwied about his cwedibiwity—"

"Drop the fucking act, Bridget! You're not a rebellious teenager anymore. This isn't *angst.* You're a grown woman who is on a path to self-destruction, and I am becoming more and more convinced that I'm the only one who cares—it's certainly evident that *you* don't!"

I blinked. Gerald had gotten frustrated with me before, but he'd never raised his voice. I stared at him, considering and discarding several cutting replies, and a couple of threats, too. I was unhappy about the sudden jangle of fear in my chest.

It wasn't the good kind.

Was he giving up on me?

Did I care?

Gerald leaned on the desk, his entire posture bristling. "One thing, Bridget. I want you to tell me one thing you've done as a result of our time together to *improve* your mental health or wellbeing. Just one!"

"I wear the stupid heart monitor when I work out, and I usually avoid coffee," I said quickly, because it was true.

But Gerald shook his head. "You do those things to keep our mutual friend off your back. I want to know what I've recommended that you've chosen to follow *for yourself.*"

I pressed my lips together and did some bristling of my own. "Are we suffering performance anxiety, Ger—?"

He shoved out of his seat and stormed around the desk towards me. Adrenaline shoved through my veins and I instinctively sprang to my feet, taking a defensive stance, assessing him—much taller and with longer arms so he could reach me easier. But there was some softness around his middle and—

He drew up short on the other side of the coffee table, his brows high and jaw slack. "Bridget, I'm not going to *attack* you... dear God."

I blinked, realizing I was in a fighting stance and he was just standing there, gaping at me.

I dropped my arms immediately, shame and self-disgust rolling through me in a wave as the anger died in his eyes to be replaced with a deep sadness. His forehead pressed to lines and he stared at me like... like he was *grieving.*

Ugh.

"Bridget," he said, then shook his head. "I'm not trying to bait you. I'm genuinely terrified that you're going to get yourself killed," he said quietly. "Every second you're late to an appointment I wonder if you're out there in a dumpster behind some dive bar where the local psycho stuffed your body. Every day I brace before reading the news in case I stumble on an article about the *body of an unidentified female.* I know you think you handle yourself—and I know you can. But… god… the *risks…*"

He kind of slumped, and my entire body ached with self-loathing.

"I don't know," he muttered, rubbing a hand over the smooth top of his head. "I don't even know if I'm helping. I don't know if—"

"I show up," I said bluntly.

"Yes, but—"

"No, Gerald that's… that's real for me," I said, folding my arms and avoiding his eyes that had snapped to my face when I spoke. "That's a thing. That's a… one thing that I've done that's good for me. I show up. I never showed up for anyone before. So that's… you did that," I admitted, squirming, because I could feel him taking that *all kinds of ways.*

"Bridget—"

"I'm not going to tell you that I'm better and all is well. But… I hear you, okay. I don't always agree, but I hear you. When you talk, I listen. Even when I *deflect.*"

His head kind of eased back and he looked at me, a little stunned. "Well… thank you for telling me that."

I shrugged, because I was very afraid he was going to want to hug me, and my skin felt too tight and I thought if he squeezed me at all my guts might actually burst out of my body and—*ugh.*

He watched me for a second, then sighed heavily. "Don't worry. I'll go back to my seat now."

And he did. When he sat back down, I did too. But I didn't know what to say, or do. I twisted my hands together in my lap and my skin itched. I wanted to *run*. It was the most uncomfortable I'd felt in months.

And the fucker knew it, and didn't talk to break the tension, he just stared at me, challenging me to flee.

I kept my arms folded and crossed my legs at the knee as well, pushing out my lower jaw to meet the challenge, because maybe I wasn't going to run, but I wasn't gonna talk first, either.

A minute later, Gerald sighed again, then picked up his glasses and cleaned them with an old-school cloth hankerchief he got out of his pocket, them put them on as he began to scribble some notes on the paper in front of him.

"Same time next week?" he asked quietly.

I nodded.

He stopped writing. "There's something I want you to consider between now and then."

"Okay," I muttered.

He looked at me and I looked back, wary, but waiting.

"I understand you're not ready to talk to your dad. But... I want you to consider whether there's anyone else in your life who's there because they care about you. Who isn't Court-ordered, or medically advised. Who doesn't get paid to talk to you."

"Like you?" I asked sweetly.

He shot me a look and kept going. "I want you to look for someone who... just cares about you. Anyone at all. An older person who maybe knew you when you were younger and has at least an inkling of what you've been through. Someone you could talk to. Even if it's not about dark stuff. But just about your day to day life... someone who cares about you, just because they care about you. Do you know the kind of person I mean?"

I did, and I nodded, though I hadn't had that kind of person in my life since high school.

"Before you come see me next week, I'm asking you to do something for me. I'm asking you to seek a person out. Maybe have coffee. Maybe lunch. Maybe just go for a walk. I don't know. I just... Bridget, I think you need someone to prove to you that you're worth caring about. Someone who doesn't have any external reason to care. They just know you, and like you. Can you give that some thought? Call it a different kind of risk."

I frowned. "What do you mean?"

He met my eyes evenly. "I mean, you need to realize that you can be loved, my girl. And the only way you're ever going to believe that is if you let someone show you they care when they don't have any other reason to be there."

I frowned harder. "Okay."

Gerald rolled his eyes, but then he smiled a little. "Just… baby steps. If it's not easy, maybe just think about who that person might be, and how you might get in touch with them. That's all. Let's say you don't need to take any action yet. Just… identify a target," he said dryly, using language I often used.

I shrugged. "Fine."

Then he fixed me with another of those stern gazes. "Bridget, you like to put yourself in situations where your body and wellbeing are in danger. I'm asking you to put yourself in a situation where someone could hurt your *heart*. Where you risk rejection. Where you might care, and they might let you down. That's the kind of risk we're looking for."

"Whatever."

"Avoiding these kinds of relationships is just one more form of self-destruction."

I rolled my eyes then. "I've told you countless times, I'm not going to destroy myself." *I'm going to let Cain do it for me.*

Gerald didn't look impressed, but he also didn't respond. "Just think about it. We'll talk about it next week," he said quietly.

"I will."

But I don't think he believed me.

6. That's What She Said

SOUNDTRACK: *Hell Replied* by Grey

~ CAIN ~

Her account was active when I logged in. My heartrate kicked up like I'd just snorted cocaine.

She was a fucking drug.

I rubbed a hand over my face and reminded myself that I'd already broken the rules, and it had to stop. Then I clicked on her profile and selected *Send Message*.

SYSTEM NOTE: CHAT ENCRYPTED END-TO-END. ENSURE ALL ACCOUNTS ARE LOGGED OFF BEFORE DISCONNECTING.

SleepingBeast: Your safe word is "Villeneuve."

SleepingBeast: It's pronounced, "Villa-New."

DeadGirlWalking: What the hell kind of safe word is that?

SleepingBeast: Good, you won't use it by accident, then.

DeadGirlWalking: We may have to renegotiate. I didn't realize I was gonna get stalked by a fancy french dude. Do you wear suspenders and a kicky beret? Is that why you don't want me to see your face? Because I'd laugh?

DeadGirlWalking: For the record, I'm literally laughing right now. I have a vision of you prancing through the forest dressed like a mime. You're frolicking.

DeadGirlWalking: Do you frolic, Cain?

SleepingBeast: Rarely.

DeadGirlWalking: So you're saying it's happened. I will need video evidence. I won't show anyone. I swear. I'll take it to the grave—you can personally make sure of that.

DeadGirlWalking: Wait… our safeword is the last name of a Canadian filmmaker?

DeadGirlWalking: ARE YOU TREY PARKER?

SleepingBeast: *Your* safeword. And no.

SleepingBeast: Also no.

DeadGirlWalking: That's what Google says.

SleepingBeast: Google is a dick.

DeadGirlWalking: So are you if you won't let me see you frolic before I die.

DeadGirlWalking: You would seriously deny a dying woman her last wish?

SleepingBeast: Apparently not, since I have a list of supplies for you. But don't open it until we're done here.

[SleepingBeast has sent you an attachment: Supply List.docx. Click here to download.]

DeadGirlWalking: So mysterious. My fingers are itching.

SleepingBeast: You should get that examined by a medical professional.

DeadGirlWalking: No thanks. I've had enough of medical professionals violating my person to last a lifetime.

SleepingBeast: Pretty sure if they're violating you, they're doing it wrong.

DeadGirlWalking: Tell me you aren't a woman without telling me you aren't a woman…

DeadGirlWalking: Anyway, why can't I look at the supply list?

SleepingBeast: Mainly because you ask an annoying number of questions and I don't want to have to answer them.

DeadGirlWalking: Am I offended? I think I'm offended.

DeadGirlWalking: Nope, it was just indigestion.

SleepingBeast: Just review the list, go find the things. Make the post when you've got everything. Don't post the picture until you have.

DeadGirlWalking: Should I take the picture in my bedroom, or my kitchen? Will you be examining it for clues to where I live?

SleepingBeast: I already know where you live, Bridget.

DeadGirlWalking: Stop. You'll make me come.

SleepingBeast: Nah. That's later.

DeadGirlWalking: OMG are you flirting with me?

SleepingBeast: Do you want me to?

DeadGirlWalking: God yes.

SleepingBeast: That's what she said.

DeadGirlWalking: *Bah dum TISSSSSS*

[DeadGirlWalking is typing...]

I yanked my hands off the keyboard and sat back in my rickety desk chair, raking my fingers through my hair.

What the hell was I doing? *Flirting?* I couldn't flirt with a mark.

I dropped my face into my hands and breathed for a while. This woman was trouble.

No, she was *disaster.*

But I didn't even bother trying to tell myself that I needed to stop and block her. I knew I wouldn't do it. I'd had every reason to after that shitshow yesterday, and I was still here. I was in. And so was she. I could feel it.

I might be a monster, but I was an honest one. Even with myself. If I was going to do this, I was going to enjoy it. Enjoy *her.*

But no more flirting.

SleepingBeast: I have to go.

DeadGirlWalking: Wait! I was playing! I have actual questions. I don't want to get this wrong. I don't want you to stop.

SleepingBeast: Just get what's on the list and we'll be golden.

DeadGirlWalking: But is there anything illegal there, or anything that I need to like, get permission, or a prescription, or something?

SleepingBeast: no.

DeadGirlWalking: Can I ask you questions if I don't know what something is, or can't find it?

SleepingBeast: You can try. The internet is free. But you're a smart girl. You won't need to.

DeadGirlWalking: So, as long as I get everything exactly as its described, we're moving ahead?

SleepingBeast: yes.

DeadGirlWalking: Can I ask you one question about yesterday?

DeadGirlWalking: Cain?

DeadGirlWalking: its not anything bad.

DeadGirlWalking: I know you're still logged in.

DeadGirlWalking: Okay fine, ignore me if you want to, but I need to know: What cologne do you wear? You smelled divine. I was thinking I'd get you a bottle for Christmas. Arrange to get it sent online or something. A message of thanks from the grave.

SleepingBeast: You need help.

DeadGirlWalking: Duh. Why do you think you're here?

SleepingBeast: Go shopping, Bridget. Post the pic when you've got it all.

DeadGirlWalking: How much time do I have?

SleepingBeast: You expect a trip to a couple stores to delay you indefinitely?

DeadGirlWalking: No, but I don't know what's on the list, so if I have to order something and wait I just want to make sure you aren't going to abandon the plan.

SleepingBeast: You can find every item on that list within five miles of your house.

SleepingBeast: Goodbye Bridget. Sleep sweet and dream of me.

DeadGirlWalking: Wait!

[DeadGirlWalking is typing…]

[You have left the chat]

    I punched the keys a little too hard to close the forum, then confirmed that I was logging out, and went through the process of turning off the VPN.
    I was breathing loud. And my heart was pounding.
    My mind conjured three different reasons why I needed to log back on and talk to her, but I shook them all off and pushed away from the computer.
    I was alone for now, but it wouldn't stay that way, and I couldn't risk anyone else catching wind of this. It had been reckless to login on a work computer at all, even though no one else was going to use it. I was breaking all my own rules and it was making me sweat.
    And it was *thrilling*.

As I made myself uninstall the software from the work computer, I kept reminding myself why it was *so* important to keep myself unentangled from her.

But it was too late.

I dreamed about her last night.

God had a sense of humor. In the dream I'd met her walking down the road with the Pitbull from the gym, because he'd apologized to her and she'd been touched, and they ended up dating. And she didn't know my face, so never recognized me. So every day I'd go in there and watch them work out together.

I woke up when I saw him lean over her and put his hand on her ass.

I woke up sweating, with a double-chokehold on the quilt, and my heart pounding so hard in my skull that it hurt.

I tried to avoid masturbating these days, but I was hard and aching and *raging.* I'd needed something to take the edge off.

So, I'd taken hold of myself and remembered how she laid back on that bench in the gym and opened her knees…

I imagined that I was standing between those pretty knees and I reached down, laying my hands over her breasts first, stroking the insides of those soft rounds as her nipples rose under my touch, then sliding down her body, gripping her so tightly my fingers made dents in her soft flesh, until I reached her stomach, then I hooked my fingers in the waistband of her workout shorts and drew them slowly down, down, until I exposed her—clearly ready for me, which made me groan—then revealed her pale thighs. Then I dragged the shorts down her firm calves, took each foot in my hand, and pulled it through the stretchy fabric. And when I had both feet free, I tossed the shorts over my shoulder.

And she smiled at me.

My mouth went dry when she grasped the underside of her sports bra and pulled it up and off, baring both breasts.

My breath got shorter. Heavier.

She arched her back as I slid both hands all the way up from where I'd been cradling her ankles, trailing my palms up the backs of her calves, cupping my hands behind her knees, then tightening my grip and pulling her legs wider as I yanked her towards me.

She squeaked, worried she'd fall off the bench, giggling as she struggled to balance on the narrow pad. But then she sighed as I sat down on the end of it, and grabbed for her, pulling her right up onto my aching lap as I leaned over her.

She bit her lip and reached for my chest as she wrapped her legs around my waist and rolled her hips to bring us together—she was already slick, and I groaned.

My hand was trembling as I slid it under the hollow of her back and lifted her hips, positioning myself, then plunged into her in a single, sharp thrust.

She arched, one hand slapping to my neck as her eyes rolled back and she gasped my name.

Overcome with the perfect pleasure of her, I lowered myself over her, arching my back, grasping the top of the bench over her shoulder and gripping it until my knuckles turned white, using that arm to brace myself and pin her to me as I gripped her hip with my other hand and pulled her onto me with each powerful thrust.

Her nails dug into my shoulders, threatening to break the skin, but I just wanted more.

And the harder I pumped into her, the more her breasts bounced. And her nipples were so hard I felt them drawing back and forth against my chest—

It had taken *seconds* before my body was convulsing and I was choking on my own cries.

And just a few seconds more before I was sweaty, shaking, and coated in shame.

No.

No, no, no, no, no…

This wasn't why I was here.

This wasn't why I'd hunted her down.

This wasn't what I was here to do.

But I couldn't stop wanting it. Wanting *her.* It was a death sentence. And not the good kind.

If I didn't get myself together, we were both completely fucked.

Or not.

And I couldn't decide which was worse.

7. Going Off List

~ *BRIDGET* ~

I was walking down the aisle at Walmart, frowning at the list. I'd gotten all the medical supplies quickly—bandaids, disinfectant, bandages and medical tape all in various sizes and lengths, ice packs, and a thermometer. Even a wrist-brace, a reversible sling, and some finger splints, which made me raise my eyebrows. But none of that was *entirely* unexpected. He'd said there would be several hunts. And since I was presumably going to live through all except the last, I supposed it made sense that I might need medical supplies in the aftermath.

The entirely black, athletic clothes were easy to figure out, but harder to find. It seemed like everything had little pops of color, visible brands, or those mesh cut-outs. Yet, I got there.

There were a few other random items that weren't hard to find, but the last few things had me stumped. I was definitely going to need to go somewhere else after this.

A burner phone I could understand, I supposed. Though they were hard to find prepaid these days. And it wasn't like there wasn't already a trail on my computer to him. I mean, it would take some FBI hot shot with a grudge to find him. But I wasn't stupid. I knew *nothing* was completely hidden anymore. Plus, I had screenshots.

But a silk sleeping mask, a tube of lanolin, four jar candles in scents that I liked—with wooden wicks and lids that could stand up on their own... and a *bible?*

I'd had to read that one several times before I was sure I wasn't hallucinating.

Then I laughed.

And then I went shopping.

And now I had everything but the bible. And that little niggle in the back of my head kept making me snicker to myself. Because it was too perfect. How had he known?

He hadn't, of course, it was a coincidence. I knew for *certain* Gerald wasn't running in any of the circles that Cain did. But it did make me look over my shoulder for a while. Because it was too perfect.

But then again, why not? Gerald would be so proud.

So, once I had everything paid for and packed into the car, I looked at my phone, decided I had time for the forty-minute drive, and set off. Because I wanted to get started. And I couldn't do that until I had all these things.

And if I was going in hunt of a freaking Bible of all things, and Gerald wanted me to talk to the one person who'd give me good advice without needing anything from me... well... two birds with one stone.

Richard would have a bible I could have. I was certain of it. And it gave me an ice-breaker when he freaked out because he hadn't seen me in several years.

I was surprised about how nervous I was on the drive. Richard had always been clear that I was welcome anywhere he was. And in recent years, he always sent a Christmas card with a handwritten note, and he'd emailed a couple of times, too.

He was semi-retired now, and so close, it was a shame we didn't see each other more. Wouldn't I like to jump in the car sometime?

Last Christmas was the first that passed since high school where I didn't get a card from him. I hadn't had an email in a few months either, though. So maybe he was giving up on me. Maybe I'd finally pissed him off by ignoring all his efforts.

I prayed to the God he worshiped that wasn't the case. It would be good to see him again. And since I wasn't going to be around much longer, it would be our last chance.

Not that I'd tell him that. But still.

When I finally found the church in the little backwater named Dayne, I was surprised by the size of the parking lot. But it was right next to the highway, and there was a big truck stop just half a mile down the road, so maybe they were the kind of place that got a lot of travelers.

I pulled the visor down in my car and checked my hair before I got out, which was stupid.

Father Richard—I called him Father Dick, which always made his eyes twinkle—had to be almost eighty by now. Or maybe he wasn't that old if he only retired a few years ago. Maybe he just felt that old because we met when I was fourteen and he already had gray hair.

Well, I was going to find out. I caught myself smoothing my shirt down nervously and stopped myself. Richard was the warmest, sweetest person on the planet. If he didn't smile when he saw me, no one was going to.

That thought didn't make me feel better.

It wasn't until I got up to the top of the stairs and realized that the arched, double front doors were locked that it occurred to me that churches didn't stay open all week like businesses.

And I felt so dumb.

I'd just driven forty minutes to stand on a step at a church alongside the highway and feel stupid. Because of course no one was there on a Thursday afternoon in August. I quickly read the sign next to the door that said services were Sunday mornings, Sunday and Wednesday evenings, and that group meets were in the hall behind the chapel.

Maybe there would be someone there? I could go look, and while I was walking around, I'd check my email and send him a message just in case he was close. Maybe he had a cellphone number on it.

Or maybe I was stupid and this had been a dumb idea all along.

I was surprised by how disappointed I felt. I'd been making excuses to avoid Richard for years. And yet, maybe I shouldn't have, because now I kind of felt weepy. That was even dumber.

"Idiot," I muttered, tucking my hair behind my ears, as I started to turn, looking for the path around the building.

"Well, that's a little harsh," a thin, warm voice said behind me. "If you'd told me you were coming I would have made sure we had the parade ready!"

I gasped and whirled to find a beaming, white-haired old man with craggy lines around his eyes, and a fully-bald pate ringed in scrappy white whiskers now. When I gaped at him, his smile got even broader, if that was possible.

"It really *is* you, Bridget! Thank God!" His eyes were misty as he threw his arms wide.

"Dick!" I squealed and threw myself into his chest.

He laughed as he stumbled back a step and almost toppled down the stairs. I gasped and grabbed for him, pulling him back up until he was steady.

He patted my arm, still beaming. "Thank you, dear. I'm not as steady as I was. But goodness... I am just so glad I left my phone here. Otherwise I would have missed you. See how God works, Bridget. We call this a *divine appointment.* And there I was muttering about the drive back to get it... Gosh, it's good to see you."

That pinch in my eyes came back as he lifted a soft, wrinkled hand to pat my cheek.

"It's really good to see you too," I said honestly. "And I'm sorry I didn't warn you. It kind of happened on a whim and... is there somewhere we can go to talk?"

"Yes, yes! Of course. Come with me—we'll go make some coffee in the manse. I have a Keurig now," he said proudly.

I swallowed a snort, but nodded and took the arm he offered because he was an old school gentleman. Then walked with him, down the stairs and around the building, through the parking lot, past what must have been the hall the sign talked about, then through a high wooden fence that looked like it had only been built recently, and down a cute garden path to a small cottage at the back of the chapel.

The whole walk—which was long because he was old—he asked me questions about my life and the people I'd gone to high school with, none of whom I'd kept in touch with. But he had. He'd been the chaplain of our fancy private school, and the only actually good person within those walls, in my opinion.

I apologized for having no gossip for him, but it didn't matter, because he had plenty.

I heard about how the class of 2015's chastity-belt wearing princess, Katrina, had eventually married and had kids with the former manwhore, Jimmy. And since there were progeny, that meant they'd definitely had sex.

Richard chuckled. "I didn't get to do the service, but they invited me to the wedding, and it was beautiful." He continued as we walked, telling me what he'd seen that day—and all the familiar names who'd been there, which gave me a strange pang... these people were all still friends?

Then he ushered me through the gate in the fence and up a short path to the cottage.

"Would you like normal coffee, or the hazelnut flavored? That's my favorite," he asked warmly as we stepped into a small, dingy, but comfortable little place, ushering me into the small entryway that was right next to an even tinier, galley kitchen,

I hesitated. I didn't usually drink coffee. It wasn't good for my heart. And, while I wouldn't really care if Richard gave me the cup that ended up killing me, I'd feel *terrible* if watching me die gave *him* a heart attack. The man had earned some time to live without dealing with other people's shit. Specifically, mine.

"I really don't need coffee," I said hurriedly. "I just wanted to talk to you Richard. I don't mind if we don't have drinks."

"I also have ice water, or maybe a coke somewhere..." he said, frowning as he bent to look in the ancient refrigerator in the corner of the tiny kitchen. "What could I get you?"

I shrugged, and it just came out.

"I don't suppose you have an extra bible?"

I had to bite my lip when he stood up so fast he banged his head on the inside of the fridge and the bottles inside clanged. Then he stepped back and straightened more carefully, muttering and rubbing the back of his skull.

"Say that again?" he said hoarsely, frowning in confusion.

Fucking priceless.

As Richard tried to get over his shock, I made up a story about just doing some research about various religions, but not knowing what books to read. Richard hurried off and got me one and talked at length about where I should start. I thanked him, but couldn't really take it in because the moment I had the book in my hands I realized... I had the whole list.

I was prepared.

I could send the image to Cain and this hunt would be *on*.

It was hard to sit for another hour and catch up, but I made myself do it because Richard was a wonderful man and I was trying to be nicer to people. Plus, Gerald was going to cream his jeans when he learned that I'd already spoken to someone like he asked.

Of course, it wasn't all easy.

At some point Richard gave me The Look—brows furrowed, eyes pinched with concern, voice spoken softly and with too much care.

"So... how are *you* doing? Have you heard from your father?"

I wanted to slap fifteen year old me for her moment of weakness when she'd shared our past with Richard who had gingerly tried to enquire about why, in the past year, I'd developed a penchant for opening my legs for a new boy every week or so. And being a complete bitch to everyone else.

"I'm fine. I'm still in counselling. Dad's still in prison. And I don't want to talk about him," I said, honestly.

Richard sighed, but nodded, and turned the conversation to other things, which helped me breathe.

I was still clutching that bible tightly in my lap an hour later, though, when I told him I had to get home. And of course, he argued and didn't want me to leave, even when I assured him that I had other commitments this evening and wouldn't be alone.

Of course, I didn't tell him those commitments included proving to my Primal Dom that I'd successfully followed his instructions, but one thing I'd always loved about Richard was that he didn't pry.

He did, however, insist on feeding me before I left. And I didn't want to argue, especially when his kind blue eyes got all pleading and sad. So I compromised and met him at the truck-stop diner down the highway, figuring at least then when I went home I wouldn't need to worry about food.

I was going to be too nervous to eat later anyway.

"Promise me you'll come again. *Soon.* And I don't mean four years later, soon," he said in the closest thing this sweet man had to a reprimand.

"I promise. I'd... kinda like to talk to you about some stuff sometime. If you have time. My, er, counsellor thinks it would be a good idea."

"Of course! I'd love to help if I can!"

And that was how I ended up making an appointment to see him again in less than a week, which felt a little bit soon, but I had his number now, so I could change it. And Gerald would have kittens when he heard that I'd gone *beyond* the necessary. So I'd made two old men happy at the same time. It seemed like a win.

As fall closed in on us, the Pacific Northwest air was getting chilly at night. But I kept my car window down and didn't feel it because I was *humming* with adrenaline. I couldn't stop bouncing in my seat, impatient to get home.

By the time I did it was already growing dark and that just made me even more excited. I had everything on Cain's list. And one thing he hadn't asked for, but he was going to get. All that was left to do was arrange it all so everything could be seen in the same photograph, post the image in the forum. Then wait.

God, I hoped he didn't make me wait.

When I got home, I made sure the garage door was closed before I carried the bags inside, which wasn't necessary. It wasn't like I had drug contraband, or something. But I was more nervous than a virgin on prom night... if the virgin was *also* horny and excited.

It took a surprisingly long time to arrange everything so that every single item could be seen in the same image. I'd wanted to make it look like a gift basket, but that just sucked. Then I thought about taking a wide shot with myself laying naked on the floor in front of it, only posting the part of the picture with the stuff in it on the board, but showing him the wider shot later. But since it was possible my death would make the news and Cain would be investigated, I didn't want *that* living in perpetuity on the internet.

So in the end, it was a picture on my hardwood floor that looked like a neighborhood marketplace picture of a bad lot from a garage sale. But it did the job.

My fingers trembled as I logged into the VPN, then accessed the forum. I mistyped the title of the post three times, and cursed until I got it right.

IT'S ALL THERE
Image.png

I sat back in my chair while the site buffered, then blinked, then the post was live.

Holy shit. This was really happening.

8. Panic

~ BRIDGET ~

My heart was off to the races.

There were a couple comments immediately, but of course it was just the trolls. Then Nate came on in my direct messages.

SYSTEM NOTE: CHAT ENCRYPTED END-TO-END. ENSURE ALL ACCOUNTS ARE LOGGED OFF BEFORE DISCONNECTING.

PurplePeoplEater: Whatcha doin'?

I chewed on my fingernail. Cain had said no one could know.

DeadGirlWalking: Just toying with the trolls. I can't wait to see what conspiracy theory they'll come up with about what it's for.

PurplePeoplEater: You're evil.

DeadGirlWalking: You just noticed? Go to sleep.

He sent back a gif of a woman sticking out her tongue, and I didn't reply.

The post was still up. A handful of trolls were debating whether it was a serial killer's play box. Only one of them mentioned something about Dom after-care—but he got shot down by the guy who pointed out that the Bible was a buzzkill.

But every time a new comment popped and my computer pinged, my heart rate went through the roof. And then, every time, it was *nothing*.

I checked Cain's profile, but it said he was offline.

I chewed on my fingernail for a minute. Then decided, *fuck it,* and clicked the direct message thread.

SYSTEM NOTE: CHAT ENCRYPTED END-TO-END. ENSURE ALL ACCOUNTS ARE LOGGED OFF BEFORE DISCONNECTING.

DeadGirlWalking: Are you online?

DeadGirlWalking: I posted the picture and it's all there. Let me know you got it.

DeadGirlWalking: And tell me how long it will be until the hunt. Please?

I waited for a few minutes in case he came online, but my blood was humming, and not in the good way. It was as if my veins pumped carbonated water and it was making my entire body swell. Like my skin might burst.

My heel was tapping on the carpet, and I bit the quick of my nail, hissing when it bled and I had to suck on it. But still… I was just sitting there staring at an empty, inactive screen.

And then it hit me. It might be *days* before he came on, or told me he'd seen it. I couldn't know.

Then the fizzing in my veins turned to sheer panic.

I really didn't know.

How long might he wait just to toy with me?

Hours? Days? *Weeks?*

Since the moment Cain had told me he'd see me, every waking, undistracted thought had been about him, and the hunt, and getting to the place where I knew he was coming. I'd been chasing that rush like an addict after a dealer. Now there was only this one hurdle left.

But it was one I could not affect.

Him.

My breath was short and shallow and my hands were beginning to shake as the dark shadows of my mind started talking, reminding me why we were here, and where this was going, and why I wanted that, and *maybe I didn't need to wait for Cain at all.*

Panicking, I quickly logged off and got the computer shut down, then tore out of my office to my room. If I sat here alone, I was going to spiral. I could *feel* it.

I had been so obsessed with this, I hadn't even showered today. So the first thing I did was make myself get clean. Then I needed to get dressed.

I didn't even hesitate.

Skin-tight jeans. Heels. A low-cut, figure hugging top that showed my shoulders and hung off my boobs and made them look bigger. Then I grabbed my phone and wallet, the one with the long shoulder-strap, and practically ran out of the house.

Because if Cain hadn't seen my post and wasn't hunting, I *needed* something to distract me.

And if he had, and he was coming for me, well… it didn't matter where I was as long as he could find me.

So that meant going somewhere public. But not easily predicted.

And I knew just the place.

The garage door rattled up and I stood in the glaring light of the automatic light for a minute, wondering if those shadows outside already hid him.

He'd said he knew where I lived.

For a minute I forgot about everything except that somewhere in the dark in this world there was a monster who knew my name, and my address, and my car. He was bigger, stronger, fiercer than me. And even though I was going to fight a lot harder than he thought, I also knew the odds.

Eventually, he would win.

And I experienced the strangest sensation at that thought—half of my heart zipping up into my throat, leaping with joy. The other half plunging to my toes and screaming at me to run.

But I didn't run. I wouldn't run.

Not until he was there to chase me.

I swallowed hard, staring into the darkness outside my garage. "Are you there, Cain?" I whispered. But there was no answer.

There was nothing but a neighborhood street and a night stretching in front of me that made me want to slit my wrists.

And I wasn't going to do that. Ever.

And that conviction put wings on my feet, and a jiggling kind of panic in my chest. I darted to get in the car, firing the engine, and tearing out there, praying Cain was on my heels.

Twenty-five minutes later, deep in the city, I made it to the dive bar owned by Kash, my ex-boyfriend. But I didn't park in that awful lot across the road where most of his patrons left their two-bit dusty, dented rattletraps until they decided to drunk-drive home. Instead, I sailed past, took the next corner, turned up the narrow alleyway behind the building to the cracked cement and dumpsters where the staff parked.

Kash hated it when I did this, but if I decided to drink I needed the car under the security cameras. And not where some drunk would piss on it.

It would make it harder for Cain to find me, too, if he showed up. If he was hunting he wouldn't want to risk getting caught on camera. So he'd have to get more creative about how he was going to intercept me.

I smiled.

And I hoped.

I fucking *prayed* he showed up tonight.

Then I shook off a new wave of panic, got out of the car, locked it with a *bloop,* and trotted up the handful of steps to the staff entrance at the back.

When I swung that heavy, industrial door open, the glaring light of the service hallway washed over me and made me squint at the same time the thumping bass, which had been little more than a dull thunder outside, became a pounding that vibrated in my ribs.

And as I hurried forward, towards the noise and distraction, I only cast one look over my shoulder towards the shadows near my car outside.

But nothing moved before the door swung close on its hydraulic hinge.

Cain, where are you?

9. Burning Up

~ CAIN ~

When I saw the post I got *butterflies.* She'd surprised me.

No one ever surprised me.

It shook me so bad, I shut the computer down and didn't let myself log back in. An hour later, I was expecting a visitor, and I wasn't properly prepared because I'd been distracted all day. Even after she arrived, I was never quite centered.

I was *obsessing* about Bridget.

I'd never accepted a mark that consumed me so completely before and it was dangerous.

Driving, working, fucking *sleeping,* I couldn't stop thinking about her and it wasn't fair to anyone, least of all the woman I was currently in session with.

And she noticed. We'd met before, so she could tell I was distracted.

It was rarely a discipline for me, but this evening I had had to *work* to turn my emotions off, to concentrate on the needs of my companion. But then, just when I was settling in, forcing myself to focus, just when my companion went deep, my phone buzzed which meant Bridget had started moving again and I had to swallow a curse. The woman I was with was halfway through a catharsis and was going to need significant aftercare.

Shit. *Shit.*

I did my best, but for the rest of the hour we remained together, more than half of my brain was screaming at me that Bridget was out there and she'd prepared and it was *time,* even though in over a dozen preys, I'd never started a hunt the same day a mark got equipped.

Not once.

When I was finally alone again, I took one look at the map to see where she'd ended up and growled a curse. Then I tore through the house to get changed and... *fuck!*

First she visits a fucking *priest,* now she's hanging out—alone—in one of the seediest bars in the city. One that was frequented by men who would kill her—or worse—as soon as look at her?

Or... what if she wasn't alone?

I couldn't decide which would be worse.

Time to find out.

Time to hunt.

I grabbed my keys and my bag and got out there like the building was on fire.

But it wasn't the building at all. It was *me* burning up.

Shit.

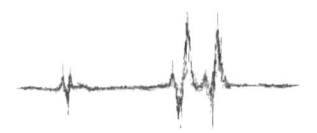

~ *BRIDGET* ~

Kash was standing in the half-dark behind the sticky bar, rinsing out glasses. He looked up to see me approaching and started shaking his head before I even got close enough to hear him over the music.

"Nope. Not tonight, Bridget. Get out."

"Don't worry," I said, rolling my eyes. "I'm not even drinking. Give me a ginger beer. See?"

He wasn't amused. He shook his head and turned around to lean down to one of the glass-fronted fridges lining the floor behind him.

For a second I saw him like a stranger would—a tall, wiry-strong, pretty handsome guy, with a beard that needed trimming because it was hiding his neck tattoos, a dark presence, and a wicked grin.

Kash and I dated three years ago and stayed friends after.

Well, I stayed friends with him. He tolerated my presence because, in his words, I was *a good fuck.*

We hadn't done that for over a year, though. I'd sworn off sex after the guy who said he liked to role-play as a serial killer but who attempted to examine my large intestine, up-close and personal.

Heart conditions and massive blood loss are not easy bedmates.

And neither are me and twelve-inch bowie knives.

I pushed away the slew of *impaled by twelve-inches* jokes that sprang to mind that only I would laugh at, and flashed a smile at Kash when he plonked a Bundaberg ginger beer on the bar, glaring at me over it.

"You drink it. You do whatever business it is that you're here to do, then you leave. I'm not playing, Bridge."

Kash had met the not-so-psuedo serial killer and warned me he was bad news. But since Kash also existed boldly in the *Mother Will Not Approve* space, I'd told him he was the kink calling the fetish "pervert."

Of course, Kash drew the line at loss of life—unless it involved his own, and a massive amount of drugs—so maybe I should have listened.

"I'm not doing business tonight," I said as I pulled the tab-top on the fat, brown, short-necked bottle. "I'm just hanging out."

"No, you aren't."

"Kash, stop."

"No, Bridge. *You* stop. Art told me what you were looking for last time. That's *fucked up.*"

"Art needs to keep his mouth shut," I grumbled, then took a swig from the bottle, appreciating the very-real, slightly spicy, ginger hit.

"Wouldn't help since you told the entire bar," Kash grumbled. "So drink your drink and bat your eyelashes at someone, then leave. I'm having nothing to do with it. I don't want those kinds of guys in my bar."

I let my mouth drop open, then very slowly turned to look pointedly at the old mob guy who sat in the corner booth here five nights a week, doing *business* because he liked that Kash played old rock music instead of "that electric crap." Then I looked back at Kash with my brows up.

Kash's jaw tightened. "*He's* never had the Police knocking on my door," he said with a pointed look at me.

"That's because they *work for him.*"

"Shut up, Bridge. I told you, drink your drink, then get your ass out of here."

"And a very shapely ass it is, too," a low voice rumbled from behind me.

For a split second my heart leaped—had Cain come for me?—but I should have known, it was just Art, the barn-sized man who worked as Kash's bouncer.

"Hey, Art," I said, giving him my most winning smile, mainly because it would piss Kash off.

"Hey beautiful—I'm glad you made it. I found something you might like."

I clapped my hands as Kash put both hands up and shook his head, backing away from the bar. "Fuck this. Just fuck it. I don't want to hear it. I'm too old for this."

"You're thirty-five," I snapped at his back as he tossed the dirty rag into the sink and stormed out to the walk-in fridge at the other end of the bar.

Art leaned over the bar to steal a handful of peanuts, then grinned and threw a few in his mouth as he watched Kash leave.

I patted his ham-sized fist to draw his attention back to me.

Art was old-school. The kind of criminal who used knowledge as power, and was more interested in ripping off *The Man,* than becoming an online culture icon. He was a vault when it came to keeping secrets, and knew a great many of the fleas crawling around on the dirty underbelly of this city. He was very useful. And he liked me. I didn't know why, but from the first time Kash had brought me here, he acted like I was his niece or something. He watched out for me, stuffed me into an uber when I got too drunk, and needled Kash to make me laugh.

I loved him.

"Now that Killjoy has left the chat, what's going on? Whatcha got for me?"

Art grinned and crunched the rest of his mouthful before he answered. "I got a dude who likes the same dark shit you like and he's trying to build what he calls an *audience.* I want you to be careful though, he's a live wire."

"Those are the best kinds. How do I reach him?"

"You walk over to the pool table, 'cause he's hustling, but he's eager to meet you."

I leaned past Art's mammoth chest to look at the slightly-better-lit alcove where the two pool tables were, and sure enough there was a guy with spiky black hair, metal punched through every ridge and orifice, a *dog collar,* and a nasty grin, looking right at me as he chalked the business end of a pool cue.

I straightened so Art was between us again. "He looks… interesting."

Art snorted. "That's one word for it."

"Exactly what kind of *shit* is he into?"

"He's working over at *Vigori*," Art said, waggling his eyebrows at me.

I sat back, surprised. "Really? *Him?*"

"Really," Art said, beaming because he got a kick out of surprising me.

I leaned past him again to take a second look at the guy, but nope. "Someone needs to tell him the eighties called and they want their punk back."

"You tell him. He doesn't strike me as the type of dude who has a feedback box."

Me either. But my mind was still turning over this new puzzle.

Vigorí was a club just a few blocks away, but one that was definitely not for public consumption. Entry was by invitation only—and you could only be invited by one of the Doms who worked there, or by long-term members. There was no signage. No website on google. No indication that a business even existed there. It was literally a door in a blank wall that anyone would walk past a hundred times without a second look.

I'd been inside many times, but not for over a year.

The thing was, *Vigorí* was the kind of place where menus didn't have prices, and the offerings were generally human in nature. The Doms called their pastimes *art,* and everyone else either watched, or participated.

And if you didn't participate on your very first visit, you weren't invited back.

"He just doesn't seem their type."

Vigorí was run by a woman named Valerie, which was the most interesting thing about her. The club catered to people with money. Rich housewives, bored executives, and their trust-fund kids. Valerie told me she'd chosen to locate on the shady side of town because rent was cheap and it made it seem *edgy.*

"When people have money, the whole world is available to them," she said in her smoking-for-thirty-years rasp. "It's not just hard ons that elude them. Any kind of thrill is hard to find—no pun intended—when all you have to do is point and whatever you want is given to you. Coming downtown makes them feel like they're in danger they can't control, which is a new experience for most of them."

Unaware of my meandering thoughts, Art shrugged. "I guess he's been in DC, decided he wanted to come west, and he's very… skilled."

"At what? Stonewashing jeans?"

"Look, I don't know. Not my circus, not my monkeys. But I thought of you as soon as I heard, because you're into that shit. And after last time—"

"Last time I was drunk. We shall not speak of it again."

Art gave me a look. "I gather our friend over there likes gagging people too, so you two will get right along," he *giggled*.

It had always taken me aback when he did that. He was such a massive man—ruthless and dangerous when he needed to be. Intimidating in the extreme when you didn't know him. But the longer I knew him, the less surprised I would be to find out he played Bingo on Wednesdays and was learning to crochet. The man was a study in juxtaposition.

"He mentioned gags?" It wasn't really my thing, but the world only existed on two planes in Art's world: Things/People Art Liked, and Everything Else. I had learned early that asking a lot of questions was important if I didn't want to stumble into some extremely unpleasant situations that Art knew only enough about to be dangerous.

Art shrugged again. "Nah, he just said he works at *Vigorí*, but I mean, that's part of the whole Dom thing, right?"

"Sure, sure," I murmured, frowning. "So, why does he want to talk to me?"

"Oh! So, last time, you were talking about looking for someone who wanted to hurt you, so I did some asking around and his name came up."

Not what I meant, but bless his heart. "That was... very thoughtful," I told him.

Art rolled his eyes. "Look, I know he's not what you were looking for. But he obviously *knows people,* and he's looking to make connections, you know? Those kinds of people are always helpful. Besides, I thought you might enjoy checking the place out."

Art didn't know I used to be a regular at *Vigorí*. But it had been a while since I visited, and if they were using dudes like this now, maybe it wasn't the place I remembered. Maybe Valerie died.

"Okay, I'll talk to him," I said, hopping off my stool and starting across the bar. "Thanks, Art!"

"Do your business and get out!" Kash called after me. I didn't reply, but raised my middle finger over my shoulder and let it talk for me.

10. In the Shadows

~ BRIDGET ~

Crossing the bar towards those pool tables, I couldn't resist letting my hips sway a little, just because I knew Kash would be watching, but of course, the guy at the pool table noticed too, and followed my progress with his eyes, so I had to pretend that was just how I walked.

His gaze dragged down my body as I got close enough and the hair on the back of my neck stood up.

Excellent!

"I heard you wanted to talk? What's your name?" I asked the guy, leaning my hip against the pool table and folding my arms to emphasize my chest.

Between the hair, the piercings, and the vintage punk look, I'd expected him to be an awkward, angry man. So it was a surprise when he shot me a dark grin, set the chalk down on the pool table and turned away from me to take his shot without responding.

I waited a second while the balls cracked, but I wasn't letting Stonewash Steve dominate me *here,* so without another word, I pushed off the table and turned around to leave.

"I heard you're looking for someone to hurt you."

Hunt, actually. But close enough.

I stopped walking and turned, but kept my unimpressed expression. "I'm looking for someone with a very particular set of skills. Not a sadist with an inferiority complex."

He nodded. "I'm happy to hear you know the difference."

"Do *you?*"

He dropped his chin and grinned and for a split second that jawline looked familiar. My pulse began to race.

No.

No way. He couldn't be Cain. Cain wouldn't let me see his face. But that jawline...

My breathing got shallower and I turned to fully face him. He noticed and his smile got bigger.

"I'm working at a local place," he said in a low, dark voice as he moved around the table to take another shot.

I nodded. "How's Valerie doing these days? It's been a while."

There was more stubble on his jaw than I'd seen reflected in that window. I couldn't tell if that made his jaw seem stronger, or if the shadows were just playing tricks on my mind.

Had Cain had his lip pierced? I didn't think so, but it was on the side that had been turned more away from me...

He arched one brow, but smiled as he shook his head. "Val is... Val. She's got a lot going on."

"Including inviting east coasters to come play with our rich kids?"

He locked eyes with me. "I have a very unique set of skills."

"Sure you do. So skilled and *successful* that you're drinking in a dive bar on a Friday."

He stared at me a second, then shrugged and leaned his pool cue against the table before reaching into his back pocket. I liked the way his bicep curled, and how his sleeves-cut-off t-shirt pulled against his chest when he reached back like that. But I didn't let it show on my face as he pulled out his wallet and opened it.

He had man-hands. Big knuckles, calluses, tendons that stood proud and continued up his forearms, a visible power that was almost elegantly reduced in fine motor-skills. The kind of hands that had dexterity *and* brute strength. They could thread a needle, or choke you to death.

I love man-hands.

My heart pattered.

Unaware of my breathlessness, the guy pulled a card from his wallet, held it pinned between his first two fingers and extended it to me.

I took it and ignored the way he watched me while I read it.

Sid Vicious
The Conductor
Invitation for One

Swallowing a chortle at the name—what was this guy on?—I offered it back to him. "I don't need an invitation. I'm already on the list."

"You will if you want to get into my den."

I blinked. "She gave you a private den?"

He smiled again and gave one of those humble-brag shrugs. "I told you, special skill set. Only limited numbers can participate on any given night."

I snorted. "Excellent marketing. You should run courses on *How to Give Rich People FOMO.*"

He smirked, but didn't respond.

I was still holding the card out for him, but he returned his wallet to his back pocket and picked up his pool cue again.

"I work Saturday to Wednesday. You should stop by."

I blinked again and prayed my shock didn't show on my face. "Valerie's letting you skip the two most popular nights of the week?"

"Like I said, only limited numbers each night. I work better with the smaller crowds."

Or you've only got a limited draw.

But then again, that fringe, niche stuff was what I usually liked the best.

He leaned down on the table to aim his cue, and with his body stretched out like and his t-shirt hugging his back muscles, he looked like a big cat... If a cat had an obsession with eighties punk rock and fashion that was *almost* back in style.

"I'll keep it in mind," I said, tucking the card into my back pocket, and not missing how his eyes cut up to my breasts when my shirt pulled tight.

Tit for tat was only fair.

"Enjoy your game," I said breezily as I turned to walk away.

He snorted, but didn't respond.

Then I stopped like I'd forgotten something and faced him again, but kept walking slowly backwards. "What's your real name?"

"Ronald," he said without missing a beat. He sent that cue snapping forward and the balls cracked on the table again, two of them finding their goals.

"Ah, that explains it," I said, turning away again, grinning.

"Explains what?" he called after me.

"Why you thought that Dom name was cool. Your baseline reference is *terrible."*

He snorted. "What's your name, then?"

"I'm sure you already know. We'll get along better if you don't pretend otherwise."

"Goodnight, Bridget."

"There you go."

"See you next week."

"Maybe."

But the way my heart was pumping, it was possible.

Especially if Cain made me wait.

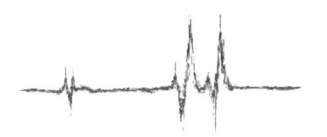

Just to piss Kash off, I sat through three ginger beers, talking to Art and flirting with the drunks who passed through.

The panic that had settled under my skin had passed—mostly. The interaction with Ronald and the potential of that whole situation helped a lot. If Cain didn't make contact, I had something to distract me.

For a second, I saw Gerald in my head, taking off his glasses and shaking his head, his lips puckered like he'd tasted something sour as he tried to come up with the right words to express his exasperation. But I pushed the image away because he might get parts of me, but he didn't understand this.

Then a shadow moved to my left and I snapped my head around, my heart racing—only to find Georgio, the mob guy's thug, leaning on the bar, smiling at me.

Well, shit.

"Hey, B. You look great tonight."

"George," I said dryly without looking at him. "You look exactly the same as you always do."

"Thanks, babe," he beamed and I had to turn away to take another swig from my third ginger beer to hide the eye roll. Poor Georgio was very big, and very strong, and not very smart.

He turned so his shoulder pressed up against mine and tipped his chin to Kash to order a drink. I shifted my seat so we weren't pressed together and suddenly became very aware that I was going to need to use the disgusting ladies room.

I always waited—or skipped those little trips if I could—because so few women frequented this place, we were lucky if Kash threw a mop around it once a week.

I'd taken it on myself for three years to restock toilet paper and wipe down the sinks every time I visited. But my bladder was swelling to near-painful proportions, which meant I was going to have to *use* the bathroom before I cleaned it. And that was going to be gross.

Better than wetting on my stool, though.

When Georgio got his Italian soda and warning look from Kash—because he was both a walking cliché *and* responsible for the mob man's wellbeing, which apparently he took very seriously—he took a sip, then grinned at me.

"It's good to see you, beautiful. You feeling better?"

That panic under my skin gave a crackle, and I launched off the stool. "You'll have to excuse me, I need to pee. Kash, can you make sure George doesn't touch my drink. I don't feel like swimming with the fishes tonight."

Kash nodded once and George snorted. But I was fleeing. I felt eyes on my back and knew Sid was still over there watching.

Would he come after me? The little hallway down to the bathrooms was almost entirely black because the bare overhead bulb had been broken and Kash didn't care enough to replace it.

I looked over my shoulder, tracked that Sid was far enough away he couldn't get to me before I got through the door I could lock, so the only real danger would be when I came back.

The bitch in me smiled at him, made sure he caught it, then turned away and hurried into the little black hallway and pushed open the sticky door into the ladies, whirling to lock it, then darted to the first stall because if I didn't I might actually piss my pants.

A couple minutes later, relieved, but still battling a small wave of panic, I washed my hands, then found the wipes and stuff under the sink and busied myself with removing the worst of the grime from around the faucets and the edge of the sink.

I couldn't bring myself to touch those toilets though, so after putting an extra roll of toilet paper in each stall, I just washed my hands again and checked my reflection in the freckled, cracked mirror, then took a deep breath.

The hallway outside this door was approximately fifteen feet long. The first ten feet or so were pitch black except for the light that came out from under the bathroom doors. When I opened it, I'd get a couple seconds of light, but lowered visibility because of the sudden change in brightness—then it would go pitch black and I'd be aiming for the place where the hallway opened to the main bar, which *would* have some light, though dim.

If Sid was coming for me, he'd do the smart thing and hide *behind* the bathroom since I'd walk out looking towards the bar.

I smiled and cracked my knuckles. *Come at me, bro.* I stood for a few seconds with my eyes closed so my retinas wouldn't be confused by the sudden change in light, then unlocked the door and strode out into the black, the skin on the back of my neck prickling as I darted towards the bar, but half-turned to see if I could make out anything coming for me from the other direction.

It all happened so fast, I'm not sure I breathed.

There was a sickeningly dark, *"Hey there,"* from beside me in the hallway that made me suck in and step sideways, twisting to evade hands I couldn't really see.

As they closed on my elbow, I whipped that arm in a circle to break the grip, grabbing the thick forearm and yanking the dude closer as I swung my leg high enough to take him in the temple—I hoped.

But even though I'd moved like a snake, my leg was only halfway up when a different shadow appeared from nowhere, grabbed me at the waist and flung me sideways.

I stumbled, getting my hands up only just in time to protect me from slamming face-first into the wall, still banging my nose hard enough to see stars for a second, blinking to clear my now watery eyes—then whirling to put my back to the wall and use it for leverage.

But then I froze.

The two shadows had melded and were grunting, moving. I couldn't see enough to know who was winning—or who I wanted to win—but I registered that *two* men had come for me and that was my cue to get the fuck out of here.

I pushed off the wall, the sole of those flimsy heels slipping on the cement floor as I tried to run, but ended up pitching back instead as my foot slid out from under me.

There was a strangled, choking sound, then the thud of a heavy body hitting the floor to my right.

Shit.

I got my feet under me and ran, but I was too late.

One thick arm curled around my middle, while a calloused hand clapped over my mouth, and I was pinned against that wall again.

My pulse pounded in my ear as I tried to scream and clawed at the hand, but then a stubbled jaw scraped against my ear and a rasping, deep voice spat, *"Run."*

A voice that I recognized.

I was flung sideways again, but this time towards the bar, and one hand stayed at my back, making sure I kept my feet.

"Fucking *run,* Bridget," he growled.

Adrenaline slammed through my system. I didn't think. Didn't look. Just took off like a rabbit with a wolf on her tail, straight through the bar, ignoring Kash's shout as I grabbed the end of the bar for leverage to take the corner faster, then sprinted down the other hallway to the staff entrance.

I hit the bar on that door with my full weight, throwing it open and running out—almost flying off the steps, then turning my ankle a little when I hit the uneven cement at the bottom.

But one look over my shoulder showed an empty, well-lit hallway and no shadow pursuing.

I dug into my little purse for my keys, hitting the unlock button while I was still running and almost pitched right over my toes and left skin on the cement when I looked over my shoulder again.

Nothing.

I caught my balance, ran into the driver's door hard enough that the bang echoed in the alley, then threw the door open and jumped inside, plunging the key into the ignition. The car roared to life and I peeled out, the engine whining as I reversed way too fast for the narrow space. But I slammed on the brakes before my back bumper kissed the building on the other side of the alley, cranked the wheel, and tore out of there and into the street, ignoring the red light one block down and pushing through and away until I saw the signs for the highway and the only sound other than the grinding engine, was my breathing, heavy, wheezing inside the car.

11. Bedtime Story

~ BRIDGET ~

I kept looking in my mirrors and over my shoulder, but I never saw anything—or anyone—following me. But how could I know if the car lights behind me were the same car, or five different ones?

I couldn't, so I kept speeding and pushing through lights all the way to the highway, and then all the way home, changing lanes several times to see if any headlights followed me.

My body was humming—that panic replaced by an electric rush. But the longer I drove with no sign of anyone following, the more I began to calm… and decompress. Which made me angry. I *wanted* the exhilaration. That was the whole point!

Then, as the adrenaline wore off and left me shaky, but calm, the self-doubt crowded in.

Had it been Cain or not? It had sounded like his growl. But there'd been none of that wonderful scent. And if he was chasing me, he would have pursued me out to the car. Wouldn't he? Wasn't that the point of the hunt?

My head spun with questions, none of which had answers.

When I took the exit to my suburb and no cars followed me, my heart took its last thump, then puttered along at a far-too-normal rate while I drove through the sleepy streets until I was almost at my place.

Halfway down the block, I clicked the button and slowed the car, because my driveway was short and my garage door was slow. I ended up sitting in the car, the nose in the driveway, still waiting for the door to rattle up, watching my mirrors and scanning my yard, my phone open and dialed as I looked for any sign that he was here and considered whether it was time.

Fuck!

Frustration rattled through me. As I'd driven up, the arc of the headlights had revealed an Amazon package on the front door, and that was a little lift. Another couple sets of the black clothes that I'd ordered same day. But more equipment for the hunt did me *no* good if Cain wasn't here.

I was nervous and angry and not having fun.

Determined to spend the rest of the night in the forum if that was what it took to catch Cain online and ask him if that had been him, I parked the car and tapped my phone a couple of times, then took a deep breath, then shoved out of it, slipping the phone in my back pocket as I stormed around the front to get the package since it was closer than going through the house—and I didn't want to detour to the living room. I wasn't even going to change until I had the computer logged on.

This fucker was going to answer some questions.

I picked up the package and started back down the short path towards the driveway and garage, my heels clicking on the cement, one hand clawed into the cardboard box, the other clenched to a fist around my little garage door remote, when something big and warm hit me from behind and took me off my feet.

And as that hand clapped over my mouth again, my heart slammed against my ribs, and my soul fucking *sang*.

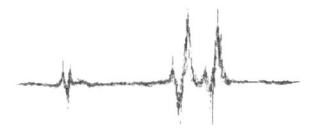

~ *CAIN* ~

Did she have a deathwish? Just walking out in the open like that in the dark?

But, of course she did.

I would have laughed, but I was too busy crouching behind the largest of the bushes between her front door and garage. I'd intended to dart into the garage once she got the door open, but she was already in the driveway, and then another car passed just as she parked, so I had to wait to be sure.

But instead of going into the house, she'd clacked her way out of the garage and to the front door to pick up the package—my backup plan. If I didn't get into the garage in time, I hoped she'd come to the front door so I could ambush her when she bent down to pick it up.

Instead, I got an eyeful of her ass as she leaned down in those heels to pick it up, then turned back the way she'd come, her jaw set and one hand clenched to a fist.

Her breasts bounced with every step and made my body tighten.

The moment she'd passed the bush, I slipped out and swept her up from behind, clapping a hand over her mouth so she couldn't notify the neighbors.

There was a moment when my arms first wrapped around her that my stomach lurched and my heart expanded in my chest. I buried my nose in her hair and inhaled as I lifted and turned her—only to have my little reverie broken by a very sharp elbow straight to the ribs.

I grunted and hunched, my next step a little unsteady because my weight shifted.

She kicked my shins with her heels and I hissed, almost screaming because that was fucking *brutal*. But delight trilled through me because she was a cat—strong, quick, and never stopped moving, clawing, yeowling behind my hand, and making it very clear what she'd do to me if she had the chance.

Panting, but chuckling a little bit too, I whipped her completely off her feet, lifting her so she was slung over my hip—*good luck kicking my shins from there, Bridget*—and hesitated for only one second at the garage door.

This was only the first hunt, but it was probably the most important of them all. For the experience we planned to be truly fulfilling, this first hunt had to achieve two things. She had to learn that she could not beat me physically. And that there was *nowhere safe.* Even her home was not a sanctuary from me.

I wanted her heartbeat pulsing in her skin every second of every day, *knowing* I could reach her if I wanted to. That she had no control—and I had all of it.

However, neither of us was going to be truly satisfied by this whole arrangement unless there was some kind of build-up. If I'd just hidden in her house and ended this the first time, there might be a rush as it happened, but we'd both be left hollow. Dead.

This first hunt had to be short, sharp, and eye-opening—the promise of something greater to come. An inkling of the growing danger she was in. And a rush that threatened more.

So, as I carried her off her feet and towards that open garage door I discarded the idea of taking her into the house. I'd already proven that I could. And since I hadn't had time to explore her home yet, there was a risk I'd get turned around or stuck.

This hunt was a taste. An appetizer. She already knew I'd found her at the bar. Now she'd learn that even when she couldn't see me coming, I'd always be there. No matter where she hid.

The automatic garage door light had come on when she pulled in. But she'd taken a moment to get out, and a few more to walk to get the package. Pulling her hard up against the side of the garage, holding her tightly while she struggled, and whispering to her that it wouldn't be long, I waited for the light to click off, then darted into the shadows of her space, pinning her up against the side of her car to give more freedom for my hands.

Her chest was heaving, her breath tearing in and out of her nose. She struggled hard as I brought her upright, clawing at me, trying to pull my hand off her face, but when I shoved her up against the car, pinning her against the rocking vehicle with my chest to her back, and one knee between her thighs, there was no room for her to engage those elbows. And keeping her feet off the ground gave her nowhere to go.

"Flatten your hands on the window where I can see them," I growled, then smiled a moment later when she slumped and did as she was told. *"Good girl."*

She shivered.

When I was sure she was secure and we hadn't been seen, I paused... and for a moment I was almost overwhelmed by the thrill of her firm, sweet flesh in my hands. Her scent in my nose.

Her strength and courage.

God, she was amazing.

And I was hard.

Swallowing, I rocked my hips just once, nudging her. "Can you feel that... feel what you do to me?" I whispered a voice that started in the pit of my balls.

She nodded quickly, her breath still coming short and shallow.

I smiled as I dropped my chin and ran my nose along her jaw, and rasped, "The only question left is... can I do the same to you? What happens if I get inside you, Bridget? What will I find?"

She whimpered as I slid a hand between her and the car, right at the button of her jeans, though I wasn't going to pop it. Not yet, not tonight. Even if the monster inside was *aching* to touch her.

She whimpered when I ran fingertips along the seam of her jeans–a simple tease–and she tried to fight once, tried to push me off the car, off of her, but the car moved more than I did. Then she slumped again, her shoulders moving up and down with the force of her breath as she was forced to accept that she was helpless.

I smiled, about to reassure her that if she was a *very good girl* she would live through this night.

But then... she *laughed?*

12. Fuck Around and Find Out

SOUNDTRACK: *Russian Roulette* by Ryan Mitchell

~ CAIN ~

I'd had a lot of different reactions from marks, but this was a first.

As Bridget sniggered and spluttered against my palm I was rocked with conflicting emotions—half of me fascinated and amused, the other half pissed off and determined to make sure she understood the danger she was in.

Dropping my voice as low as it would go and keeping it harsh, I growled in her ear. "You think this is a joke?"

I leaned my full weight against her, pressing her hard enough against the car that it would be difficult for her to breathe.

She tensed and shook her head frantically under my palm, but her breath was still coming in snorts.

I had to know.

"I'm going to remove my hand from your mouth. But you make one sound to alert your neighbors, and it will be the last you'll make. Do you understand? Blink twice."

She quickly squeezed her eyes closed, opened them, then squeezed them tight again.

Slowly, poised to clap my hand back over her mouth if she was deceiving me, I loosened my grip on her face and gave her room to breathe, then to speak.

She was panting heavily, but even those tearing breaths were broken by waves of *giggles*. She struggled one more time, but she was already losing strength, I just shook my head.

"F-fuck you're strong," she gasped, then she snorted. I huffed and I gripped the back of her neck, pressing her head against the car as a warning. She tensed. "Don't-don't-don't! Imma n-nervous laugher." Then she was overcome. She had her hands up on the car and covered her face with one, spluttering and snickering. "You saw the p-post, I guess?"

"You did well," I admitted gruffly, keeping my voice in that rough rumble.

"D-did you like the p-present?"

I'd seen it immediately, of course, laid out on the floor in front of the first aid kit and the disinfectant. It was a floor-plan of her house, printed and annotated, with notes on entries and exits, and ways the house varied in reality from the plan logged in the city's system.

That jangle of pleasure screamed through my veins. I wanted to high five her, but kept my face straight and my tone disapproving. "You think you're funny," I growled.

She shook her head, her eyes still covered by her hand. "Have you had a chance to check it out yet?" she whispered, still sniggering.

"I've seen enough."

"Are you s-sure?"

"Why do you care?"

"Because," she gasped, giggling. *"You're going to need it."*

I frowned. "What the fuck are you talking about?" I snarled.

Then she took her hand away to look at me. I was literally breathing down the back of her neck, far too close for clear sight, and I was wearing a silk mesh over my face that obscured my features, but let me see. With my hand on the back of her neck and her temple pressed against the car, she could only look at me from the corner of her eye—those startling, sparkling eyes that were light blue with a jade rim around the outside of the iris. I knew she couldn't see my face distinctly, but our eyes locked.

"I g-gotchu," she breathed.

I raised an eyebrow and smirked. "I don't think that word means what you think it means," I rumbled.

But she smiled. "I called the cops when I was driving up the block. Told them I suspected I had an intruder in my house."

She bit her lip as adrenaline flooded my system.

She was lying.

She had to be.

I leaned into her ear, letting my voice drop into the abyss. "You *trying* to piss me off, Bridget?"

"No," she whispered. "You said I could fight. In fact… you encouraged it."

Then she lifted her right hand, the one that had been clenched into a fist when she was on the path outside, and something metallic flashed in it.

Instinctively, I shot my free hand out to clamp her wrist and slammed her hand into the car.

She gasped with pain, but even though the little remote tumbled out of her grip, it was too late.

A warm light flickered on overhead and I ducked my face against her shoulder as the garage door creaked, then began to rattle slowly down.

I was still cursing about being in the light when she started squeezing words out of a clenched jaw because I still had her head pinned against the car.

"If you studied my notes on the plans you know all the external doors in this house are combination locks. You w-wont get in or out without the code. You've got about twenty seconds before the gap under the big door gets too small for you to fit," she said through her teeth, because I had her head pressed against the car. "You could break a window, I suppose. But there's only about a minute before the cops show up. I dialed the number, but didn't talk after I told them someone was here, and didn't disconnect the call. Their procedure is to send a unit no more than five minutes after the start of an open call."

"You're just trying to—"

"Look at my phone in my pocket." Then she arched her back a hair, bumping me with her ass. "It's right there."

Vixen. I growled a warning to her, but slid a hand between us slowly, I reached into her back pocket to find the phone locked, but there was an active-call notification at the top with the scrolling words…

EMERGENCY CALL

My blood ran cold as I hurriedly hit the end-call button, then pressed her harder against the car.

"Tell me you're joking, Bridget," I hissed.

She shook her head, then snorted again and there was an edge of hysteria in it. "Not joking. Just fighting. The best way I know how."

I stood there, frozen in shock—and admiration—for about three seconds. The garage door was about halfway down, and she wasn't joking that pretty soon the gap under it would be too small for my frame.

Then the soft glow of car lights appeared, growing closer from somewhere down the street.

Shit. *Shit.*

I didn't entirely believe that she'd done it—but the risk of being trapped in her house when the Police arrived was too great. Bridget wanted this—wanted the services I offered. But she was quick and reckless, and completely unintimidated by authority.

She wouldn't give a fuck about possibly getting charged with wasting Police resources. But I gave a great many fucks about being caught by law enforcement in a strange woman's house.

I hissed a curse, then shoved away from her as she gave an unhinged laugh. I dove for the gap under that garage door and rolled underneath it just in time, then straight to my feet, sprinting into the front yard because there was a hedge for cover from those lights that had almost reached the driveway, and were slowing.

Vaulting the neighbor's fence, then turning immediately to follow it to the back of their house, where no lights were shining, I turned at a right angle with the fence, then up and over the six-footer on the other side of the house and through that neighbor's property, too.

Five minutes later, finally certain I hadn't been seen and wasn't being pursued, I crept out of the bushes around a house two blocks away, yanked the mask from my face and ran a hand through my hair to straighten it as I stuffed the wad of thin material into my pocket.

I took a long time to circle back to my car, keeping eyes and ears alert for law enforcement, though I avoided the streets that took the most direct route to her house from the highway.

By the time I reached my vehicle and got inside, my heart rate had almost returned to normal.

I sat there for a long time, parked under a huge maple that had to be twenty years old, and whose branches extended halfway over the street, blocking out the streetlights and casting the car into deep shadows that would keep me safely out of sight.

And then I breathed.

And stared at the street ahead, and in the rearview mirror, always checking just in case. But there was nothing. Just a quiet, suburban street, hiding a monster.

Sliding my hand into my pocket, I pulled out her phone, turned it to airplane mode, then completely off, before I sat there, staring at it, stroking the face of it with my thumb, imagining her looking for it.

Bridget was going to be my best hunt yet. She was fearless and wicked. And a clever bitch.

But not as clever as me.

Then I started laughing.

13. He's Coming

~ BRIDGET ~

It wasn't until I'd gotten all the way back to my room that I realized he'd taken my phone.

Fucker!

But it made me smile. I wondered whether he'd be able to crack my phone and figure out that had been a dummy number. It was one of those information lines that had a message that looped infinitely, so the line would stay open. I'd named it EMERGENCY CALL in my phone for purposes just like this—to intimidate people who needed a wake up call. But all he'd have to do was look at the contact in the call log to see that it was a 1-800 number.

That car coming up the street at that time had been such a stroke of luck, I decided maybe God did have a sense of humor. I didn't think I'd ever seen a guy move so fast.

Definitely ex-military. Or some kind of training. He'd moved like a cat—so smooth and quick. No hesitation.

And now he was gone.

That thought made me sigh.

But my entire body still hummed with the adrenaline he'd set coursing through me. I was on a high because he was everything I'd hoped—strong, intelligent, sneaky and…

well, I didn't know if he was handsome, but he certainly *felt* like it.

I closed my eyes, remembering the feeling of his body pressed against mine, hard and unrelenting as steel, pinning me to the car.

My breath got faster.

Yanking my heels off, I began to pace the floor of my room, reliving each moment in my mind—that scuffle at the bar, fleeing home in the car and being disappointed because I thought he hadn't come after me. I'd only set up the phone on pure *hope.*

Then, when he jumped me, it was such a rush, I got shaky remembering it.

I couldn't stop seeing that moment in my mind when he'd cursed and thrown himself away from me to dive and roll under the lowering garage door—straight to his feet on the other side and sprinting away.

I shivered just thinking about it.

I needed more.

I didn't know how far away Cain was from his home and his computer, but I was going to try and make contact— after all, he had my phone.

So, after a quick shower and change into sleep-shorts and a t-shirt, I ran to my office and turned on the computer, praying that he didn't live far away and would be online already. It had been half an hour since he left and my adrenaline was fading.

My heart spun in my chest when I logged into the forum and the first notification was a DM from him, but then it sank when I realized he'd sent it before he came for me.

It was a list of after-care instructions, along with detailed lists of which of the things to use in any given situation.

There were even links to video tutorials that showed things like how to properly clean a scrape, how to wrap a wrist, or ankle, how to properly set a sling.

I was oddly touched.

Then my adrenaline skyrocketed again, because the little green circle over his profile picture suddenly blinked alive, which meant he was online. I grabbed for the mouse to hit *message* so fast I almost knocked my keyboard off the desk.

SYSTEM NOTE: CHAT ENCRYPTED END-TO-END. ENSURE ALL ACCOUNTS ARE LOGGED OFF BEFORE DISCONNECTING.

DeadGirlWalking: You have something that belongs to me.

SleepingBeast: You'll get it back.

DeadGirlWalking: When? My life is on there.

SleepingBeast: I know. And soon. Don't worry.

DeadGirlWalking: People are going to try and contact me.

SleepingBeast: Relax. I've got all your calls and texts diverting to the burner phone—so it better be charged like the instructions said.

DeadGirlWalking: Well, aren't you clever. That was quick.

SleepingBeast: This isn't my first rodeo.

DeadGirlWalking: I always thought that saying was odd— like, how many rodeos *should* a person have ridden? Because if this is only number two or three, I'm still not trusting your process.

SleepingBeast: Change subject.

SleepingBeast: From this point forward, any time we meet and you're injured and I'm forced to leave before we're done, you send me pictures of the wound, and how you treated it. Every time, D. Including now.

DeadGirlWalking: I mean, sure. If you want harm porn, I'll help you out. It's the least I can do. But I'm not hurt right now. A couple sore spots that might bruise, I suppose.

SleepingBeast: You sure?

DeadGirlWalking: I'm sure. You were just so gentle.

SleepingBeast: I'll make sure and correct that next time.

DeadGirlWalking: Yes, please.

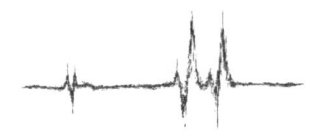

~ *CAIN* ~

I clawed a hand through my hair and cursed.

My marks were always consenting participants in our little game—they always came looking for me, not the other way around. They were always thrill seekers, and sometimes masochists. But Bridget's eagerness had a unique edge that was fascinating to me. And a very bright red flag. She wasn't frightened of me. At all.

The others came to be *because* they were scared. They *wanted* to be scared. In their fear, they found the thrill.

I'd hunted many different women. Some were trying to face a fear to overcome it. Some were drawn to violent men and wanted to take control by inviting it in, instead of having it inflicted on them. All were self-destructive and taking control of their own destinies.

At first I'd thought Bridget was just one of the latter. But now I wasn't so sure.

I was beginning to think that she was truly dark like me.

And I couldn't decide if that was the best thing that had ever happened to me, or was going to be my downfall. Because I didn't usually *chat* with a mark.

I'd told myself I was only getting on here to make sure she took care of herself in case I'd hurt her, carting her around and shoving her up against the car.

But we'd covered that in a few lines, and yet... here we were.

DeadGirlWalking: So how long until I see you again?

SleepingBeast: This isn't a date, D. We won't be syncing schedules.

DeadGirlWalking: I know. But still. How long?

SleepingBeast: The whole point is that you don't know when I'm coming for you. That's what makes it fun. I'll never tell you when I'm coming.

DeadGirlWalking: Ah, the luxury of being a man—no one has to question if you'll come. It's only ever a matter of time.

I was just taking a drink of coffee and almost spat it over my keyboard.

SleepingBeast: You have trouble coming, D?

DeadGirlWalking: Sometimes.

SleepingBeast: Challenge accepted.

DeadGirlWalking: I didn't realize you were a sweet-talker.

SleepingBeast: No, just a giver.

DeadGirlWalking: A primal dom with manners? That seems counter-productive.

    I caught myself grinning at the screen like an idiot and stopped typing.
    This was sick what we were doing—what we planned. Why was she so engaged in this? With *me?* And why did I love it?
    Why was I this way? And why was she?
    I started to type, "What happened to you?" but caught myself halfway through and deleted it.

SleepingBeast: I gotta go.

DeadGirlWalking: Wait! No! We were just getting somewhere!

SleepingBeast: Sorry, D, but I got work in the morning.

DeadGirlWalking: Wait, you work?

SleepingBeast: We aren't all independently wealthy. Some of us have to make an honest wage so we have the resources for our very dishonest pastimes. Hunting isn't a cheap hobby.

DeadGirlWalking: So, I'm a hobby now?

SleepingBeast: Goodnight, D. Picture tomorrow if there are bruises. And use the Arnica.

DeadGirlWalking: I will, but wait!

[DeadGirlWalking is typing...]

    I swallowed hard and almost gave in, but the first trickle of sweat started down my spine. I quickly logged out, then got off the computer, shaking my head at myself the whole time.

She was dangerous. *So* dangerous to me.

But maybe that was the point, I realized. She wasn't the only one who needed the risk to feel alive.

I did too.

I just never confused the hunt with *feelings* before. I'd always sworn I wouldn't.

But she was hilarious, and smart, and bold, and fearless and…

When the screen went black and the computer's hum stopped, I rubbed both hands over my face, asking myself if it was worth it—if *she* was worth it. Because I was breaking all my own rules. And that meant I had to have an honest conversation with myself.

Was she worth it, if she was the one that brought me down?

My soul answered without hesitation that she was.

I looked at the clock on my phone and cursed. Almost 2am.

I wasn't lying to her. I had work in the morning. I needed to get some sleep.

But first, I had a phone to mirror.

Digging around in my bag, I drew out her phone and took it to the little workbench in the corner where I already had another, brand new phone in the same make, model, and year as hers.

And then I went to work.

14. Can You Feel It?

~ BRIDGET ~

That silk sleeping mask he'd made me buy was over my eyes, so I couldn't see anything. But my other senses were heightened.

"Can you feel that, Bridget? Can you feel what you do to me?" Cain rasped in my ear and my belly trilled as he rocked his hips and I felt the hardness of him under his jeans, pressing against the crack of my ass.

"Yes," I breathed, gripping the top of the car to give myself leverage as he cupped both my breasts over my shirt, then dragged his hands down, down, down my sides, then under the waistband of my yoga pants, his callouses scraping on soft skin, his hands so large that his thumbs pressed on my lower back when he cupped my hips.

Then his hands were moving and he was sliding my pants down, dragging my underwear with them.

The cool air of the garage shocked my heated skin and raised goosebumps that made him growl, long and low, burying his face in my neck and sucking hard as he bared me.

Then he had my pants and underwear past my hips and they dropped, puddling around my feet so I could step out of them, kick them off to the side while he kept his chest pressed against my back, his breath harsh in my ear. There was a clink as he unbuckled his belt and he leaned back slightly to give himself room to wrestle with his own jeans.

Bare from the waist down, I was already frantic for him and arched my back, bumping against his hands and breathing his name until he gave a guttural groan and grabbed for me, pulling me back against him and I gasped as the thick length of him slid between my thighs and teased at my most sensitive skin.

Gripping the rail of the rack on top of the car, I dropped my forehead against the glass window, then reached back with one hand to bury fingers in his hair as he groaned and growled, pressing, sliding, teasing until it was little more than a parody of what I really wanted.

"Cain... please—"

Face still buried in my neck, his lips and tongue dancing just below my ear, he reached around with one hand, between my legs, and pressed himself hard against me, still rocking, sliding, promising what was to come.

My body came alive, pleasure zinging from my slick flesh where he played and pressed, through my body, all the way out to my limbs. My skin sang in time with the rhythm of his toying.

Then he passed over my core and almost took me.

I sucked in, dropping my head back. "Oh, god..."

Cain brought his other hand up to cup my throat, holding my head back, as he nipped and sucked at the sensitive skin under my ear.

The jolts from where he pressed against me crackled through my bloodstream to meet the waves of pleasure washing down my back from his lips.

I was trembling, arching, begging for him. And Cain was shaking with me, guttural groans bitten off, his teeth scraping on my skin, his hands grasping, body jerking and twitching as he tried to hold himself back.

Then with a muttered curse he straightened. Before I could complain, he grasped both my hips and pulled me back half a step, nudging my knees wider.

"Are you ready for me, Bridget?" His rasp echoed in the garage.

"Yes!"

With a low rumble of need, he slipped two fingers into me and when I tightened on him, gave a husky chuckle that sent goosebumps up my spine. "Yes, you are."

Then, without any further warning, he planted a hand at my lower back and pressed down as he plunged into me in a single thrust from behind. He filled me so quickly and so perfectly, I felt it all the way to the soles of my feet.

Cain bellowed and snapped forward over me, his hand clamping over mine on the roof rack, his chest hard and hot against my back. His fingers clawed between mine, gripping my hand and locking it in place—and then, with his other hand on my hip to control me, he dragged himself slowly out so that I felt every slow inch, my body humming and shaking with sheer, animal delight.

He dropped his chin, opening his mouth and biting down where my shoulder met my neck. The sounds that ripped from his throat belonged in a national geographic documentary—animalistic, brutal—those low snarls vibrating in his chest against my back.

As he picked up the pace and all I could do was brace to meet him, I reached back with my free hand, fisting his hair and holding him to me as he began a punishing rhythm that tore a cry from me with every pounding thrust. The pressure building deep inside me, and a growing promising pleasure that glowed on the horizon like the rising sun.

"Cain... Cain!" *I gasped, struggling to keep my feet as my knees began to shake.*

He growled and let go of my hand and shoulder as he snapped upright again, grasped my hips and began pulling me back onto him with each thrust, so hard that the sound of our bodies smacking echoed in the garage.

"Fuck, Bridget."

"Don't stop, I'm going to co—"

He snarled and pulled out of me so fast I blinked, then grabbed my shoulders and turned me around to face him. I had to grab for his broad shoulders so I wouldn't fall, but he'd already lifted me and plunged back into me, slamming me back against the car, grabbing that rack and pinning me as my back arched against the cold door and braced one hand on his chest, as he began to pound again.

I was pinned, utterly at his mercy. I hooked my ankles behind his back, gripped his shoulder and planted a palm on his chest, and focused on bracing to meet him. And in seconds he was grunting and that wave of promised pleasure was glimmering at the edge of my blackened vision again.

But that blindfold over my eyes was suddenly an unacceptable barrier. I needed to see the way his muscles corded, the tendons on his neck, the shaking of his shoulders when he came.

"I have to s-see you," I gasped, needing his eyes on mine when I reached that peak.

"Fuck, Bridget, no."

"I have to," I breathed. "Have to. Cain… please."

Bridget—" he hissed.

Still braced on his chest with one hand, I grabbed for the blindfold and started pulling it down, just as he roared.

All I saw was the flashing blade, the dim garage light catching on it in his fist as it descended in an arc. I screamed as it plunged into my chest—

—and sat bolt upright in bed, screaming, sweating, my clit humming, my heart rattling in my chest at a hundred miles a minute.

I blinked several times, gasping, grabbing for my naked chest, checking myself and…

And it was just a dream.

And my heart felt like it was going to explode.

With a groan that was half-disappointment and half-relief, I let myself slump back down onto the damp pillow and started my breathing exercises that were supposed to help my heart regulate.

But the adrenaline was flooding through me. The high of the arousal, the shock of terror, and now the ever-present threat of my body that could fail me at any time.

After a few minutes, when it appeared I wasn't going to die, I made myself throw back the blankets and get out of bed. I stumbled to the shower, my body still humming with need and ended up standing under the spray and rubbing myself to a climax in seconds as I replayed that dream in my head—except for the part where he stabbed me.

God, please… before I die… let that dream come true.

I was still trembling a little an hour later when I'd finished drying my hair, dressed, and had breakfast.

My body wanted more.

My body wanted *him.*

But he'd said he had work today.

Did he work all day? Or just in the mornings?

Somehow I knew if I messaged and asked him, he wasn't going to tell me. He'd already refused to say if he'd start hunting again immediately.

But I needed him to.

After yesterday, I knew he was following me. At least at night. And now he had my phone. He'd probably find the logs on it to tell him everywhere I went.

That was fine. I *wanted* him to show up.

It seemed like a good day to run errands and go to the gym and basically stay on the move. Tempt him to follow. Entice him to come for me.

It wasn't like I had anything else to do.

So I didn't even log in to the computer. Just grabbed my little purse and keys, and darted out to the car.

I couldn't help watching the rearview mirror as the garage door rolled up. But the only thing that showed up in my garage this time was bright sunlight, because I had slept in and it was almost lunchtime.

I reversed into the street a little faster than necessary, then rolled towards the highway, biting my nails, praying he was keeping track and would show up. My own tortured words in that dream coming back to haunt me.

Please, Cain… please.

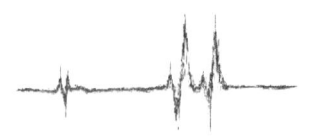

CAIN: Someone's busy today.//
ME: Stalker.//
CAIN: True. But let's not forget that I was invited to this hunt.//
ME: I need my phone back. I also need you against my back again. Soon.//
CAIN: Shameless.//
ME: If it's shame you want, come treat me like a naughty girl. And you don't have to be gentle this time.//
CAIN: Tempting as that is, sadly I already have plans for today.//
ME: Do those include chasing me and railing me against a tree? Because I'm up for that.//
CAIN: Such a flirt. Patience.//
ME: I don't have time for patience. Imminent death, remember?//

He didn't answer that one right away and I was frustrated. Because I *wanted* him. I'd known this whole game would turn me on, but I hadn't ever had a dream that graphic and... *hot* before.

ME: Suddenly shy about the death part?//
CAIN: No. Working. You aren't the only thing in my life, Princess.//
ME: Apparently not. You have my phone as well. Why?//
CAIN: I needed to do some research. Don't worry, you'll get it back.//
ME: Next time, just ask. You don't have to steal. I'll let you have anything you want.//
CAIN: Temptress. Is that a challenge?//
ME: Try me.//
CAIN: I plan to.//

ME: I look forward to it.
CAIN: You need therapy.
ME: You are my therapy.
CAIN: Well then. You're fucked.
ME: I hope so.
ME: Now come get me.
ME: Please?
ME: You like it when I beg, don't you?
ME: Cain, where are you?
ME: Anything. I'll give you anything. All you have to do is show up.
ME: God, you're annoying.
ME: Also hot.
CAIN: Not as hot as those rotisserie chickens you're standing next to.

I gasped and looked up from the phone, scanning the entire deli and produce section where I was shopping. I turned a full circle, but there was no one in sight that could even *maybe* be Cain.

ME: Where are you?!
CAIN: I told you. Even when you don't see me, I see you.
ME: Well, I hope I'll see you at the river park. That's my next stop. For a picnic. All by myself.
ME: You're welcome.

15. I Feel Seen

SOUNDTRACK: *Running Up that Hill* by Placebo

~ BRIDGET ~

Come get me. Come get me. Come get me.
My heart was thumping so hard I felt it against my ribs.
If he was close enough to see where I was in the store, then he must be hunting?

There was only one way to find out. I sent that text telling him where I was going, then hurried to the checkout and paid for my groceries, throwing them in the back of the car and peeling out of the parking lot. My heart hadn't slowed, and my breathing was quick and shallow. My body *hummed.*

The hair on the back of my neck kept standing up as I drove. Because I could feel him watching? Or just anticipation of what was to come?

When I reached the river park, I grabbed the bag of food, then practically ran from the car, across the parking lot, to the trail that went into the woods.

My phone pinged and I almost dropped it because I was so frantic to get it out of my pocket.

CAIN: I thought running wasn't good for your heart?
ME: Being alive isn't good for my heart. But I've calculated the cost/benefit risks and decided running from you is worth it.

He didn't answer immediately, so I kept moving.

There weren't many places near the city that were truly private in daylight, but this little section of greenbelt had been protected by the town planners. It butted up against the river and in the spring it was the mating ground for a protected breed of water-bird that I couldn't remember. But this time of year it was little more than a path for joggers and dog walkers.

I'd explored this park countless times, and a couple years earlier, discovered a hidden little clearing deep in the woods. I'd only been able to find it by GPS and had never seen anyone else there. I'd never told anyone about it either.

Cain was either going to follow me and discover it, or lose me.

I smiled.

Come find me. Come find me. Come find me.

Once I was in the trees, I couldn't see anyone. I knew there'd be people at the park itself, and probably along this path, but I couldn't see any of them.

Then my phone pinged again.

CAIN: How many men have you lured out here?
ME: You're the first.
CAIN: I don't believe you.
ME: I'm not a liar either, Cain.

The little voice in the back of my head nagged that the statement wasn't *entirely* true. But I didn't correct myself.

I left information out sometimes, but only when it was important. Not about little things.

When he didn't answer right away, I reluctantly put my phone back in my pocket and kept jogging, darting between the trees. I'd been out here enough now that I could find it without the map. Which was good. Because Cain's handiwork on the phone meant it got all my emails, texts, and calls. But I was missing a lot of other stuff.

Which made me pull the phone out and send him another text.

ME: You better have brought my phone. I'm missing my games. And some other stuff.

CAIN: Your collection of ab shots? What's with that? Not a single dick pic in there. So vanilla. I was disappointed.

ME: You like dick pics? Is there something you want to tell me?

ME: Sneaky bastard. How did you figure out the password for that?

CAIN: Disappointed in *you*

ME: Some things can only be appreciated in the flesh.

ME: I mean that in every way you heard it.

ME: For the record, the hottest part of the male anatomy is actually shoulders and arms, but very few men refine their forearm porn. So chests and abs it is.

I had slowed in my running because I was so busy texting. I heard a crack in the bushes nearby and squeaked, shoving my phone into my pocket and sprinting forward, laughing.

Come find me. Come find me. Come find me.

My phone buzzed in my pocket again, but I made myself wait until I'd found the big, felled tree that was a landmark on my route before I turned to follow it and slipped the phone out again.

Then I stopped dead, panting and gaping at the phone.

Cain had sent me a picture.

Holy shit.

He'd stopped in the shade of one of the big pines that had a bare trunk for the bottom twenty feet, and taken off his shirt.

He'd lifted the phone high to take a shot of his back and shoulders, one arm bent up, shoulder muscles rigid and tendons proud on the back of his hand that he'd clamped on the back of his own neck. Sadly, his forearm bent out of frame, and I couldn't see his face at all, only the nape of his neck—his hair was dark and needed a cut—but his hand was thick and strong, and his shoulders…

Desire hummed between my legs because he had the kind of muscles that didn't come in a gym, or from a needle. The kind of muscles that were useful and raunchy, because they were carved by hard labor.

The kind that didn't disappear in the off-season, because there was no off-season.

There were scars here and there all over him, including an ugly pucker of skin right below his ribs.

My mouth watered as I imagined licking that scar. And the ridges of muscle down his side.

When I found the presence of mind to text back, it was only one word.

ME: More.

Then I remembered where I was, and I started running again, slinging the bag of food over one shoulder and sprinting because the clearing wasn't far from here and I *really* hoped I'd make it before he found me.

When I broke through the trees into that little light-bathed oasis of pretty, I was ecstatic.

I dropped the bag of food and darted into the center where the sun was high enough to bathe the thin grass in a warm glow. There was another couple fallen trees here, not as big as the one I used to point me, but big enough to sit on.

I couldn't sit down, though. I was panting, my heart thumping, my senses shrieking.

He's here. I know he's here.
But where?

I stopped, held my breath, tried to hear the sounds over my pulse pounding in my ears, but there was nothing. No crack of a foot on a twig. No rustle of a very muscular body pushing through the leaves.

I turned a slow circle, trying to breathe deeply, but quietly, trying to catch any sound or flicker at the corner of my eye.

Where was he?

I wanted to pull the phone out again, but all the hair on the back of my neck was standing up.

He was here. I was certain of it.

"Feeling shy, Cain?" I said to the trees, smiling.

Nothing.

Humph.

"I know you're here. I saw the forest in your picture. Thank you for that, by the way. I'll cherish it. I hope it'll show up on my phone. You've got my phone, right?"

The phone in my pocket buzzed again and my adrenaline shot up a notch.

Still keeping my eyes on the forest around me, still turning slowly, scanning for any sound or sight of him, I pulled the phone out of my pocket and tapped the screen.

One glance, and my smile got broader.

CAIN: Look on the stump.

I whirled to face the stump of one of those fallen trees. It wasn't very big, maybe a foot in diameter. But the tree had clearly snapped because there were jagged teeth of wood standing up from it.

Still watching and listening, I approached the stump slowly and peered behind those spikes of wood to find the light reflecting on a black screen.

My phone.

I kept my eyes on the trees behind it as I reached over to pick it up. "Thank you," I said in a normal voice. "Now… don't be scared. I brought enough food that you can have s—"

A weight slammed into me from behind, knocking the wind out of me so a strange, strangled choke erupted in my throat.

Then we were tumbling to the sodden earth, big hands, thick arms curling around me and turning me as we fell so I went down to the left of the trunk, not on those wicked spikes sticking out of it.

We hit the ground and it thumped like a drum, the carpet of pine needles and leaves almost cushioning the fall. But there was a thick, steel arm under my ribs, and a heavy weight bearing me to the ground. So even though we bounced a little, the last squeak of air my lungs had retained was gone on impact.

I lay on the forest floor, my arms pinned to my chest by his, his breathing in my ear. And mine… non-existent.

I couldn't breathe. At all.

I couldn't breathe.

And my heart was *vibrating,* it pumped so fast.

Cain was here. He was finally here—grasping at my body, growling in my ear. And we were alone. It was everything I'd been hoping for. I just prayed I wouldn't have a heart attack and die before I could enjoy it.

Because I couldn't… fucking… breathe.

16. Takedown

~ BRIDGET ~

He'd rolled me onto my stomach and had me pinned to the dirt, one arm around my chest keeping me from using my arms, the other clapped over my mouth, though he had left my nose free so I could breathe. It wasn't what was stopping me.

My body quivered, demanding oxygen. But my thoughts were oddly calm and everything felt… weird.

He gave a snarl in my ear and my heartrate ratcheted up another notch because he sounded so feral—exactly how I'd hoped he would be.

But then he noticed I wasn't struggling and he went still. I felt that large body over mine, suddenly freeze. Poised.

"Bridget?"

He had been panting a little, but his breath stopped for a moment as he listened—and obviously confirmed that he couldn't hear mine.

"Bridget, breathe… *Bridget, fucking breathe!*"

The world spun as he flipped me over and I found myself laying on my back, staring up the sky, the sunlight

123

angling through the hole in the treetops above. Then all of it was shadowed by a *huge* guy, leaning over me.

For a split second my eyes widened—was I going to see his face? But I should have known. When his face came into view it was shrouded by some black mesh facemask—some kind of protective gear for sports, I thought. It circled his entire face and was strapped on underneath his hood. I couldn't see anything but the shadow of his features under it, which was disappointing. But not the most important point of fact in that moment.

I needed to fucking inhale.

My chest began to pump in and out, but my lungs wouldn't inflate. And my heart was racing so fast I wondered if it was finally going to give out.

"Bridget, look at me. Is it your heart?"

I shook my head and thumped my chest awkwardly with a shaking hand, but I wasn't sure if he knew what I meant.

"Shit. *Shit.*"

He'd kept his voice in that low rasp—half whisper, half growl. But I thought I heard a hint of his real tone when he swore the second time.

All sense of danger and predation dropped from his posture and suddenly, he was nothing but business. With another muttered curse he leaned down and shoved an arm under my shoulders, pulling me up to sit with low, firm instructions.

"Your diaphragm is in shock."

Not the kind of diaphragm I had hoped you'd shock for me, I thought and wished I could say. Wished I could see if he smiled under that mask.

"You need to sit up—brace your hands on the ground… Good. Now, lean forward."

I did as he said, but my lungs still wouldn't inflate. I clawed one hand into my hair, the other into the dirt under me.

"It's just a muscle spasm. Don't panic."

I wasn't. I was still eerily calm. But my vision was beginning to tunnel.

"See if you can cough—hard. Push air *out* so your diaphragm will reset."

I tried, but it seemed I didn't have any air left. That second impact on the ground after he tackled me had taken care of the last of it.

Then my heart pinched, and for the first time, a trickle of fear entered my bloodstream, because my heart would do all kinds of crazy loops, skips, and dips, but it didn't usually *hurt*.

One of those calloused hands flattened on my back and began to rub, first in firm-but-slow circles, then from the base of my spine, up, then back down.

"You need to relax, Bridget," he graveled. If I could have breathed, I would have giggled because it occurred to me that he sounded like Batman. "Let your shoulders drop. Relax your hands—don't grip. Tell your body that you're ok—"

Suddenly, without warning, as my chest fought to expand, my lungs caught and I sucked in a huge wheezing breath.

"Oh, thank God. No, don't sit up—stay leaning forward. Just breathe. Concentrate on keeping it slow and deep, in through your nose for a count of four, out through your mouth. The last thing you need is to hyperventilate now…"

He continued issuing instructions in that deep husk of a voice, but I stopped listening.

The moment I caught my breath my vision cleared. My hands were still shaking, but I thought that was from the adrenaline more than anything else.

I kept my head down just like he said, but as soon as I was breathing normally, I started to plan. Five more breaths, then I was going to run.

But then he started checking my vitals—fingers pressed at my carotid artery as he watched the timer on his phone and counted the beats of my heart.

He got close and peered into my eyes, touched my forehead. He lifted my hand and checked the color of my nails.

"I think you're okay... I think you're okay." He sounded *relieved.*

"I know you're s-supposed to k-kill me, but I didn't think it would b-be this quick," I quipped breathlessly.

He grunted and put his hand to my back without a word. I took a second to realize he was counting my breathing rate.

Which meant pretty soon he was going to realize I wasn't out of breath anymore. Which meant I needed to get ready to run.

"Just take your time," he growled, sitting back on his heels and finally taking his hand off me. "You've got a waterbottle in that bag, right?" He pushed to his feet and started trotting towards the shopping bag I'd tossed to the edge of the clearing. "Don't worry, we can go back to our game when the time is right, but you need to be checked—"

I pushed to my feet and sprinted in the opposite direction from where he'd gone.

Behind me, I heard him hiss a curse, then heavy footsteps raced after me.

I laughed, but kept running and didn't look back. I needed to focus on putting each step in the right place so I wouldn't turn an ankle, and conserving energy to make this chase as long as possible. I was fast, but he was going to catch me. It was inevitable.

Thirty seconds later those footsteps were gaining fast and I knew it was time for evasive maneuvers. But I waited until I heard him pounding right in my wake and the hair on the back of my neck stood up, then I juked him and darted between two trees that had plenty of room for me, but were close enough to slow him down a hair.

"Sonofabitch!"

I snorted, but kept running, eyes on the ground to avoid getting tripped by a tree-root, snickering to myself because I was getting a little lightheaded. But my heart was full and slamming in my chest in the *best* way.

Of course, it couldn't last forever. I could feel him gaining again, the ground vibrating under my feet with his heavy steps. I'd had to slow because we were off-trail and I was worried about falling, spraining something. Plus, after the oxygen deprivation, my body was tiring fast. Even though I was pretty fit, I didn't get a lot of lengthy cardio.

Clearly Cain did, because even though he was a lot heavier than me, he wasn't slowing down.

There was a moment when I could *hear* his panting. Then he gave the most delicious chuckle and rasped, "Got you."

I tried to juke-step again, but I was too late.

A steel bar of an arm whipped around my stomach and suddenly I was running on air, stomach swooping as Cain grunted and whirled me around, curling his other arm around me too and slowing to a walk.

He'd pinned one of my arms against his body, but the other was free, so I used it for leverage, locking against his shoulder and shoving out and away, not giving him the chance grip me close to his chest and take control.

But he just hitched me a little higher on his body, held tighter with the first arm, then used his steel forearm to knock my wrist upwards so I lost my leverage.

He chuckled when I hissed and spat like a cat, struggling and kicking, but now that he had me without traction, he'd turned me over his hip again, clearly remembering how I'd kicked him in the shins last time.

Then he turned back in the direction we'd come from, but after a few steps, he hesitated, and turned again.

I clawed at his arm, trying to break his grip around my waist. But he was wearing a thick hoodie and even though I knew I was pinching him, I couldn't seem to cause enough damage to even make him swear, let alone let me go.

"Put me down, or I'm going to scream!" I wheezed, still fighting.

"No you aren't. You want this as much as I do," he growled in that low rasp and my stomach trilled.

I stopped fighting for a second and looked up at him. "Ohhhhh, do we get to do the fucking before the killing?" I whispered. "I thought it was all teasing before the Big Event. But I'm definitely up for that."

"Fucking shameless."

"Lee."

He looked down at me and even though I couldn't see his face, I knew he was staring at me like he was confused. "What?"

"Lee," I repeated. "Fucking shameless*ly.*"

He snorted and started hauling me deeper into the trees. "Dear God, you have problems."

"Said the pot to the kettle."

He was shaking his head, but before I could come up with anything else to keep him talking, he carried me through a thicket of bushy trees that caught at my hair and scratched my skin.

"Ow! Where's your chivalry? Push the branches away with one of those ham-sized fists, please."

"Oh, *that's* the part you protest?"

"Only because I don'want to—*oh!*"

I stopped with a gasp because Cain had brought me to a little clear area surrounded by those thicker bushes and trees, and he'd lifted me upright, shoving me against one of the larger pines, and used his thick body to keep me there while he wrestled with me to grab both my hands that I'd gotten free again when he repositioned me.

It took him a second, but in the end, his brute strength won.

When I stopped struggling, I was pinned against the truck of a big pine, both wrists clamped in one of his hands, his fingers unyielding, like manacles, and locked together above my head. He'd stretched my arms high so I couldn't get leverage, so I was arched back, hands pinned and body bowed against his.

We would have been nose-to-nose, but he was wearing that mask, so instead I was staring at a black mesh with vague shapes behind it that I knew were a nose and eyes and brows… but I couldn't make out any actual features.

"Well," I whispered. "Now you've got me, what are you going to do with me?"

He gave a predatory rumble in his chest and arousal exploded behind my navel.

My breath got shorter as he brought his free hand up to my throat and clamped it there, not placing enough pressure to stop me from breathing, but the inherent threat was there.

And delicious.

I swallowed hard and felt my throat press against his calloused palm.

He brought his thumb to the point of my chin and pressed it higher so I was looking down my nose at him. Then he leaned in, that mask brushing the side of my jaw as he whispered in my ear.

"The question is, what *won't* I do with you, Bridget?"

"My first guess is taxes."

A little splutter burst from him before he caught himself. "You're a smartass," he rasped.

I shrugged as best I could, trussed up like a turkey. "One man's obnoxious is another man's endearing."

"This man finds your humor both hilarious and utterly inappropriate. You really aren't scared of me, Bridget?"

"Not especially. I mean, I know you could snap me like a twig, but *urgh—*"

"How about now," he whispered as he clamped that hand on my throat hard enough to cut off all my air.

My body fought reflexively—I writhed and for the second time in minutes, tried desperately to suck air through gritted teeth.

"I've given you too much freedom and not enough warning," he whispered in that husky rasp. "I am not to be toyed with Bridget. Do you believe me?"

Then he released my throat enough that I could gulp a lungful of air and nod frantically. "Yes, yes, I believe you," I gasped, that heady mix of terror and arousal twisting my chest into knots and my belly into coiled need.

"Good, then keep your mouth shut, and listen. As long as you don't speak, I'll allow you to breathe, do you understand?"

"Y—" I started to answer and he clamped down on my throat again so the word cut off in a strangled yelp.

"I said, *as long as you don't speak,*" he hissed. Then he released my neck again, slowly this time.

I panted, chest heaving, my breasts rising and falling right under his chin because of the way he had me arched back.

Then he pulled his head back far enough to look me in the eye, though I couldn't see it through that mask.

I nodded without speaking, *thrilled* that he'd actually made me feel cautious to speak.

"Good girl," he rumbled warmly, rolling his hips against me so I could feel his growing erection straining against his pants. My body *throbbed* in response. "Now, as tempting as you are, I'm not ready for this hunt to end yet. So we have a little problem, because you're trying to run this game, and it's not yours to control."

I looked up, towards where he had my wrists clamped, and down towards his hand on my throat, then returned my gaze to that mask to remind him that I had very little control at all.

He gave another husky chuckle that made me want to bite my lip.

"I'm a patient man, Bridget. But this is *my* hunt, and I will not let you steal it from me. So we now have a new rule…"

17. Gotcha

~ BRIDGET ~

"Are you listening?"

I nodded again, strangely enjoying the sensation of his hand on my throat.

"From now on, you tell me *nothing* about where you will be, or what you're doing. If you do, you will only guarantee that I will go dark. You need to learn is that I can *always* find you. I am *always* prepared to take you. And no one will choose the time and place but me. Not even you."

I nodded again, thrill and fear trilling in my stomach.

"If you try to lure me out again, I will disappear from your life. I am the hunter. You are the prey. You do not choose when we meet. You do not choose where. And you have *no* say in the moment our arrangement ends, are we clear?"

I nodded again, my heart racing when he leaned in.

"Unless you'd like to use the safeword? That is the only control you'll have in this little dance."

I shook my head as best I could.

He growled his approval, deep in his chest, then his thumb came up to trace the line of my jaw again. And his voice dropped to a whisper.

"Such a pretty girl... so fragile. You think you're strong, Bridget. And in this world, you are. But not in mine. I can do more than just steal your air."

There was a split second when niether of us breathed, then the universe spun.

Limbs completely out of control, I wasn't even sure which way was up until I landed on the ground with a thud and a grunt—immediately followed by another as a heavy weight landed on my lower back and massive hands pinned flat against either side of my skull and pulled me back until my spine was arched and I was looking up at that mask as he straddled my back and stared down at me.

Hands clawing in the dirt but unable to give me any traction because I was bent backwards to my limits and all I could think was *don't break my neck!* I caught myself, swallowed the sounds back just as I was about to plead with him to stop.

He huffed. "So you do have *some* self-control. Very good. You've pleased me."

I tried to plant the heel of my hand on the dirt to give myself some support, but my arm slid out because of the angle he'd bent me into. My heart was beginning to hammer with fear again.

"Now, remember that I told you I don't lie? Here's an important truth. I could snap your spine right now. Just a few pounds more pressure and the right twist of your neck," he tightened his grip on either side of my skull, "and this game would be over. Finished. The only reason you're still alive is because *I* choose it."

I couldn't nod, or speak, so I just listened, fear and thrill clanging through me.

Then he dropped his chin and his jaw brushed my cheek as he leaned down to whisper in my ear again.

"You're mine, Bridget. No more of this teasing. No more trying to tempt me out. No more begging. I will come for you when *I* choose. I will *take* you when *I* choose it. You have no control. None. And if that isn't what you want, then when I disappear, you run home and send me that safe word."

His breath was growing harsher, and I could feel his arousal pressing against my lower spine, it made tingles radiate between my thighs even as my body screamed terror because he had me stretched so taut I didn't doubt at all that with just a small jerk, he could kill me on the spot.

Then, to my surprise he moved, releasing my head only to slide one hand back down to my throat and keep me bent backwards that way, while the other dove down the front of my shirt, and under my bra, to grasp my breast.

I thought he'd be rough. I thought he'd grab and twist and punish me for my insolence. So it was a surprise when he cupped my breast, his hand so much bigger than my boob, and stroked the inside of it with his thumb, then began circling his calloused palm over the painfully hard peak of my nipple which had been straining against my bra this entire time.

He gave that deep, approving rumble again and rocked his hips to press his length against my spine, but easing back the pressure on my throat just slightly so it was a touch easier to breathe.

"If I touched you, what would I find?" he rasped, the edge of that mask dragging against my hair. "I think I'd find you slick and ready for me. Am I right, Bridget?"

I gave a handful of short, quick nods because I only had about half an inch of movement before his hand would cut off my air.

He rumbled again and I started panting.

"It's going to be good between us, Bridget. So very, *very* good."

Then he lifted that hand out of my bra and stroked the side of my face, then took his thumb and traced it along my lower lip.

And that was when I realized his fingers were trembling.

I swallowed—which was hard to do, craned back like that—and stared up at him, right to where I thought the shadows were the depths where his eyes would be.

And then I licked my lips.

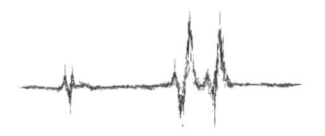

~ *CAIN* ~

Fuck!

I'd just schooled her. Pressed her about having no control. Taken from her so she'd know it was true. But even though she'd submitted—and the beast in me was *roaring* about that—the little minx still found a way to reach me.

When that pink tongue darted out to trace her lower lip, I had to swallow a groan. And all my plans to bury her face down and make her count to fifty while I got the hell out of there dissolved like smoke on the wind.

She was stunning and ballsy and hilarious, and I couldn't leave without a taste.

Easing off on the pressure so she could breathe properly, I stroked her throat and lowered my grip as I murmured instructions to her, and to my fierce relief, she complied.

As I lowered her back to the dirt she stretched her arms wide and high above her head, turning her head so her temple rested on the ground, which was when I clamped that hand at the base of her neck again, though not hard enough to stop her breathing.

I was genuinely worried about her heart and had almost pussyed out on stealing her air. But she had to learn. *Neither* of us were safe if she didn't learn the fucking lesson.

Seeing her so compliant now, I knew I'd done the right thing, and it was thrilling. My heart was banging in my chest, and my hands trembling slightly with the anticipation and arousal of her—her shining eyes, her wet tongue, her quick, harsh breaths.

She wanted me.
The feeling was mutual.
But I couldn't. Not yet.
God, help me.

Still, I had to have something. It was far too soon to risk the whole show, and she wasn't scared enough yet, but I was a man obsessed, and I'd stopped fighting the battle with myself over how dangerous she could be.

She was going to be mine. Period.

Just not right now. At least, not entirely.

So I urged her to lay flat, to keep her palms to the ground, and not to move or speak unless I told her to. Because if she did, I would make her pay.

She nodded and did as she was told, until I had her laying flat on her stomach, arms wide and hands high above her head so they wouldn't give her any strength. Then I nudged her thighs apart, clamped one hand on her shoulder and pinned her down as I knelt between her knees, covering her, rubbing myself against her ass once or twice, applying pressure there, just to get her going.

She whimpered, but I decided it didn't count as speaking and let it slide.

Also my hand.

Sliding down her back, under the waistband of her leggings, underneath her underwear, and down, down, down, following the line of her beautiful ass, down until I found her, heated and slick—so slick that my fingers slid straight into her with only the slightest pressure.

We both exhaled heavily and she clamped around my fingers so beautifully, I almost lost control, tore her pants down and plunged into her.

I had to drop my head as my body shuddered, *demanding* her. But I couldn't do it. Not yet. It was too soon.

So I gathered all the self-control I'd accumulated in over a decade as a Dom, and made myself focus on taking just a taste, and giving her a taste, *teaching* her that it was worth obeying. That I would always make it worth it to her.

The move was easy to get wrong, and not every woman enjoyed it, but I had a feeling she'd like it. So, spreading my hand wide, I pressed the pad of my thumb just below her asshole, inserted my second finger inside her, and as I pushed into her, slid my forefinger down until I found the base of that swollen nub.

And then I began to massage all three, thumb on her taut skin, thickest finger inside her, curling it to beckon her orgasm as best I could, and forefinger sliding onto her clit, then down, over and down…

Her entire body twitched and she gasped. Her fingers clawed into the dirt. But she did as she was told and didn't try to move—though her back arched and her breathing came in short, sharp gasps.

God, she was beautiful, mouth open and eyes screwed tightly shut as she tried to press into my touch, but without any real space to move.

Her lips kept making silent words as she stopped herself speaking because I'd told her to—and that just made me want her more.

"I know what you need, Bridget… what you want," I rasped, picking up the pace of my strokes as she tightened around my finger. I couldn't resist rolling my hips and rubbing myself against her, though the harsh catch of fabric on my aching cock was as uncomfortable as it was tempting. "But you have to trust me to choose when you get it," I hissed through gritted teeth as she began to writhe under me, exhaling every time I drew my fingers out and down and sucking in and holding every time I pressed in more.

She was whimpering again, biting down on her lower lip, her breath tearing in and out of her nose in time with my stroking, and I was beginning to shake, achingly hard, desperate, the only thing stopping me taking her right then was knowing that it was far too soon.

Then I felt her body tense and her breath stopped.

"Yessssss, Bridget," I hissed. "Come for me, beautiful."

Her head jerked back and she cried my name as I stroked and slid and pressed and almost came myself out of the sheer thrill of seeing her cheeks flush and her body shaking in my thrall.

God she was beautiful. So fucking beautiful.

Then she sucked in a huge breath and her hips bucked as she tried to escape my touch because she was too sensitive now.

With a groan, I stroked her once more, almost laughing when her body jolted, almost weeping because I wanted her so badly, then made myself slowly draw my hand away.

She was breathing hard, blinking, her eyes glazed, as I leaned down, almost forgetting the mask, almost dropping a kiss to the soft, vulnerable skin on her neck.

"You're mine now," I rasped in her ear. "I will choose what you get, and when. And I'll choose what you need in between. Are we agreed?"

She nodded quickly, her shoulders shifting up and down with her panting breaths.

"Good girl."

She shivered and I smiled.

"Now… you're going to lay here and recover. You're going to count *slowly* to fifty before you so much as raise your head. And I'm going to know if you defy me—do you believe me?"

She nodded again.

"Good. Then you just rest. And I will see you again—I will touch you again—when the time is right. But until then… dream of me."

She bit her lip as I shoved off of her and ran—uncomfortably because of my erection—but quickly and efficiently, taking a winding route through the trees as silently as I could, then slowing to a walk before I reached the trail.

I was forced to stand against a tree for half a minute, breathing and focusing, until my body softened. Then, when I was sure there was no one nearby, I flipped the mask back and shoved it under my hoodie, stepped out onto the trail with my chin low and hood over my eyes, then walked as quickly and directly to my car as I could, paying attention to no one, and praying none of them paid attention to me.

18. More

~ BRIDGET ~

My heart was still thundering in my ears when I got home, my body still humming from that incredible orgasm. But I also felt hollow inside and itchy on the outside.

I wanted more.

I wanted more *Cain.*

It was like being in love. I was giddy. And nervous. And excited.

And terrified and insecure.

And thrilled.

I found myself driving miles without registering any of the passing time or space, because my mind kept returning to those moments in the forest with him. In no time at all it seemed I was back at my house—and there was another Amazon package on the front step.

My pulse, which had only just dipped back into normal ranges, raced away again and as I pulled into the driveway and waited for my garage door, I looked in every direction, and in all the mirrors, trying to see where Cain might be hiding.

I didn't make a dummy phone call this time, just dove out of the car and out of the garage and up to the front door to grab the package and turn on my heel, half-expecting to see Cain explode from behind the bushes, or leap out from hedge. But there was nothing. Just a normal, mostly-sunny afternoon, with the rush of cars rolling past on the street, the occasional door slamming or dog barking in the distance.

My body refused to believe that he wasn't there, watching me. But after a little while standing on my own front step, staring like a moron, I started down the path to the garage again, still looking over my shoulders and eyeing bushes, just in case he could somehow fold himself into one of those little shadows in daylight. But… nothing.

As I stepped into the garage, I turned and started walking backwards towards the internal access door to watch for him to dart in as the roller-door slowly lowered.

But a minute later, I was standing inside my dim garage as the final inches of the garage door clanked into place, and then the mechanism stopped humming and… soon the interior light clicked off too.

Nothing.

Was he in the house somehow?

That itch started again between my shoulder blades as I marched into the house gripping that Amazon box and searched every room and closet, even checking behind the obscured glass in the shower, just case he'd found a way to blend in with my tile.

Nothing. Nothing. *Nothing.*

Finally, when I was forced to accept that either he hadn't followed me home, or if he was watching, he wasn't hunting anymore, I took the box into the kitchen to get a penknife to slice through the thick tape and cracked open the cardboard box, holding my breath, to find a bubble-wrapped block.

I reached tentatively into the box like something might close on my fingers, but tearing the plastic off revealed that it was just my phone, bubble-wrapped and charged and clean—so clean, it looked brand new and untouched, though I *knew* that wasn't the case.

I dug through the box looking for a note, or anything, but underneath that ball of bubblewrap was a round tin holding... a dozen cinnamon rolls?

I gaped at the puffy, delicious-smelling pastries, confused and delighted.

What the actual fuck?Cinnamon rolls?

How the hell had he known?

I pulled one of the rolls out, mentally noting the perfect stretch of the soft bread, and the sweet, rich sugar-smell wafting up from them.

One bite told me they weren't just any cinnamon rolls, either. These had either been homemade or baked by a chef. They were just too bouncy and fresh, the frosting too perfectly cream-cheesed and the buttery cinnamon sugar too intense to be from a supermarket bakery.

Licking the fingers of my free hand after pulling a roll free from its brothers, I turned my phone on and took a bite of the delicious pastry as I walked towards my office, my eyes still darting left and right, ears still perked for any unexpected sign of a hot, talented, strongman who'd hidden himself inside my house.

But deep down, I knew the truth. He wasn't here.

My heart was returning to its normal, slow thud. And the adrenaline rush was dissolving faster than the sugar on my tongue.

Determined to hold onto that precious exhilaration as long as I could, I trotted into the office and put my slowly-booting phone next to the keyboard as I got my computer going and tapped my way, one-handed, through the VPN and masking until finally I was in the forum... and there was no message waiting for me. And no little green circle underneath his profile picture to say he was online waiting for me.

Damn.

I typed out a quick message.

DeadGirlWalking: Cinnamon rolls? Who told you my secrets?

I didn't mention the phone that had clearly been wiped for prints and any other evidence he might have left behind. Not because I was going to get it tested, but because I knew it would bug him, wondering why I didn't mention it.

But then I was just sitting there, staring at his profile, willing him to come online, chewing a sweet treat that made me feel warm. Which was good, because there was nothing else to do but wait. And since he'd warned me that I couldn't tempt him to chase me again, that meant I was utterly at the mercy of his whims.

And that thought made me itch.

I needed to do something. My head was scrambled, but as I mentally searched for a task, a mission, *something*, my eyes fell on my phone sitting innocently on my desk and I smiled.

Oh no you don't, Cain. *No you don't.*

Then I tapped through to Nate's profile.

SYSTEM NOTE: CHAT ENCRYPTED END-TO-END. ENSURE ALL ACCOUNTS ARE LOGGED OFF BEFORE DISCONNECTING.

DeadGirlWalking: NATE! I need help.

PurplePeoplEater: What's going on?

DeadGirlWalking: How would I tell if someone's added some kind of tracker on my phone, or is getting my messages, or something.

PurplePeoplEater: What did you do?

DeadGirlWalking: I tell you someone did something to me and you decide it's my fault?

PurplePeoplEater: Babe, it *always* starts with you.

DeadGirlWalking: Fair enough. But it's too long a story, so right now, I just need you to tell me how to check my phone and get rid of any viruses or tracking apps, or anything I might not know are there.

[PurplePeoplEater is typing...]

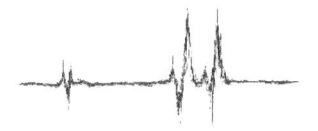

~ *CAIN* ~

My phone was ringing as I burst in the door at home, but I ignored it, throwing the door closed behind me and rushing through the house that was half-dark because I hadn't opened the blinds this morning before I left.

My body was urgent. Demanding. *Insistent.*

After watching to make sure she got back safely and found the package, I'd spent the entire drive home buzzing. I'd thought it would pass, but every time I'd start to calm down, I'd get an image in my head of her spread-eagled on the ground, or hear the memory of that cackling laugh when she knew I was coming after her.

I'd remember her scent and my cock would twitch.

I stalked through the house, half-blind with lust, and straight into the bathroom, stripping off and leaving my clothes on the floor because I was already running late and I had a meeting and I had to get cleaned up, but *dear God, I needed her.*

Stepping into the hot spray—that should have been cold, I should have been turning my mind *away* from her—I groaned and took myself in hand.

A few seconds. I would give myself a few fucking seconds to just be with her, and then I'd go back to normal life.

Normal responsibilities.

Normal. The act… the pretend I was forced to play every day that I didn't have to play with her and *oh fuck.*

Planting one hand on the shower tile, the water streaming off my back, I let my mind turn back to the sight of her, utterly surrendered, spread-eagled, and holding back her own sounds of lust as I touched her.

She was devastating.

And I began to pump into my own hand like I was thirteen again.

Seconds—seconds of her full lips, parted, her panting breaths, her body slick for me, her back arched—seconds of remembering the *feeling* of her holding herself back because I'd told her to, and I was bellowing, gasping, shooting all over the wall, my body trembling…

And then I sagged, resting my burning forehead on the cool tile and gritting my teeth as my body slowly, slowly came back under control. As my mind slowly cleared, and in the wake of all that delicious *need,* the shame and fear of what I was doing washed back over me, coated my skin so I felt thirteen again, but this time curled up in a corner trying to stop hearing my father's drunken rant.

No one is ever going to want you, you freak.

I don't want you. You're a fucking disgrace.

Shaking for entirely different reasons this time, I shook my head and pushed away from the wall.

No.

No.

No. I wasn't giving him that power anymore. Never again.

Swallowing curses, desperate and frantic and lost, I made myself go through the motions. *Pick up the soap, rub it all over my wet body, rinse, repeat, then turn off the shower and get out.*

I grit my teeth and dried off, focusing on the work meeting I was late for, and refusing to think further than that, because the truth was, I knew I was fucked. My entire life was unequivocally *fucked.*

I'd given her far too much control, let her way too far in. And now I had broken every rule I'd ever set for myself *precisely to avoid this exact scenario.*

The chances of me getting to the end of this without losing were so small, I didn't even consider it.

Whether Bridget lived or died, my life as I knew it was over. It was only a matter of time.

But then the sound of her laughter echoed in my head and I sighed because… even if she was the drug that I was going to overdose on, even if she was the noose that was going to tighten around my neck, the other truth was… I was going to die smiling.

19. Make a Plan

~ BRIDGET ~

EMAIL FROM: The Dick (Richard Fitch)
TO: Bridget
SUBJECT: Don't forget that coffee!
--
FROM: Asshole (Jeremy Haines)
TO: Bridget
SUBJECT: What the fuck are you up to?
--
EMAIL FROM: Asshole (Jeremy Haines)
TO: Bridget
SUBJECT: Answer me
--

Checking my email was a smorgasbord of *nope*. There was a reason I didn't have this account linked to my phone. But it had been three days since I had seen or heard from Cain and I was losing my mind. I barely slept last night. I was checking my DMs obsessively. And the itch between my shoulder blades was starting to feel like a fist planted and trying to shove me forward.

Cain had said he would choose where and when he came for me. He'd said I couldn't try to entice him, or he'd never come back. But with every passing, neurotic moment, as my skin felt too tight and the darkness over my head began to press down, I got closer to doing something stupid.

Gerald tried to tell me this was a panic attack. He claimed I confused thrill with connection, and was unconsciously trying to soothe my loneliness and distract my brain from trauma by weaponizing adrenaline.

"You're self-medicating, Bridget. Just without the pills."

I grimaced at the sound of his voice in my head. I wasn't panicking. Not really. I was bored. And didn't like being alone in silence.

In the past I would have already been out looking for some fun—and found it. But this past year I was starting to find most of those distractions were so hollow and unsatisfying, they did little more than keep my body moving for a few hours.

Gerald had applauded when I told him I'd virtually stopped my *risky, promiscuous coping behaviors* as he liked to call them.

I called it *going a little crazy,* and I'd only stopped because the behavior stopped achieving the pay-off of soothing the itch. Of course, that also meant that life had become very… uneasy.

Hence, toying a little with Jeremy. And my search for Cain.

But now I was pacing my own house like I was caged, and that wasn't fun at all. And it was only Tuesday. The first few hours had been fine, getting Nate's help to clean my phone. I'd slept like a baby, with a smile on my face, knowing whatever Cain had been monitoring was now sadly lacking in access.

I'd been certain when he realized, he'd either come for me out of sheer rage, or at least message me so we could banter about it. But *nothing.*

It was driving me nuts.

I bit my lip, staring at the computer screen that was still benignly staring back with *zero* contact from Cain and I made the decision.

If he didn't get in touch, or start a hunt today, I was going to have to find something else to distract me. And I couldn't tell him about it because he'd think I was trying to draw him out.

And then I remembered.

Hurrying back to my desk, I yanked open the drawer where I threw stuff that wasn't important, but I wanted to keep. I had to dig through a little to find it because I'd been looking for a pen the other day, but then I uncovered that little cream card under the pamphlet Gerald had given me about *Borderline Antisocial Behaviors* and I relaxed a hair.

Sid Vicious
The Conductor
Invitation for One

It *was* only Tuesday. And Ronald worked Saturday to Wednesday.

I smiled and grabbed my wallet, sliding the card into a slot for safe keeping. Not that I planned to use it. It might be a challenge to get into his den without it, but I had contacts, and testicular heft. If Cain didn't show up today, I'd set myself a little challenge to get in and see Ronald work tonight.

That itch between my shoulder blades that had been making me squirm, eased off and I blew out a breath.

I had a plan.

Either way, tonight was going to be fun.

But then I deflated because that just meant that I had a lot of very *unfun* hours to kill between now and then.

Reluctantly, I sat back down at the computer and opened the first email from Jeremy, biting my lip as I scanned the first one quickly, which started as little more than his usual whining, but then at the end…

...if I can't trust you to be in this with me, then I'm ending our arrangement. This isn't what I signed up for, Bree. You're making me look bad.

Shit.

I really *did* panic then. I wanted to keep Jeremy close without actually having to touch him. I didn't want him to find someone else!

I hurriedly clicked into the second email, my heart beginning to race. But he hadn't put anything in the body of the email, just that subject line.

Answer me.

Muttering a curse, I clicked *Reply* and hammered something out in a rush.

--

FROM: Bridget
TO: Asshole (Jeremy Haines)
SUBJECT: RE: What the fuck are you up to?
J, calm the fuck down. I don't have your email on my phone because it's not secure.
Remember I told you about Dick, the old chaplain from high school? Well, he's shown up again and now he's actually an old man. I'm going to see him today. Then I've got my weekly flaying from Gerald tomorrow. You know that takes it out of me. I'll be in touch on the weekend when things have settled down. But stop panicking. Nothing has changed. I'm just working on stuff, that's all.
--

After I pressed send, I opened Richard's email, wincing because it was days old, and didn't even bother to read it since I knew why he was messaging—he'd thought I wouldn't show.

--

FROM: Bridget
TO: The Dick (Richard Fitch)
SUBJECT: RE: Don't forget that coffee!

Hey Dick, I haven't forgotten you. I'll see you after lunch today. Promise.
--

I sent that one then shut my email down immediately so even if Jeremy responded right away, he'd know I hadn't opened it. Then I jiggled my foot the whole time I was quitting the masking and VPN and getting the computer secure and shut down.

The hours of the day stretched ahead of me, and I felt like my skin was so tight it was threatening blood flow. Options kept flooding my mind—but I had to discard them because they were only going to get me in trouble. But even that thought pissed me off, because why did Cain and Gerald get to decide what was good for me?

I recognized the anger as a panic response and shook my head as I dove out of the office chair and out of the room.

I was going to be a *good girl*—I shivered, goosebumps rising on the back of my neck as those words echoed in my head in Cain's deep, approving growl. But only until tonight. If Cain didn't show up tonight when I was on my way back from seeing Richard, I was going to head into the city.

That meant I needed to wash my hair, which meant a real shower. And I'd have to bring a change of clothes since no one but the richest and most powerful got into *Vigori* unless they dressed the part. Valerie was unwavering on that. It added to the risk for those who wanted to remain anonymous—and I was pretty sure she used it for marketing.

There was no signage on the old industrial complex that housed that den of iniquity. But anyone who was paying attention wouldn't miss that wealthy and freakish looking people wearing a lot of leather, silk, masks, and cloaks showed up in the area at all times of day and night. Though most of the truly wealthy just had drivers drop them off at the doors, then speed away.

Still. I didn't have a driver, which meant I had to walk on the sidewalk like a normal person. I needed to be prepared.

At least when I saw Gerald tomorrow I'd be able to tell him the *very real* story of going to talk to my old high school chaplain.

Twice.

Hopefully, that would get him so excited, his ancient brain wouldn't register that I hadn't relayed any stories of my evening escapades.

God, I hoped Cain would show up tonight.

I had one fleeting glance back towards the computer, my finger twitching to send him a message.

Then I remembered… I could text him! He hadn't said I couldn't contact him, only that I couldn't try to entice him.

But then I couldn't think of anything I could send him that wouldn't be either a temptation, or a straight-up plea. So I growled another curse and went to make myself a late breakfast.

20. Seize the Day

SOUNDTRACK: *Atlantic* by Sleep Token

~ BRIDGET ~

Look at me, eating breakfast, seeing old men, *listening* to advice. God, if I wasn't careful, I was going to turn into a pearl-clutcher.

Maybe that's the costume I needed to prepare for tonight.

I snorted at the mental visual of turning up to *Vigori* in a cashmere sweater, pearls, and with a little dog clutched under my arm.

I wondered what Sid would do with *that*.

Heart beating a little faster, and smiling because I couldn't help it, I hurried into the kitchen to make a smoothie.

I had a plan now. My body was still jittery, but the panic was passing.

Either I was going to be hunted tonight, or I was going to have some fun. It was a win-win.

I kept telling myself that all the way through my breakfast, shower, drying my hair, and packing the bag for *Vigori*.

But that little voice in the back of my head didn't want to leave me in peace.

Cain, it said. *I need more Cain. These other guys are just… hollow.*

But I didn't get a choice with Cain.

Even "Sid Vicious" was better than another night alone in the dark.

Maybe after I watched him work I'd finally be able to sleep…

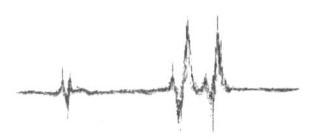

When I got to the little church near the highway, I was surprised that there were several cars there already, and the doors were open. And even more surprised to see a little handwritten sign out front that said MEMORIAL with an arrow pointing to the open doors.

Shit. I hadn't read the email from Richard. Maybe he'd been changing the time?

Halfway across the parking lot from my car I hesitated as an old couple got out of their vehicle in one of the disabled parks and tottered towards the ramp alongside the main stairs to the door.

Was I going to be intruding? But one glance towards the fence at the back revealed Richard's car. So he was definitely here. I turned on my heel and headed to the little house behind the chapel, but I knocked three times and there was no answer. Which meant Richard was over in the church.

After a moment's pause, I decided to go ahead and go inside. There weren't a lot of people here. Either Richard was running this service and I could just sit at the back and wait for him to be done—he'd probably need a drink after that—or he was just over there being nice, and I could wait for him until he was ready to go.

The sun was bright enough outside that when I stepped in the door my eyes took a moment to adjust. The pretty chapel inside looked very dark—the long, wooden pews in regimented lines designed to seat a couple hundred people held maybe a dozen—just pairs and singles scattered here and there around the sanctuary, all with gray hair and wearing tweed or sweaters. All old.

As my eyes adjusted, I caught sight of one younger guy in a white collared shirt under a slim-fitting black sweater and black pants, squatting in the middle of the aisle, murmuring comfort to a couple old ladies. But other than that, it looked like a poorly attended rotary club meeting.

I swallowed hard and started scanning the chapel and pews again to see if I could find Richard, probably praying with some old lady in a corner. Or maybe he was being forced to do the service and he was in the back room getting changed into a funny hat or something?

I'd never seen him wear a funny hat, but I'd always imagined he had a closet full of robes and hats and whatever else men of the cloth had to use when they were called on to give last rites, or whatever.

Then my mind threw up an image of me convincing Richard to let me borrow one of those pope gowns and sashes, then showing up at *Vigori* dressed like that, and I kind of spluttered.

The young guy in the aisle turned to look, saw me standing at the top of the aisle and quickly got to his feet, leaning in to whisper something to the old ladies before trotting towards me looking apologetic.

I took a quick second to admire the broad shoulders and limbs so muscular even the could-have-been-a-waiter outfit couldn't hide them, before seeing the cross hanging around his neck and realizing the guy was obviously another priest.

Then he got into the light from the door behind me and I had to blink because with that dark hair scattered over his forehead and rugged good looks, he didn't *look* like a priest.

"I'm sorry, I'm sorry I wasn't here to greet you. Mabel just needed a quick prayer. Thank you for coming."

"Oh!" I said, taking an instinctive step back. "No, no, I'm sorry. I'm not here for the memorial, I'm just looking for Di—I mean, Richard. I didn't mean to disturb the service."

The guy's heavy brows pressed down, forming a V over his nose. "You're... *looking* for Richard?"

I nodded and scanned the church again. "Yes. We had made an appointment for a coffee. A... a counseling session, I guess you could call it," I said, laughing nervously because this guy's gaze was penetrating and he was *exactly* my type. Physically. I couldn't say I'd ever been drawn to the spiritual type. Though it might be fun to try and corrupt one...

I shoved that thought out of my head, suddenly pissed off with myself. The guy was a *priest* running a memorial service, and here my brain was already painting pictures of taking him into the back room and throwing him down on the funny gowns and hats and—

Stop.

I blinked and looked back at him, surprised to find him staring at me like he was scared.

God, he couldn't read thoughts, could he? Did God do that? Tell His people what others were thinking?

"I'm sorry to interrupt," I said quickly, licking my lips quickly—not missing when his eyes cut down to watch that, then he forced them back up to meet mine. "It's just that he's not at the house, so I thought he might be here."

"He is," the guy said, then looked over his shoulder, then back to me. "Why don't we just... why don't you sit down here at the back?" He opened one of those muscular arms towards the nearest pew, which was empty.

I frowned. "I don't mean to make you go get him. You're obviously busy. If you could just tell me—"

"No... look, I'm sorry, I've been thoughtless," he said, running a thick, calloused hand through his hair in a way that made my mouth go dry. "I'm not at my best and you took me by surprise. I apologize—let's start again. What's your name?"

"I'm Bridget. I'm one of his old students from years ago. I came by last week. He might have mentioned me—"

"Bridget, sorry to interrupt you, but... I really need you to sit down."

I stared at him as he kept that arm open towards the pew, but used his other hand to gently cup my elbow and usher me towards the seat.

The first flicker of real unease began in my chest as I plonked myself down on the edge of the pew, staring at him.

"Okay," I said. "I'm sitting down. What? What's going on? Where's Richard?" I kept my voice to a low hush, but my tone was snappish.

The young priest knelt down at the end of the pew, just like he had for those ladies deeper in the church, and his forehead furrowed.

"Bridget, I'm really sorry to have to be the one to tell you... but Richard had a heart attack a few days ago. He's... he's the reason we're gathering here today."

21. No Good Surprises

~ BRIDGET ~

"I'm sorry... what?" My voice came out squeaky with shock. I was difficult to surprise, but if he was saying—

"Richard... he was almost eighty. He had some heart issues. He hadn't been feeling well for a while. It's why he was retiring. I'm sorry to be the one to have to tell you, but it's been a shock for everyone. They asked me to come cover until they could find someone to shepherd here permanently. I didn't meet him, so... I am hearing such wonderful stories, though. You said he was your high school chaplain?"

I nodded dumbly, strange things happening in my chest. Awkward, difficult feelings that I was struggling to put words to.

Disbelief.

Unease.

A strangling kind of fear.

Rage?

It made no sense. Except for our meeting last week, I hadn't talked to Richard for years, and even with the correspondence we kept up, he hadn't really been a part of my daily life since I was seventeen years old.

I felt sad that he'd died. I hoped he hadn't been in pain for long. I hoped his heart didn't...

His heart.

Right.

That uncomfortable squeeze in my chest got tighter.

"...didn't have the chance to check his schedule and warn you. This all happened really fast and they called me in because they haven't found his replacement yet..."

I realized this man had been talking the whole time, while I was off in lala land and I put a hand up to stop his babbling.

"I'm sorry, I kind of tuned out there. What's your name again?"

He looked down with a wry smile, shaking his head. "No, *I'm* sorry. This isn't my usual, uh, audience. My name's Sam. And your shock is understandable."

I nodded and swallowed hard. "Thanks, I... Richard emailed me just... just days ago. We were supposed to meet and talk and... I'm just... he was just a really sweet man."

The only man I'd known when I was young who was really sweet without an ulterior motive.

"Yes, that's what I keep hearing. A very loving, very kind man. They don't make them like that anymore."

I nodded again. To my surprise, my eyes blurred and my throat pinched. My hands started to shake and my breath got short. And not in the fun way.

"I have to go," I said abruptly, standing up like I'd been launched out of the pew. Sam shot to his feet too, hands up to catch me like I might fall.

"You don't have to go—"

"Yes, I do," I breathed, turning my shoulders to push past him.

Sam's arm shot out to catch me around the middle, which made my eyes widen. But then he yanked his hands up and took a step back, shaking his head.

"Sorry, sorry. It's reflex. I usually serve in a prison ministry and we have to be... it doesn't matter. I'm so sorry. I didn't mean to scare you... I'm not trying to stop you if you want to go. I just think you should let the shock pass before you drive. That's all. If you don't feel safe, I understand. I'm sorry. That wasn't my intention…"

He trailed off, looking so miserable and stressed, raking his hand through his hair so it stuck up in five directions, his eyes darting left and right.

Even with all these competing emotions, I almost laughed.

"You're fine," I said, then my breath hitched because I was starting to cry. I *hate* crying. "I just… thank you for telling me."

Then I bolted.

He stepped out of my way and didn't try to stop me. But as I whipped past, he murmured, "I'll pray for safe travel. Please be careful."

I nodded, biting my lip as I fled.

When I got out to the car I pressed the wrong button on the key twice, so I was cursing by the time I got the door open. Then my shaking fingers made me fumble and drop the keys trying to get it into the ignition. Then I hit my head on the steering wheel when I tried to bend down to reach for them.

Somehow, I ended up sitting there, both hands on the wheel, my forehead buried in the crook of my elbow, weeping.

Weeping for the loss of a man I barely knew, but who had been the only man in my life that cared about me without wanting to have sex, or being paid to be there.

And even though I wouldn't have named Richard if someone had asked who my closest friends were, it turned out that I very suddenly, and very acutely felt the hollow space he left in his passing… much more than I would ever have imagined.

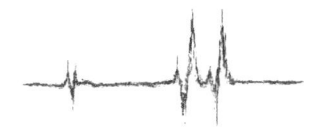

Some time later, I'd stopped crying, but I was still feeling strangely fragile and afraid to face the world. I hadn't looked up or got the keys, or anything. Then there was a rap on the window next to my shoulder and I startled.

When I snapped my head up, Sam was standing at the window, looking apologetic and very tired, with deep lines around his eyes and mouth, and a sexy stubble darkening his jaw.

I had the sudden thought that if they made all priests like this, probably more people would want to come to church. But I swallowed back the slightly hysterical snort and rolled down my window.

Sam leaned one hand on the top of the car and spoke as if this was a continuation of our conversation in the chapel.

"I'm really glad you didn't drive," he said quietly. "I was worried. Look, everyone's leaving now. Why don't you come in and I'll make a pot of coffee? I know I could use some."

I stared up at him for a second through aching eyes. Then shrugged.

I didn't know why this news about Richard was hitting me so hard. But this guy was cute and obviously had a good heart. And the thought of the drive home just to walk into my empty house alone seemed... too much.

Why not?

I didn't speak the words, just pushed the door open and, as Sam stepped back to give me room, got out, remembering to lean back in to fish the keys from off the floor and close the window, before turning and following the muscular priest across the parking lot, to that fence behind the chapel, and into the magical little garden, then up to the cottage door.

As Sam pulled a key out of his pocket, he grimaced. "I only arrived this morning, so I haven't had a chance to box up his things. Just wanted to warn you."

I shrugged and followed him through the door into the entryway, then that little galley kitchen.

"Take a seat, I'll get the coffee going. The bathroom is around the corner then down the hall if you need it. This ancient thing will take a few minutes, I'm afraid."

I nodded, then shuffled through the little house to use the facilities, then back to that little, formica dining table where Richard and I had sat to talk last week, when his wispy gray hair was fluttering and his eyes still twinkled.

And then, as I watched the strangely rugged but beautiful man frown and fiddle with the coffeemaker on the counter, I wondered why I could feel *so sad* for Richard when I was completely unconcerned about myself.

22. The Strange Weight of Grief

~ BRIDGET ~

It took several minutes, but eventually Sam walked towards the dining table where I sat and placed two mismatched mugs of coffee in front of me.

I slipped my fingers through the handle of the closest mug and wrapped both hands around it, sliding it towards me like I would hug it. I needed something to hold onto.

Sam frowned as he took his seat. "Oh... Do you take creamer or sugar?"

I shrugged one shoulder. "Usually, but honestly, I'll drink it however it comes." I wasn't supposed to drink coffee at all, but right now I felt like I needed it.

"Let me see what we've got. I haven't had a chance to look through things yet. Just a sec."

The chair scraped as he pushed away from the table again, returning quickly with a little sugar bowl and a bottle of ready-made creamer from the fridge.

I made my mug creamy and sweeter than it needed to be, then took a sip and nodded. "It's good, thank you."

"No problem."

Sam took a sip of his black coffee, and sat back in the chair. I could feel his eyes on me, but I was still feeling so weirdly fragile—like if I moved too fast, or the wrong way, a piece of me would break off. And I definitely *didn't* want to start crying again.

But Sam had that same weird, comforting presence that Richard had, and he had hot coffee. I needed something to help me focus before I started driving.

So even though it was weird, I didn't say anything, and I was surprised when he didn't either. Usually when I sat down with a guy, he either got nervous at silence, or he let me carry the discussion and just gave me one word answers and listening noises.

But Sam just sat there, watching me without any apparent concern about the fact that neither of us was speaking.

He'd taken off the sweater and cross necklace he was wearing before and rolled up his sleeves. I hadn't really paid attention before, but while I was sitting there, staring at nothing, my gaze fixed on his arms—he had nice arms, the strong, tendony kind that I fondly referred to as forearm porn—and tattoos.

I almost spat out the mouthful of coffee I'd just taken.

Instead I swallowed uncomfortably, coughing and spluttering while he jumped back up to get some paper towels and hurry back to me.

It wasn't until I'd stopped coughing and stared at him, red-eyed, and croaked, "They let Priests have tattoos?" that he went a little still and his eyes went wary.

His mouth tightened as he leaned down to wipe up the little spray of coffee on the tabletop where I'd coughed a little too hard.

"I'm not a priest," he muttered, then shrugged like he was trying to loosen the muscles in his neck. "If the tattoos bother you, I'll cover them up. I just thought—" He put down his coffee and reached for the first sleeve to roll it down, and I almost choked on my coffee again.

"No, no! That's not what I meant—I like them! I just… I'm just surprised. I thought the church frowned on that kind of thing. Don't the old ladies think it's the devil imprinted on your skin, or something?"

Sam hesitated, his eyes locked on mine like he wasn't sure whether to trust me or not. His Adam's apple bobbed, but he stopped pushing the sleeve down.

"Some parts of the church do. The wrong parts, in my opinion," he said quietly. "I try not to flash them around, but they're a very real part of my past, so I'm also not ashamed of them. I just… I don't want to make people uncomfortable. Like I said, this isn't usually where I work." He grimaced, gesturing back towards the chapel.

"Where did you get the tats? And where do you usually work?" I asked uncomfortably. I wanted to know, but he used words that seemed so alien to me.

"In prison," he said sheepishly.

I waited, but he was taking another swallow from his coffee.

"The ink? Or the work?" I asked.

"Both," he said a moment later, then his eyes cut up from the cup to me, like he was watching to see how I'd react.

"You went to prison?"

"Yes."

"For how long?"

He frowned. "I was in for almost four years. I was supposed to have six, but they let me out early for good behavior. But it was enough. I didn't want to go back—at least, not on that side of the bars. By then I'd already met Jesus and was starting to help the other inmates. So they took a chance on me, I guess."

"The prison? Or the church?"

He huffed. "Both, again," he said, scratching the back of his neck. "I had to find a job when I got out, and it's funny how working is supposed to be part of demonstrating your rehabilitation, even though most businesses won't hire a convicted felon. I was in touch with the pastor at the prison and told him how I was struggling, and he said the guys missed me and… yeah, it kind of went from there. Now I've been out and serving… four… almost five years?"

My brows rose. "You're the Priest at the prison?" Then I looked down at his forearms and tipped my head. "I suppose that makes more sense, though."

"I'm not a Priest."

I gave him a skeptical look. "You were praying with old ladies. You wear a cross. And in the middle of the day on a Tuesday, you're in church." I pointed at him. "Priest."

He arched one brow in a *heavenly*—no pun intended—boyish charm expression. Then he shook his head and counted his points off his fingers. "I don't have to be celibate, just married for sex. I don't wear collars, or swing incense. And no funny hats," he said pointing towards his own head. "No one has to call me Father. I just talk to people. I'm a shepherd. A mentor. A coach… a spiritual advisor. The church calls me a Pastor."

"Pastor, priest. What's the difference?" I asked with a snort.

"You'd be surprised. A lot of being a priest is ritual—how you look, what you say, what you do. Most of my job is about the heart. How you feel, why you make the choices you do, why God cares… that kind of thing."

I let him see on my face that it was a dubious distinction, but I wasn't going to argue with a man of the cloth. "Well, you don't look like a Priest, so maybe you're right."

"Oh? How should a Priest look? Like Richard?"

I shrugged. "Yeah. But trust me, that's not a compliment. I think if more Priests looked like you, there'd be a lot more people ready to go say prayers on a Sunday," I snorted.

He chuckled. "Well, then, I guess… bring your friends?"

I actually laughed at that. This dude was wild. And I needed something to distract me from everything else right now. "So, seriously though, you work out at the State Penitentiary? And they called you *here?*"

Sam gave a grim smile. "Yes—and *yes*. I guess they were in the middle of looking for a replacement for Richard to work here, and there's not a lot of pastors with part-time schedules out this way. So they asked if I'd spend a few weeks here until they could appoint a new pastor."

"Tell them to keep you on," I said seriously.

His eyes went wide and he physically leaned away, waving his free hand in protest. *"No.* This isn't the place for me. I mean, don't get me wrong, these people love Jesus and I'm happy to serve. But… just no. I'm not the right shepherd here. I'm just helping out. And trust me, no one was more surprised than me when they asked me to do it. I'm more used to gang bangers than quilters. Some of the old ladies were a little intimidated this morning," he said with a self-deprecating twist on his lips. "I don't want to be the reason someone *doesn't* come to God."

It was weird, seeing that expression on his lips and hearing that tone. I *knew* that feeling. And for me it had nothing to do with God. It was just straight judgment.

People took a look, or learned something, thought they knew what they were seeing, and acted accordingly.

And it sucked.

The ghosts of my past wanted to float up then, my brain conjuring images of the things that happened to and around me, and all the ways it made people afraid of me. I shivered and shook my head.

"Well, I don't know about the God part, but I get that whole judgment thing. And I'm glad that's not how you… work."

"I'm hardly in a position to judge others—convicted felon, remember?"

I nodded and took another sip of coffee, staring at him over the rim of my mug.

He gave a flat little smile. "Just ask. I'm not scared to talk about it."

"What were you convicted of?" I blurted.

"Assault and battery, sexual assault on a woman, and voyeurism."

I blinked. Sounded like my kind of party. "Seriously?"

"Seriously."

"How long ago?"

"It happened a decade ago. I was convicted eight years ago, give or take."

"And... now?"

One side of his mouth tipped up in a wry smile. "Now, I'm proud to say that not only have I not touched an unconsenting woman since I was sent to prison—present company excluded, sorry about that little slip earlier—but I think I can confidently say I've helped quite a few other predators turn their lives around, too."

"And the church people still judged you?"

He shrugged. "It's not like I've had t-shirts made. I don't usually get the chance to lead with that. I still look like trouble, and the ladies of the bridge club know it."

I shrugged, but deep down I was impressed. "Not all heroes wear capes. If it's any consolation, the world doesn't just judge the tough guys. I mean, look at me."

Sam smiled. "So, you're a hero just in your Clark Kent era?"

"No," I said emphatically. "The opposite. I mean, you've got tattoos and... the rest of this," I said lamely, flapping my hand at him. "But... I can relate."

He tipped his head. "Can you?"

"More than you realize. My tats are just on the inside, that's all. So my judgment arrives by stealth. I don't have t-shirts either. So people have to spend time with me to realize they think I'm... wrong," I said, reflecting his wry smile and *oh well,* shrug.

He didn't take the bait to move on though. He took another sip from his coffee, but his eyes remained intent on me. "What are they judging you for?"

I stared at him, surprised that the urge was there to tell him the *truth.* That never happened. But I caught the words before they tripped off my tongue, though my heart started hammering because that had been close.

When I didn't answer, Sam's expression went serious, and he shook his head. "You don't have to worry with me, Bridget. Trust me, it would have been better if I'd never gone the route I did. But I can't change the past. All I can do is walk into a different future. And I've made it my purpose to help anyone else along the way who wants to."

I almost choked on my coffee again. It was *so close* to some of the stuff that Gerald had been saying to me for years and...

God, all the cold and brittle things I'd been able to ignore for a few minutes sank their teeth back in. I put my coffee cup down, suddenly tense and needing to move.

I needed to get out of here and go home, but home felt so empty, and I just *didn't want to.* Except, I had nowhere else to go. I wasn't feeling sexy. *Vigorí* and my new friend Sid were going to have to wait.

But that just left me sitting in a priest's cottage, deflated and strangely afraid of being alone.

I stared at my half-empty coffee mug and suddenly felt *overwhelmed.*

"Bridget?"

I blinked and looked up at Sam who was staring at me intently. "Can I help *you?* Somehow? It's kinda my job now. And if it matters... I understand the judgment of others, but I don't offer it. Promise."

I shook my head. "Thank you. I just... my problems are different, that's all."

"So try me. That's one thing about being a God guy, you'd be surprised by the stuff I hear. I bet I have stories that could curl your hair."

I raised my eyebrows. "Ditto."

He chuckled and went back to his coffee, but I saw the smile stick even when he was drinking. And even though he'd looked away, his eyes came back to mine even before he'd swallowed his coffee.

"I think you do need a t-shirt," he said gruffly.

I folded my arms, but I was smiling. "What would it say?"

"Oh, nothing except *Trouble.*"

"We could start a club."

He snorted. "I'm trying to help others *out* of trouble now, remember?"

I mock-pouted and glared at my coffee. "It's so stupid that it has to be one or the other. There are some kinds of trouble that don't hurt anyone. Why can't we do that stuff without getting smited?"

"Oh, don't worry—God won't smite you for the stuff that doesn't hurt you or others, Bridget. The problem is people... struggle to see the difference. I know I do. So if they see something that *feels* dangerous, they back away. And they're wary of the person who made them scared. I wish life wasn't that way, but I'm getting better at accepting things the way they are, rather than how I want them to be."

And that reminded me of Richard—who used to say stuff like that to me in high school.

A memory drifted into my head—Richard sitting across from me in his Chaplain's office looking concerned and trying to convince me that I was more than the things that had happened to me. No matter what other people thought.

And *that* made me teary again.

Damn.

"Bridget—"

"You just sounded like Richard for a minute there," I said hoarsely, dashing the tears away. "That's all."

"Well," Sam said, sitting back in his chair. "From everything I'm hearing, that's a compliment. Thank you. Everyone who knew him said Richard was a good man and..." I could feel his eyes on me, but didn't want to meet that penetrating gaze. "Bridget, if it's any comfort to you, I'm *confident* that Richard is in heaven now. So don't be sad *for* him. It's sad to miss him from here. But he's never going to feel darkness or pain again, and he's always going to have joy. That's a beautiful thing."

I did look at him then. "Is that where you're going when you die? Even though you did bad things?"

He nodded. "And I'm very grateful that's the case. If you'd met me a decade ago—"

"So, what you did before just doesn't matter to God anymore? He's like, you're being good now, so we'll just forget about the rest?" I asked bitterly, the memory of that letter floating through my head. I knew I was lashing out at my father and Sam didn't deserve that, but my skin was too tight and my heart was racing, and I was *sad,* and—

"No, Bridget. God isn't like people. It's not all or nothing. It's not just good or bad. God accepts my darkness, but shines light on it. And… I don't know how to explain it except… he uses it."

I arched one brow at him. "God uses your *darkness?"*

Sam nodded slowly. "Don't get me wrong, He's not pushing me towards it—quite the opposite. But… just like this conversation. He uses my past to help me connect with people. That's why I serve in a prison. Usually," he scratched the back of his neck. "Because those guys know about what I used to be. And they can see what I am now. And I'm not perfect—not even close. But they can see the difference. God takes what used to be ugly in me and turns it into something useful. I don't forget where I came from. Ever. But I'm free of it. Most of the time."

"Most of the time?"

He shrugged. "I struggle sometimes. You can't live the way I lived for twenty-five years and just walk away without… carrying the marks of it." He tipped his head towards his tattoos. "That's what the old ladies feel when they get close to me. That's what scares them. They can sense it on me. I wish it wasn't true, but it is."

"But that's just baggage," I said bitterly. "Doesn't matter whether you're different or not. Doesn't matter if you *wanted* what happened. It only matters that it's there. They're judging you!"

"And sometimes I do things I'm not supposed to. We all have our issues, right?"

"Darkness."

He nodded and leaned forward, folding his arms to rest on the table. "From God's perspective, it's like your shadow—everyone's got one. It's just that, the more light there is, the less you can see it."

"But then, they're judging you for things that they have too!"

173

"Yep. But my shadow's easier to see than theirs. So sometimes they forget because theirs doesn't show up as much. That's all."

"You're being very nice to the bridge club bigots."

He shrugged. "I'm *glad* that God sees all the ways I'm dark and doesn't reject me. He doesn't get fooled by whether my shadow's showing more or less. He just cares and helps me, regardless. It's the people who point and judge. But if I reject them for that, I'm no different than they are. Just choosing a different darkness to care about. I get things wrong. So do they. If we reject everyone who ever does the wrong thing, we'd never stay in a relationship with anyone."

I went very still, staring at him, because it was a weird way to see the world and God and this whole issue. It appealed to me for my own flaws... but for monsters like my dad? They should *never* get a pass, no matter what.

Something in my chest kept pushing forward, wanting to talk to Sam about my past and see what he thought of that—would his eyes go wide, then shutter closed? Or would he shrug it off and not care?

Or something else?

I licked my lips and his eyes dropped again, but he yanked them manfully back up to meet mine with an intensity that made my breath shorter.

Then it struck me that I was sitting next to a fucking *Priest* and my heart was thrilling when he looked at my lips and... dear God, what was wrong with me?

But before I could make an excuse to leave, there was a sudden crash of tinny music and Sam muttered something and pulled his phone out of his pocket, answering it before he put it to his ear.

"Yeah, it's me. What's up?"

Sam listened for a second, then blinked, muttered an apology to me and got up from the table, wandering into the kitchen and asking a couple quick questions before saying, "I'll be there as soon as I can. I had a memorial today and... it just might take an hour. Just... hold on." Then he hung up the phone with a frown and turned towards me, rubbing his face.

"I'm really sorry, Bridget. But I have to—"

"I have to get home anyway, don't worry about it," I said quickly, pushing out of my seat, wishing I could slap myself for the way I'd been sitting there gawking at him like he was dessert. He was a fucking *Man of God.*

That thought didn't help me want to corrupt him less.

I really was broken inside.

Ugh.

"Thank you for the coffee and the talk," I said without really meeting his penetrating gaze as I got into the kitchen where he was standing.

But to my surprise, he put himself in front of me, blocking my passage when I was about to step past him.

"I want to finish this conversation another time, if you're willing?" he asked quietly, watching me intently. "I think Richard would want me to try, at least?"

I wasn't used to someone who held bald eye-contact like that. Except Gerald. But I was pretty sure piercing gazes were a psychiatrist's bread and butter.

Maybe that was a thing for priests too.

Pastors. Whatever.

He didn't wait for me to respond, but pulled open a drawer and pulled out a little notepad and pen, scrawling something on it, then ripping it off and holding it out to me. "My number," he said. "I think I'm going to be here a few weeks, but I don't know. Even when I'm at the Prison, I'm within driving distance though. How about we have coffee next week—we can talk about Richard. Or… whatever you need."

I folded my arms. "Father Sam… are you asking me out?"

"I am *not* your father." He raised an eyebrow like a warning, but his lips slipped up on one side. "And no." Then he waved the paper a little bit, urging me to take it. I didn't break eye-contact, but when I took the little piece of paper from his fingers, his smile got wider. He stepped back to give me space, opening an arm towards the door. I took the cue and walked past him to the door, opening it.

"Not *yet,*" he added quietly as I stepped over the threshold .

My breath caught and I hesitated, midstep. But I didn't turn around. Didn't let him know I'd heard him. And as I got moving again and trotted across the carpark to my car, I caught myself smiling a little bit.

23. Give Me Your Word

~ BRIDGET ~

FROM: Asshole (Jeremy Haines)
TO: Bridget
SUBJECT: No more bullshit or I'm pulling the plug
--

Shit. *Shit.* I *knew* I shouldn't have checked my email.

I usually ran headlong into trouble, rather than away from it. But seeing those words from Jeremy sent my already screaming body into full-on rage-panic.

The temptation was there to ignore the email and just go get drunk or something, but I knew Jeremy didn't make empty threats. I had to know what he was saying, so I made myself click into it and read it quickly, my heart banging harder and faster with each of the brief sentences that boiled down to one, hard fact: Unless I started keeping contact every day, he was walking.

Fuck!

I tapped out a quick message pointing out that I *had* replied to his emails.

It took him seconds to reply.

--
FROM: Asshole (Jeremy Haines)
TO: Bridget
SUBJECT: RE: No more bullshit or I'm pulling the plug
I'm not doing the back and forth anymore, B. We need to meet. You name the time and place, and I'll be there.
--

Nononononononono. Shit. Fuck. *Shit.*

I hated that he had this kind of control over me. Absolutely despised it—and he knew it. Usually he was pretty good about not using it. But when he did, like this, it made me want to run. Just take what I had and go and never see him or anyone else I knew ever again.

But then, that would mean losing Cain. And I wasn't prepared to do that yet.

My fingers trembled as I tapped out another reply, taking a little bit more time with this one because I couldn't push him, but I needed more space than he wanted to give.

--
FROM: Bridget
TO: Asshole (Jeremy Haines)
SUBJECT: RE: No more bullshit or I'm pulling the plug
This isn't back and forth. I can't meet. Not yet. But we will. I just found out yesterday my old Chaplain from high school died. I'm seeing Gerald tomorrow, then have a meeting with the priest the next day. I can't really focus on anything right now. Please. I'm not saying no. I just need more time.
--
FROM: Asshole (Jeremy Haines)
TO: Bridget
SUBJECT: RE: No more bullshit or I'm pulling the plug
How am I supposed to know if I can trust you when you don't give me anything? For all I know, you're out there rage-fucking some dude and hiding him from me.
--

I shrugged to myself. I mean, he wasn't wrong. That had been my modus operandi since I was fifteen. Until a couple years ago, at least. But I was growing up now... or growing cynical. I wasn't sure which. But the end result was the same, and Jeremy had been around long enough to know I was changing things now. Even though he was an asshole, he was logical. He would listen to sense. Usually.

--

FROM: Bridget
TO: Asshole (Jeremy Haines)
SUBJECT: RE: No more bullshit or I'm pulling the plug
Come on! Two years ago, maybe. You know I've been changing things. Losing Richard really fucked my head up. I'm not ready to see you right now. But I'll tell you as soon as I am. I give you my word.
--

The next reply took a few minutes. He was probably in the office. Or just being a bastard and making me wait, because he knew I was sitting here, sweating.

--
FROM: Asshole (Jeremy Haines)
TO: Bridget
SUBJECT: RE: No more bullshit or I'm pulling the plug
You agreed to these rules—or should I say, got me to agree to them. Now I'm the fuckwit? You got yourself here, B. No more silent treatment, or it all stops. All of it.
--
FROM: Bridget
TO: Asshole (Jeremy Haines)
SUBJECT: RE: No more bullshit or I'm pulling the plug
Blackmail? Seriously?
--
FROM: Asshole (Jeremy Haines)
TO: Bridget
SUBJECT: RE: No more bullshit or I'm pulling the plug

I've been doing everything you asked, staying away, leaving you alone, not pushing for months. And nothing. You haven't left me any choice.
--

The rage that washed over me then was *devastating*. I wanted to raze the world. Set fire to the house with him in it. I shouted a curse at the screen and shoved out of my seat, pacing my office for a minute before I answered.

Let the fucker sweat like he was doing to me.

I kept pacing back and forth, glaring at the screen, but I knew he'd wait for me to answer now. Because he always knew exactly when to leave me stewing.

Shit.

The blackmail made me want to cut off his balls, but what could I do? I didn't need the money, but I did need Jeremy. He was my protection. And the one who'd make me legit if I didn't die—and that was a big *if*. But just in case, I needed a safety net, and he was it.

Which meant... I couldn't avoid him forever. But something told me I *could* still avoid him for now.

--
FROM: Bridget
TO: Asshole (Jeremy Haines)
SUBJECT: RE: No more bullshit or I'm pulling the plug
Okay, fine. I will email every day. Check in. And as soon as I have the mental space, we'll meet.
--
FROM: Asshole (Jeremy Haines)
TO: Bridget
SUBJECT: RE: No more bullshit or I'm pulling the plug
We'll meet before the end of the month, B. Either we have a date, or I just find you. The choice is yours.
--

Fuck!

We went back and forth a few more times—him pushing, me dodging, but in the end I didn't have to actually commit to more than emailing him every day… for now.

The fact that I'd gotten out of that conversation without making a date was a huge relief. But it also left me a little desperate.

I was starting to freak out. Losing all my balance.

I tried to message Cain, but he wasn't online and since I couldn't say anything that he might see as a *temptation,* I was reduced to inane nothings like, "What's going on?"

When he didn't reply—of course—I was left sitting there, once again staring at my computer and feeling that tension twisting tighter and higher inside me.

This always fucking happened when Jeremy wanted to see me. I *hated* this part.

I shuddered and pushed the asshole right to the back of my mind in a way Gerald had warned me against, but it was necessary for survival.

When I got the computer secure and turned off, I swung away from my desk, swearing.

I needed something *good* to happen.

Where the fuck was Cain? It had been *four fucking days!*

My entire body hummed with unspent tension. My heel jumping up and down. Hands shaking. Heart hammering—and not in the good way.

Then I thought about everything that was going on, and everything I'd decided yesterday, and said fuck it.

It was already early afternoon. *Vigori* opened in a couple hours.

I could go and maybe see what this Sid character was doing. I would challenge myself to getting into his den without using his invitation, if I could. Though I hadn't talked to Valerie in months. She might still be pissed at me.

But then, maybe I'd just play some games and come home. At least I wouldn't be alone tonight. And I wouldn't be the freak.

So I darted out of the office and into the shower.

An hour later I was dressed up, ready for anything, glossy, and driving into the city. And praying that Cain was watching and would intercept me before I got inside. Because I needed *something* to happen tonight.

Anything.

24. I See You

SOUNDTRACK: Bad Choices by Kode

~ BRIDGET ~

As it turned out, Valerie wasn't even on site when I got there.

I had to show ID to the *Vigori* security guards, but I was still on the list, which meant I got the little wristband, and ushered inside with a dry, "May all your nightmares come true."

It was a play on the club's motto, *Live your dreams, live happily* which was written *in latin* on the napkins and anywhere else Valerie printed the logo, but I knew what it meant.

The industrial nature of the building was unrelenting when you first walked in. Security kept a gray box of a room just inside the door from the street. The only doorway into the club was locked with a code, and it wouldn't be opened unless you were on the list. That door opened to a long, narrow, black painted hallway with no lighting except strips of purple LED lights along the concrete floor.

But it was when you opened the door at the other end that the magic of *Vigori* came alive.

On its other side was the main lounge of the club. A massive, wide oval room wallpapered in red-velvet, lit by dim but sparkling chandeliers, and peppered with thick, brass-riveted leather couches, solid wood tables, and discreet waiters who ran back and forth between the patrons and the bar at the end, making certain that everyone had any social lubricant they could want.

The secret menu at *Vigorí* included every recreational drug known to man, including many things I'd never heard of before coming here. But at this time of day, only the die-hards were here. The men and women with serious money, and no jobs. And they didn't need substance-assisted courage. *Vigorí* was their life.

Even though this wasn't my first choice for a playground, I got it. *Vigorí* was a place where a person's secret, internal needs could come to life without judgment.

And that thought made Sam swim to mind—that boyish grin in stark contrast to the tattoos and rugged strength. I wondered what he'd make of a place like this.

But it was impossible to know, so I put that thought aside and pushed back the hood on my cloak as I scanned the room and tried to decide what I was going to do first.

The cloak would look costumey anywhere else in the world. But it fit perfectly here. And it served the dual purpose of hiding my half-naked body from the men—who were almost always predators—and giving me a flair that was applauded in this place.

I started a slow circuit around the main lounge. I'd get a drink before too long—something to do with my hands. But first I had to decide if I was going to look for Sid first, or if I'd wander around a bit.

Vigorí had five main dens, two more lounges aside from this one, countless shadowy alcoves, and a few lockable rooms for which only a handful of the patrons could retrieve the keys.

Over the years I was a frequent visitor here, I'd been inside every nook and cranny of this place—I thought—but the main dens changed Doms every few months, which meant the content of each Den changed too. If Sid was new, he was probably in the eastern quadrant. I started drifting in that direction, still unsure if I was going to look for him right away, or not.

I actually loved this place. The darkness of it suited me. And it was one of the few environments where I felt *vanilla* compared to most of the other regulars. I felt comfortable around dark people in a way I never felt outside these walls. Probably because I knew they were all more dangerous than me.

I had my skills—I could take care of myself when I needed to. But mostly, I enjoyed being forced into submission. A practice that was very common here at *Vigorí*. Yet, whether I was playing the game, or just watching, I loved this place because no one would judge me here. I could be a silent observer, or an obnoxiously loud participant. Whatever I felt like—because I didn't always feel like the same thing. And no one would bat an eyelid.

I used to spend a lot of time here for that reason. But then stuff happened and I got tired and… I hadn't been back in almost a year.

Valerie was going to shit herself when she saw the security logs.

As I made the circuit of the room and got closer to the fifth den—the one that changed doms most often—there was a small cluster of people at the door, obviously speaking to someone inside.

I had Sid's invitation secreted in a pocket inside my cloak, just in case. But I had challenged myself to see if I could talk my way in without using it. Just because I knew it would piss him off.

Doms *always* hated it when you beat them. In anything. Except the ones that liked to switch, and so were always looking for someone to best them, then take over. But Sid hadn't struck me as that kind of guy.

I pulled my hood back up as I got closer, dipped my chin to keep my face shadowed, and slipped up behind the people standing in the doorway.

"…shows at five, eight, eleven and two. But we're full for the late ones, and you have to be screened."

I smiled when I heard that voice and sure enough, as I took a spot behind two women in bondage gear, and a man in a wrinkled but clearly expensive suit, David, one of the Protectors here, looked at me suspiciously, then his eyes lit up.

"Hey! You're back!"

I nodded, smiling wider. "Good to see you."

He wouldn't use my name—no one in *Vigori* used names, except in private. This was supposed to be a place where anyone could come and remain anonymous. A trait that was necessary because it was frequented by a lot of politicians and celebrities.

"You said there's a show at five?"

"Yeah, yeah. You've been in before?"

The others' heads kept turning back and forth between us as they watched this conversation. I considered lying for their benefit, but that would make it too easy. "Not this show in particular, but Valerie—"

"Oh, even Val is saying you have to be assessed. You can't get in unless he's talked to you first."

I frowned. "He? Sid?"

"Yeah. This is the line for assessment. I think he's got like three or four gaps."

I gave David a look. "Wait, there's actual numbers?"

He frowned. "Yeah, you didn't know?"

"He mentioned limited places, but I just thought he didn't know I'd been here before."

"No, no. He only takes twenty per session—at the most. He'll take less if he doesn't have the right people there and assessed."

The whole exchange was baffling for me—since when did a Dom assess *audience?* It had to be a marketing ploy? But the end result was that I was told to wait for assessment and stood there with the others for a few minutes while David closed the door and went to retrieve Sid.

The two women had their heads together and kept whispering. They were young like me, and their costumes looked like something out of a movie. I suspected they were just rich and looking for an experience they could tell stories about, rather than being in the lifestyle. But who knew? *Vigorì* attracted all kinds.

The guy was older, and kept looking at me and running his hand through his hair. Like something was bugging him. Me? Or was I just under his eyes? In the end I decided it didn't matter. I kept to myself, waiting for that door to open again, and when it did, I let the others hurry forward, trying to look like they weren't hurrying. I kept my chin low and peered out from under the hood—only to find Sid standing in the doorway grinning at me.

"I knew you couldn't stay away."

I shrugged, but couldn't deny that the predatory grin on his face had made my heart beat faster.

"You first," he said, crooking a finger at me and ignoring the others, who were forced to step aside to let me reach him.

Sid said something to David as I passed through the doorway, then it was closed behind me and I was in the short hallway that was the entrance to each of the Dens. I pushed my hood back as soon as the door was closed since Sid already knew what I looked like, and I was curious what he had set up in here. But as I walked into the Den proper, I was frowning.

If I hadn't known better, I'd say I had just walked into one of those small amateur theaters that only seats thirty people, and the chairs climb up from the floor—which doubles as the stage.

There were nice touches here—red velvet covered seats with leather arms, the hardwood floor had been revealed and refinished, and the area I would have called the stage was surrounded by luxuriously red curtains that hung in thick folds so there was no wall visible.

At the center of the stage was a massive, four-poster bed in a deep, dark mahogany.

When I first saw it, I thought it couldn't possibly be real. But I should have known Valerie didn't cut corners. Not only was the frame made from solid, heavy wood—I couldn't even make the bed jiggle when I grabbed one of those posts and leaned my entire weight against it—but the bed was covered in genuine silk sheets, and thick furs.

I took it all in, looked at the audience chairs, and frowned as Sid came to stand behind me with his arms folded.

He wasn't dressed like a punk today—his spiky hair was brushed down and flat, and most of his piercings were out, or subtle. He wore a black collared shirt open at the throat, black slacks, and a black belt. All of them fit him like they'd been custom made, and he stood, welcoming my perusal, smiling like he knew that shirt made his shoulders look even broader and his muscles deliciously tight.

I scanned slowly to his leather boots, then back up to his sly smile.

"Bondage and voyeurism?" I said to him over my shoulder. "I mean, I won't deny I'd like to see the show, but it's hardly earth shattering. You're reducing audiences, why? To choose only the richest or most attractive? Give them a sense of being elite and others the feeling that they're missing out? Smart, but it won't last long. Someone will start talking and pretty soon they'll all know you're just peddling garden variety bondage—"

"My show is far from garden variety," he said, but he was still smiling. "Why'd it take you so long to show up?"

I turned to face him and matched his stance, arms folded and head slightly tipped. "Last time I saw you, you tried to tackle me."

"Did I? I saw a scuffle and your boyfriend come to your aid. Is that your kink? You're bait and he comes in to play the hero on whatever idiot you suck into your lies?"

"Actually no." But I also wasn't telling him the truth because it was none of his fucking business.

He waited. But when I didn't speak further, he smiled wider. "Art told me you had sass. I like it."

"I have that effect on men a lot," I said with a shrug, sweating because it wasn't actually true. Most men found me intimidating, or wanted to break me.

"Okay, I'll bite. Why are you here?" he asked, his smile fading as he offered a glimpse of his dom persona—the take no shit, you're on *my* turf, kind of Alpha that a lot of the doms strived for, but there was something about him that, oddly, pulled it off.

That jawline caught my eye again. He was clean shaven today, and I once again found myself questioning the familiar line of it.

But I'd seen Cain fight him.

Hadn't I?

I frowned and made myself focus. "I'm here because I'm bored and you talked a big game. So I thought I'd come see what you were doing."

"And you wanted to prove that you could."

I shrugged. "Maybe."

He snorted, and relaxed, letting his arms drop to his sides and walking past me as he spoke, leaning over the bed and running his hands down the posts and along the head and foot as if he was checking it for weakness. "Well, you did it. David vouches for you, and didn't get your invite, but still put you on my list. So you won. Well done."

"All you would have had to do was refuse to assess me."

He looked up from where he was squatting near the back of bed and peering at the carvings. "Why would I do that? I want you here."

"You don't even know me."

"I know enough."

I rolled my eyes. "Look, I get that we've got this thing going where we sniff around each other and both of us try to be the more mysterious one. But it's kind of dumb, and… not really what I'm looking for. Do your assessment, see if you'll keep me in the room. I want to stay and see your show… possibly," I said, frowning at the very luxurious, but otherwise very normal looking bed.

Sid got to his feet again and opened his mouth, then closed it again, his eyes narrowing. "I think I'll let you come back for the show," he said slowly.

I blinked. "That's it? Your assessment is just… *meet* people? What the hell is going on here? And why is Valerie going along with this shit?"

He gave me a sharp look that made the hair on the back of my neck stand up, but then he softened those warning eyes with a smile. "No… I'm not going to assess you. I said, I'm going to let you in. I guess you'll have to come back tonight to see if you like the magic," he said with a one-shouldered shrug.

I cut him a look. "I said I was done doing the intentionally mysterious thing. It's melodramatic and juvenile."

"Then call me the drama, I guess?"

He didn't say anything more, just remained standing there, smiling at me. For whatever reason, it pissed me off.

"Look, I don't want to waste my time. Tell me what you're doing here—if you don't, and I show up, and it's boring or you're doing two-bit street magic tricks with sex, I'll just walk out. And I won't be quiet about it."

"I'll take the risk," he said, though he didn't smile anymore.

Prima Donna Dom didn't want his little show getting interrupted. So he was an *artist?* I looked around the space again, shaking my head. "What game are you playing?"

"Come back at five and find out."

I glared at him, frustrated because there was something about him that told me he wasn't bluffing. And he wasn't safe. I'd always been really good at picking a show-boater, and even though this dude did a lot of things that were designed to make people look at him, he didn't have that flimsy kind of presence—the kind that stunk of desperation and folded as soon as they took off the makeup and turned on the lights.

"Fine," I snapped and turned on my heel, heading for the door. "See you at five, I guess."

"Do me a solid and tell the guy who was waiting to come in when you leave? And tell David that the girls are a no."

"I'm not your fucking messenger."

"No, but you're someone who chooses when they break the rules. And you don't like being impolite to polite strangers, because there's still a part of you that crumbles under that kind of disapproval. Especially from men."

"What?!" I whirled around, stopping dead, gaping at him from halfway down that short entryway.

He was standing next to the bed, hands in his pockets. No longer smiling, but not looking tense either. "You heard me," he said quietly.

I snorted. "You don't have a fucking clue about m—"

"Something bad happened to you, and it's held a cloud over your entire life. Now you keep trying to outrun it, but you can't. You're not bored, you're scared. And you didn't come see if I put on a good show. You came to see if I could make you feel something."

My jaw dropped. "Who the *fuck* have you been talking to?!"

Art didn't know about my dad. Sid didn't know Nate. And no one local except Gerald and Cain had a clue about the other stuff.

Sid just stared at me, his expression unconcerned, but serious. "Bridget, what you see at five is going to scare you. I'm not sure if that'll make you run towards me, or away from me. But either way, I'm in."

I stared at him like he was crazy. *"In* what?"

"I know what you're really looking for," he said, and he did smile this time. "You wouldn't be my first. I'm saying *yes."*

"Yes, to fucking what, Sid? And if you vague-post this one, I'm leaving and not coming back."

"No, you aren't, because you're half-scared and half-fascinated now, so it'll drive you crazy until you find out whether I'm full of shit or not, but don't worry, I'm not going to make you wait. I know that you want to be *hunted.* And I can tell you that, yes, it will make you feel alive. Maybe even alive enough that you don't want to die anymore. It's something I only do on the side, but I'm saying… yes."

I looked at that jawline again and those broad shoulders. He didn't look as big as Cain had—or maybe it was just the clothes. Black was slimming after all. And all this unrelenting black was deceiving to the eye, especially in this dim lighting.

I didn't think he was Cain.

But what if he was?

What if this was part of the hunt?

I swallowed hard, my heart beginning to patter faster.

"I haven't asked a question," I croaked, way too late.

Sid smirked. "Sure."

"I just came to see what you're doing here, and why Valerie is keeping you around."

"Then come back in about an hour and get that question answered. Or... Stay after the show and I'll answer *any* question you have."

He dropped his chin until he was staring at me out from under heavy brows, and his smile was dazzling—and terrifying—in this half-light. It made a shiver skitter down my spine. The genuine jolt of adrenaline made me have to fight a smile of my own. But I did it because I wasn't going to give him the satisfaction.

"Cool your jets, Sparky," I said, trying to sound like I thought he was nuts. "You don't know everything you think you do. I'll see you in an hour, though."

"Yes, you will."

I turned away and stalked back to the door, each step just a little faster than the one before.

And I kind of hated myself, but I passed on the message that the girls had been turned away, and the guy was to go in and talk to Sid.

David nodded and asked me if I was coming back for the session.

"Yeah," I said, my palms beginning to sweat, though I couldn't exactly have said why. "I think I am."

"Great! See you in an hour then."

And then I fled to the bar to get a drink and maybe watch someone have sex in one of the alcoves with those little windows because I needed to keep my brain busy until then.

What you see at five is going to scare you...

I fucking hoped so. Otherwise it was going to be the biggest anti-climax since Cain disappeared.

And I didn't think I could handle another one.

25. The Conductor

SOUNDTRACK: *All by Myself* by Lexxi Saal

~ BRIDGET ~

I sat at the back of Sid's little theater, unmoving, jaw slack, my mind racing.

When I came to the door just before five, David and a couple other guys were there. One of the other men had a clipboard, and as each person approached the door, we were assigned a seat.

Like some kind of fucked up movie-theater.

There were only fifteen people there, each of them handing over a piece of paper before they were given their tickets.

Then the doors were opened and we filed in—some whispering quietly with others, everyone looking at their tickets, which were just plain, blank pieces of white paper with a seat number printed on it.

I was the last one through the door, and I leaned close to David.

"What's the paper they're all handing over?" I whispered to him as he found my ticket and ripped it off. I didn't have whatever the others did and I was worried this was going to be Ronald's ploy to win the little scuffle over my access.

But David just winked. "Legal waivers," he said with a small smile. "Sid says he's not going to touch you, so you don't need one."

I frowned, but took the ticket David handed me and walked into that little hallway.

I'd been given seat eighteen.

I frowned harder when I read that, because there were only fifteen people here. But I followed the others without a word and walked in, found my seat—in the center of the back row—and waited.

What unfolded in the thirty minutes following that moment was possibly the most fucked up, mind-boggling thing I'd ever seen. For reasons I couldn't even articulate.

Ronald, the man who called himself Sid Vicious, *The Conductor,* wasn't just a Dom. Though the room had several more furniture pieces in it now that made it look less like a stage and more like a den, along with chests and satin-finished wooden boxes that were obviously filled with his newly-sterilized toys.

Still, there was nothing earthshattering—I'd seen *far* more intimidating pieces in some of the other dens in the past.

But my skepticism was short lived. Because it turned out, Ronald was a mentalist.

He spent the first ten minutes of this little pageant hypnotising everyone except me… or something. I wasn't sure. All I knew was that the first three rows of this room were full of people who, one by one, were placed in some kind of trance.

And then he had started talking. Asking questions. And smiling a lot.

Like he'd fed them all some kind of truth serum, these people each answered his very delving, very personal questions.

Secrets. Secrets within secrets.

Fears.

Hidden fantasies, hidden desires, hidden fetishes.

They all came out. And as each person spilled their darkest thoughts and fears, Ronald made notes on a clipboard just like the one the Protectors at the door had used.

At first I just gaped—was this some kind of therapy disguised as a Dom session?

But then he'd been through the fourteen other people in the rows ahead of me, and he lifted his eyes to meet mine as he put the clipboard down.

He must have caught the question in my eyes.

"Don't worry, Bridget," he said with a sly smile. "Today you get to just watch. But I want to see what you think at the end, and if you ever decide to come back and participate, as I said, *I'm in*."

I was so stunned I didn't even answer, just stared at him as he leaned over a woman in her forties from the first row, gently tipped up her chin and made her meet his eyes.

"Are you ready, Penny? Do you want to try?"

Penny nodded, quick and jerky, like she was both nervous and excited. And as Ronald took her hand and drew her out of the chair and began to work his... whatever this was, I saw why.

Now, fifteen minutes later, she was on all fours, staring up at Ronald like he'd hung the sun in the sky. She crawled towards him slowly—afraid of his rejection. Because he'd warned her it might happen. Not like an asshole. But like... like he was *taking care* of her.

His eyes *blazed* with a heated kind of satisfaction. He hadn't even touched her except when he helped her out of the seat. Yet, she was now naked, her breathing short and shallow, and she'd admitted that she'd cheated on her husband several times, and was now considering divorce.

And that she rarely orgasmed when she had sex.

And that she was scared of Ronald.

That part had made him smile broader.

When she said that, my stomach clenched so hard I got nauseous. Yet, his response surprised me.

"If you fear me, Penny, why are you here?" he asked in a low drawl, that was very calm, but very intense.

I watched her face, saw the flicker of awareness in her eyes and my breath stopped.

She swallowed audibly, but her eyes never left his. "Because the whole point of this is to face fears, right?"

Ronald nodded like she was a good student who'd pleased him. "You're absolutely right, beautiful. So tell me…" For the first time since this started, he drew close to her, standing over her, but cupping her face like a lover. "What was the boundary in your mind or body when you walked in this door?"

Her breath whooshed out of her. "Anal," she said quickly, like she wanted to get away from the word.

My eyebrows went up. Seriously?

"I hate it," she said, then licked her lips and gazed at him like she was pleading.

"Why?" he asked quietly.

"Because when I was fourteen my brother used to rape me that way because he said there was no way I could get pregnant."

Ronald nodded and stroked her cheek. "Have you ever told anyone that before?"

"No."

"Why did you tell me?"

"Because seeing you made me feel like… like I wanted to get rid of the fear."

He beamed at her, then squatted in front of her, took her face in both his hands and stared at her like she'd just given him a gift. Then he leaned in and kissed her and I couldn't quite believe what I was seeing—the gentleness in him, the fascination. Like she was a prize. What the hell was he—

"You are safe here," he purred. "Every single one of these people was personally assessed by me and they will not tell your secrets. They will not reveal anything you say or do here. You're free, Penny. Do you believe you're free?"

"I want to be."

"Good girl. But your heart is racing, and you're beginning to sweat. Tell us why."

"Because I'm afraid you're going to fuck me up the ass."

He gave a low, husky chuckle. "That's because I am, darling… but not until you ask me to. Not until you *want* me to. We'll face your fear together so that you can walk out of here and never be afraid again. Are you ready?"

She stared at him like he'd just revealed a profound truth, then she nodded.

He leaned in and kissed her again, then murmured, "Now, let's get started."

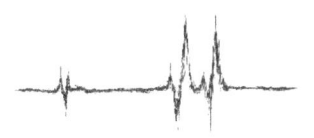

It was like watching a high quality porn movie with the premise that the Dom was a psychologist, using sex to work his clients through their issues…

Except it was real. And, at least here and now, it was working.

I tried to imagine what Gerald would think of this *theraputic approach,* and almost choked on my own spit.

I told myself it had to be a party trick. A two-bit hypnotist magician who could make people think they wanted something they didn't actually want, and I almost fled.

But then I remembered his words.

Bridget, what you see at five is going to scare you. I'm not sure if that'll make you run towards me, or away from me. But either way, I'm in…

And then, as I sat there, bolt upright in my seat, I watched that woman turn into his sub. Give herself into his hands.

My adrenaline started pumping the moment a panting, sweating Penny, who'd been pawed and pleasured and seduced, bent herself over the bed and begged Ronald to take her by the back door.

My heartrate rose as I watched him prepare her body, ready her physically, and her mind as well. His hands gentle and coaxing, while his voice remained low and calm, the murmured assurances, the reminders of truth… as if there was no one in the room but them.

It was fascinating.

My belly began to tingle when he finally decided she was truly ready and—still whispering comfort to her, positioned himself behind her and swept her hair up with his hands, murmuring reassurance to her as he applied lube, then wrapped her wavy brown hair around his fist.

I was panting when he trailed his other hand down her spine to grab her hip and take a firm hold on her for the first time.

My belly fluttered when his eyes rolled back and he groaned softly while her eyes went wide and her mouth dropped open because he'd entered her. The startled joy on her face was as if he'd just introduced her to a world she'd never seen before.

My body pulsed with need and want as I watched the patience he showed in easing into her, talking her through it, and praising her when she relaxed… The affirmation never stopping until he was drawing in and out of her, and her slightly-sagging breasts began to swing.

Which was when I tore my eyes off the pair and scanned the other participants—who stared, eyes bright and wide, shoulders rising and falling with their quickened breaths, but none of them made a sound.

And when Penny began to keen, then shriek, when she finally arched and froze, resisting him for the first time as her body began to twitch and shake… and then she slumped onto the bed… weeping.

And he didn't come.

He drew out of her, calming her, stroking her, whispering in her ear in ways we couldn't hear, but he mopped up her tears, then helped her clean her body, then dressed her and ushered her back to her seat, holding her face for a long moment as he *thanked her* for trusting him… then he took the hand of the man to her right and brought him to stand in the center of the floor.

I lost all track of time as he walked that man through a repressed desire to dress in women's clothing and be blown by another man—and the change in Ronald was stunning. With this man he laughed and cajoled and reassured, but accepted no backwards step. He pushed and challenged, and eventually, fallated him to climax.

I forgot that the world existed when he started working with another woman who was a high powered executive, and all she'd ever wanted was to be helpless in the hands of someone stronger than her, but she'd never found the man who could—or would—intimidate her.

The need in me grew tight and urgent when Ronald's countenance changed.

He never raised his voice. Never *overtly* dominated her. But no one in the room missed it as he suddenly embodied an unwavering, ruthless Dom.

She would listen, and she would obey.

She would take what she was given, and she would learn the freedom of losing control.

At one point, even in the trance, her nerve broke, and just as he was challenging her, she started scrambling away. My body reacted as if it was me he was chasing. My heart was pounding in my skull, adrenaline flooding me.

I almost came when he tackled her to the ground.

Then, with arm locked around her middle, he pulled her head back, his hand clasped around her throat, pushing her chin high as he growled in her ear and I saw shades of that moment with Cain that raised all my questions.

"Try to free yourself—you can't," he snarled.

She shuddered and struggled, squeaking with the effort to get out of his arms, but then she stopped, panting. A moment later she swallowed with some effort, then shook her head. "I can't," she rasped because of the pressure he had on her throat.

I was leaning forward in my seat, wishing I could masterbate because the ache between my thighs was so great it was almost painful.

Every moment was a struggle, she didn't let him take anything without a fight. But eventually he had her bent over too, and even though no one moved, and no one spoke, the air in the room went *tight.*

And just as he finally had her positioned, he turned his head, just for a moment.

It was the first time I'd seen him take his attention from the person he was dominating.

He looked right at me as he entered her and I actually gasped.

It was as if my vision *zoomed in.* I was locked in that gaze, need and want twisting together, tighter and tighter in my belly as the woman began to cry out, then scream, and the room echoed with the sound of their bodies meeting and her cries.

I was quivering, right on the edge of coming myself, but it wouldn't happen without *some* kind of stimulation.

I leaned forward, tempted to get out of my seat and go join them, but even though Ronald smiled at me, he dropped his chin and shook his head once. And when I froze, he turned back to her, holding her so tightly she couldn't breathe until he pounded her to her climax.

She was a mess at the end—as chaotic and shaky and *grateful* as I was.

My hands were actually trembling.

None of the others affected me that way. But by the time we left that den, two hours after we entered it, he'd fucked or fiddled with six of the attendees.

And everyone that he didn't touch, slumped with disappointment when a high, resonant chime echoed through the room.

Clearly it was the signal of the end of the session.

Ronald finished with the dude and his wife who'd come to the club together because they were bored.

By the time Ronald led a round of applause for their display and wiped the sweat off his brow, I felt about a strong as a cooked noodle.

He stood near the exit, speaking quietly with each person before they left—but when I started to get out of my seat as the row in front of me made their way out, he caught my eye again and shook his head.

I sat back down with a thump.

And fizz of need in my belly.

And I waited until the very last person had walked out.

I watched him stand in the entrance to the hallway and watch them go, then pull a cloth out of his back pocket and wipe his face, then his chest, and take a deep breath, before he finally turned and faced me.

And his eyes were hard as flint, and bright as the sun.

26. Who Are You?

~ BRIDGET ~

"So, Bridget," Ronald said quietly. "I await your cutting commentary with baited breath."

I stared at him, my body thrumming and my mind spinning. I couldn't decide whether I'd just seen something *horrifically* fucked up, or... really, really cool.

"What did you do to them?"

Ronald arched one brow and walked towards me, still rubbing his hands on that little cloth. "You saw *everything* I did—"

"No, before. They were all... they were all in some kind of trance or whatever. What did you do?"

His lips pulled up on one side. "When I assess a person, Bridget, I'm exploring whether they're ready for this— having their boundaries *willingly* breached. I discuss with them what happens here, and see if they can be hynotized. And if they can, I *do not change their minds*. Without any hypnosis in place, I tell them what I am willing to do, and ask them if that's what they want. Their waivers are personalized to their personal fears, goals, and boundaries, and they sign a new one every time they enter this den. They come to me because we've already discussed what I will do to them if they are chosen."

"So, some of them come and you never work with them?"

Ronald snorted. *"Many* of them never work with me. Some of them lose their nerve and stop showing up. Others get too demanding and get banned. But most… most will have their moment if they keep showing up and play by the rules."

I swallowed as he mounted the shallow stairs alongside the seats and started up, his eyes locked on mine like a cat on a bird.

"You didn't assess me," I said breathlessly as he came to stand at the end of my row.

He nodded once. "You weren't ready."

"Then why did you let me in?"

"Because… you're one of the ones who needed to see what I do. You're chaos, Bridget. I'm not going to have you freak out and steal my future from me."

"What? I wouldn't do that. If I don't like something I just leave—"

He edged up the narrow space between the rows of seats until he stood right at my knee, then he stared down his nose at me, his eyes piercing and intent, like he was examining me.

"One thing I don't allow in here is lies, Bridget," he said darkly. "There is freedom in truth—even dark truth. The world you're living in doesn't understand that. They're so busy pushing everything under rugs, or into closets, or renaming it to make it more palatable and pretend it isn't what it is… they never let themselves learn how much freedom comes from just admitting the truth.

Then he leaned down, one hand each on the arms of my chair, his eyes locked on mine, and his breath fluttering across my face.

He smelled like mint and smug-satisfaction.

"I understand the world, and I can play by the rules. But this is *my house.* And here we don't bullshit ourselves, or anyone else."

I swallowed. "I wasn't—"

"Your head is so chaotic you throw yourself into danger on purpose, then scream when the monster comes after you."

"Are you the monster, Ronald?" I asked seriously, because there was still a part of me that wondered if he was Cain.

"Only if you need me to be," he said, then smiled.

I should have rolled my eyes.

I should have made a joke about monster sex requiring multiple-peens, or some kind of tentacle that could knot inside me and pound me stomach-first.

I should have sneered and told him he wasn't the first Dom I'd known and wouldn't be the last, and his little tricks were intriguing, but not truly earth-shattering.

But I couldn't make my voice work. And the fucker just stood there, all up in my space, and waited. And out of *nowhere,* my skin began to itch.

"I'm going to leave now," I said, suddenly deeply uncomfortable.

He tipped his head. "Are you?

I nodded.

"Okay."

He didn't move. And neither did I.

And then he was smiling again. "Ask me, Bridget."

"Ask you what?"

"Whatever secrets your clever little mind is trying to uncover. Ask me."

Are you Cain?

Is this a set up?

What would you do to me if I said yes?

"I don't believe in coincidences," I said hoarsely.

"Neither do I," he said in a voice so deep I felt it in the soles of my shoes. "Ask your questions, Bridget."

"I… Have we met before?"

"Not that I know of—not until the other night at the bar."

"Were you the one who came at me in the hallway outside the bathroom?"

"No."

I blinked and eased my head back. "You said you didn't lie." *Something else that Cain had emphasized.*

Ronald's eyes went flinty again. "I don't. Your mob friend came for you. I was watching from the bar to see if you could handle yourself when your boyfriend showed up."

"He's not my boyfriend."

"You might want to tell *him* that."

I huffed and a little of the tension left me, but Ronald's face got tighter.

"Ask me, Bridget. Or if you prefer, *tell* me. Tell me what you need. If it's not me, I'll tell you."

The strange, high laugh that came out of me then sounded almost insane in that empty, echoing room.

He was still leaned over me, both thick, man-hands clasped on those arms, and his arms locked as surely as his eyes. If I tried to run, he'd have me. That woman he'd taken was inches taller than me, and strong. Ronald wasn't a weak man. But that wasn't what scared me.

That was when I realized this *sleek* version of him was different. He'd taken out most of his piercings. He'd flattened his hair down. He was dressed not for attention, but to emphasize his body.

When I'd seen him at the bar, he'd seemed ridiculous. Now he seemed much more deadly—but less himself.

And just like that, I was done.

"I don't trust you," I said bluntly.

His brows pinched over his nose. "I've never spoken a false word to you."

I shrugged. "Maybe not, but… I don't trust you. There's something in you that sets off all my alarms and I trust my instincts. I grew up with a monster. I learned how they hide. And you, sir, are hiding *something*."

He didn't like that at all. His jaw jutted out and he pushed off the arms of my chair, turning away and stalking towards the door, grabbing that cloth again and rubbing the sweat off the back of his own neck.

"You never came," I said, like it made sense.

He shrugged, but broke eye-contact. "I have three or four shows a night. I need to keep my… *energy* up."

I shook my head. "That's not why."

"Oh really?" he snarled. "What childish, jacked up *insight* do you have to offer, Bridget? I'm all ears."

"It's a loss of control," I said, more confident with every word.

He rolled his eyes. "I'm a Dom. Control is what we do."

"Nah. You're... you're not a Dom. A *true* Dom is playing out their own fantasies, not someone else's."

"You don't get to define words for me. Especially if you aren't willing to play the game."

"See," I said, pushing him and swearing at myself because I really needed to just leave. "You call it a game. It's not a fucking game for some of us."

He frowned. "You're a switch?"

"No, that's not what I meant—I meant... You say you're telling the truth here, but the reality is, other people are telling you their truth, and you're using it."

"I'm *helping them with it,* actually."

"That's such bullshit. If you believe that, you're stupider than I thought." He opened his mouth but I kept going. "Penny didn't heal from her brother's rape just because you brought her to orgasm."

He sneered "I'll be sure to ask her when she comes back and asks me to take her again."

"I didn't say she didn't enjoy it. I said she didn't *heal.* Now the next time she wants that because it felt good, she doesn't have any way to process the fact that it's also connected to the memory that fucks her up. This isn't facing fears, it's twisting trauma. In the long run—"

"Get out," he snarled, turning away to start towards the stairs. "I've got another show in an hour and I need to eat."

I launched myself out of the seat and down the opposite aisle, rushing so I'd be ahead of him.

"Coward," he muttered, just as I reached the entrance to the hallway that would take me out of that place.

I stopped dead, pissed with myself for flinching at the barb, but I turned and frowned at him.

"*I'm* the coward?" I challenged, aware that I was slowly inching back along that hallway, every instinct screaming at me to get away from this guy.

"You heard me."

"You're *literally* playing on people's fear to make them admire you."

His expression went dark and he started towards me. "You're an idiot if you think I didn't help those bitches break through fear. You saw—"

"I saw you push them past their boundaries—"

"Which they agreed to!"

"—but do absolutely *nothing* to help them beat the reason they were afraid in the first place."

"I'm not a fucking therapist."

"No. You aren't."

Neither was I. But I was regurgitating things Gerald had confronted me about in my own behavior. He would have been proud of me, I thought.

"Goodbye, Bridget," he growled, stopping at the edge of the hallway, scowling.

"Goodbye, Sid."

"Don't try to come back, I'm adding your name to the banned list."

"Now who's the coward?" I snapped, then turned on my heel. It took everything in my body not to *flee.* To make myself stay at a walking pace. Ears perked, heightened senses, everything aware, listening, waiting for movement behind me, or the rush of air, or pounding footsteps... until I reached the very normal looking door and clasped the cool metal of the handle, pushed it down and stepped out into the blood red lounge of *Vigorí*.

My heart was *slamming* in my chest.

But no one came after me as I darted through the space and towards the exit.

I'd had enough thrill for tonight.

27. Into the Night

~ BRIDGET ~

I hurried through the lounge, ignored by most—people wearing cloaks and moving quickly wasn't really noteworthy in this place. Plus, with Ronald's den having just emptied and some of the other shows finishing at similar times, there were a lot of people milling around trying to figure out what they were going to do next. I knew it was sometime between seven and eight—there were no clocks here and I didn't want to stop to dig my phone out to be sure. But Ronald had another show at eight, so it was earlier than that.

Valerie had told me in the past that this was when the night started to pick up. But it wouldn't be until the ten and eleven o'clock shows that the crowds would arrive. Those were the most popular, any day of the week.

I was just grateful that there were a lot more bodies around now, and that none of them cared enough to stop me or enquire why I was *fleeing* a den.

Mainly because I wouldn't have known what to say.

Nothing had gone wrong. I hadn't been threatened—frankly, I would have enjoyed it more if Ronald had come at me. But he didn't.

So I didn't know why I was feeling *so* exposed and *so* uncomfortable. I'd been looking forward to coming here, and even though Ronald's "show" hadn't been what I expected, it also wasn't traumatic.

I'd watched consenting adults letting other consenting adults push their boundaries. It was the entire point of this place, and something I usually applauded.

But I kept seeing Ronald's intense gaze, his smug smiles, and I kept feeling that itch at the back of my neck that screamed danger.

Why?

A Dom who was full of his own importance was almost *cliché.*

A Dom who considered what he did to be important and who got butt-hurt when you didn't agree was little more than garden-variety arrogant.

Regardless of *why* my body was quivering like a religious virgin on the altar, the fact of the matter was that I didn't want to stick around for any more shows. So I only lifted my head to navigate the path through the furniture and people, making a beeline for the exit hallway.

Except, as I broke through the ring of couches and chairs in the center of the large room, a husky, female voice rose to my right.

"So the guys weren't playing a prank on me. You're really here?"

I knew that rasp. That voice, molded by fifty years of smoking and too much of any vice or substance you could imagine, belonged to Valerie. The owner of this fine establishment, and *not* someone I wanted to talk to when I felt like I was about to split my skin.

But it had been a year, and I didn't want to lose my privilege, just in case. So, I made myself stuff the feelings down and stop, turn on my heel and look for her.

She was a short woman who, at well over sixty, had cut her hair short so she didn't have to wash it very often. She didn't usually wear make-up, and lived in black slacks and frilly blouses that looked like they belonged in a Walmart *Seniors* Department.

She'd aged since I last saw her, but I pretended I didn't notice.

"Valerie! It's great to see you."

I would have hugged her, but she lifted her hand—clutching a vape—and pointed at me with a stern look on her face.

"You come in after a year away and don't even knock on my door? I'm hurt, Bridge."

I grimaced. "I'm sorry. I had heard about Ronald and I was kind of obsessed with seeing what he was doing, so I just… I'm sorry."

"Whatever. So he let you in, I take it? I can't think of anyone else here that would make you run like your shoes were on fire."

"I wasn't running."

She gave me a skeptical look, but didn't comment. "What did you think?"

I swallowed. "It was… not what I expected."

She snorted. "I swear, every word that comes out of your mouth is either barbed, or completely understated. That guy is a mind-fuck. In fact, that's what we should name his show. I need to get marketing on it."

I snorted. "It's actually really good."

"Don't sound surprised. It takes more than a pretty face to make a place like this work." Valerie used that extended arm to slip around my shoulders and turn me away from the exit, and head me towards the nondescript door that would lead us to the back office.

Shit. "I'm sure it does, but I really need to—"

"I'll let you go in a minute, but I need something from you."

I blinked. "You do?" She was ushering me towards that door. "Yes. You're young, right? I need someone to help me with auditions, because I only took the Monster guy because we had a gap, but he's proving to be the most popular with the under-thirty crowd, and now I'm feeling like I'm losing touch."

I looked at her. "Monster guy?"

"Yeah, he's got all those hollow dildo things that he straps on and fucks you like he's an alien, or something. I don't know. It's not my cup of tea, but you know me, I won't yuck your yum."

"Right."

"So, I was going to call you, because you're young, but not *too* young—God, I cannot stomach a giggler. And I was thinking if you wanted to come help me with casting next month when we do the next round, I could make it worth your while."

"That's a really generous offer, Valerie, but—"

"You don't even know what the offer is yet."

"Yeah, but I know you. I know how generous you can be," I said carefully, praying she wouldn't get pissed off with me. "I just have a lot going on right now and I'm not sure I'd have time—"

"Please, it's two days every three months. Even you can swing that. And I'll give you a month's notice."

"I know you would, I'm just—"

"I'll call you in a couple weeks and we'll talk about it then," Valerie said like I hadn't even spoken.

I opened my mouth, but my brain was short-circuiting because what she described would be *fun,* but if I was getting hunted I would want to focus… but what if I wasn't?

"I… okay," I said helplessly as we reached the door into the back offices. "You give me a call, but I have to go now, okay? I have a date."

Valerie chuckled, which devolved into a hacking cough. "Sure you do. But I get it. I'm old."

"No, Val, that's not—"

"You help me with the recruitment and I'll forgive you."

I slumped, shaking my head. "I'm beginning to see why these people never get around you," I grumbled.

Valerie chuckled again. "Smart girl. So, talk in a couple weeks?"

"Sure."

I was just relieved to finally be free when she squeezed my shoulder, then let me go. "Then you go have your date. Don't do anything I wouldn't do!"

"That doesn't narrow my options at all," I muttered, which made her laugh. But she walked away smiling and pushed through that door, leaving me free.

I heaved a sigh of relief and darted back to the exit and out, through the security room, then onto the street.

I'd had to park three blocks away because there was no parking for *Vigorí*, and no businesses nearby that offered public parking. So, I turned left out the door and started down the street.

My skin was still itching, but it wasn't as bad as it had been at home. And maybe... maybe it was because of Ronald now? Maybe when I got home I'd feel *better?* Or maybe Cain would finally have sent me a message.

Or maybe he was hunting me now and had only been waiting for me to get out of the club!

That thought made my breath catch, and I instinctively looked up and over my shoulder just in time to catch the very masculine shadow separating from the corner of the alleyway between *Vigorí* and the neighboring building, and launching at me—arms extended and man-hands clawed.

"Holy sh—"

I tried to twist and avoid the grip of those long arms, but only managed to turn enough so he grabbed my hair instead of my shoulder, snapping my head back at the same time he lifted me off my feet and turned me, slamming me backwards into the side of the building in the shadows.

I struggled to break free, heart hammering, spitting curses and trying to kick him, but he had me off my feet, my heels against the wall, and his thighs pinning mine so there was nowhere to move to get a swing on him.

I looked into the shadow of his hood, trying desperately to see his face, but the dim glow from the distant streetlight on the next block only silhouetted the edge of his jaw.

Cain? I sucked in a huge breath.

But then he tossed his head back and the hood slipped off, revealing the smiling face of Ronald, teeth gleaming, eyes ablaze.

"I told you I was in," he whispered, then smiled in the way that made my stomach go cold. Then he glanced over his shoulder, and his smile got broader. "So... you really did come alone. *Good girl,"* he purred. "And don't worry, I won't tell your boyfriend you came looking for me."

28. Terms and Conditions

SOUNDTRACK: *Stalker* by Stevie Howie

~ BRIDGET ~

I didn't move or struggle any further, but I locked eyes with him and made my tone as calm and flat as I could.

"Ronald, this isn't—"

"Call me Sid, or we're going to get nowhere."

I took a breath. *"Sid,* let me be really clear with you—this isn't a game. This is a no. There is nothing to be *in."*

He raised one brow. "Don't play games, Bridget. You want to be hunted. I told you I could help. You came to see me work. Here we are."

"No, Ron—Sid. That's not how this works, and you know it." *Heart slamming.* "You have your assessments and your waivers, I have my arrangments." *Gotta breathe.* "But you and I haven't agreed on terms. I don't have a safe-word. This is *not* part of a game," I said very clearly and firmly, not lowering my voice. And definitely not letting him see how I was *about to have a fucking heart attack.*

Ronald tipped his head and reached up with one hand to push my hair back off my face. I jerked away from his touch, but held eye-contact. Submission could be deadly with a Dom on the hunt.

"This *is* our game, Bridget. You and I both know you don't need a safeword. I know your boyfriend, and I'm not surprised he's not... *satisfying you.* Don't worry. I'm here now. And I'll make sure you—"

"Ronald, *no.* This isn't part of the game—there is no game for us. I'm saying no. I don't want this from you."

He smiled and nodded like I'd just said something profound that he agreed with.

I stopped breathing when he leaned in and his lips brushed the corner of my jaw, his breath thundering in my ear as he whispered, "Boundaries understood. Now... let me help you. And don't worry, we can take our time. I won't even hypnotize you. I think you're brave enough without it."

Shit. *Shit!*

Then he pulled back, locking eyes with me again, chin low and his lips pulled up in a wicked smile that turned my blood cold.

"Your heart is beating *way too fast,* Bridget. Take a breath. In a second I'm going to let you go so you can run and we can get started. I know you'll fight—I love that part. But I give you my word, I won't let you down. You won't get away... I *promise."*

I gaped at him, rage and frustration and *abject terror* coursing through me as I looked in every direction and realized there was no way to get through him.

He really thought I'd come to him for help. He wasn't going to hear my clarity—he thought it was me stating my fears.

Fears that I wanted him to help me face.

Head spinning and heart thumping painfully in my skull, I just stared at him as he slowly, carefully set me back down on my feet, then took half-a-step back, though he could still reach me easily.

Then he brought one of those strong hands to cup my jaw and stroke my cheek with his thumb. I raised my chin, turning from him without breaking eye contact, letting him see my teeth, but his smile just got wider.

"Now… *run,*" he whispered like it was a lover's caress.

Every system in my body screamed high alert and time slowed.

Valerie had once told me that all men have animals inside them. Predators. But that modern life had stifled those instincts so firmly, the only option left to most men was to become caged in their own rage.

Doms, she postulated, had found an outlet for the animal inside.

"Never run from a predator unless you want to be his prey," she'd warned me once a couple years ago, as we sat drinking in the lounge, watching the rich, the perverted, and the self-indulgent come and go from her lair. *"Never ever run from a man you don't want to chase you—because unless he's a complete pussy, you'll just wake up the animal inside him."*

And now I stood here, staring into the eyes of a predator who'd had his pride hurt and had somehow twisted our interactions in his mind. If I ran, he'd chase me. But if I didn't, I was already in his grip.

There was no winning.

He was going to kill me.

And very, very suddenly, I didn't want to die.

Not like this. Not with him. This wasn't the end I'd fantasized about.

A tiny, distant screaming voice tried to shake me awake to something in that moment, but there was no room for deeper thought. All I knew was that, at least for tonight, I wanted to survive. And I wasn't quite sure how to do that.

My head felt numb. I was terrififed in all the wrong ways—and as Ronald tipped his head and his eyes flashed warning, breathing became a struggle.

"Bridget, I said—"

"I'm not running from you, R-Ronald," I managed, breathlessly. "You've read this all wrong."

He shook his head and chuckled. "No, babe. You're just not as smart as you think."

His expression hardened for a blink, then suddenly those hands had me again and the world tipped and spun. I squeaked as the cement under our feet came rushing for me, curling my head into my arms to protect it, trying to tuck and roll.

But then I was on the ground, heart thundering, unable to breathe, with an immense weight over me and all I could feel was the fear.

On my back, on the ground was the way I'd always been weakest, the position from which I'd always struggled most to take back control. A tiny sob broke in my throat as I clawed at his face because he'd only managed to pin one of my arms, and for a split second I wanted to scream.

What the fuck was wrong with me? Why did it always end like this?

But just as Ronald cursed and grabbed my wrist, wrenching my shoulder with the force he used to pin that hand to the ground, suddenly the weight on my chest was gone. There was a second shadow, another muttered curse and I was scrambling backwards, crawling, crying, wheezing, pushing myself back back back back away from those figures—both of them big, strong, angry, and *dominant*.

My back hit a dumpster, and I coughed and almost threw up, but as one of those figures growled and the other hissed and a very heavy body flipped through the air to land with a sickening thud on the ground, I was pushing to my feet, grabbing the sticky, stinking dumpster to help me stay upright on very wobbly knees.

And then the shadowy figure on top grabbed the other one, leaned into his face and snarled, *"You need to learn some fucking boundaries."*

My heart was in my throat as the lower figure slumped and then the other guy was on his feet, and his hands were gloved, and his hood was up, so I couldn't see which of them was grabbing for me and forgot every piece of training or self-defense I'd ever learned and just screamed and ran straight for the main street, praying there would be a car or a cop or *something*.

He cursed and footsteps pounded the sidewalk behind me.

I knew to my bones that this was going to end because too many parts of me hurt, and I was fast, but not that fast.

Yet, I tried. Goddamnit, I tried—I made my hands flat and ran the way I'd been taught. But I still couldn't breathe.

Then, midstep, I was whirled, one firm, calloused hand clapped over my mouth, and as I sucked in a breath through my nose, I blinked because that heavenly smell—faint, like he'd been wearing that cologne earlier in the day, but it had faded—washed over me.

And that scent broke through the haze of fear.

Cain. This was Cain.

Thank God.

He'd dragged me to a stop, his chest heaving from the fight, then the run. There was nothing on the street. No one. But it would only be a matter of time.

"Did he hurt you?" That rough, rasping voice snarled in my ear.

I shook my head. "Not in any way that counts," I squeaked.

We were both still for a moment, just breathing. And Cain cupped that hand over the top of my head and just pressed his face into my hair.

It was so unexpected, so *sweet,* that to my horror, like the messy, weak little bitch that I was, I sank into his grip, shivering and fighting tears. And when he sighed, I turned in his arms and every muscle in my body turned to water. I sagged against him like a sack of pathetic potatoes.

He caught me with a curse.

"Bridget... what—"

The choking little sob I made was so pathetic, I hated *myself.*

But Cain just swung me into his chest, curled me up like a child in his arms, then carried me away.

29. On the Mark

~ CAIN ~

Bridget was shaking worse than me.

Thank God I'd brought the mask. This area was industrial. No handy bushes or trees, very few doorways that weren't gated off. No parking along the street. *Way* too exposed. And I'd been waiting hours when she finally came out. Thank God I'd hidden in the alley.

Thank God she was so clear with her words.

That fucking *bastard* broke every rule of the game.

I was proud of how she handled him, trying to break through. But he'd made up his mind and was just saying what he needed to say to justify it to himself. That wasn't being a Dom, that was being criminal.

I don't know what she had said or done inside that place—no doubt being her smart-ass, bratty self—but the upshot was that he'd decided he had something to prove to her.

I'd waited to make sure it wasn't one of Bridget's games. But when he refused to listen and took her down, I saw red. I didn't even remember tackling him. But I came back to myself when I had him on the ground, holding him by his shirt. I almost killed him. Almost flattened the back of his skull like a ripe watermelon on that cement.

But Bridget was there, and watching, wobbling like a baby deer and…

And then she ran.

Thank God she realized it was me.

Thank God she didn't fight, because if even one car came along while I handled her, it didn't matter what arrangement we had, I'd be going to jail.

But none of that mattered. I'd gotten her to my car, bound her ankles and wrists in front of her and sat her gently in the passenger seat. And now we were getting the fuck out of there.

I was on the highway and considering my options, discarding each one because *she was fucking sinking.* I could feel it. She was losing touch with reality. I needed to bring her back without scaring her completely out of her mind.

So I kept driving until I made a decision, and nodded to myself.

It wasn't until we were halfway there that I realized I could smell her.

I glanced at her from the side, shaking my head a little. I would have smiled if she didn't look so out of it.

What the fuck was she doing wearing a cloak? *Vigori* didn't require that—was this her kink? When I'd first been tying her I'd wondered if she'd be naked underneath it, and my body tightened. But she wasn't. The heavy fabric came in handy, though, because she was going into shock. She was cold and shivering, her lower lip loose, her eyes glazed and fixed in the distance.

My heart wouldn't stop racing.

She was here. In my space.

Holy *shit.*

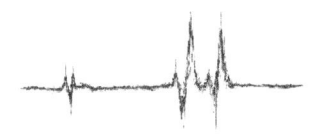

~ *BRIDGET* ~

At some point I could breathe again.

A few minutes later I could sort-of think.

I couldn't move much though.

Then I realized I was in a car, and I recognized the passing highway and distant city.

I made myself breathe the way the doctors told me too—long, slow breaths in through my nose, long slow breaths out through my mouth. Counting and focusing, flooding my body with oxygen.

I was shaking. I lifted one hand to pull a strand of hair off my lip that had stuck there, but both my hands came up—he'd tied my wrists.

The bonds were padded though. I could probably slip out of them if I had time, and privacy.

I swallowed as my heart rate went up another notch and I had to do the breathing exercises all over again.

"You okay?" His voice was low and husky, that gravel he used to hide his true tone from me.

I turned my head, struggling to focus. He was looking at me, but he was wearing that mesh mask again and I couldn't see anything because the mask obscured the shape of his face, and the hood hid everything else.

He turned away first, eyes back on the road. But I saw his shoulders rise and fall with a deep breath.

"Is this it?" I tried to ask, but my voice was so thin and hoarse, I had to clear my throat and swallow a couple of times to wet the roof of my mouth again. I coughed, then sighed. "Where are you taking me?" I was pretty sure he was on the way back to my house, but it was entirely possible he'd set up a lair somewhere nearby and he was taking me there. "Are you going to kill me now?"

"This was *not* a hunt," he growled, shaking his head.

And I slumped with relief—then my eyes welled again. What the hell was wrong with me?

I rested my temple against the window, blinking, swallowing, working to get my body back under control. And eventually, when I could trust my voice, I spoke to him quietly.

"Thank you for… intervening."

He grunted as if he didn't approve, and I *felt* him bristle. I sighed.

"I never made an arrangement with him, Cain. You're the only hunter I'm talking to… now."

His head snapped towards me again, and again I wished I could see beyond that mask—read his eyes, his expression, get inside his head. But I couldn't and I was way too tired to talk, so I let myself slump against the window, closed my eyes, and tried to breathe deeply.

Twenty minutes later when his car rolled into *my* driveway, I wasn't even surprised.

I also wasn't surprised when he used a little clicker on his visor and my garage door began to rattle up.

I was starting to feel like nothing would surprise me tonight.

Oh, how wrong I was.

As soon as the garage door was down and we couldn't be seen from the street, Cain pushed out of the car and trotted around to pull me out of the passenger seat. He didn't speak, just slid his hands under my knees and behind my shoulders, then turned me bodily to slip me out of the car, giving me a couple little bounces to get me balanced properly in his arms… then took me inside my own house. Still tied up.

My house looked strange to me. As if my eyes had been replaced with the eyes of someone who'd never been in here.

Suddenly I could see through the patina of middle-class wealth to the shit underneath.

The stains on the carpets.

The dust in the corners.

The lack of art or any other kind of decoration on the walls.

I wasn't surprised when he walked confidently from the garage, straight back through the house, beelining to my bedroom.

I tried to drum up the adrenaline, the anticipation, to feel good about that. This was what I'd wanted! But my body suddenly had nothing to give.

Even when he sat me on the bed and began untying the knotted laces at my throat that helped keep the cloak in place over my shoulders, my heart barely sped up.

No. *No.* This wasn't the way this was supposed to happen.

I started lifting my hands, trying to bat his away—but bound the way I was, all I did was look stupid, trying to push his big, strong hands aside when I couldn't even move mine independently.

He huffed at me, but didn't speak. And the moment he got the cloak off, he knelt to remove my shoes.

I sat there, gaping at him, aware of how gentle his grip was on my ankle while he pried off first one shoe, then the other.

And I didn't miss the way he cupped his large hand under my leg and let it slide up my calf a little before he let go.

But as soon as my feet were bare and my shoes tossed aside, he straightened and lifted me again, throwing me over his shoulder this time and carrying me, ass first, into the bathroom.

I wanted to make a joke about that. But my brain wasn't working. I couldn't think of one.

Then he leaned down to sit me carefully on the countertop.

He stepped away for a second and I saw his head turn to the shower, then the bath, like he was trying to make a decision, and I tried to drum up some adrenaline.

He decided on the bath, figured out the faucet and got it loudly pouring into the enamel bath before turning back to me.

"You gonna get n-naked too, Cain?" I whispered through numb lips, keeping my arms bent up and against my chest because I felt cold. "You c-could untie me so I could t-trace the lines of your muscles. I p-promise n-not to touch anything I shouldn't."

I wished my voice sounded more alive and my teeth weren't chattering, but Cain snorted and I tried to smile.

Then he stripped me in short, efficient tugs at my clothing. He muttered curses when the bonds made it impossible to get my clothes off, so he was forced to untie them, and hold my wrists in one hand while he stripped me with the other.

I considered fighting, but my entire body felt like a wrung out rag.

And when he had me down to my underwear, he stopped.

He was staring at me through that mask. I could tell. Though I couldn't see his eyes.

"You gonna fight me now, Bridget?"

"Are you g-gonna k-kill me?"

"No," he rasped firmly. "No way does that fucker get a vote in our arrangement. That's between us."

"I c-can't decide if I'm f-flattered, or off-fended."

"You aren't offended," he whispered, then picked me up off the counter and lowered me into the still-filling bath. "You are in shock, though. So let's get you warmed up."

Once I was in the bath, the water lapping around my stomach, he hesitated. Then he straightened and that masked face turned like he was meeting my eyes.

"I'm going to get you something to eat—you need sugar. And where's your after-care kit. Can I trust you to stay here? Or do I need to tie you again?"

"You d-don't need to tie me. And it's in the hallway cupboard."

He didn't respond for a moment, just stayed there, very still. Then, as if he'd made a decision and wasn't going to let himself examine it, he turned on his heel and marched out of the bathroom.

I considered getting out and going after him for about three seconds. Then my throat pinched and my body panged, and I just… I couldn't.

He was probably going to steal something. Or put a camera in to watch me.

And I couldn't drum up the energy to care.

With a heavy sigh, I let my head sink back on the edge of the tub, closed my eyes, and asked God why I still wanted to cry when it was all over and nothing bad had actually happened.

But, unsurprisingly, God didn't answer.

I must have fallen asleep, because I woke to the soft sounds of little plastic wrappers being opened, and found Cain, still dressed and masked, opening some of the medical supplies he'd had me buy.

"Whatcha doin'?" My lips didn't want to move so the words were a little slurred.

"You've got some scrapes. I'm going to clean them."

"I do?"

The mask bobbed up and down as he nodded, laying out bandaids, a gauze, a sticky bandage, a little bottle of disinfectant and some cotton balls in an extremely neat row on the countertop.

"Oh, God. Are you OCD?" I groaned.

He snorted again. "No." There was a pause, then, "Drink, then eat something please. You need to get your blood-sugar up."

I frowned, then realized he'd brought in one of the dining chairs and placed it next to the bath. There was an oven-tray sitting on the seat with a plate of cookies and a steaming mug of… something.

"Lemon honey," he said, like he knew what I was thinking.

"Always the perfect accompaniment to cookies," I said dryly, but my heart wasn't really in it. I picked up one dripping hand to grab the mug by the handle and took a sip. Then another. Then a gulp.

It must have been sitting here for a little while, because it was warm, not hot. So I could drink it comfortably.

Then I grabbed one of the cookies and took a bite.

The lemon honey tasted *very* bitter after that, but I made myself choke it back, because it did make me feel better.

And a few minutes later, with the drink gone, and two cookies in my stomach, I could actually think.

Which was when Cain walked over to the bath, leaned over and reached in to cup the back of my calf and lift my leg out of the water.

I blinked—the gentle, cupping touch at odds with the perfunctory lift of my limb.

He hooked my knee over the side of the bath, which spread my legs and *should* have made me feel very vulnerable. But I was wearing black underwear, and even though he had the mask on, I could tell that he wasn't looking at me.

All his attention was on that red, slightly swollen scrape on my knee.

When he touched it with the cotton ball, I hissed, because there was something on it that stung.

"You know, bathwater is super unhygienic. Your aftercare is for shit."

He shrugged, still dabbing at the scrape, the stinging scent of disinfectant filling the room and making my nose wrinkle.

Then I stopped breathing as a low waft of air floated over my knee... and I realized he was blowing on it through the mesh mask.

"Are... are you—"

"Shut up," he muttered, unwrapping one of the larger bandaids to lay it gently over the wound, his big fingers flattening it to my skin, then his palm resting over it for a moment before he moved onto the next scrape—on my elbow—and repeating the process.

"Do you feel warm now?" he asked gruffly, his voice still rough and harsh.

I nodded.

He helped me out of the bath, wrapped me in one of the towels from chest to thighs, then made me sit on the edge of the bath while he patched up the other side.

As my brain and body came alive again, it was hard to be sure I wasn't still in shock, because it was *so* surreal to have his muscular bulk moving so easily in my room, in my house. I just stared at him.

Then, when he was done with patching me up, he straightened and started to clean up after himself.

For real?

As he tossed the wrappers and used gauze into the trash, then washed his hands, I remained on the side of the bath, staring at him.

Then he dried his hands on my towel—I decided I'd never wash it again—and turned to face me and went still.

I stared at that mask, wishing desperately that I could see the face behind it. Then I licked my lips, because my heart was beginning to race again.

"Is this how you lull me into a false sense of security so you can ravage me and kill me?"

He gave a spluttering little laugh. "You aren't secure—at least, not after tonight. Tonight… tonight is a freebie."

"But—"

"I told you, Bridget. That fucker doesn't get *one say* about what happens between us. And *no one* gets their hands on you, except me. Remember that."

My heart gave a painful thud and I smiled, but he was turning away like he was going to leave.

"Wait! You can't just—" I pushed to my feet, gripping the towel so it wouldn't fall, but hurrying after him out of the bathroom and into my bedroom—but he didn't stop there, either.

"You'll see me again," he growled without looking back.

"When?"

"Soon."

"But how soon?"

"Goodnight, Bridget. Sleep sweet. Dream of me."

Then he slipped around the corner outside the bedroom door and was gone from sight. By the time I'd rushed into the hallway, the only hint that he'd been there was the click of the door into the garage. And even though I'd run to open it because the garage door was rattling up and he couldn't leave for a few seconds, he was already in the car.

The engine roared as I threw the door open and tried to call after him. But he must have activated the door while he was still in the house, because it was already up, and the car tires squealed as he peeled out of my garage.

I got a vague impression of a nondescript, tan sedan—Oregon plates, but with one of those screens over it that reflected light and stopped it from being readable—before it turned, ass-end into the roadway, then roared down the street.

I stood there in the internal access door, staring at the street, heart thumping for a long time. But he didn't come back.

And by the time I pushed the button to close the garage door and turned slowly back into the house, my heart had stopped pounding.

30. Sleep Sweet

SOUNDTRACK: *Goddess* by Written by Wolves

~ CAIN ~

She lay in the bath, head resting on the back of it, wrists draped over the edges, but her eyes bright and locked on mine.

With a low growl, I shucked off my jeans and threw them into the corner, then braced one fist on the edge, near her knee, and leaned over the bath, dropping one hand into that steaming water to find her ankle, sliding fingers around it, then up the back of her leg, her calf, the back of her knee, where I paused.

Her eyes hadn't left mine, but her lips were parted now and her breath shallowed.

When I stroked the inside of her knee with my thumb, she bit her lower lip and let both knees fall apart to rest against the edges of the bath and bare herself to me under the water.

The rumble in my chest started in my cock.

"Beautiful," I rasped, not having to be careful to obscure my voice with that false husk because she made me want so badly my voice graveled on its own. I let my hand

play down the inside of her thigh until I found those soft folds and slipped two fingers between them.

She stopped breathing when I found the core of her— and I groaned, because even under the water it was clear she wanted me.

The water rippled as I pushed one finger into her and she arched her back, her eyes closing for a moment.

She was smiling.

Dear god.

A second finger, and her breath got shallower, faster. I had a flash of worry for her heart, but she rocked her hips; I felt her tighten on my fingers, and my cock almost exploded with the urge to be inside her.

Forcing myself to patience, I beckoned with those fingers inside her, smiling when her jaw went slack, then using the pad of my thumb to slide from where I was touching her, up, until I was sliding over that bundle of nerves that made her whole body twitch.

"Cain..."

"Just breathe, Bridget. You've had a shock."

"I need more. I need you."

"Breathe, beautiful, just... breathe."

I played and teased and experimented until I found the amount of pressure that made her breath catch, the rhythm that made her hips roll, and then I was finger-fucking her and I was shaking.

She gripped the side of the bath harder, her knuckles turning white, and her breath turning from pants, to small pleas, to cries when I hit just the right spot.

And just when she was clenching on me, just when I had to decide whether to take her all the way, or clamber into that steaming water with her, she let go of the sides of the bath and grabbed my arm with a cry, holding me there and riding my hand, her head thrown back, mouth wide, and cries echoing through the bathroom.

I almost came when she did, she was so beautiful—skin flushed and sheened in sweat, small tendrils of hair curling around her face, sticking to her cheek, and that soft, soft skin still in my palm. She shuddered and her breath stopped entirely. Her back arched and one of her heels squeaked against the floor of the bath.

I swore.

Then she slumped, her chest rising and falling so her beautiful breasts bobbed on the surface of the water, her rosy nipples hard and peaked from her orgasm.

But I was still panting, my breath rasping in my throat. And she was still holding my arm.

Then she blinked and her head snapped up. She stared me right in the eye and—

"More," she demanded. "More, Cain. I need more."

With a delighted growl, I removed my hand from her, but only to brace on the other side of the bath and clamber in, water splashing as she pushed up onto her knees and grabbed my shoulders, pulling me closer.

"Quickly. Quickly!" She whispered, looking past me to the door as if someone might interrupt us. "Quickly! There's not much time!"

The water made a wave that splashed over the side when I finally got my ass into the bath, but we both ignored it as she clapped a hand to the back of my neck and crawled into my lap, whispering my name like a mantra.

I grabbed a fistful of her hair with one hand, pulling her close, taking her mouth deeply, desperately, as I reached down to cup her ass with the other and pull her into position.

"Cain! God!" She hissed, reaching between us to find me. I shuddered, breaking the kiss to moan into her mouth when she stroked me.

Then she rose up on her knees, positioning me. My entire body jolted with electric need as she sat down on me and I slid into her, right to the hilt, and for the first time we were—

I came awake.

Literally.

My own shout woke me and I sat bolt-upright, startled, my body shuddering. My orgasm detonated at the base of my spine and rushed out to my limbs in a mind-spinning mix of sheer joy and bald shame as I came all over the sheets, bellowing and panting, every instinct shrieking alarm, shrieking danger.

It took several seconds of clutching at the quilt and blinking to remember where I was and what had happened… and then I groaned for an entirely different reason, clawing my hand over my face as I slumped back on the pillows and shook my head in disgust at my own lack of control.

It had been like this all night—who was I kidding? It had been like this since the moment we met.

Thoughts of her plagued my waking mind to the point of dangerous distraction. Dreams of her tormented my sleep.

And I had no one to blame but myself.

I'd known the moment I saw her.

I should never have agreed to this. Now I was living in a hell of my own making. Because the only thing I wanted to do was steal her from her life, insert her bodily into mine—in every way possible. Take her forever.

But if I did what *she* wanted, she was out of reach.

And if I didn't, she'd leave me.

Forever was a long time. And I only had forever options.

I couldn't do this. I couldn't let her in… even if I wanted to. But that was the problem. I *did* want to.

Muttering a curse, I looked at the clock. It was only four. But I knew I wouldn't sleep anymore, so with a low groan, I got out of bed to strip the sheets and start the laundry, feeling grim.

By the time I was sitting out in the chill morning watching the sun rise, I knew my life was fucked.

And not in the good way.

31. Service for One

~ BRIDGET ~

I was woken by a pounding on the door that startled me out of sleep and sent my pulse through the roof.

And because the sound broke me out of a nightmare, it took several seconds to remember that Ronald *wasn't* outside my house, and he *hadn't* killed Cain.

But then the pounding started again—on the front door—and I realized it was real.

I threw back the covers and raced through the house, grabbing my hoodie from the foot of the bed and throwing it on over my pajamas before I got to the door.

When I opened it, there was a balding guy with a potbelly stomach, holding a clipboard and looking annoyed on the other side. The morning sun was bright—I'd slept in—and there was a huge truck in the street outside my house… with my car on the bed in the back of it.

I blinked, first at him, then at the car, then back at him.

He thrust the clipboard towards me, tapping one spot on it with the pen he held in the other hand. "Your car, right? You gotta sign here that you received it safe," he growled.

I blinked again, then took the clipboard from him and scanned the paper quickly.

Tony's Tow

"Wait… you towed my car?"

The guy grunted. "Your boyfriend paid for it to be towed here, said you couldn't drive last night."

Cain? Or Ronald because he was wracked with guilt?

My hands were shaking as I signed and I couldn't breathe right. But as soon as I handed it back to him, he took it without a look, then whistled at the guy in the truck.

I stood on my concrete path in bare feet, feeling a little faint, and hugging myself as they maneuvered the truck into my driveway and rolled my car off the back of it.

Then they were gone—ignoring my wave—and I walked back into the house rubbing my eyes and trying to feel like I was real.

The world seemed distorted.

After that initial shock wore off, my heart felt sluggish, like my blood was too thick and cold, and my skin was too tight, pulling against me, trying to suck me out of myself.

I tried to eat, but a wave of nausea hit on the first bite, so I put the yogurt back in the fridge and took a shower instead.

And then I put on sweats and a loose hoodie because I couldn't stand the feeling of anything tight on my skin, and I paced the floor of my living room for an hour.

My mind kept flashing back to that moment that Ronald had me pinned on the ground and I couldn't breathe. And my lungs would freeze.

Then I'd remember how Cain tore him off me, and my lungs would inflate again.

Over and over.

I tried logging into the forum, ignoring the DMs from Nate and a couple others, only checking to see if Cain was online—but he wasn't. Or at least, he wasn't visible.

And I didn't know what to say, even if he was. So I said nothing. And I thought about what Gerald would have to say about me not having words.

And then I remembered I was supposed to see Gerald that afternoon, and my entire body recoiled.

No no no no no.

And then I remembered why I'd fled to *Vigorí* yesterday and my breath whooshed out of me.

I had to find it—buried in a pocket of my cloak—but got my phone out and dialed Gerald's office.

He'd given me his personal number to text in an emergency last year, but I ignored that. I did *not* want to talk to him.

"Doctor Fisher's office, this is Natalie! How can I help you?"

I faked a smile because I knew people could hear it in your voice, and spoke as calmly as possible. "Hi, Natalie. I'm supposed to see Gerald this afternoon, but I'm going to have to cancel this week's appointment. A family friend passed away and I have to go visit his, er, people today."

"Oh! I'm so sorry to hear that! What was your name and I'll get that taken care of."

"Thank you. This is Bridget."

There was a very still, very silent moment at the other end of the phone, and I closed my eyes and mouthed a swear.

"Bridget? Bridget Thompson?"

Was that the last name I'd used with them? I thought so. "Yes."

"Ah, I see. I'm so sorry to hear about your friend, Bridget."

"That's okay. It's just one of those things."

"Of course, of course. I know that Doctor Fisher would still want to talk to you—"

"I know he would too, but tell him I haven't missed an appointment in over a year and I won't miss next week. This is a very real loss. It's my old high school chaplain. His name is Richard Fitch. Gerald can look it up if he wants to."

"Oh, I'm sure that won't be necessary, but look, Bridget, Doctor Fisher has been really clear that if you're canceling an appointment he wants to speak with you personally, so if you could just hold for a brief moment—"

"No, I can't. I have to leave right now. I was up late and my car was towed and it's a whole thing. But I have to leave. I'm sorry. Please tell Gerald I'll see him next week. I'm going to see Richard Fitch's people—tell him that. He can look it up."

"I know but—oh, look, Doctor Fisher is here now—"

"Goodbye, Natalie. Thanks for your help."

I clicked the END button on the phone before she could have time to hand it to him, and muttered a curse as I turned the phone off completely. The battery was nearly dead anyway. I'd need to charge it while I was driving. I would tell Gerald about all these details next week. They were *true*.

Then, just to make it *all* true, I grabbed my keys and purse and ran out to the car that was still sitting in the driveway and started driving to the little church on the side of the highway, praying that the hot Priest didn't mind drop-ins, because there was no way I could stomach talking to Gerald today—my skin would actually split and my guts would fall out.

But it would use up a lot of time to drive out there and beg the tattooed priest for some time. And that would solve the problem of Gerald.

Right?

Right.

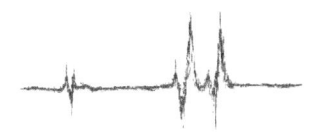

I was standing at the closed double-doors of the church, rattling the knob and swallowing hard. I knew I was acting weird, but I'd lost my nerve for just walking up to that little cottage and forcing the Priest to deal with me. I'd had the idea that if I could get someone at the church then it was their job and—

"Bridget? Are you okay?"

I whirled, clutching one hand to my chest—see, I was learning to be a pearl clutcher already—to find Sam standing there at the bottom of the steps.

He was in jeans. And a slim-fitting sweater. His hair was tousled deliciously. And he was looking at me like I was crazy.

"I wasn't trying to break it!" I shrilled.

His brows rose slowly. "I know... were you looking for me?"

"Yes! I mean, no. I mean... Well, just someone. I was... thinking about Richard and... I don't know!" I wailed, then dropped my face into my hands and took a step back because I was embarrassed and now *deeply* wished I hadn't come, because he was looking at me like he was worried for my mental health and wasn't that probably right? I mean, I was a hot mess. But not the way he probably thought, and—

"Bridget?"

I lifted my face out of my hands and realized I was crying when his eyes widened and he rushed up the steps to get an arm around me and usher me back down and around the building.

"Hey, hey, it's okay. You can be here. That's what we're here for, I promise. It's fine. Don't cry—I mean, cry if you need to, but... you don't have to. You don't have to do anything..."

He was babbling almost as much as me and I started laughing because it was so ridiculous.

A person who'd never been to church being escorted through an old-people's parking lot by a priest who was a felon and both of us completely clueless about how this was supposed to work.

Oddly, his discomfort made mine less, so I was already blinking away tears by the time he got me into the cottage and practically shoved me into one of the dining chairs, before he marched back into the kitchen to make coffee.

"Now," he said a couple minutes later while the machine was bubbling away. "Why don't you tell me what's going on? Is it just about Richard? I was thinking about you yesterday because I found something I thought you'd want. Wait... wait right there. I'll go find it."

I sat there, wiping my face on my hoodie sleeves, and snorting a little because we were both being kind of stupid. But he was back a minute later with a little book in his hands.

"I hope... I hope you don't mind. I wasn't... I wasn't prying," Sam said nervously, clawing a hand through his hair as he took the seat next to me. "I was trying to figure out if there were any other people I needed to notify of Richard's death. We haven't been able to unlock his phone yet. So I was going through his journal and diary, looking for names and... well, yours came up."

He passed me the little book, open to a specific page he'd had his finger stuck in and I saw pages of Richard's scrawled handwriting.

"Wait... Richard wrote about me in his journal?"

Sam nodded, and gave a sad smile. "He wrote really wonderful things."

He pushed the book closer and I caught one word on the page.

Bridget.

I leaned back in my chair like he'd just pushed a snake across the table.

"I... that's really sweet of you to... to show me that. But I don't think... Right now isn't a good time. I just—"

"He's not telling anything personal, Bridget. He's talking about how much he cares about you."

"That's *worse!*" I blurted, then clapped a hand over my mouth, staring at Sam, wide-eyed over my hand, as he stared back.

Then he blinked and shook his head like he was clearing it. Then he gave an adorable, self-deprecating smile and leaned his elbows on the table, resting his face in his hands.

"I'm sorry, Bridget. That's a lot. I just put a lot on you. I'm sorry. I'm still... finding my way with normal people. I'm—"

"I'm not normal!"

Dear God, please sew my tongue to the roof of my mouth forever. Thank you. Amen.

Sam dropped his hands and looked at me, grinning. "That's great. Because I'm not either."

We just sat there, staring at each other for a second.

And my heart started to beat faster.

I swallowed hard. "I'm sorry to just land on you like this," I said, trying to keep my voice lower and quieter so I wasn't shrieking at the poor man. "It's been a rough couple of days, and I think… I think it didn't really sink in the other day when we talked about Richard and I just… I needed to get out of my house," I said, embarrassed, and gesturing towards my loose sweats.

"This is the part I know for sure, Bridget. I'm glad you came. I *want* to help you if I can. And most people take some time to process when they get news like that. So, at least in that, you *are,* in fact, normal."

I snorted, and he grinned and my heart beat a little faster still.

"So," he said, watching me carefully. "Why don't we start again? I'm glad you came. What brought you here? Was it just Richard? You said the last couple days have been kind of rough. Have you had other bad news as well?"

"I found out that… I mean, I *think,* but I'm not sure. But… I think I don't want to die."

Sam blinked. "Okay. Just in case you aren't sure, that's also normal—"

"No, I mean…" I groaned and dropped my face into my hands again. And I remembered what Gerald had said about talking to people to see if they cared and how that was a risk, and one I was scared of. And he was right. I knew that. But I also thought… I thought this guy was kind. And kind of hot. And he did a job that most people couldn't do. And I was kind of at the end of my rope and…

"Do you guys have like… attorney client privilege, or something? But like, the god version?" I asked bluntly.

Sam's eyebrows shot up. "Do you mean you want me to tell me about a crime? Or—"

"No, I mean… if I tell you something that's kind of… odd… do you have to keep my secrets?"

Sam's mouth curled up in a sweet smile. "Bridget, I will keep your secrets—unless you're going to hurt someone, or yourself, in which case I'll try to convince you not to—I'll always keep your secrets. And any pastor who wouldn't isn't listening to the God they claim to serve."

"Okay, cool. Then… you might want to get your drink because I think this might take some time."

Sam shrugged. "Sounds good. Do you want a cup?"

"I better not. I'll explain why. But it's kind of a long story."

"Well, then. Why don't you start talking while I get myself a drink and we'll see where this goes?"

Oh, it's going deep, Sir. Better clutch your rosary or whatever.

"Great, okay, so… have you ever heard of *Vigori*?"

Sam frowned as he got out of his chair. "What's that?"

"It's a sex club in the city. Except, like, a hidden one. You have to be invited and I've been a member for about four years, because I have issues."

To his credit, he didn't miss a beat. But he also didn't turn to look at me as he walked into the kitchen.

"So… for the purposes of being a man of God, I need to tell you… I don't need your sex stories, Bridget. I just… you can tell me what you're struggling with in general terms, but I don't need details, right?"

"Are you sure?"

He huffed as he pulled a mug from the overhead cupboard. "I am *certain.*"

"Okay, then well… Are you familiar with Doms and subs and all that kind of stuff?"

He went still, spooning sugar into a mug, then cleared his throat. "I mean, I understand the concept."

His ears had gone pink. How adorable. A whole lot more of his skin was going to flush before this story was done if he was already embarrassed.

Was it a sin to embarrass a priest? Well, hopefully not.

"Great, so just so you know, I'm not technically a sub, but… I like being dominated, just… in a different way than most people want to be. And I've been looking for a very specific kind of Dom. And I think I found him, but there was this other guy too, and I wasn't sure if they were the same guy…"

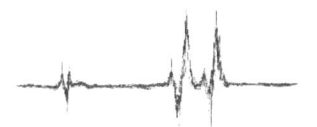

Sam sat at the end of the table, staring at me intently, his brow furrowed, the mug to his lips, though I was pretty sure his coffee had to be cold by now.

"You asked him to *kill* you?"

I nodded and licked my lips because his eyes shadowed. But was it with judgment, or grief?

"Bridget… why would you do that?"

"Because I don't want to be here anymore. But I don't want to kill myself. I want to die. I just… I want to feel alive first."

He put the mug down and sat back in his chair, one hand extended to the table, tapping on its top, his expression firm. "You're telling me that you *like* being hunted? By men?"

"Yes. Not just any man, but one in particular."

"Why?"

"Because it makes me feel alive."

"Killing yourself makes you feel alive?"

"No… it's the threat I guess? Or… look, my psychiatrist says all kinds of things. But I'm pretty sure what he means is that my brain and body are messed up and I only feel excited when there's very real danger. So… I go looking for it."

"But death… death isn't a thrill, Bridget. It's the *end.*"

"I know. But that's okay too."

"No, It's not."

"Yes, it is," I said firmly, not letting my gaze waver. "You know what prison is like, right?"

"Yes. And it's hell. Definitely do not recommend."

"Exactly. But that's the problem. I got put in prison—inside myself—when I was a kid, and now, no matter what I do, I can't get out. If my health doesn't kill me, my thrill-seeking will. And if I don't die, I have to keep facing all this

243

other shit—sorry for swearing—and… there's just nothing left that's fun anymore. Except this."

His lips twisted like he wanted to say something, but he was stopping himself. "How long has this been going on?"

"I've been kind of dabbling around the edges of it for a few years, but about a year ago there was a guy who wasn't the right one so that made me a little gun shy—maybe knife shy is the better term, anyway—just recently… I found the guy. Except, like I said, in the process of finding him, I also found *another* guy. And when the first one didn't show up this week I kind of panicked and went and found the *other* guy and… turns out he's not the cool kind. He's… just an asshole."

"Wait… wait…" Sam sat forward, pinching his temples between his hands. I got to admire his big knuckles and the tendons on the backs of his hands for a second which was nice. "There's three guys?"

I snorted. "There's been *lots* of guys, Sam."

He shot me an unimpressed look that reminded me a lot of Gerald. "That's not what I meant. These… Doms. These guys that are willing to kill you… there's three of them?"

"Not quite. There was one last year that I thought was the right kind, but it turned out he actually just wanted to murder me—whether we matched or not. So once I got rid of him I kind of stopped looking for a while. But then things got worse and I went back, but more carefully and—"

"What things?"

"Hmm?"

Sam's expression was gentle. "What things got worse?"

"It doesn't really matter, the point is—"

"No, Bridget. I disagree. I know you're in a… situation with these men. But what put you there? Because if you solve that, the rest will go away on its own."

I thought of Cain and smiled. He wasn't going away. "I don't want them to go away."

"I've gathered that. What I want to know is… why? What has happened to you that makes you *want* to put yourself in danger?"

"I told you," I deflected. "It's what makes me feel alive."

He stared at me for a moment. "Bridget, if you don't want to talk to me about this, you don't have to. But you said you're having a tough time. And you said you discovered yesterday that you don't want to die."

"I don't want to die *like that.*"

His lips thinned. "So, what I'm telling you, as someone with some real life experience and a relationship with God that showed me the difference between a symptom and a cause, is… I know there's a *reason* you don't want to live anymore. And that's the real cause of whatever pain or anxiety you're having now. So if you want some help… I think that's where we should focus. It's up to you, of course. It's your story. But I'm telling you, I want to know. What happened to you?"

I opened my mouth to give him the *poor little rich orphan girl* line I gave everyone else, because people wanted to believe that. They wanted to believe that having money didn't really make you happy—which was true—and also that no one with money *really* had a reason to be unhappy—which wasn't. And I'd been telling that story for so long, I didn't even think about it anymore.

But when I opened my mouth, he tensed and that made me hesitate and we were just looking at each other and suddenly my heart gave a little kick.

Gerald's line that he'd repeated countless times over the years came back to me, echoing in my head in his deep, pompous tones.

The only way to know if a person can be trusted is to trust them—which is why we're so scared to do it. We have to take the risk before we can know if we were right to do so. You're a risk taker, Bridget. Try it.

I'd always ignored that last part.

But as I readied again to tell Sam the lie, my skin did that thing where it closed in on me, and I felt the hand on my throat and…

And for the first time ever I decided maybe it was time to stop caring if people looked at me differently, or wondered if I was crazy.

Maybe *this* guy would be different.

And so I swallowed back the lie, pulled my hands in my lap, and tried to figure out how to tell him at least part of the truth.

"You said you're a felon?" I said quietly.

"Yes. Assault and battery, sexual assault on a woman, and voyeurism. It never gets easier to say that, but it does get easier to live with myself every day I don't go back to it."

I nodded and swallowed hard, my entire body poised for flight, my heart pounding, and my thoughts beginning to skitter. But I found I wanted to do this. I *wanted* to finally be honest with someone.

"So, um, my dad is a felon too."

"Here in State?"

I nodded. "You might have heard of him. His name's Gordon Reynolds."

Sam frowned at the wall. I waited.

It was a pretty boring name, but anyone who lived in the Pacific Northwest and was alive twenty years ago knew it—even if they couldn't remember *why*.

I'd had to tell this story before—against my will, or for legal stuff. You could always see the moment someone's brain made the connection on my dad's name. Because they did exactly what Sam was doing now.

First he went very still.

Then his eyes went wide and cut to me.

32. The Story

~ BRIDGET ~

Sam gaped at me. "Gordon Reynolds. He killed his wife—"

"In front of his daughter. Yes," I said, settling into that oddly numb place I always found on the other side of revealing this little nugget.

Sam just kept staring at me, and I kept waiting, because I knew he'd get there.

Then he sat back in his chair like he'd been shoved. His handsome brow furrowed, and his eyes went deeply, desperately sad.

"You're his daughter? The one he took with him when he went on the run? Or was that a—"

"No, it was me."

"Oh, *Bridget*..." He was aghast. And even though I'd been coached by counselors and psychologists and countless therapists over the years that the look on his face was not *pity,* not an assumed *weakness,* it still always felt that way.

So I did what I always did and pretended I didn't care. I flapped a hand to dismiss him from having to say anything and spoke to the false grain on the formica table.

"Look, I know it sounds dramatic—"

"Bridget—"

"I've had over twenty years and a dozen therapists to try and fix this, but... it turns out that when you're seven years old and your dad drives you around for a month on a killing spree, holding a gun to your head, and threatening to kill you in your sleep—and you've had the evidence in front of you *seven times* that he's capable of it—it does something weird to your developing brain. I don't remember the medical term. But... the short story is, my blood got toxic and my brain rewired and ever since, I *can't* feel safe. Not really. If I even *kind of* feel safe, my body just... dies inside. But then the moment there's a threat—real or imagined—I come alive. Except..."

"Except what?" Sam asked hoarsely.

"Except that it turns out fear is a bitch. And a few years ago I figured out that whether I was safe and dead, or afraid and alive, I was miserable. Period. Merry Christmas to me, huh?" " I made myself meet his eyes then. Sam opened his mouth but I kept going. "Look, I don't want to do this life anymore. But I also don't want to just sit in my house and swallow a bullet. I want to go out *fighting."*

Sam raked both hands through his hair, but he didn't do that thing a lot of people do, which is try to find a positive thing to observe about me like, *Oh, but it's made you such a strong person!* Or, *What an incredible story you have to tell—you should write a book!* Or, my personal favorite, *What doesn't kill you makes you stronger...*

No irony there. No sir.

Bitterness and rage bubbled up in my throat because all I'd ever wanted was to be normal. To be worried about things like boys or clothes or whatever. But since I was seven years old, I'd had to worry about dying—or about people I loved dying. Or being killed. Because it happened. And once that happens to you, your body remembers that it's possible. And no one warned you it was coming, so you better always be ready...

"Fuck," I muttered and pushed out of my seat. I needed to move. I stormed into the little living room off to the right and started pacing, back and forth on the old carpet.

"Bridget—"

"Trust me. You can't fix this. And I don't want you to try. I'm only telling you so you understand that my whole life is fucked up and I'm so tired! I just want it to be over—and don't start telling me you'll pray for me either. Trust me, been there, done that, got the bloodspattered t-shirts to show for it. Monsters exist in this world and once you know that, you can't unknow it, no matter how much therapy you get."

"I know," Sam said wearily.

"Good. Then let's not do that thing where you start counseling me—"

"I wasn't going to. At least, not about that."

"Good. So—wait, what do you mean, not about *that?*"

"I mean… well, I know you don't want to hear this, but I absolutely see divine intervention in you being brought to my door—the fact that I'm here is a miracle by itself. But that it happened right when you showed up too… I see God's hand in that."

"Oh really? Then where was God's hand when my father was murdering my mother, then driving me around for a month killing everyone he hated, and threatening to kill me as well?"

My raised voice echoed briefly in the little cottage, and I swallowed hard.

Sam blew out a breath. "All I'm saying is… I haven't lived what you've lived—my darkness was more self-inflicted—but I know that look people get when you tell them stuff, right? That understanding you had of the judgment people bring? Yeah, I get it. And here I am, in a place I shouldn't be, but I know how that feels, and I'm used to living with and talking to and ministering to men just like your father. I don't think that happened by accident."

I rolled my eyes and kept pacing. "So you're saying God cares enough now to want to give me therapy, when he could have just stopped my dad from killing anyone?"

"I'm saying… I'm so sorry that happened and you've been carrying it your whole life. I can't even imagine the kind of fear that would give a child. It scares the shit out of me, and I'm a grown man."

I stopped pacing and gaped at him. "You swore!"

Sam grimaced. "It seemed appropriate."

"Better not do that in front of the blue-hair ladies. They'll wet themselves—one way or another."

Sam coughed and scratched the back of his neck, but the moment passed and I started pacing again. I didn't know what to say. It was always like this. On the rare occasions I'd ever chosen to tell anyone this story, I got so agitated that in the end I just bailed on the conversation—and usually on that person too. Funnily enough, they never hunted me down later, so it must have been the right choice.

"I should go," I muttered and turned towards the dining room.

Sam immediately raised his hands like he was surrendering. "No, Bridget. Please. I'm so sure I'm the right person for you to talk to about this. You won't shock me. You won't freak me out."

"I thought you were scared shitless?"

"I was—at the idea of what you must have witnessed and how that would affect you. But trust me, if there's one thing I can confidently say I *am* good at, it's dealing with the people who've lived with violence—or been the violence. That's me, remember?"

I stopped walking just a couple steps from him. He licked his lips like he was nervous, but then he spoke.

"There's also something I know about stuff like this that a lot of other people probably don't think about."

"What's that?" I asked suspiciously, folding my arms.

"I know that what you just told me is not the end of the story. But that it's where most people stop when they ask you about it, or where you stop when you tell them. Because everyone thinks, well, that's the climax right? Everything else is nothing compared to that. But that's not true... is it?"

I blinked. "No."

He nodded. "Okay, so... you can keep walking if you want to, or you can sit down. I want to know what happened *after* that? When they got you away from your dad. What happened *then?*"

He backed away and sat back down at the table, still staring at me. Expectant.

I almost laughed.

What was wrong with this guy?

"It's not a fun story," I said hesitantly.

"Those are usually the most interesting kind," he replied.

I frowned. "I'm not going to, like, give you some scoop for a news story or anything."

He put up his hands again, shaking his head. "Call it… Sacred Privilege, Bridget. I give you my word that I will not speak to anyone else about what you tell me today without your express permission."

I was going to scoff. But then I remembered the tatts, and his discomfort with the old ladies, and his comments about not fitting in that had resonated with me so much and…

And to my surprise, I didn't want to leave.

"You better stay sitting down," I warned him. "Because I won't."

"Whatever you need," he said quietly and even though the wasn't the first person who'd ever said those words to me, for the first time ever, looking into those eyes, I think I believed him.

33. The Rest of the Story

SOUNDTRACK: *Atlantic* by Sleep Token

~ BRIDGET ~

"When the police caught up with us, he shot one of them before they got him," I said first, pacing Sam's living room again. I couldn't look at him while I talked about this stuff, because it always made the words freeze in my throat when people got freaked out. "Luckily the officer lived, but it added to his charges."

I was seven. I didn't know anything except my family, my life. My Dad had guns. The Police had guns. Ergo, men had guns.

I thought the Police were just as bad as him. So when they shot him, I screamed and tried to run. And they had to chase me down.

I thought I was being kidnapped.

It took them four hours to get a woman officer—in plain clothes—to come help with me. I didn't know she was a Police Officer. I thought she was someone coming to help me.

She was nice, but a little cold.

She arranged for my aunt to come be with me. My aunt that I barely knew. The aunt my mother had always said was a bitch, but she was super-nice to me. She treated me nicer than any adult in my life ever had.

She let me sleep on the floor in her room every night because I always had nightmares.

She got mad that I kept crawling into her bed in the middle of the night, then wetting it, but other than that, it was pretty good for the first few months.

But I kept having to talk to the Police. They told my aunt to change my last name before I went back to school—a new school—because otherwise the kids would all want to hear my gory stories and it might retraumatize me.

Instead, all the warnings about not revealing who I was made it feel like a dirty secret. Like there was something wrong with the real *me. Probably because there was.*

I never made any friends at that school.

Then the Police told me I was going to need to testify. And they kept bringing me into the station and reading me things I'd said in the first few days, and even though I didn't remember them, I just kept saying yes.

By then I was nine and Aunt Pattie got a new boyfriend, so I couldn't sleep in her room anymore, which meant I didn't really sleep much at all.

By the time I was ten, I was a zombie, failing elementary school, and getting molested by her boyfriend.

He never fucked me, thank God. But he was a pervert who touched me and snuck into my room at night—one more reason not to sleep—and it was one more secret. And he stole the one person I'd been able to talk to about my real life—my aunt. He told me if I told her what he did, he'd kill her. And I believed him. After all, men have guns, right?

So, she was off limits.

I pulled away from her.

I started acting out at school because I was so fucking tired, and so fucking angry all the time.

And I didn't even have my real name anymore.

But then I had to testify against him and I did it. I was so fucking proud of myself. I had just turned eleven years old and I hadn't seen him for that whole time.

Dad looked fatter and older. And he never once looked me in the eye.

I cried, and felt stupid about it, but the judge was really kind.

He got convicted, and I got told by a lot of adults that I was strong.

But I wasn't. So it was one more lie that I lived.

Then I hit puberty, and the ticking time bomb of my life finally detonated.

My aunt found her boyfriend in my room during the night and blamed me. At least, that's how it felt. She kicked him out, but she always looked at me with rage in her eyes. And nothing I did after that was ever good enough.

She fed me, clothed me, and showed up at the school when they asked her to come in to talk about my behavior. Which got so bad in middle school that she—very reluctantly—started paying for a private school that was better equipped to help me.

I was the weird girl there, but it was better. I met Richard. I made a couple of friends. They weren't close, but I had people to sit with at lunch.

And then my aunt bought me a car when I turned sixteen.

It was the nicest thing she'd ever done for me, and I was really touched. It was a cool car, too. A truck because she said it felt like I'd want something I could run people over with.

She wasn't wrong.

Trucks also had "beds," which at that point in my life, was very useful.

Everyone knew I was a slut, and I didn't give a fuck. Or rather, I gave too many—according to everyone else. Richard was the only man who ever talked to me about it without telling me to be ashamed of myself. He was more worried about why I did it.

But he was old and out of touch and even though I started to trust him, I never really let him see everything.

Probably because, soon after that, I started thinking.

Why had my aunt—who still looked at me every day like I was a roach that crawled across her floor—bought me the car? It was my sixteenth birthday, sure, but... she hadn't been kind since those first couple years. Why now?

As my teachers always told me—I was very intelligent and clever, but didn't want to apply myself to academics.

I sure as shit applied myself to investigating my aunt's motives though.

It took a few weeks, but eventually, while she was at work, I found the box of papers she'd hidden.

Lo and behold... my mother's life insurance wasn't just enough to provide for me...it was a fortune. And some clause in my father's meant his got paid out too—if he had a medically determined date of death. My aunt went to court to argue that life without parole was a medical date of death and... I guess she won. And it made her a rich woman. Because she was named as the trustee to my *inheritance, which gave her free rein to spend on "my behalf."*

Suddenly the bathroom renovations and that cool leather jacket, and all her "business trips" took on a whole new light.

And the car? It was a fucking guilt gift.

She'd never told me that all of this was waiting for me. I would have bet everything I owned that she wouldn't have told me ever. If I understood the paper, when I turned eighteen she would become the executor of my mother's will, and the person who had to manage my small fortune.

If she hadn't spent it all by then.

I seriously considered murdering her in her sleep. But the urge inside me to actually remove her life was a wake up call for me. That was the day I realized I had the same monster my father did, and I was flat-out determined never to let it out of its cage.

So I faced it inwards, instead.

At Richard's urging I got into martial arts and was remarkable at it. Mainly because I didn't give a shit if I got hurt.

Turns out a girl who doesn't care about breaking a leg or getting bruised can scare the shit out of other girls.

I won the age-group for sparring in the first tournament I entered. Everyone said I was awesome. I was just raging and unafraid of pain.

And I was planning.

Junior year of high school, I had almost everything in place—I'd spoken to a lawyer, convinced my aunt that I needed money to visit colleges early so I could do early declaration and get more scholarships.

It was a test.

She had tons of money. Or rather, I *did. But she'd never told me.*

She could have said, "Don't worry about scholarships, you're provided for."

She didn't.

She gave me money to travel to college campuses and fuel for my car. And I used it all to pay the lawyer who was getting ready to emancipate me and subpoena her for the financial records.

Then I got kicked in the chest at Karate and after a few hours at the hospital, found out that sparkling in my vision wasn't my rage. It was my heart warning my brain that I was about to die if I didn't get more oxygen pretty quick.

All those pretty lights in my eyes that I used to love were a sign that I was dying.

Who knew?

Then my whole life changed. That is to say… it got worse.

So, a heart condition meant there wasn't going to be any more karate, or kicks to the chest for me.

Running? Also bad.

In fact, anything fun was a bad idea.

We had great insurance (shocking) so my aunt made sure I got all the fancy tests, and they found out the cancer genomes were there too.

I was the walking dead. Even the doctors looked at me with wary eyes.

The medications were awful and I had to miss a lot of school. But at least my aunt was motivated to make sure I got what I needed so no one would ask questions. Before I graduated high school, she'd found an experimental vascular treatment that helped my heart without making me feel sick or weak all the time.

Then I found a sketchy property manager who'd sign a post-dated lease to a minor as long as I slipped him some extra cash to cover the rent until I was eighteen. And then, when I had my birthday—two weeks after graduation—I walked back into the lawyers office and told him to do the subpoena.

Turned out the bitch was investing and everything. Hiding money left, right and center. She'd still never told me about the inheritance at all. I was still driving the Toyota she bought me when I was sixteen. She was driving an Audi.

It was a mess, but in the end, I had an apartment in another city where I would attend college. A car that wasn't tied to her insurance. And enough money to keep me alive longer than my body was likely to. If I wasn't stupid about it.

I barely remember college.

I have a degree, but I've never used it.

All I remember is that it was during those years I discovered the dark web and other people who thought like me, even if their experiences were different. I found my tribe. And I've been walking deeper and deeper into that world every year since.

It's true, I've fucked half of California.

It's also true I stopped, because it stopped feeling good.

It's true I want to die, because what's the point?

It's also true that when Ronald came at me and I saw that light in his eye, it reminded me of the serial-killer dude from last year and everything I had to go through to get rid of him.

So yes, maybe I don't want to just die for the sake of it. Because I've had two chances now, and didn't take either of them.

But that just means I want to die on my own terms. And they weren't it.

When I met Cain it was obvious he was different. More like me. And I find that fascinating. He's got the monster, I can tell. But then again, lots of men have.

Am I fooling myself? Maybe.

But I've kind of stopped caring.

This life is nothing but isolation and pain. Even the fun parts are only fun for moments. Everyone is hurting. They have enough on their plates dealing with their own lives. They don't even know where to start with mine. And I can't blame them.

My life has been fucked since the moment I came into this world to an abused mother, and a psycho dad.

So let's not even talk about whether or not I'm going to die, because I am. If Cain doesn't get me, my heart will. Or the cancer will show up. But I don't want to wait that long. The idea of facing one more Christmas like this is… God, it feels like I'm suffocating.

I'm done.

I'm just done.

And if Cain's going to help me let go, I'll ask God to forgive him for whatever the sin is, because in my mind, he'll be doing me the biggest favor anyone ever did.

I'm exhausted. This world is terrifying. And it's not even the fun kind of scary. Now I'm just starting to create pain for other people, instead.

It's time.

34. End of Story

~ BRIDGET ~

"Bridget... don't you see that dying will hurt others—the people who care about you?" Sam asked in a voice that edged on torment.

I blinked and stopped walking, turned to look at him, a little shocked because I'd gone so deep I'd kind of forgotten I was talking.

So I just stood there, staring at him, shaking my head.

"Don't deny it, Bridget. If you died, anyone who cared about you would be hurt by that."

"I'm not denying that," I said finally. "I'm just kind of shocked that you haven't figured it out yet."

Sam frowned. "Figured what out?"

I raised my brows. "That there *is* no-one who cares. Not really."

I kind of blurted it out, so it wasn't until it was out there, hanging in the air between us, that I realized what I'd said.

I would have been nervous, felt vulnerable, tried to backpedal and reassure him really quickly, but he didn't immediately rush into the void telling me how many people loved me and God was there and blah blah blah.

No.

This strange, double-sided man stared at me for a few seconds, then his eyes narrowed and his entire body *quivered* with rage. "Is that true?"

Welp. "I mean, there's people who get paid to care. And they're diligent. They'd notice if I was gone. But the biggest gap I'd leave would be in their calendars. And there's a few people who'd show up at my funeral. But their lives wouldn't miss a beat. I don't have family. I don't *really* have friends. Not the kind that fly in when you're in the hospital, or whatever."

I shrugged, feeling uncomfortable because his eyes were very intense, and he looked like he might launch out of that chair and come to me, which I definitely didn't want. I never wanted to be touched after I talked about my dad, or any of that shit.

"You aren't a hugger, are you?" I asked him warily when he didn't speak. I was also struggling with his fucking *silence.*

"I can be," he said, but his voice was dark, flat.

"No, no, that's not… I mean, you're good. You just looked like… like you were about to move."

Sam's jaw rolled and he clawed a hand through his hair. "Seems like maybe you've needed more people to move faster for you your whole life."

I had to fight not to roll my eyes. But he kept going.

"So, did that step-uncle or whatever he was ever get convicted?"

"No. First I took his girlfriend, and then her money. Worst punishment for both of them."

Sam's eyes went flat. "Debatable," he muttered. "Are you still in touch with your aunt?"

Ugh. "Only once a year. She's the executor of my parents' estate. She can't touch the money anymore—that's mine until I die—but that bitch knows she gets the money if I go, so she has to have proof of life every year."

"Proof of life?"

"Yeah, she legally has to have proof that I still breathe. So every January she flies into the airport, I drive there and walk past her, flip her the bird, then walk away. It's a very sweet reunion."

"That's fucked up."

I spluttered. "Don't you have to do a hail mary now, or something?"

"Not a priest, remember?"

"So you're allowed to say *fuck?*"

"I'm not supposed to," he muttered, grimacing and looking away from me like he was mad at himself. "I told you, I'm not good at normal people."

"That's okay, I'm not normal."

He looked back at me and there was something in his eyes that made my belly-button flutter. For a moment we just stared at each other.

Then I realized I wasn't pacing, that I'd just been standing there while we were talking for the past little while, and that was weird. Especially because I didn't feel like I was caged anymore. Didn't feel like I *needed* to move, which is how I usually felt after these conversations. Even ones that weren't as revealing as this. Usually I couldn't sit still for *hours* afterwards.

"Bridget?"

"Yeah?" I bit my lip nervously and his eyes cut to that, then back up to mine.

"That whole story… that really sucks. Like… I can't believe you're still here. So… well done."

My head jerked back. No one had ever *complimented* me about that story before. I snorted, because I didn't know what else to do. "You're right. You don't do normal well."

He shrugged. "What would be normal?"

I gave it some thought, because I'd only done this a few times. "Either, ask for increasingly gory or private details about all the fucked-upedness, or to put your hand on my arm and tell me how awful that is and how much you care about me because of it."

"I guess I'll skip the part where I'd weep quietly about the girl you could have been then?"

I did laugh then. "Oh dear, so you've been through this too?"

He shook his head. "Nothing like that. I'm just the product of an occasionally violent, always neglectful home. The local gangs were my friends, and organized crime suited me because I'm not dumb. But I got out. In fact... well, you kind of make me feel like a pussy, if I'm honest."

"Am I corrupting you? Or do you always talk like this?"

He gave a little smile. "I usually work with guys in prison. They're a lot more colorful than *pussy,* trust me."

"You're saying I talk like a felon?"

"I'm saying you haven't corrupted me. Yet."

There was a split second where his eyes locked on mine and something crackled behind my navel. But it was there and gone so fast, then he was turning away, picking up his mug, and getting out of his chair, so I wasn't sure it had actually happened.

"Did you want a coffee yet?"

"Probably not a good idea."

"Oh, right, the heart thing." He sat back down, plunking the mug in front of him and shaking his head. "That's a helluva story, Bridget."

"I'm a helluva girl," I said and winked.

Sam cleared his throat and looked away, grinning, but I saw the way he was rubbing his hand on his thigh, and I smiled too.

He liked me.

"Look," he said a moment later. "I get that your life is *far* from normal. And I can even understand why you... want what you want. But... isn't there something in this life that gives you purpose? Something that would make it worth sticking around for a while? Or at the very least, not *hiring* a guy to kill you?"

"I didn't hire him. He was very clear. No money is going to change hands."

Sam cut me an unimpressed look. But the fucker didn't speak, just sat there in silence. And I wanted to curse because that meant he'd already figured out that I could handle a lot of messed up conversations, but silence would kill me.

Metaphorically.

I rolled my eyes. "Look, like I said, I wanted to be hunted, right? And I thought… I thought if someone else killed me I wouldn't feel guilty about killing myself."

"But?"

I winced. "No but."

"Yes, there's a but."

"No, for real, I just—"

"You just told me that you realized you *don't* want to die! Are you just going to ignore that?"

"No. But I also told you that I realized I didn't want to die *that way.*"

"What difference does it make?" his voice was still quiet, low. But there was a hint of menace in it and it made my stomach flutter again.

"The difference is… I find it thrilling."

"Being hunted? By a human being?"

"Yeah."

"So find a guy who will hunt you without killing you! There must be a kink like that?"

"There is, but… this isn't my kink, Sam. This is—"

"Of course it's a fucking kink. Wake up!"

He didn't yell, but the words were so aggressive, I blinked and my heart started to race.

I thought he'd back down and apologize, but instead his jaw got tighter.

"Bridget, I don't do *normal* well, but I live and work with these kinds of guys—right on the fringe of society. I used to be one! They're real people, but they keep the veil over their true lives. Inside, most of them are *animals.* It's always only a matter of time before a guy like that goes too far."

"I mean, hopefully."

He gaped at me and I stared back, and I wanted to start moving again, but I was frozen in that gaze. Because it wasn't angry or confused.

It was… sad. And that made me mad. "I was being cute. Do *not* pity me."

Sam rubbed his face with one hand. "I wasn't pitying you. I was—"

"You think I don't know what these guys are like down deep? Hello, *Gordon Reynolds was my dad.* Trust me, *no one* understands these kinds of men better than me!"

"Then why would you put yourself in their hands? Why would you let them destroy you? They aren't worth it!"

"Because they're the only ones who *will!*"

"That makes no sense."

"Bullshit, it makes every kind of sense. I can't kill myself. I don't want to. But I don't want to be here anymore either. So finding someone else who has the balls I don't have—"

"He's got a lot more than balls you don't have," he scoffed. "And I'm sure that's exactly what you're going to find out. These guys are *toying* with you, Bridget. You've already found one who wanted to cut you to ribbons—"

"I believe the exact quote was, *open you like a zipper,*"

Sam didn't respond, just stared at me like he was mad.

"Why are you angry right now?" I asked him, genuinely curious. "Why do you even care? You don't know me."

"I know enough to know you're worth more than dying in some alleyway in the hands of a monster."

"That monster is going to be kinder to me than any man who was ever in my life before." *Except Richard.*

"Then you're meeting the wrong men," Sam said bluntly.

I hacked a humorless laugh. "You'll get no argument from me there."

"But—then why? You said you went looking for these guys—"

"Because once one of them has fucked you, none of the good ones want anything to do with you!"

Sam frowned, but now *I* was mad.

"Don't decide you know me—I know *you.*"

His brows popped up. "You do?"

"Yeah, I do—you're the redeemed villain. You might get judgment from the Pearl Clutchers, but the rest of the world *loves you.* You show up at the gym and you're a beast. You go to college and you're a man of hidden talents who turned his life around. You go for an interview and you're the, *did you see the new guy's tattoos–hot! guy."*

Sam huffed. "That's not entirely—"

"You know what happens when the high school slut turns up at the gym, or goes to college, or turns her life around?"

He went still. "What?"

"She's still just a slut."

Sam's lips pressed thin. "So, first of all, *no.* And secondly, none of that matters if you're putting yourself in the path of these guys. Of course you're going to get treated like meat if you jump in the cage with the wolf. You're playing with fire, then complaining about getting burned!"

That made me suck in. "No," I said firmly, glaring at him when he looked like he was about to argue. "I mean… that's true about some of them, sure. But not this one. He's different."

Cain carrying me through the house and laying me in that bath…

Sam actually scoffed. "Bridget… you can't seriously believe a guy you found on the dark web who's willing to kill you is actually a *good man?"*

"No," I said, folding my arms again. "No, he's not a good man. But I'm not a good woman, either. He gets it. And unlike some people, he doesn't judge me for all the ways I'm broken."

Sam slumped. "I'm not judging you, Bridget. I'm worried about you. These men are monsters."

"No. Not this one," I said, a little breathless because my heart was banging so quickly. *Cain's gentle fingers on the bandaids, pressing them so carefully against my skin.* "This one's just… broken the same way I am."

Which is exactly why I need him.

The thought was weird and out of nowhere—as if it didn't come from my mind. But it felt so true, I almost hugged myself.

"Bridget—"

267

I couldn't breathe for all the right reasons this time. "You've been really helpful, Sam. Thank you. But I have to go."

"No—please, I'm sorry I got angry, I was feeling protective for you—"

"I know, Sam. It's fine. For real. You're a good man. Clearly. I shouldn't have put all of this on you. But I did. So... just forget about it, okay?"

I started walking, darting past the dining table when he got to his feet and out through the kitchen, his voice bouncing off the walls behind me. But I didn't look back, and I didn't answer.

I ran out to my car and got inside and started it.

And texted while I drove.

ME: You said I can't try to entice you out, so I won't. I'm just saying I think I need another bath.

It was a huge relief when he texted back so quickly.

CAIN: That was one-time only. Limited edition.
ME: Cain, please. I NEED you.
CAIN: I have that effect on women.
ME: I'm starting to believe it. I want to change the rules.
CAIN: Not going to happen.
ME: Hear me out.
CAIN: Are you giving me the safe word?

My heart slammed against my ribs and I almost dropped the phone I texted so fast.

ME: No!
CAIN: Then nothing changes. This is it, Bridget. This is the game. Live with it. Or die with it. The choice is yours.

And no matter what I sent after that, he didn't respond, until by the time I got home I was almost in tears out of pure frustration.

268

35. Lucky Night

~ CAIN ~

I *knew* that fucking priest got in her head and gave her a conscience. If he put out her light I'd take a knife to *that* fucker.

When I listed the Bible in the kit, I thought she'd buy one at Walmart. I never expected it to send her to church—how had I missed that part of her life in my research?

Easy... I'd been so fascinated with her, I got sloppy. *Which was all the more reason I needed to turn around and go home.*

But I kept driving, my phone open on the dash, watching her tracker progress as she drove, shaking my head and cursing the whole way. But I didn't speed. I couldn't. No way was I fucking this up by getting pulled over.

I needed to let her get home and think the day was done. Start to relax. She needed to have given up on seeing me today. Because she couldn't be allowed to think she could just text me and I'd come running. That wasn't how the hunt worked. Lucky for both of us, I'd already decided to come for her tonight.

But she was having second thoughts. She never got the words out, but I knew it. I could feel it. Especially knowing she sent that message when she left the priest.

Confession was a bitch. And I was *mad*.

This wasn't the way to start a hunt. It was dangerous because it clouded my vision. I knew that. But I'd given up fighting the urge to keep her. I'd accepted my obsession.

One way or another, she was going to belong to me forever. And if that meant I had to remove that fucking priest, well… it could be arranged.

I smiled grimly and came to a full and complete stop at the stop sign. My mother would have been proud.

I circled the car around the little shopping mall a few miles from her house until I was sure she'd gotten home, then I drove very carefully to her neighborhood.

I didn't usually invade the home so soon, but we needed to talk, and I needed to make sure we wouldn't be interrupted. When I was just blocks from her house, I parked in the shade of that big tree again since it wasn't dark yet, and checked my kit. I wouldn't get out of the car until it was dark, but I needed to be close in case—

The little blue dot on my phone screen that was her car suddenly started moving again. I cursed and grabbed it, heart pounding because she wasn't supposed to move. Where the fuck was she going?

She better *not* be going back to *Vigorí*. I hadn't killed that idiot who'd tried to take her yesterday even though he deserved it. He better not tempt me a second time. I was beyond any kind of mercy.

Then I realized that dot was coming around the corner a couple blocks from where I was parked—she was going to pass me!

I didn't hesitate, just flipped my car seat back so it laid flat and I was completely out of sight from the street. My breath came faster and the hair on my arms stood up as I heard the rush of her vehicle passing a minute later.

She was *right there.*

Shit.

It was torture watching my phone until she'd gone around the corner further down the street and was out of sight, then I sat up and got the car going, working hard not to drive like a crazed man because I didn't need to keep eyes on her to follow her.

Where the hell was she going? And why had she gone home, then not stayed there?

Five minutes later she was stopped at a light and I was getting dangerously close because of the light sequence. But it didn't matter, she'd get a green before I got to that block.

Except, she didn't.

As I drove down the street, staying in the flow of traffic, her dot didn't move, even though we were creeping up on that block... I kept my hood up and tried to sit normally in my car as I got closer and closer—cursing when I realized she'd stopped at a gas station and I was going to drive right past her.

I didn't even turn my head, but I caught sight of her car parked in one of the slots for people using the convenience store as I rolled past and kept going two more blocks before I turned off the road to watch until she started moving again soon.

It took every ounce of will not to follow closely, but I couldn't risk her catching sight of me, so I waited until she was more than a mile away, before I followed, and stayed well away until the car had stopped again, this time in a neighborhood park.

My skin began to prickle. Had she somehow figured out that I was hunting her and come here because she wanted to run?

And did that mean it would be a fun hunt, or did I need to turn around?

She'd thwarted me once already—dummy number, or not, she'd gotten the upperhand the last time I actually hunted her. And last night...

Last night had been a shitshow.

I needed to know that she was okay, and watching her run was a great way to make sure she wasn't lying about...

who the fuck was I kidding. I wanted to hunt her, chase her, take her down because she was a fucking *prize*.

I smiled.

It wasn't the first time I'd had to hunt in a new area. This would be fun.

I made myself stay to the speed limit until I reached the little park and could roll past just to see where she was.

Her car was parked alongside the road, right where the suburban homes opened up to a park that was probably about an acre, and hedged in trees. There was a playground for little kids at the front, some picnic tables and benches, and a big grassy area behind it all that stretched to the trees hiding residential fences lining the back.

And a lone figure sitting on the top of a picnic table just behind the playground area, with her back to the streets.

My heart panged as I drove past because she looked so small, hunched over like that, watching the sunset fade over the trees, drowning in baggy clothes which made me frown.

What was going on? Had the Priest gotten to her? Or was she just bored?

She was out of sight in moments and I was reminded that I needed to formulate a plan.

Take her now?

Or leave her alone?

Making her wait would show her she didn't have control. But if she had too much time to think, she might send me the safeword.

Fuck.

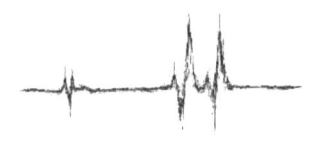

~ *BRIDGET* ~

The minute I got home that itching in my skin got worse. And it definitely wasn't because of Ronald this time.

I'd barely made it to my bedroom before I changed my mind, grabbed a couple things, then turned right back around and stormed out to the car again.

I wasn't prepared for *Vigori*, and frankly, wasn't sure I wanted to try that again. I'd pissed Cain off with wanting to change the rules, so he wasn't going to show. Sam would try and convince me not to let Cain hunt me anymore... there was really only one choice. Because I needed to sleep tonight and get rid of this tension.

So I drove to the little convenience store a few miles away, bought a bottle of cheap, sweet wine, and took it to the playground.

I'd said after last time I got drunk I wasn't going to do it again. It always made me feel like crap, and my heart banged around too much for the crappy hangover to be worth it. Especially when hangovers included Art putting me in front of psychos like Ronald.

But it was also true that last time I got drunk I put that post on the forum where Cain found me.

So it wasn't *all* bad.

I would be good tonight. I wouldn't drink all night. I wouldn't even drink that much.

Just to make sure, I only took enough cash with me to buy the one bottle, then I drove to the little park that wasn't too far away because if I sat with my back to the road, it was just grass and trees and the sunset, and I could kind of pretend I wasn't so lonely. Just choosing to be alone.

The effect was kind of ruined by the rumble of cars passing behind me, but at least they were never there for long. Suburban dads coming home from work, soccer moms driving their kids back from sports. As the darkness descended, warm lights would pop up here and there from the houses where people were together and eating and talking and fighting and...

God, I sounded like such a wilting flower. Even *I* didn't want to listen to me. Was it any wonder no one else did either?

Which was when I remembered Gerald, and how I'd hung up on his office earlier today and I knew he'd be freaking out. I hadn't even looked at my phone since then, so, as I climbed up onto the picnic table and plonked my ass down on its top, I pulled it out of my pocket and looked at my notifications.

Then I winced.

Two missed calls from Gerald's office, one from his personal cellphone. Three voicemails. And who knew how many texts, because the notification icon was multiplied.

Yeesh.

I cleared all the notifications, didn't read any of them, just pulled up Gerald's cellphone contact and tapped the message icon.

ME: I'm fine. Its not what you think. You'd like the priest I talked to today. He sounds a lot like you. I'll be there next week.

My phone buzzed as I put it back in my pocket, but I didn't look at it. I couldn't deal with Gerald's *careful wisdom* tonight.

I had to figure out what I was going to do. Because talking to Sam had been a bit of a wake up call. He hadn't said anything I hadn't heard before. But it had helped me clarify what I was feeling. And that wave of frustration that washed over me when Cain wouldn't even *listen* to what I wanted to change...

I sighed and twisted the top on the wine bottle and opened it to take a swig, wincing at the terrible, overly sweet flavor. But that immediate, warm rush of the alcohol was a balm. I took another swallow, then two more, and my head gave a tiny little lurch.

Good.

I didn't want to do this sober.

Gerald had been telling me for years that I processed by talking. And that if I was trying to make a decision, I should say everything I was thinking out loud. To an empty room.

I figured an empty park was just as useful. Except it made me feel a little nuts to just talk to nothing, so I stared at the ground and pretended my mom was sitting there, listening.

I could still remember what she looked like.

I didn't know how she'd feel about all this, because obviously she'd been attracted to dangerous men, too. The *most* dangerous.

But she'd been weak, too. Weaker than me. I thought.

Was I fooling myself?

There was no way to know.

I took a deep breath and another swig of the wine, but this wasn't going to stop being stupid, so I needed to just do it.

I cleared my throat and imagined that she was sitting on the ground with her knees drawn up and her arms around them, looking at me.

"I don't want to live anymore," I murmured quietly so there was no chance I'd be overheard by a suburban kid whose life hadn't been ruined already. "But I also don't want to die." It was true. And I hadn't admitted that to Sam because I knew he wouldn't let it go if I admitted he was right about that part. Plus, I wasn't really clear on how I could feel both of those things at the same time. Which was why I was sitting here, drinking wine, and talking to a blade of grass like a crazy person. "I'm afraid all the time. And I'm lonely. And… I feel like the only people who like me are the ones who are even more fucked up than me." *Like Cain.* "They're the only ones I can really be myself with. But they scare me."

I pretended they didn't. Gerald had called me on that once, telling me he knew I wasn't quite as "unperturbed" by the dark people I surrounded myself with as I pretended.

I'd asked him if the snooty attitude was genetic, or something he'd cultivated.

We'd moved on.

"I want Cain to hunt me," I murmured. "But… maybe I don't want him to kill me. Except, what's left if—"

"Sounds like it's your lucky night."

I dropped the bottle of wine so that it clunked on the seat under my feet and bounced, spraying cheap sticky red liquid all over my sweats, but I didn't even care.

I started to whirl, to look, because that voice was *right* next to my ear, but I was already being pulled backwards off the picnic table by those thick, steel arms.

Cain was here, and he was snarling.

Maybe there really was a God.

36. Change the Game

SOUNDTRACK: *Chokehold* by Allistair

~ *CAIN* ~

Wrong. It was all wrong.

She gasped and startled like she should.

She dropped her wine, and tried to turn to look at me, but I caught her too fast.

But as I dragged her off that table and over towards the shadow of the trees, well-outside the cone of light from the streetlights that had flickered on as the sun went down, she didn't *fight*.

I growled, tightening my grip around her so she couldn't budge, until I had her deep in the shadows and no one was going to see us from the road.

If she screamed, there were dozens of houses where they'd hear if they were outside. But the moment I took her, I could tell she wasn't going to.

Something was wrong.

When I got her under the trees, I leaned her forward, hunching over her, checking the street, listening beyond my own panting to make sure that no one had seen me take her.

But except for a dog barking down the street, and the rush of cars on nearby roads, there was nothing.

"Thank God," she breathed, bent forward over my arms. "Thank God you came. I was losing my mind."

My chest tightened at those words. I blinked, uncertain how to respond to that. But she just sagged in my grip so I was taking all of her weight, and sighed like it was a welcome hug.

"Bridget," I rasped. Except, I didn't know what I was going to say.

"My friend died," she said in a very small voice. "And my mom died when I was little. And I think it's just hitting me and that's making me want—"

It was instinct, because *she couldn't say those words.* I clapped a hand over her mouth and pulled her upright so her feet dangled, but her ear was next to my lips. "Shut. Your fucking. Mouth."

She tensed and that predator in my chest went on alert.

"Now... *run,*" I snarled and threw her away from me with such force that her arms pinwheeled and she stumbled when her feet found the ground, falling almost completely to her knees.

But even though she caught her weight and got her feet under her, she didn't do as I'd instructed and flee.

She just stayed there, crouching like a runner about to start a race, her shoulders rising and falling quickly.

And she didn't look at me.

"Fucking run, Bridget," I spat.

"But—"

I stepped forward, *furious,* and grabbed her hips, throwing her forward again with a snarled curse. "I said *run.* That is the game. That's why I'm here—that's what *you* asked for—"

To my relief, when she caught her balance, she looked back once over her shoulder, then took off like a hare, and I was surprised again at how quick she was on her feet. But the rush of the hunt was on me, and as she darted along the line of trees, staying in the shadows, the monster inside me came alive and I took off after her with a stifled roar of joy.

I got lost in the strawberry scent of her, the blood pulsing in my veins, and the delicious sound of her panting breaths tearing through the falling night.

She almost reached the back of the grounds before I caught her—cackling as she sidestepped my swipe, then squeaking when I caught her around the middle and took her to the ground. My shoulder was grateful for the soft-earth and grass, but I would have taken her anyway, even if it was cement.

I curled one arm around her head as we went down, making sure she didn't get beaned by the force of my tackle, rolling us until we were on the ground and she was hissing like a cat and trying to keep her arm free because I'd only managed to pin one of them to her side in the tackle.

There was an awkward struggle when she planted that hand on the ground and tried to push me back at the same time I reached for that wrist and we struggled.

But then I had her… on her belly with one of my arms around her and my weight pressing her down hard so she couldn't get her right arm loose. Her other wrist was in my grip and I held it almost at her shoulder so she couldn't get any leverage with that elbow.

"You'll never win, Bridget," I growled as I braced and then rolled us over so I could get to my feet without losing my grip on her.

She struggled again, cursing under her breath as I kept her to my chest and got us up, pulling her right to the back of that little park where a six-foot, solid-wood fence rose behind the trees, offering both darkness, and a place to pin her.

She called me every name under the sun as I carried her, even getting a couple good shots at my shins with her heels, but we both knew her heart wasn't really in it.

And it was pissing me off.

When I passed the trunks of the thick cedars, under the shelter of their branches, to the fence behind, I whipped her around and shoved her up against the fence so hard her head thunked back and she blinked a couple of times.

But I had both her wrists gripped in one fist, and used my body—one knee between her thighs and my hips against hers—to keep her pinned to that fence.

"What the fuck is wrong with you?" I snarled, my heart pounding. "Fight!"

"I am!"

"No, you aren't."

"I'm just glad you're here—"

Furious, I slammed that hand to her throat, gripping her hard enough that her words cut off in a strangled squeak.

And as she hung there from my fist, clawing at my forearm, her mouth opening and closing like a fish, I leaned into her ear.

"What *the fuck* is going on with you?"

I loosened my grip on her throat just enough to let her wheeze a few words. Words that I expected to be pleas for me to change the rules, or garbled explanations for what the fuck was going on in her head. But instead…

"Keep going."

I blinked and stared at her, so off-balance that I cut off her air again for a second, just so I could think.

But now it was *my* heart that wasn't in it. I released her almost immediately because it suddenly felt like her skin burned my palm.

She dropped to her feet, wheezing, sucking at the air, while I stood in front of her, gaping behind my mask.

"What. The. *Fuck?"*

She'd leaned forward slightly and I would have sworn she rested her forehead on my chest for a second as she gathered her breath, but before I could flinch, her head snapped up and she looked up at me.

"We're the same. You and me."

I stared at her, every alarm in my head screaming.

She swallowed and continued, her voice hoarse. "The others scare me. But you don't."

"What the fuck are you doing, Bridget?" I was frozen. My feet nailed to the dirt and scraggly grass. The monster in me roaring that she *would* fear me, but the other side of me suddenly desperate to hold her and keep her close and put myself between her and the world that scared her so much and—*fuck!*

I tensed, about to run, when she caught my arm and shook her head. She was still panting and had to swallow before she could speak.

"I'm not... I'm not going to give you the safeword. *Ever.*"

"Then, what—"

"I just want *more,*" she whispered, then stood to her full height—which was still below my shoulder—and took the half-step to stand between my feet.

I couldn't move as her pretty little hands slid up my chest to the top of the zipper on my hoodie and drew it down in one quick swipe—and then she was tugging my shirt out of my jeans, and reaching for my belt—

I caught both her hands with a snarl and pushed her back.

"No, Cain, *please—*"

I shoved her back up against that fence and she hissed like I'd hurt her, but her eyes never left my mask—I knew she couldn't see my face through it, but it still made adrenaline pulse through me like I'd been shot up.

Catching both her wrists in one hand and pulling them up above her head, I had her arched back and her nose only an inch from my mask.

"What are you doing, Bridget?"

"I'm not scared of you. You're like me."

"That's bullshit."

"I want to play a new game."

"No."

She stared at me, her brows pinching over her nose, her eyes trying to search mine, but she couldn't see anything.

But having her like this, so close, her body not tense, but liquid... it was intoxicating. And *so* dangerous.

Her throat bobbed and I wanted to bite it.

And then I realized... she wasn't fighting me at all. The wall behind her forced her to arch, but her body was loose and her hips... she was pressing her hips against me.

I growled and she sucked in a breath as I rocked my hips, thrusting hard. Her eyes widened and her jaw went a little slack, but she didn't say anything. And *that* was fucked up.

"I'm not scared of you, Cain. I want you. I want to know you. I want you to know me. I'm—"

I exhaled on a shudder and snarled at her to shut up, but I wasn't even thinking. The twang of desire jolted through me at her words, and if I'd let go of her wrists, my hand would be shaking.

She tried to roll her hips against me again, but I had her pinned too tight, too close, no room to move.

It hit me that I wasn't shaking because I was afraid. And I wasn't shaking because I was mad. I was shaking because I wanted her more than I'd ever wanted a woman in my life. And it was *not the way this was supposed to go.*

Yet, I was already in too deep to say no. To either of us.

"One move and I'm gone," I snarled at her, then pressed my free hand firmly over her eyes and the bridge of her nose, making absolutely certain that she couldn't see anything before I released her hands.

She obviously thought I meant she had to keep her arms up, because they didn't drop to her sides when I let them go with the other hand so I could reach for my mask.

Deep in the back of my skull a small voice was screaming, snarling, shoving at me that *this was too dangerous.*

But she was *right there*, and I was quivering with need, and…

Pushing the mesh frame back so it sat on top of my head like a catcher's mask, I waited, unbreathing, to see if she'd try to break free. But she didn't. And I didn't move. Just stared at her lips, that lower pillow slack as she stood there, unable to see, but her breath rushing in and out of her throat.

Pink lips, sweet, warm breath, breasts pressing against my chest with every expansion of her lungs.

It was too much.

"Bridget—"

"I want you, Cain," she whispered, tipping up her chin.

And I broke.

I took that mouth, devoured it, entwined my tongue with hers, sucked in a breath so deep and rough it seared my throat because she kissed me back. Her arms fell, one hooking around my neck, the other sliding under my hoodie to grip my back and I didn't stop her.

I didn't fucking stop her.

I just kissed her harder, deeper. Tilting my head because I couldn't get deep enough, couldn't eat those lips, couldn't swallow that tongue, had to suck at her soul instead.

And then I realized what I was doing.

I had my mask off. I was *holding her,* only one palm between me and a police artist's sketch of the masked man. And I was kissing her like she was fucking crack.

I tore out of the kiss, pressing her back so hard on the fence, she gasped, but she was smiling.

I was panting and so was she, so I took a moment to catch my breath and sear the memory of her body willingly pressed against mine, the sweet taste of her tongue, and the song of her heavy breathing deep into my memories.

Then I took hold of myself, closed my eyes because I thought it would help with the temptation—it didn't, I still wanted her like I wanted oxygen—then leaned in, inhaling her scent, before I rasped in her ear.

"Bridget… do you want to live?"

She tensed for the first time and didn't answer immediately. Then she swallowed and I growled, almost unable to resist leaning down to taste that delicate throat.

"Yes," she breathed.

Every muscle in my body turned to stone.

This is over. It has to be over. She's done.

Soul screaming in protest, I grabbed my mask with trembling fingers and pulled it back down over my face before removing my hand from her eyes and taking one step back.

But the moment I moved, she reached for me, even before she blinked and opened her eyes that were wide with alarm.

"Cain, you have to understand, I want to live *with* you in my—"

"Goodbye, Bridget."

"No! Cain—!"

I turned and ran, letting her increasingly desperate calls fuel my feet until I was flying across the ground, teeth gritted, arms pumping, and my heart shivering.

"Cain! Please!"

But I tore across the grass, past the playground, over the neighboring fence and through one property after another, praying that I'd be able to find my car, because all I could do was flee. I wasn't even thinking.

I had to get away. Had to *make* myself keep running. Because if I stopped I'd go back and she'd reveal me.

I'd *let* her.

And that just wasn't possible.

Goodbye, Bridget.

Goodbye.

Good-fucking-bye, beautiful.

I wish it didn't have to be this way. But we had an agreement, and you broke it.

I'd never forgive myself if I broke you.

37. Too Much Talk, Not Enough Cain

SOUNDTRACK: *Still Here* by Digital Daggers

~ BRIDGET ~

Cain disappeared.

He didn't answer any of my DMs. He didn't respond to any texts.

It had been five days and I was coming apart at the seams.

He was never online—or at least, he wasn't letting his profile show it if he was.

I was haunted by scenarios in my mind where he was finding another woman to hunt.

By day six I got so frantic, I asked Nate to help.

SYSTEM NOTE: CHAT ENCRYPTED END-TO-END. ENSURE ALL ACCOUNTS ARE LOGGED OFF BEFORE DISCONNECTING.

DeadGirlWalking: I need help.

PurplePeoplEater: I thought we established that a while ago.

DeadGirlWalking: Shut up. I mean it. I need actual help in the real world. I need you to use those hacker skills for me.

PurplePeoplEater: You told me if you ever asked me to stalk a guy for you that I was supposed to say no.

DeadGirlWalking: That was a stupid attack of conscience brought on by sleep deprivation and tequila. And besides, this isn't stalking. Not really.

PurplePeoplEater: Spoken like a true stalker.

DeadGirlWalking: STFU.

DeadGirlWalking: I need you to see if you can track a phone for me.

PurplePeoplEater: So we're just breezing right past the fact that that is the *literal* definition of stalking?

DeadGirlWalking: I don't want to find him physically. I want to make sure he's alive… And maybe find out if he has other phone numbers.

PurplePeoplEater: Unlikely to be in his real name if it's a number he gave people like you, but I can try.

DeadGirlWalking: You're a good friend, Nate.

PurplePeoplEater: No I'm not. A good friend would drag you into therapy.

Shit. Gerald.

I looked at the calendar and swore loudly and repeatedly.

DeadGirlWalking: You aren't going to believe this, but I have to meet with my guy this afternoon.

PurplePeoplEater: You're making this up. Or setting me up. Do you get extra crazy on therapy days just to bait me?

DeadGirlWalking: No, but you have a bad habit of reminding me. I like to repress the memories of him anytime I'm not in his presence.

PurplePeoplEater: Seems like he's doing a bang-up job of helping you.

PurplePeoplEater: /sarcasm

DeadGirlWalking: I don't need your judgment. Just your skills.

PurplePeoplEater: Well, just don't shoot the messenger, okay?

DeadGirlWalking: I won't. I'll listen to anything you find. I just need to figure out what's going on with him.

PurplePeoplEater: What's going on with him is that the number you just gave me isn't in service anymore.

DeadGirlWalking: HOW THE HELL DID YOU FIND THAT OUT ALREADY?

PurplePeoplEater: Because I called it. Seriously, Bridge. You're smarter than this.

I stared at the screen. I couldn't believe I hadn't even *thought* about calling the phone.

Maybe I really was losing my mind.

And maybe I was going to cry, because a pit opened in my stomach the minute I read that and now I felt shaky and fragile.

He'd cut off the phone?

He was really leaving me?

DeadGirlWalking: I have to go. Let me know if you find anything else out.

PurplePeoplEater: Will do, but with no ongoing activity on the device, it's going to be a little harder.

DeadGirlWalking: Like I said, I won't hold you responsible. Just… whatever you find out.

PurplePeoplEater: Will do. Have fun at therapy.

DeadGirlWalking: STOP REMINDING ME

PurplePeoplEater: Jesus, Bridge. No need to shout. You hurt my eyeballs.

DeadGirlWalking: Sigh

PurplePeoplEater: You okay?

DeadGirlWalking: No. But I mean, are you?

PurplePeoplEater: Of course not.

DeadGirlWalking: Cool. Let's lose our minds together.

PurplePeoplEater: I'll race you.

DeadGirlWalking: What do I get if I win?

PurplePeoplEater: Anything you want since you can just make it up and hallucinate it into reality.

DeadGirlWalking: Why haven't I thought about this before? Life would have been so much easier.

PurplePeoplEater: You're welcome.

DeadGirlWalking: Seriously, Nate, I owe you.

PurplePeoplEater: Yes, you do. I'll look forward to receiving my blowjob forthwith.

DeadGirlWalking: Aaaaaaaaaand now you're just gross.

PurplePeoplEater: That's *His Majesty, King of Gross* to you. Get it right. I like my subs mindless and worshiping.

DeadGirlWalking: Did I ask for a favor? I changed my mind.

We bantered back and forth a few more times, but my heart wasn't really in it. And Nate could tell. But I deflected more questions and told him I had to get ready to see Gerald. By the time I logged off the message thread, I was so flat, my limbs felt heavy. My heart sluggish.

Cain had cut off the phone?

Then my email popped a screen notification because I was logged on, and I groaned out loud and dropped my face into my hands.

FROM: Asshole (Jeremy Haines)
TO: Bridget
SUBJECT: (blank subject)
Vigori, B? Really? You said you were done with that shit. Do we need to discuss terms again? Why did I have to hear about this from Val?

Shit. *Shit.* Why the hell had Valerie told him?

The question was rhetorical. I knew exactly why she'd done it, but it still pissed me off.

But just as I was tapping the reply button, I had an idea that might serve the dual purpose of diverting Jeremy and keeping me in his good books.

FROM: Bridget
TO: Asshole (Jeremy Haines)
SUBJECT: Re: (blank subject)
I met a guy and thought he was all talk. Turns out he wasn't.

FROM: Asshole (Jeremy Haines)
TO: Bridget
SUBJECT: Re: (blank subject)
Were you planning to tell me at any point?

FROM: Bridget
TO: Asshole (Jeremy Haines)
SUBJECT: Re: (blank subject)
You jealous?

FROM: Asshole (Jeremy Haines)
TO: Bridget
SUBJECT: Re: (blank subject)
No more fucking games, B.

FROM: Bridget
TO: Asshole (Jeremy Haines)
SUBJECT: Re: (blank subject)
Fine. Have you heard about Ronald, as in McDonald? He's got quite the show. Very exclusive. And it turns out the guy is unhinged.

FROM: Asshole (Jeremy Haines)
TO: Bridget
SUBJECT: Re: (blank subject)
Take me.

FROM: Bridget
TO: Asshole (Jeremy Haines)
SUBJECT: Re: (blank subject)
First, no. I don't want to see him again.
Second, you're getting secrets from Val. You don't need me.

FROM: Asshole (Jeremy Haines)
TO: Bridget
SUBJECT: Re: (blank subject)
You and I both know exactly why that's not true. What are you worried I'm going to find out?

FROM: Bridget
TO: Asshole (Jeremy Haines)
SUBJECT: Re: (blank subject)
Nothing. I just have better things to do than be your arm-candy.

FROM: Asshole (Jeremy Haines)
TO: Bridget
SUBJECT: Re: (blank subject)
Actually, you don't.

Fucker.

I scowled at the screen and *almost* logged off just to be petty. But if I pushed him too hard there was every chance he'd just show up somewhere unannounced. And I did *not* like surprises. That would be a whole lot worse than meeting him on purpose.

FROM: Bridget
TO: Asshole (Jeremy Haines)
SUBJECT: Re: (blank subject)
Wow, you really are a charmer.

FROM: Asshole (Jeremy Haines)

TO: Bridget
SUBJECT: Re: (blank subject)
Cut the fucking games. Are we still in this, or not?

FROM: Bridget
TO: Asshole (Jeremy Haines)
SUBJECT: Re: (blank subject)
I have a choice?

FROM: Asshole (Jeremy Haines)
TO: Bridget
SUBJECT: Re: (blank subject)
Not for much longer. You better think this through really carefully, B. We both know you need me more than I need you.

> Did I?
> Probably.
> Fuck.

FROM: Bridget
TO: Asshole (Jeremy Haines)
SUBJECT: Re: (blank subject)
Take the stick out of your ass. You know I'm all talk.

FROM: Asshole (Jeremy Haines)
TO: Bridget
SUBJECT: Re: (blank subject)
I used to. Then I find out you're back at *Vigori,* and meeting fresh psychos without me.

FROM: Bridget
TO: Asshole (Jeremy Haines)
SUBJECT: Re: (blank subject)
It was unplanned, a personal thing, and I'm not going back. The dude is dangerous.

FROM: Asshole (Jeremy Haines)
TO: Bridget
SUBJECT: Re: (blank subject)
Those are my favorite kind.

I rolled my eyes, but I also swallowed, because he wasn't joking.

He was, however, taking the bait. A tiny tingle of anticipation began to thread behind my navel.

FROM: Bridget
TO: Asshole (Jeremy Haines)
SUBJECT: Re: (blank subject)
He's a normal psycho. Born with an inferiority complex to go with his delusions of grandeur. But he folds like cheap paper under pressure. You'd be moving on in a couple hours.

FROM: Asshole (Jeremy Haines)
TO: Bridget
SUBJECT: Re: (blank subject)
You might be surprised. I'm not getting any younger. I could use a palate cleanser. So let's do this. I need to lay eyes on you to make sure you're alive and I'm not just talking to a really good AI.

Got him.

FROM: Bridget
TO: Asshole (Jeremy Haines)
SUBJECT: Re: (blank subject)
How about a compromise: I'll get you in—but without me. If he sees you with me, he's going to have his guard up. I'll get you in for his assessment. You can do… whatever it is you want to do. Then if you need me later, I'll come.

FROM: Asshole (Jeremy Haines)
TO: Bridget
SUBJECT: Re: (blank subject)
What did you do to him that he'd put his guard up with you?

FROM: Bridget
TO: Asshole (Jeremy Haines)
SUBJECT: Re: (blank subject)
Didn't want him when he thought I did.

His reply took a few extra seconds, which made my stomach dip.

FROM: Asshole (Jeremy Haines)
TO: Bridget
SUBJECT: Re: (blank subject)
Did he hurt you?

FROM: Bridget
TO: Asshole (Jeremy Haines)
SUBJECT: Re: (blank subject)
And you call me dramatic. Dear God. No. He didn't get the chance. He just introduced me to his crazy before I got out of there. Seriously, J, I'm telling you, this one isn't anything interesting. But if you want to go and find out for yourself, I'll make it happen.

FROM: Asshole (Jeremy Haines)
TO: Bridget
SUBJECT: Re: (blank subject)
I'll go check him out. But if he's interesting, you're coming with me when I go back.

My body washed in relief. I was pretty sure Jeremy wasn't going to find what he was looking for in Ronald, but since it was Thursday and he had to wait for an invite, it was going to take him a few days to even get in there.

We went back and forth a few more times as I explained Ronald's *assessment* and that Jeremy needed to not be an asshole or he'd get nothing. That if Val was backing Ronald against the rich dudes, she was *definitely* taking his side against Jeremy.

But that was the thing with Jeremy. He was an asshole, but he wasn't stupid. And even though I didn't want to see him, the truth was, if I was ever going back to *Vigorí*, short of having Cain there, Jeremy would have been my next choice.

He might look like an aging Ken doll, but the dude was *deadly*.

When I finally got him to accept that he couldn't sidestep the process, I immediately texted Val.

ME: Val, I need a favor.

VAL: You're in luck. As you know, I run a charity.

ME: Ha ha. I need you to let Jeremy visit and see Ronald.

VAL: Sid? I thought you two weren't getting along?

ME: That's exactly why I need you to let Jeremy come in without me.

VAL: I hate him.

ME: So do I. But he won't cause trouble you can't handle. And it will put me in your debt.

VAL: You give me your word you won't dodge out of helping me with recruitment next round, and I'll let your little cherub come.

ME: Fine.

VAL: He knows he has to participate to get membership?

ME: I'll make sure he knows.

By the time I'd sent Jeremy the details to tell him how to get in, which days and times Ronald was working, and how to get assessed, I felt like a wrung out rag. But at least Jeremy was going to be preoccupied for a few days.

I just prayed he didn't want to take me back to *Vigori*. There was too much chance either Ronald or Cain would challenge him, and that was *never* going to end well.

When I could finally log everything off and shut the computer down, I was exhausted. And then I remembered I had to go see Gerald.

God, what was it with all the wrong men in my life *requiring* things of me?

The surprise though, was that when I got out of the shower, my phone had two notifications. My heart trilled, praying it was Cain. But of course, it wasn't.

(555) 238-9090: Bridget this is Sam. I'm really sorry I upset you last week. I've got some of Richard's stuff for you.

(555) 238-9090: I found your number in his diary. I hope you don't mind me using it. I could bring this stuff to you, or you can drop by. I'd like to apologize in person.

I read the messages, then read them again.

He was such a *nice* guy. How did someone go from what he'd been, to this?

Was it an act?

I didn't think so. I had a very sensitive radar for the darkness in men, and even though Sam gave me the flutters, it lacked punch. Because even though he had the exterior and the past that gave him an edge, the reality was, he was nice. Thoughtful. *Gentle.*

I'd destroy him.

I didn't know what to say, and at that point I really did need to get to Gerald's office, so I just left the text unanswered.

With any luck, it was an old diary of Richard's and he'd think it was an old number. Or maybe I would answer another time, because I kind of did want to read Richard's journal. Just... not in front of Sam.

I didn't know, and couldn't decide, so I pussied out and ignored the text.

I'd think about it tomorrow.

Or at 3 am in the morning when I couldn't sleep anyway.

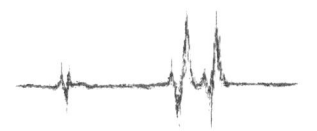

SOUNDTRACK: *Hold Me (Demo)* by Bryce Savage

~ *CAIN* ~

I watched her drive away from her house. I was all hunched down in my car looking out from under a baseball cap like a fucking pervert.

But I didn't do what I'd been vowing to do for days and turn around and go home.

No.

I waited until she was a mile ahead, then started following her dot on my phone, slamming the gear-shift into first and gripping the steering wheel with white knuckles while my guts twisted up like an old-school phone cord.

I'd done everything I was supposed to do once she said she didn't want to die.

I left.

I didn't respond to her messages.

I killed the phone.

And I stopped hunting.

That should have been the end of it. That should have been the moment I walked away entirely and watched for the next mark. But I couldn't. I could *feel* her in my hands, and it made me come alive.

If only I hadn't kissed her and tasted that poison mouth.

If only I could sleep without dreaming about her.

If only I wasn't on the verge of losing my mind every time I thought about never seeing her again.

I hadn't showed up for work in three days.

Yet, I had been everywhere Bridget went. And she had no idea. Which was how it should be. Except...

Now she wanted to live.

But now I had a new problem. How the hell was I supposed to live without *her?*

38. Gotta Want It

SOUNDTRACK: *You Don't Know What It's Like* by Sleeping Wolf

~ BRIDGET ~

Gerald was pouting. If I hadn't been so strung out myself, I would have been taunting him relentlessly.

He sat in a chair across the coffee table from where I usually sat, legs crossed and his jaw rolling.

"I didn't lie to you, Gerald. I really was at the church. You can call them and ask if you want. I have the Priest's cellphone number. You can stop being butthurt now."

He sighed and made a note on his papers. "You refused to speak to me when you canceled the appointment, you didn't answer your phone for the rest of the day—not even a text, Bridget. You have my number too. And then when you did finally text, you didn't respond to my questions."

"I was… preoccupied."

"Were you? Or did I touch a nerve last time and you're retreating? Because we've been here before. And you told me you wouldn't play childish games again." He pinned me with a gaze over the top of his glasses.

I glared back. "I'm *not* playing games. I'm the same loveable hot mess I've always been... just a little extra itchy."

"Which is all the more reason to be here with me."

God, I wanted to strangle him sometimes—and not in the good way.

"No, Gerald, it's not. Because you don't get it and that's fucking hard work when I'm already spinning out."

He leaned forward, eyes locked on mine, his expression grave. "No, Bridget. That's where *you're* wrong. The whole reason you *think* I don't get it is because you always run when you disagree with me so you never face the questions in your head." He started counting things off on his fingers. "You don't trust my motives, but won't ask me what they are. You don't like how easily I read you because it makes you vulnerable, so you run instead of asking me if I can *help*. That means we never take the next step—"

"That's bullshit."

"One time, Bridget. Tell me *one time* you have actually *asked* for my insight? One time you've *sought* anything beyond my analysis?"

"Are you seriously playing the victim right now?"

"Don't be ridiculous—"

"You *get paid* for your fucking *insight* and *analysis*—an extremely noble undertaking, I'm sure. But you and I both know Jeremy only insists on this to save his own ass if I off myself! If he stopped paying you, I'd never see you again. Don't tell me I don't know your fucking motives!"

Gerald's mouth was tight, and he was shaking his head. "Seriously? You think I gave you my personal phone number for the *cash?* You aren't *that* lucrative, Bridget."

"Oh please, I might be unhinged, Gerald, but I'm not stupid. I'm a poster child. One whispered word about my dad and suddenly everyone wants to hang on every word you say—"

"I have never told a soul that you're my client—"

"Not even at your clinical conferences? Really?" I needled him.

He arched one brow.

"Really, Bridget. Because I do actually *get it*. A lot more than you realize. I understand that in your world you've always been a commodity—either an asset or a liability. I get that you grew up in a home where you were used as a pawn in your father's game against your mother. I get the *severe* trauma of what he did to you. And I get that you retreat from people because you *think* you've never found anyone who gave a shit just because they cared about you. And I do actually *get* that you think I'm just one more cog in that wheel. But I'm not. I give a shit, Bridget. I give a great many shits. I didn't sleep for three days last week. And no one was paying me for *that*."

I broke his gaze and glared at the wall instead, because even though I knew he wasn't the noble giver here, he also wasn't an asshole and…

"I thought you'd be proud of me," I said through my teeth. "I did what you told me to do the week before, and I was excited to come tell you about it because I thought it would make you happy and prove… prove that I don't just sit here ignoring you all the time. But then *shit happened,* and that's real. It was a shock, and it made me really shaky, and…"

Gerald dropped his pen and clawed both hands over his bald pate and through the whisps of hair that circled his skull. "Don't you see, Bridget? That's *exactly* when I can help you most! Why won't you let me? You really think I don't care? You think I just want to use you? Have I not proved myself to *you* before now?"

I turned back at him, a venomous cutting judgment on my tongue—a torrent of hilarious blades that would emasculate or marginalize or make him small to get him *the fuck off my back*. But just as I opened my mouth, it hit me…

Judgment.

I hated it. *Despised* it when people took one look, or heard one story, and decided they understood me. It made me rage when someone decided for me that they knew what I could or couldn't handle.

And it finally hit me that that was exactly what I was doing to Gerald. Had been doing to him for two years, in fact.

Shit.

To his credit, Gerald clearly figured out that I was having a moment, because he closed his mouth and just watched me, one hand white-knuckled on his notebook in his lap. And then I saw his throat bob. Like he was nervous. Or scared. Or... *something.*

"You really want to hear it all, Gerald? Because it seems to me like you're going to lose more sleep, not less," I said quietly.

He nodded slowly. "I'd rather know. I'd rather have a chance, at least a shot at helping you through it, Bridget. If you're ready to tell me, I'm ready to listen."

"And what happens if you can't deal?" I asked him honestly, surprised by the pinch in my throat. "What happens if I tell you and it's just too much? I'm just too fucked up. What then?"

He leaned forward, his brow creasing. "Have you forgotten that I've met your father? You will not shock me, Bridget. I have zero doubt you're going to scare me, but you won't shock me. Tell me. Let me show you that you don't have to do this alone."

My heel was jumping up and down like the fucking Energizer Bunny. I had my hands twisted together in my lap. But I couldn't break that gaze.

My guts were twisted up and I was having trouble breathing. But I was fucking *done.*

Maybe I was the one who couldn't deal.

Maybe this was just going to tip me over the edge. And maybe there was something freeing in that.

"Better strap in," I said through clenched teeth because it felt like they'd chatter if I tried to speak normally.

"Bridget, I've been buckled up for two years. Please, it would be a *relief* to know what's really going on with you."

I snorted because I doubted that, but I was suddenly feeling reckless and a little bit unhinged, so I threw up my hands and told him.

All of it.

The dude last year that scared me so bad I stopped sleeping with strangers, which Gerald *kind of* knew about, but didn't really. Not the bloody details.

Then my father's letter that I'd never told anyone about, and the way I just wanted to be done with him.

Gerald slumped in his chair when I reached that part.

I told him about the gathering darkness. And about getting drunk and losing my shit a few weeks ago. And the post on the dark web forum. I even described the bar—and Art introducing me to Ronald.

He tensed again when I got to the drunk night, and his eyes narrowed when I described Ronald.

Then I just kept going and told him about Cain and the arrangement we'd made.

Gerald's eyes got kinda wide, which made me nervous. So I had a decision to make.

But then, because I remembered what Sam said about always stopping at the climax, I made myself keep going. And I talked about Richard. And Sam...

Gerald's lower jaw went slack when I described actually talking to Sam, and how he'd let me put it all out there. His head dropped when I told him I ran.

"...and then it's just been... hell. So, now I'm here," I said in the end, clearing my throat because my voice was a little hoarse.

By this time Gerald had his head in his hands. There was a moment where he didn't move or speak and nerves twirled through me. But then he cleared his throat and lifted his head, and his eyes were a little red.

"Have you heard from Sam since you told him your story?"

My teeth clenched because Gerald knew it had been my experience that people fled from me after they heard about my dad, and I let them go.

I shrugged. "He texted."

"And what did you do?"

"Nothing. I haven't answered him yet."

"Why not?"

303

"Because I don't know what to say!"

Gerald swallowed again and picked up his pen. "Have you tried... *thank you?*"

I squirmed in my seat and looked away from him. "No. Because I'm not sure that's true."

Gerald raised his chin. "You aren't grateful that he listened and cared without judging you?"

"I don't know. I mean... I'm glad he didn't judge me. But he was trying to tell me how I was wrong and..."

"Bridget—"

"Don't."

We stared at each other and I hated this part, because I could feel him being careful, being nervous, worried that he'd upset me and I'd run. And even though that was exactly what I wanted to do, I was so *fucking sick of people acting like I was going to break because it just made me feel even more fragile.*

"See?!" I hissed at him. "You want me to tell you and then when I do, you get scared and now it's *Does She Need an Institution?* Well you can fuck right off, Gerald. You know Jeremy wouldn't allow it."

Gerald's lips twisted. "I don't think you need an institution, Bridget. I think you need a *hug.* And as for Jeremy..." He huffed and shook his head, and it was the first time I felt like smiling, because Gerald thought about as much of Jeremy as I did. It was the one subject about which we'd always agreed.

Then Gerald took a deep breath and shook his head like he was clearing it. "Okay. Okay, fine. So that's where we're at. I'm... grateful that you told me. But I want to ask some questions, because I want to understand how this works. Cain will only kill you if you give him the right signal?"

I slumped in my seat and let my head fall back on the chair, staring at the ceiling. "No," I said. "He was waiting for a safe word to *not* kill me. But the other night... the other night he asked me if I still want to die, and I said no because I thought he could take it, but he ran. And I haven't heard from him since."

Gerald frowned. "Wait… You're saying the guy who was supposed to kill you *left you alone* when you told him you didn't want to die?"

I nodded without looking at him. "But the problem is, without him… now I want to die again."

Gerald gave a little grunt, like he'd been poked with something sharp. "Bridget, please… please don't—"

"I don't want to kill myself, Gerald. I want to die. They're different."

"And you told this Cain person that?"

I sighed and sat up to meet his eyes—which were locked on me and more intense than I thought I'd ever seen from him.

I didn't know whether to be touched, or irritated. But I swallowed and answered.

"Yes. But… that night… before he ran, he kissed me. It wasn't until I admitted that I wanted to live, that he ran away. And he hasn't come back. I think he's gone and I'm falling apart. He's like me, Gerald. I can *feel* it. He's the only person I've ever met who felt like that for me and it's… God, I wish I could just be with him all the time. But now that I want to change the rules, he's gone. He cut off the phone. He hasn't showed up anywhere. Hasn't answered any messages—I haven't seen him on the forum… it's like he never existed." I swallowed the sudden lump in my throat. "And it's so *fucking* unfair—when I finally find something that makes me feel like life is worth living, he doesn't want me unless I'm dead and… You have to help me, because he made me want to live, but I don't want to *want* to live. And how fucked up is that?"

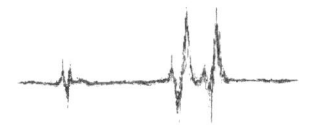

I was home and pacing my living room, Gerald's words running loops in my head.

...Find a different life. Replace the dark thrills with healthy ones and discover that they can satisfy you... keep talking to the priest...

None of it sounded like what I wanted, but I was literally shaking. And I didn't know what else to do, so I pulled out my phone and added Sam's contact to my phone, then clicked the message icon to reply, which brought up the thread.

SAM NOTPRIEST: Bridget, this is Sam. I'm really sorry I upset you last week. I've got some of Richard's stuff for you.

SAM NOTPRIEST: I found your number in his diary. I hope you don't mind me using it. I could bring this stuff to you, or you can drop by. I'd like to apologize in person.

Biting my lip, I tapped *reply*.

ME: Can we talk?

My phone rang seconds later, and I blinked, my heart thudding and bumping in my chest.

"Hey, Sam, I'm sorry I didn't—"

"It's fine, Bridget. It's really fine. I'm just relieved you want to talk. I've been really worried about you."

I huffed and scratched the back of my neck. "You don't have to be. None of this is new for me."

"But—"

"Look, I... I went to see my, um, therapist today and he thinks you sound like a pretty insightful guy and... he wants me to spend more time with people who are like that. So... thanks for not giving up on me."

There was a beat of silence on the other end of the phone. "I get it, Bridget. More than you realize."

I nodded, then realized he couldn't see that. "I know. I mean... I could tell you're good with the crazy stuff."

He gave a little chuckle. "Bridget, I *am* the crazy stuff. Or at least, I was. I just..."

"It's okay, Sam. You don't have to fix this. I mean, you'll be happy to know that I told Cain I don't want to die and he disappeared, so… problem solved, I guess?" I wished I didn't want to cry when I said that.

He sighed heavily.

"That's… I'm glad."

"I'm not."

"Yeah, I gathered."

Both of us were quiet for a while. I got tense because I could feel him trying to find the right words, and I was afraid they wouldn't be. And then this would get awkward, or ugly and I didn't want it to go that way. In my head he was sitting at that dining table in the cottage, shirtless, tats out and drinking coffee and…

And suddenly, I wished I was there too.

"Bridget—"

"Sam, can I ask you something?"

"Yes. Sure. Of course."

I almost lost my nerve, but then I just blurted it out. "Can you be my friend? Or something? Can you just… be a person for me and not a priest? Are you allowed to do that?"

There was a stunned silence on the other end of the phone and for a moment I thought I'd lost him as well, I clawed a hand into my hair. "I didn't mean to be weird, I just—"

"No, no, that's not…" I could hear the smile in his voice. "I'm just happy. Yes, Bridget. I can. I can be not-a-priest in your life. But even more important… I *want* to."

When I got off the phone fifteen minutes later we had made a plan for me to go have lunch with him tomorrow, and I realized I was smiling.

And scared shitless.

And *alive*.

39. Not Normal

~ BRIDGET ~

Sam's house—the one he lived in when he wasn't covering for Richard—was an hour out of the city and close to the prison, which made my skin crawl. But I tried to ignore it.

Driving to his house my heart wasn't pounding, but it fluttered. A lot. It beat too fast, but light and quick, like a bird. Which was dumb. He had said we'd just have lunch and hang out. It was nothing.

I would have used that as a euphemism.

Except… with him, it wasn't. I knew it wasn't.

So, when I'd pulled into the driveway of the simple, old but clean little house with a lawn that needed to be mowed, and patchy weeds in the flowerbeds, I almost backed out and left again.

I was still sitting there, engine on, when the front door opened and Sam leaned out and my heart beat faster, and a little harder and I knew I wasn't going to leave.

He stood in the doorway, watching me. He was wearing a slim-fitting t-shirt and a pair of distressed jeans. His hair was scattered across his forehead, dark and shiny like he'd just gotten out of the shower. His arms were bare so I could enjoy his tattoos. And when he stepped out of the house to walk down the little cracked cement path, my mouth went dry because that shirt hugged him in all the right places and revealed that the *not-Priest* was definitely still working out.

I still hadn't turned the engine off on the car when he got to the door, so I rolled down the window and looked up at him, trying to smile, but knowing I wasn't really pulling it off.

He leaned over me, gripping the door of the car where the window should have been closed. It made the tendons stand up on his hand, and his muscles flex. I had to swallow.

"You okay, Bridget?" he asked quietly, his voice warm... and a little bit worried.

I shook my head. But I couldn't stop staring at him.

"Do you need some time? Or do you want to come inside?"

I looked past him at the house and wondered where this was going to lead.

Not priest.

Lots of muscles.

A shirt that I could get my claws into and—

I swallowed hard. "I'll come in."

Sam smiled and reached down to open the door for me, opening it and waiting until I got out, before closing it too.

He gestured for me to walk ahead of him to the house, so I did, the skin on the back of my neck prickling because he was a lot taller than me and staring down and me, and I liked that feeling.

Then we got inside and the door opened straight into the living room and it was... normal. A little bit dusty. Very plain. But... normal.

Thick couch against the wall under the window.

Television on the wall with cords falling down, and an Xbox.

Old bookshelves filled with books.

An open archway that gave a glimpse of a small kitchen.

Sunlight coming through the windows.

Normal.

"Do you want a coffee or… something else?" He asked as he closed the door behind me, then walked towards the kitchen, flapping a hand for me to follow him. But I didn't at first. I just stood there awkwardly in the middle of the floor, uncertain if I was going to flee.

"I'm fine," I said, then bit my lip when he walked past me and I got to see how those jeans hugged his ass.

You did good on this one, God.

"Well, I'm just going to get a cup… come through here. I've got lunch on the dining table. We can eat when you're hungry."

I followed him through the little galley kitchen, then I kept walking to the dining room on the other side—small. The table would only seat four. But there was a lovely big window and the sun beamed through it, revealing an ill-kempt, but cute garden and back lawn behind the house.

"This is a cute place," I said carefully, uncertain how a man would feel about it being described that way.

Sam shrugged as he pulled the coffee pot out of the machine and poured himself a mug.

"I like it. It's… calm," he said, then looked up at me with a smile that was small and a little nervous.

Which just made me more nervous.

Shit.

"What did you end up doing yesterday?" he asked as he picked up the coffee and started towards me.

"I had to go see my therapist."

His brows pushed up. "So that was real? I thought—"

"Yeah, I told him about you," I said. "I wasn't joking."

"Only good things, I hope," he said.

I laughed more than it needed, then shrugged. "Yeah. Like I said, he thinks you've… got a good head on your shoulders. I think that's how he phrased it."

Sam shrugged humbly, but then took a sip from his coffee and we were just standing there and it was awkward as hell and I didn't know what to do. So I turned away from him to look out the window again. And then I lost my nerve.

"You know, I'm actually pretty tired and I'm sure you're busy. I wonder if we should do this another time and—"

"Bridget, don't," he said, his voice low and dark in a way that made my ribs go tight. I turned to look at him and heard the clunk of the coffee mug being plonked on the table, then he stepped right up to me, his expression serious.

"Don't what?" I asked lamely.

"Don't run."

"I'm not. I'm just—"

"I'm not unsure how to do this, I'm just being careful with you because you've got a lot going on and I don't want to make that worse."

I frowned. "How would you make it worse?"

"By moving too fast, or in the wrong direction. It doesn't matter, look, I'm just saying, every conversation we've had has been in the middle of some crisis. I want to talk to you. Get to know you. Just… be normal," he said with a wry twist of his lips that was *fucking adorable.*

But I winced. "I don't really do *normal,* Sam."

"I know. I don't usually either. Let's have an adventure together," he said quietly, smiling, but his eyes were intense and locked on mine.

My heart rate slipped up another notch and I swallowed. "I like adventures," I offered carefully.

He nodded. "I gathered. Have you heard from… your friend?"

My breath whooshed out of me and I slumped. "No," I muttered, cursing myself for the fierce reaction I had at any thought of Cain.

"Good."

"It's not good!" I said sharply, then closed my eyes. "I didn't mean to—"

"Yes, you did," he said dryly. "But that's okay. I'd rather you were honest than trying to pretend."

"I'm not much of an actor, unless it's role play," I said—unable to resist.

Sam's brows rose a hair and he went still. His Adam's apple jumped. "Is that what your *arrangement* is with Cain? Some kind of... role play?"

I shook my head. "I don't really want to talk about him—"

"Neither do I, but he's the fucking elephant in the room," Sam muttered, clawing a hand through his hair, then folding his arms and looking at me like he was getting angry.

There was a little burst of *something* behind my ribs, and I folded my arms too. "Don't you start judging me—"

"I'm not!"

"—you knew when you asked me—"

"Yes, Bridget. But here's a shocking fact. When you care about what happens to someone, it's kind of impossible not to worry when you're told there's some monster out there getting ready to kill them!"

I blinked as it hit me that I hadn't told him about seeing Cain that night...

"I... he's... I don't think that's going to happen anymore," I admitted miserably.

Sam frowned, but his eyes flashed. "Why not?"

"Because... because I saw him that night after I talked to you, and he got mad because I told him I wanted to change the rules. So he left. And he hasn't shown up since. Not even a message."

I wish saying those words didn't make my blood run cold.

Sam clawed both hands through his hair, then shook his head. "And you're *disappointed?*"

"Yeah! I told you, I like an adventure—"

"Bridget, that's not—" He cut himself off and turned away, but then whipped back around almost immediately. "Tell me what I'm supposed to do here, please? Because you keep talking about this guy and what he's supposed to do like it's a *good thing*. Is this a cry for help? Did you come here because you need help? Because I'll help you. Do you want me to call the Police? Or—"

"Don't you dare. That is *not* why I came here! You said you'd keep my secrets!"

"And I will! But it feels like I'm shadow boxing with a ghost—a ghost that you have the hots for."

I actually felt my cheeks heat and ran my hand through my hair again to try and cover. "He's not a ghost, he's…"

"What? What is he, Bridget?"

He'd taken a step closer, but his expression was tense, bordering on anger and he loomed over me.

My heart beat faster. I looked up at him and licked my lips, swallowing to wet the roof of my mouth again so I could speak.

"He's… like me."

"What does that even mean?"

"I thought you understood…"

"That's the problem, Bridget. I think I understand better than you do," he growled like he was frustrated and leaned down into my space. "You say you want an adventure, but I don't think that's it. I think you want someone who's going to *hurt* you."

"Yeah, I told you—"

"Stop playing dumb!" he snapped.

I blinked and after a tense moment where shadows flickered in his eyes, he muttered a curse and stepped closer, pushing into my space so I was forced to walk backwards or let him overwhelm me.

"I'm not playing anything—" I started, lifting my hand, intending to plant it on his chest and stop him, but quick as a flash, he caught my wrist.

Shocked, and turned on, I stared up at him, my heart racing faster when I saw how dark his eyes were.

"You don't just want a hunter, you want an abuser, is that it? Someone to treat you like shit?" he growled, gripping my wrist so I couldn't get away.

I struggled to free myself, but my heart was hammering and I was backing away, thrilled when he followed.

I came up hard against the wall, but he just stepped right up, pinning me against it, staring down at me, *glaring.*

"Is that it, Bridget?" he breathed, his nose almost touching mine now, his eyes flashing with anger and hurt and something else I couldn't pin down. "You want some guy who's going to mistreat you—does that give you a *thrill?*"

I could hardly breathe. It was fucking fantastic.

"I don't want… that," I said, swallowing hard. "I just want a guy who treats me like I'm not breakable."

He flattened my wrist against the wall, pinning it there with his clamped fist and leaning slowly against me until I felt him hard against my thigh.

My mouth opened a little because I was shocked—he'd been so careful with me. So… gentle before. This man in front of me didn't seem like a not-priest. He seemed like a felon.

A dangerous felon.

I liked it.

I smiled at him and tipped my head. "Maybe what you're mad about isn't that I like it rough, Sam. Maybe you're mad because you like it that way too?" I breathed, reaching down with my free hand to tickle my fingertips up the inside of his thigh, intending to stroke him.

That light in his eyes became a gleam and his gaze dropped to my smiling lips. I was just about to close my eyes, certain he was going to kiss me, when he suddenly tensed, then muttered something under his breath and let me go, backing quickly away, shaking his head.

"Sorry. I'm sorry. That was completely inappropriate—"

"No, Sam—"

"—I should never have… *God, help me.*" He clawed both hands through his hair.

"Stop!" I snapped, stepping up closer—but then he almost tripped, backing away so fast, and suddenly I was following him in a parody of what we'd just done, only in reverse. "Stop looking at me like that!"

"You don't want me to look like I'm sorry?" he spluttered.

"No! Like… like I can't take it!"

Sam stopped backing away and I didn't anticipate it, so ran into him, fell into his chest. He wasn't breathing as he searched my eyes, his forehead furrowed.

"That's not what I think at all," he said quietly, deeply.

My heart slammed against my ribs. "Then what—"

"I think you *shouldn't have to,* which is totally different. Bridget… abuse and adventure are really different things. But it seems like… it seems like you want both."

I blinked, then relaxed. I took a step back smiling.

Sam watched me intently, his forehead still creased with worry, but his eyes never leaving my face.

"You know what, Sam? You're absolutely right. Gerald was right. You *are* wise."

Then I took the bull by the horns, leaned up on my toes and brushed a soft kiss to his stunned and slightly open lips. I pulled away quickly, started to turn. But he caught me, his eyes still searching mine, then pulled me back in, took my face in his hands and lifted my chin, turning that sweet, soft kiss into something much, much deeper.

When we broke apart a minute later I was gasping and his chest was rising and falling quickly under my hand.

We stared at each other for a long moment, then it hit me what I was doing, and I panicked. I blinked, then turned on my heel and ran out of his house.

40. Now Who Doesn't Get It?

SOUNDTRACK: *Crush* by Saint Slumber

~ *CAIN* ~

I watched her car pull away from the priest's house and almost went after her, but I made myself sit there and wait.

She wouldn't lose me. I still had the tracker on her car. She wasn't going to get away. But it was a teeth-gritting effort not to just take off after her, run her off the road, pull her out of the car, and shake her.

Did she seriously not get it?

The Priest was still a man. He wouldn't be able to resist her—not in the long run.

Was that what she wanted?

I swore.

It didn't matter what man she went to, it didn't matter what environment they were in—she was one of those elusive women with that indefinable quality that said she was unattainable—unreachable. It was bait to a predator, and crack to a normal guy. But she made out like she was clueless. Like she didn't see the way male eyes tracked her down the street, or male heads turned whenever she passed.

But I was always following her. So I did.

I'd been convinced she was faking how oblivious she was to her effect on men, pretending she was so caught up in her own angst, she didn't realize the power she had. Had I been wrong? Or, was this all a game?

Was I the fucking loser here?

When I finally let myself put the car in gear and tear off after her—not that she'd know I was following—I *almost* called her. *Almost* let her know that I was coming for her. The battle for self control was hard and fast and I almost lost it.

But I knew I couldn't. I had to see where she was going. I had to make sure she was safe—not hiding from me. Because even I knew this was the start of her escalating. She believed that I wasn't coming back, so who knew what she'd do? Certainly not her.

But who was I to judge? I was barely sleeping, because when I wasn't fucking her in my dreams, I was desperately trying to save her life *by staying out of it.*

I was tormented in life, and tormented in sleep as again and again she put herself in the hands of fuckwits like *Sid Vicious,* heedless of how those assholes would treat her—would try to *possess her.*

No one was supposed to do that but me.

But she'd lost her nerve, so going after her now wasn't part of the game. If I took her after she'd said no, I'd be no better than that punk-vamp-wannabe cocksucker who thought he could take over the world.

I refused to be *that guy.* But that left me here, sneaking around, desperate and aching, always in her shadow, never under her eyes and even I knew this wasn't sustainable.

It took her almost an hour to drive home and I spent the entire time furious and fearful that at any moment she'd turn off the highway and head into the city, or god-knew-where-else… And if she did, what the fuck was I going to do? But if she put herself in the path of another asshole I was going to *have* to get out of this car…

It was a physical relief when she took the exit for her own suburb, and wound the car through the maze of streets to her home.

But I didn't breathe easy until she'd been home for two hours with no sign of moving.

Thank God.

Thank fucking God.

But night hadn't even fallen yet. So I wasn't going anywhere.

I parked in that spot a few blocks away, under the tree, let my seat back down and laid there, waiting. Watching the tracker on my phone, waiting to catch her if she tried to leave.

Like a fucking spider.

At some point during my vigil it hit me...

I'd been terrified of what she could do to me if I let her in. But... what if the danger here was actually me?

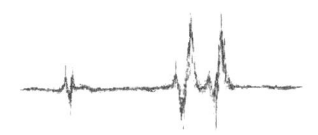

~ *BRIDGET* ~

SAM NOTPRIEST: Bridget, I know that was a shitshow, but I want to try again.

ME: You may have noticed, I specialize in shitshows. Try what?

SAM NOTPRIEST: I am asking you out. On a date. No pinning against walls. No hunting. Just two people with a mutual attraction having dinner to see if they can find common ground. And I'm going to find someone else to counsel you since I can't do that because I'm catching feelings. I'm just going to man-up and admit it. I'm attracted to you and I can't stop thinking about you. Will you go on a date with me, like a normal person?

ME: But I'm not normal.

SAM NOTPRIEST: I think we already established that neither am I.

ME: Well, okay. Next week?

SAM NOTPRIEST: Whenever you're free. Just make it an evening that's not Wednesday.

ME: Sunday? 7pm?

SAM NOTPRIEST: I'll pick you up. Send me your address.

And even though I knew I shouldn't, I did.

41. Reality Bites

~ BRIDGET ~

The next day was Saturday and I was exhausted, but by evening I was also sick to death—no pun intended—of the sight of my walls. I should have told Sam tonight, but a Saturday felt like too much pressure, so I'd pushed it out a day. Now I was regretting it, and I needed to move. So I bit the bullet—also no pun intended—and went to the movies by myself.

I was leaving the house for the first time in over twenty-four hours, and it was natural to look over my shoulder, to scan my mirrors, to see if I could find that nondescript sedan somehow in the twilight before night fell for real.

But there was nothing, of course.

It had been over a week since Cain kissed me and I wanted to cry whenever I thought about it, because the rush I'd felt when his lips were on mine and he let me wrap my arms around him...

But then that got me thinking about Sam and how confusing *that* whole thing was and what was I thinking agreeing to go on a date with him?

What was I thinking *wanting* to go on a date with him?

It was a good thing I was already at the movie theater when the darkness hit, because if I'd been at home alone I wasn't sure what I would have done.

I made myself go into the theater and buy a ticket for some stupid romcom that wouldn't make me sad. I even bought popcorn and candy. Then I trudged down the hall to the screening room, up the stairs to the second-to-last row because I hated feeling like I was trapped against the wall. Then I waited while the ads played, and the trailers. I watched three different couples find seats in the lower rows, and then, just before the movie started a group of people drifted in, chatting and laughing and started up the stairs just as the entire screen went dark and that weird sound thing started that made it feel like you were in a jet or something.

When the screen lit up again the group had all taken seats two rows below me, and I was relieved. I ate a few pieces of popcorn and made myself watch the credits… until I caught that scent and my entire body tensed.

No way… no fucking way.

Then something brushed the side of my neck, like a finger pulling my hair back on that side, but when I snapped my head to look, there was nothing there. The voice, when it came, whispered in the other ear at the same time a heavy hand landed on my shoulder, keeping me pinned in the seat.

"A romcom, Bridget? Really?" he rasped.

My heart trilled and adrenaline flooded my veins. I almost laughed when he reached over my shoulder, grabbed the popcorn bucket, and set it on the seat next to me.

"Don't turn around. And don't make a sound," he whispered in my ear, his breath fluttering against my neck.

I bit my lip, beaming as his hands slipped under my armpits and he lifted me from the seat, dragging me back… and into his lap in the seat behind mine.

I was shameless, already breathing harder, letting myself fall back against him, almost weeping with relief when he slid one hand into my hair and brought my head back against his shoulder, and the other wrapped low, around my stomach.

"Cain—"

"Shhhhh..."

On the screen, the woman was flustered and running around, sweaty and stressed, frantically trying to find the missing bride at a wedding. When his arm around my stomach began to retreat, I reflexively grabbed it, needing to feel the warmth of him, but he only huffed in my ear.

"Keep your eyes and your mouth shut. Just... let me touch you. I need to touch you, Bridget."

Oh, God, yes.

Smiling wide, I let myself slump against him, the back of my head resting on his shoulder, his hand in my hair, and his other hand...

Oh, fuck, yes, his other hand slid under the hem of my hoodie and up my stomach. The thrill that shot through me was so potent my stomach pulled in and his hand tensed on me as if he thought I was going to run. But when I relaxed again, he blew out a breath in a whoosh next to my ear.

Then he drew his hand so slowly up my stomach, only his fingertips drawing trails on my skin, but the tingling, fizzing pleasure was so intense I almost sobbed, almost grabbed his arm and pushed it higher, because he was moving so slowly.

But then, thank God, he finally got up there and those fingers dragged up the underside of my breast and I sucked in a breath.

I slid both of my hands back, trying to see if I could reach his jeans behind me, but he immediately tightened both arms around me, holding me so I couldn't even budge.

"Cain, please, let me—" I whispered.

"Don't. Move," he growled.

"But, I need to kiss you again," I whispered. "I'll keep my eyes closed, and—"

"I said... *don't move.*"

When I slumped again, he waited a moment, then both hands dropped to the hem of my sweatshirt and I almost fist-pumped when he started lifting it up, over my head. I didn't care that I wasn't wearing anything except a bra underneath. I didn't care that if anyone in the theater looked over their shoulders they'd see me. All I cared about was lifting my arms so he could pull my hoodie off—and then I wanted to squeal because he flipped the hood open over my hair and eyes, then pulled the drawstrings tight behind my neck to keep it there. There were small gaps around my nose, but I couldn't see anything in front of me.

"Cain—"

"Shhhh."

He lifted me up then, urging me to put my feet down and turn around, and when I was facing him, standing between his knees, I heard a very low rumble in his chest as he pulled me back into his lap, facing him this time and finally I could touch him.

As he settled me into his lap, I had to feel my way up his chest, then his neck, my belly tingling with the sheer joy of having my hands on him, and then I found his face and that stupid mask. I pushed it back, off his head, and he grabbed it to pull it away.

So I cupped his jaw on both sides and pulled him into a kiss so desperate I was afraid I would eat his lips.

Cain whipped an arm around my back and pulled me hard against him, his other hand cupped over my head, keeping the hood over my eyes, but also directing my head, tipping it so he could take the kiss deeper.

And I was *so fucking mad* that we were in a public theater, because my body was on fire. I didn't just want him. I felt like I'd die without him. I sucked on his tongue and clawed my nails into his skin, and he didn't flinch.

His arm at my back became a steel bar, pinning me to his chest. And I could feel him, hard under me. I wanted *more*.

Pushing him back until his head thunked against the wall behind him, I tilted his chin up and devoured his mouth, whimpering with the sheer relief of having him back, rocking my hips when his one hand came down to cup my ass like he was going to spread me and take me—but I was still wearing my sweats and—

"Bridget... *fuck.*"

"Yes, please."

It wasn't a joke, and he knew it. With a low growl, he brought that hand around to find the underwire of my bra and slip under it, his calloused palms cupping my breast. I arched into the touch, gasping a little when he tweaked my nipple. Then the other hand left my head and came to my other breast; I ground against him, dry-humping him like a fucking high schooler, and I didn't even care.

My breath was tearing in and out of my throat, but all I could think about was the sensations of his touch, his kiss, my head spinning with plans to get him out of here and into a dark closet or *something,* so that he wouldn't torture me anymore. Still kissing him like a leech, I clawed my nails down his chest and abs, letting my fingers scrape against the lines of his muscles, panting as—*holy shit*—he slid one hand down into my sweats and found me there, slick and wanting, heated and needy.

I whimpered and ground against his hand, urging him on, pleading silently with him to *please keep going.* And for a moment, it seemed like he would. He curled a finger inside me and I shuddered and almost came that easily.

I'd forgotten about touching him, I was just clutching his head and pulling him into me.

With his other hand he pulled down my bra and opened his mouth on my nipple, biting hard enough to make me gasp and throw my head back, and then everything happened too fast.

With my head back like that, those little gaps around my nose gave me a sliver to see him. But he had his head down and his mouth open on my breast, so all I could see was a shock of messy hair and his shoulders. I couldn't even tell what color his hair was because the light from the screen turned the wall behind him a bright gray, but cast his face in the deep shadow of me.

He turned to the other breast and I caught the tiniest glimpse of a heavy brow and peak of his nose, but then he sucked *hard* and my eyes rolled back because the jolt of pleasure from his mouth working on my nipple jangled through me to meet the roar between my legs where he was touching me and I couldn't focus on anything but wanting *more.*

There was a crescendo in the music and Cain groaned my name as he gripped the back of my neck with one hand, then plunged a third finger into me with the other and sucked hard, dragging his teeth over my breast so the sizzling pleasure from both zinged through me to meet behind my navel and suddenly, with a rush, I was coming, shaking, gasping, biting back his name, swallowing sound as my body twitched and jerked, riding a wave of joy that stole everything but my smile…

And then, when that shock of bliss finally broke, I slumped forward, buried my face under his neck, pulled his hand out of my pants so I could reach him—but he was thick and full in his jeans, and there was no room between us. I tried to pop the button, but he grabbed for me, pulling my hands away, and we struggled for a moment.

Then he growled, *"Bridget!"* and wrapped me in both steel arms, pulling me down to grind on him as he lifted his hips, thrusting against me. I couldn't move. Mouth open on his neck, I was pinned, pleasure crackling through me because he was rubbing himself against me so that even through my sweats and his jeans, my over-sensitized skin screamed ecstasy and my breath stopped.

There were a few moments of confusing wonder—the movie roaring in surround-sound, Cain's breath shuddering in my ear as he gripped me so hard I couldn't do anything but move with him and suck on his salty skin. Our bodies jerking as we both clung with a desperation that bordered on violence.

Then his hips shot up and he bowed under me, his head snapping back. I felt the vibration in his chest as he made a noise that was covered by the music and every inch of his body turned to marble.

And then, the theater was dark, the sound was gone, and we were sitting there, clinging, clawing, and unable to move or make a sound, because even a breath could be heard by anyone else in the room.

As the light slowly increased on the movie, and dialogue—much quieter and without the music behind it—began in the sound system, Cain turned his head so that his lips were right next to my ear—his stubble raking on my cheek because he was panting and I was clinging to him so hard, I moved up and down with every expansion of his ribs.

"Bridget..."

I tensed, blinking back tears, terrified he was going to—

"This wasn't a hunt," he rasped. "I'm..." He swallowed and I felt his throat bob against my chin.

I sucked in and sat up, thoughtlessly, about to ask him if *he* was having second thoughts—but he exploded into motion, gripping the hood and pulling it all the way down my face as he let me go so quickly and shoved me off his lap. I stumbled back and almost fell.

I had to catch myself on the row of seats in front of me—and then duck behind them because one of the couples below us turned to look. But their eyes were drawn by Cain's hunched form, darting away from me to the steps at the side, then down—so fast he was almost sprinting. Everyone turned to look at him—which gave me a chance to pull that hood off and look at him.

But he had his own hood back up, so all I could see was a thick, muscular body hugged by a non-descript hoodie and jeans, sprinting down the stairs, catching the railing at the end and whipping around the corner into the entryway that hid him from view completely.

It was tempting to run after him, but I knew I wouldn't catch him, and I needed to get my hoodie back on. I let myself drop back below the level of the seats, because a few curious people were turning to look. And when I was sure no-one would be looking anymore, I yanked the hoodie back over my head and tugged it down—shivering when my hand passed over my breast where the skin was scraped and sensitive from his teeth—then got slowly to my feet because my heart was still pounding and my knees felt weak.

I crawled back over the seats, almost falling on my face when I hooked my toe on the back, but managed to catch myself and drop into the one where I'd been sitting before, still breathing hard and shaking a little.

I stayed for the whole movie. But I didn't see a thing.

At some point my phone buzzed in my pocket and I pulled it out.

The text was from an unknown number, but only one word.

PRIVATE NUMBER: Soon.

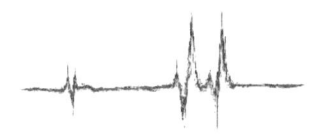

SOUNDTRACK: *Trouble* by Camylio

~ *CAIN* ~

We were in the movie theater again, but I didn't give two shits if anyone saw us, or heard us. I didn't give a fuck what happened except that I had to have her.

I pulled her up and out of her seat, dragging her over the back of it and into my lap. She gasped and I clapped a hand over her mouth because I loved keeping her quiet when she didn't want to be.

Her breath tore in and out of her nose, rushing over my hand, but her body was liquid in my arms.

I was hard as a rock and struggling to get myself free because she kept writhing against me, but finally I got loose of my jeans, then pulled her head to the side so I could bite down on her neck, then rasp in her ear.

"You make a fucking sound and I'm never coming for you again."

She nodded quickly, blinking fast like she was scared, but when I took my hand off her face she just pulled in a deep breath. She didn't say a word.

Then I used both hands, grasping her sweats at the waist and tugging them down as she braced on the arms of the chair and lifted her hips to give me room to push them past her hips, down her thighs, until she was free and—thank you, God—she wasn't wearing underwear.

With a low rumble in my chest because the beast inside wanted out, I grasped her hips and lifted her, positioning myself, then pulling her down onto me, hissing through my teeth to stifle the roar I wanted to give as I finally, finally had her, finally owned her.

A small cry broke in her throat, covered by the sound of the movie, and I held her to me, pumping into her twice, three times, hard so her body jolted and her head tipped back. But even as she arched her back, she leaned against me and reached back like she'd claw a hand into my hair.

But that wasn't how this was going to go.

Growling a warning to her, I wrapped one arm around her waist, then planted the other hand at the back of her neck and shoved her forward, bending her in half even as I pulled her hard into my next thrust.

Her jaw dropped and she groaned, so I clapped that hand over her mouth again, leaned over her, and began to pound.

"You're mine," I rasped into her ear as she threw her hands forward to brace on the seat in front of us and push back against me, which only took me deeper. "No other man... no doctor, no priest, no fucking Dom *will take you— you're mine, Bridget," I snarled hoarsely.*

I felt her voice, muffled against my hand and knew she was affirming me.

The roar began to build in my chest, wanted to tear out of my throat, but I held it back.

"No one chooses for you, but me. No one gets a fucking say—"

She was talking again, and I gave in, releasing her mouth, clamping that hand over her shoulder to keep pulling her back against me as I thrust.

"Yessss," she hissed, sucking in a breath. "It's you... it's only you."

I felt her start to clench around me and the last shred of my control snapped. Grunting like an animal, I grasped for her breast, clawing fingers into her skin and saw her head snap back, eyes closed and her cheeks pressed up in a smile.

I clapped that hand over her mouth again, just in time because she came like a freight train, her entire body bowing and shaking, riding me as I fell over that cliff just half a breath behind her.

The world disappeared. The entire fucking universe was reduced to the warm plump of her ass and the softness of her skin, the strawberry scent of her, and… then the phone started ringing and I cursed, because I was still coming. Still inside her, still—

The phone was ringing again and I couldn't ignore it because I hadn't been to work all week and now people were *worried.*

Body still shaking with the throes of my dream, I rolled over, slapping a hand to the phone on my nightstand and blinking at the too-bright screen in the darkness because there were blackout curtains on the windows, before groaning and taking a deep breath to try to slow my heart before I accepted the call.

"Yeah?"

I listened, grimacing, rubbing a hand over my face as the real world came crashing back in and everything in my body got heavier… emptier because this wasn't a dream. And I couldn't just tell the world to fuck off so I could take her. And I couldn't keep avoiding reality.

"Yeah, I hear you," I said, my voice low and gravelly with sleep—or lack thereof. Bridget would have recognized me, talking like that. "I'm feeling a lot better. Set her up for eleven. I'll need to catch up on some stuff, but… eleven should be fine."

When I ended the call, I lay there in bed, sticky and ashamed. Then I closed my eyes and remembered, just for a moment, the feeling of her hands on my body, and her kiss—frantic and needy—and my heart thrilled and just like that, I was hard again.

She was a fucking drug.
And I was addicted.
And it was going to kill me.

I groaned as I threw the blankets back and made myself get out of bed. I was going to need a long workout this morning to get rid of this tension if I was going to have any shot at being able to focus today… on anything that wasn't her.

42. It's a Date

~ BRIDGET ~

Sunday I was as nervous as a cat in a waterpark. I spent the whole day deciding I wasn't going to meet Sam and picking up my phone to text him, then throwing it onto the couch, or my bed, or shoving it back in my pocket and trying to forget.

I was so stressed, I got online to see if Cain had messaged—which, of course, he hadn't—but there were three emails from Jeremy, so I had to spend an hour answering his questions about Ronald, and praying blessings on Val for telling him that he needed to come to *Vigori* on the slowest day, which was Tuesday.

By the time that was done, I needed to get in the shower.

I cut myself shaving twice, then swore at myself, because why the fuck was I shaving?

Then I'd remember that moment when Sam had caught my wrist so quickly, and the burning darkness in his eyes and I'd remember *why* I was shaving and *holy fuck I was just going to tell him not to come.*

By the time my doorbell rang, I was a jittery mess.

I stood on the other side of the closed door without answering it for a full minute. He'd rung the doorbell twice by that time. I couldn't make myself turn the knob to open it.

But then I heard a foot scuff on the other side and thought he was leaving, and my chest went tight and I couldn't grab the handle fast enough.

I swung it open like a madwoman, ready to call after him, but he was standing there, head down, his phone in his hands.

There was a split second when my brain registered everything—the tight shirt with the sleeves rolled almost to his elbows to reveal his tattoos, the strategically messy hair, the trim-fitting black *from head to toe*—and my heart actually lurched.

Then his head snapped up, his eyes bright and shining, and he smiled when he saw me. He straightened, slipping his phone back in the pocket of his pants and did that thing guys do where they kind of stand back to scan you from head to toe and I thought I was going to see Sam-the-Felon—I thought he'd rub his jaw and nod and say something hot.

But instead he kept his chin down, his eyes came up to meet mine, and his smile got warmer. "I thought maybe you'd changed your mind," he said quietly, in that low, soothing voice that he'd used when I was upset, except now there was just a *hint* of an edge to it and I swear it vibrated right in my lady-parts.

"No, just weird," I blurted, then wanted to close the door and turn back time and start the whole thing over again because I ruined it.

But Sam's smile got wider and he quirked one eyebrow. "My kind of woman," he offered.

I think I blushed.

I know I stepped out of my house and checked that the door was locked before I took the arm he offered to lead me back down the path to his cheap little car and I only thought of Cain one time, when I passed the bush that he'd hidden behind that first time…

Then Sam opened the passenger door for me and held it while I got in, then trotted around the car to the driver's side.

The car's suspension wasn't great, the whole thing dipped when he sat down, but right after he turned the key and it roared to life, he turned his head and looked me in the eye.

"You look beautiful, Bridget."

I *definitely* blushed that time. "Thank you. You look hot. Are priests allowed to do that?"

God, the lopsided smile got me every fucking time. "I told you—"

"I know, but I have joke-tourettes and I can't stop saying it."

He kind of huffed a laugh and shook his head, as he put one hand on the wheel and lifted the other to hold the back of my seat in a deeply masculine move that *always* made me shiver as he looked backwards to reverse out of my driveway.

And then he did the whole thing.

The whole *normal* date thing.

I hadn't been on a normal date since Homecoming when I was fifteen—and even that was just me and Ryan Speelman going through the motions before we fucked.

I hadn't thought men still existed who opened doors and reserved tables at cute hole-in-the-wall italian restaurants that were owned by a family, and paid for the meal and looked you in the eye instead of the chest.

But Sam was… different.

Of course, I wasn't.

I spent most of the night blinking because he'd ask me something and I'd catch myself sitting there wondering what his chest looked like under that shirt, and I'd have to take a second to remember what he'd actually said. Which was usually a question about me, or an adorable observation about someone in the restaurant.

It was all so fucking *wholesome.*

Twenty minutes after he picked me up, my belly fluttered because our knees brushed under the tiny, round table we were sharing.

Ten minutes after that my stomach sank because he smiled at the waitress and asked an intelligent question and it hit me that he knew how to do this, and I didn't.

I was desperately uncomfortable, barely talking, and it was making *him* tense.

Five minutes later my heel was bouncing under the table and I was looking at the exit over his shoulder.

"...wondered if you're comfortable talking about your past—the normal stuff, I mean. I wondered how it felt to change your name so young."

I grimaced, fiddling with the knife and fork on the tablecloth, turning them over and over. "That made me feel dumb," I said.

"Dumb? Why?"

"Because people would say my name and I'd forget and think they were talking to someone else, and then I'd make up stupid excuses and... everyone just thought I was weird and kind of psycho and I mean... I kind of was..." I said lamely.

Sam tipped his head. "That's a lot for a kid."

I snorted and grabbed a piece of the very yummy free bread. "That was nothing. The weird part was instead of playing sports, I was put in twice-weekly self-defense classes—when I was ten—and forced to have monthly meetings with law enforcement because everyone thought my dad's people were going to try and come for me, so they wanted me to have people I could feel *comfortable* to talk to," I said, making my eyes big because it was such a farce.

"Law enforcement?" he asked, his voice a little tight because, *felon.* "You mean, Police?"

"No, I mean *law enforcement.* That's what my aunt always called them. I know now that they were FBI, but she never told me."

"The FBI came to your house when you were a kid—?!"

He cut off because my knee shot up to bang the underside of the table and make the glasses and silverware clatter—and I overreacted, my hands shooting out to catch the wine glass so it wouldn't spill, and instead I accidentally knocked the water glass clean over, so it splashed all over the free bread.

336

"I'm sorry!" I gasped, shooting to my feet—but that made the table rock and then the wine glass really *did* tip over, and even though I caught that one, it still spilled a little over my hand and the tablecloth and my heart kind of shattered. "Sorry—*sorry!*" I squeaked.

Sam was chuckling. "Bridget, it's fine—"

"No, it's not. I'm sorry, I don't talk about this stuff and I don't sit around with people over a glass of wine and… I should never have said yes to this," I breathed, tearing away from the table towards the bathrooms.

"Bridget—"

He started to get up out of his seat, but I was hurrying. I caught one of the waitresses on my way and whispered something about cleaning up my mess—saw how her eyes found Sam behind me and lit up and my stomach clenched, and I fled to the little bathroom at the back of the restaurant.

I was having trouble breathing and knew this was all just a dumb idea, so I got out my phone and texted him.

ME: I'm sorry. This isn't going to work. You should leave. I'll get an uber home.

But he didn't answer. Because he was a good date and had his phone on silent? Or because he'd already given up and left?

I don't know how long I sat in there trying to get my hands to stop shaking, but when I finally got up the courage to walk carefully out, our table was empty and a bus boy was clearing it.

I felt relieved and really sad at the same time.

I stood there in front of the bathroom door for a minute watching a spotty kid clean up the table I'd destroyed and reminded myself that there was a *reason* I didn't do this stuff. There was a *reason* people like Cain felt like I belonged to them. And I needed to stop fighting that.

I was still close to tears when I pushed out of the swinging restaurant door—and stopped dead, because Sam was out there, leaning against the hood of his very cheap car, frowning at his phone.

There were some bushes and a couple trees in the garden that ran alongside the sidewalk between us, so I was only seeing him through the gaps. And he hadn't realized I was there. So I got to just look at him.

If I'd seen him without any context, I would never have picked him for any kind of spiritual man. I wouldn't have thought he was wise, or thoughtful, or gentle.

My stomach trilled at the sight of him because he was thick and strong and had that air about him that men who could be dangerous always had—an underlying confidence in their own strength, combined with a subtle wariness.

He must have felt me watching, because his head came up and caught me staring. For a second we just looked at each other. I hadn't moved away from the door because I didn't know what to say. But he pushed off the car and straightened, his expression a question… and a little fear.

"I'm sorry. I know that was weird," I said. "I just… I'm just not good at this stuff."

Sam shrugged. "I don't care. I just want to talk to you."

"But…" I made myself walk along the little path around those trees to the parking lot, my hands clenched to fists at my sides. "There's no way this is going to work," I said, flapping a hand back at the restaurant.

Sam frowned. "So, let's try something else?"

Was he serious? "Like… what?"

Then he reached behind him for something he'd left on the hood of the car then held it out.

It was a big paper bag with the restaurant's logo on it, clearly full of boxed up food.

"You must be hungry?" he said, just loud enough for me to hear it over the rush of cars on the street behind him.

I know I protested, but somehow I ended up back in his car that immediately filled with the smell of rich, delicious food. And after a few minutes of silence and very calm driving on Sam's part, we pulled off the road and into a park.

I got out of the car without his help this time because he was getting some stuff out of the trunk.

A few minutes later we were sitting on a blanket under a tree, next to a manmade pond with a single fountain spray at its center, and I didn't even care that I splattered marinara sauce on my dress after the second bite.

"When I was a kid," he said around a mouthful of food, "I thought the men that came to visit my father were his friends. They always showed up in pairs. And after I'd yell at my dad that they were there, they'd always be nice to me and ask me questions."

I looked at him warily. "Law enforcement?"

He shook his head. "Mob."

I nodded, chewing a mouthful of some very nice alfredo out of one of the trays he'd spread between us. "They aren't all bad."

His brows rose. "You're connected to the mob?"

I shook my head, and couldn't help but smile a little bit. "No. But one of the, er, Dons has meetings at my ex-boyfriend's bar. He's always been nice to me. He said I remind him of his daughter."

Sam thought about that for a second. "Well, the ones who came to our house and were nice to me were just using me to get information because I was a naïve kid," he said darkly. "My father owed them money."

I winced. "That sucks."

He shrugged. "They really did like me. I mean, they got me away from my dad when I was a teenager."

I stared at him. "You worked for the Mob?"

"I was always on the outer fringes because I wasn't family, but yeah."

I watched him carefully. "So, maybe you weren't so naïve after all?"

Sam just shrugged and changed the subject.

It was a habit of his, I realized as darkness fell and the food got cold, but we didn't move. He was engaged, and thoughtful, and *talking*. But every time I'd turned the conversation towards the darker side of his life, he shut the door and moved on.

And left me sitting there in the shadows by myself.

Because he didn't want to admit his darkness? Or because he didn't want to be dark anymore?

"Both," he said bluntly, then looked at me.

I had to swallow. I hadn't realized I'd asked him the question out loud.

"I, uh, didn't mean to pry," I said.

"You didn't. I'm just... I'm just being honest with you. I hate my past. I hate the parts of me that got molded by it. But they're there. So the only thing I know to do is... not bring them out. Because they're my past, not my future," he said with a strange little squirm that made my instincts prick.

43. There is No Choice

~ *BRIDGET* ~

I watched him, but he was finding a reason to look out at the water.

"You can't tell anyone the things I told you," I blurted suddenly.

That brought his eyes back to me. "I won't," he said simply. "On one condition."

That made my instincts scream. I went still and wary, but he brought his hands up as if to soothe me.

"I didn't mean it like that," he said quickly. "I meant… I meant, I want to ask you not to meet this Cain guy again without talking to me first."

Everything in me deflated. I shook my head "I'm not going to do that, Sam. I barely know you and he's… I don't know if I'll even see him again—" My head echoed *soon,* proving me a liar, but I ignored it—"but if I do… that's between me and him."

Sam sat back, propping up on his arms. It made his chest and shoulders pop, and his shirt cling to his flat stomach. "So… if we work this out… if we got together… you'd still see him?"

I wasn't eating, but I choked like I'd inhaled the Fettucine. "No. Not like *that*... I mean... *no*. But I... you can't... that's not—"

"I like you, Bridget. I feel like we get each other. And I know I'd be a helluva lot better for you than some monster in the dark who's indulging his fantasies."

"That's not what's going on," I croaked, still trying to clear my throat.

"Whatever, I just... If I learned anything in the past few years it's that playing games and dancing around things can be fun for a time, but it gets old fast. I'm trying to get away from thinking that way. So I'm here. I'm telling you that I like you. But if we're... if we become something, I don't want to share you with some dude in a mask creeping around in the dark."

All the protests and excuses rushed up my throat, ready to be thrown at him. But he was sitting there, just baldly staring at me, waiting to see what I'd say.

"Why?" I rasped.

"Why do I not want to share you?"

"No. Why me?"

He shrugged. "I don't know. But I can't keep my eyes off you. And when you're not around, I wish you were. It's really that simple."

I just stared.

"But... you're *good.*"

He sat forward, shaking his head. "Depends on the day, honestly," he said, clawing a hand through his hair. "But I try. I mean, more than I ever have before."

Then he met my eyes again and I felt the light in his eyes. It crackled in the air and in my chest and made my heart beat faster.

I couldn't remember what we talked about after that because my head was spinning, and I spent the whole time arguing with myself about whether I should take him seriously, or whether I'd destroy him.

At some point he got to his feet and offered me a hand to help me get up. I thought for a second he might pull me into his chest when I got up, but after a moment's hesitation, he let me go and reached down to stuff the trash into the bag, then gather up the blanket that he slung over the arm closest to me as we walked back to the car.

I was confused.

He'd declared himself, hadn't he?

But now he was walking along, staring at the ground and acting like we were just friends out for a walk.

He opened the car door for me, then drove me home.

But neither of us really talked, and I couldn't decide if the silence was tense with awkwardness, or anticipation. Because I didn't know what he was doing.

And apparently neither did he.

When he pulled up at my house, he got out quickly and trotted around to get my door, then walked me up the path to make sure I got in.

I unlocked the door with trembling fingers, then just as I turned the knob, I looked over my shoulder at him, about to invite him in to see if I could get a look at the rest of his tattoos.

But even though he stepped closer, when I swung the door open, he caught my elbow, and pulled me back from the stoop to stand in front of him on the porch.

"Sam… What are you doing?" I breathed.

"I don't know," he said honestly. "But it feels right." And his eyes were gleaming.

I grabbed his arm, flashed him a grin and started to turn towards the door, pulling him with me. But—

"Bridget, no, I'm sorry."

He held back and I couldn't move him.

I turned to face him again, my breath coming fast and short. "For real?"

He scratched the back of his neck. "Not a priest, but… waiting for marriage now, remember?" he asked sheepishly.

I actually laughed. "You can't be serious?"

His eyes flashed. "Deadly."

Want pulsed through me, zinging in my chest, even though I was completely off balance and *so unclear on what was going on here.*

But I made myself hold his gaze, though I folded my arms across my chest because it felt stronger. "Okay then," I kind of laughed. "So what *is* allowed?"

He sidled right up to me, watching me with a question in his eyes, then slowly lifted his hands to cup my face. And when I didn't break his gaze, or pull away, he leaned in slowly and… kissed me. Softly at first, his lips barely brushing mine. Gently. His tongue barely sliding beyond my lip, but that tender need stole my breath.

I unwrapped my arms from myself and gripped his forearms, holding onto him not to stop him, but because I suddenly felt like I might topple over if I wasn't holding onto something.

And then he groaned softly, tilted his head and deepened the kiss—still keeping it slow, but intense, his lips dancing with mine, his tongue flicking, our breaths mingling…

I got lost in that kiss. I hadn't had a guy kiss me without grabbing me somewhere since I was in high school. But somehow… somehow the innocence of it only made it hotter.

I leaned into him, slowly letting go of his wrists to wrap my arms around his trim waist.

But just as I leaned in and began to press myself against him, he broke the kiss, but didn't let go of my face.

We just stood there, a bare inch apart, staring at each other.

I discovered that I was half-blind with need, and half-terrified.

Then he muttered a curse and suddenly, I was pinned up against the house, his hands in my hair, his body pressed against mine from chest to knee, and his breath thundering on my cheek.

Every thought that had been spinning in my head just flew out. The world was suddenly made up of nothing but his warmth, his strength, and *that tormented kiss.*

Sam was shaking under my hands. As I wrapped arms around him and pulled him in, I felt him quiver. When he slid a knee between mine and pressed it right up high and firm at the apex of my thighs, I gasped and dropped my head back.

With a rasped, *"Shit, Bridget!"* he dove for my throat, and I clawed a hand into his hair, pulling him tighter against me as goosebumps washed down my arm and side.

I rolled my hips, pressing myself on his thigh, and it made my breath stop.

He shuddered again, and want *exploded* in my belly.

I reached down with both hands, scrambling for his belt-buckle, mentally mapping the route through the house to my bedroom, then deciding that was too far, and I'd tell him to hike me up on the sideboard in the hallway. But there was a couch in the living room that was closer and—

With a muttered curse, Sam suddenly tore away from me, and the night chill rushed into the gap he left as he stumbled away from me, practically fell down the step off my porch, rasping, *"I'll call you tomorrow,"* then turned and *fled* to his car.

And to my shock, I was left there, panting and flustered, as the car screeched out of my driveway, then down the road, the gears grinding and engine whining because he was accelerating so hard.

I stood there, shocked and horny, for too long, still somehow convinced that he would come back.

But he didn't.

When I finally accepted that he wasn't going to, I turned on trembling knees and stumbled inside as the fierce disappointment and lingering sense of rejection slowly roiled inside me.

With a burst of spite, I almost left the door open, half-hoping that Cain was out there somewhere, watching all of this unfold. Half-hoping that he'd show up, pissed and needy, and finally take me.

But then, part of my heart screamed that wouldn't be fair to Sam—who was being up front, and not leaving me in the dark…

And yet, I liked the dark. I *liked* it when Cain didn't ask, just took what he wanted.

I wanted to be wanted like that.

But didn't Sam want me like that? Wasn't that what had just happened? He'd wanted so much, he had to *flee?* Or was it all just some weird religious thing?

I made myself close and lock the front door, but not without a look out into the dark in case a shadow moved and separated from the rest of the night... but there was nothing.

As I walked slowly back to my bedroom, the two men flickered through my mind... like yin and yang—one light, one dark. Both touched by the other.

Cain felt like my evil twin—dark, aggressive, dangerous, And yet... I remembered Cain putting me in that bath, and cleaning my wounds. There was a touch of light in him. Something that made me safe, just for the necessary moments.

Sam felt like sunlight—he brightened the day and made it safer. His quiet strength fed something in me that had been screaming and alone for far too long. And yet... he still possessed that edge that stole my breath. When he'd let himself give in to it...

Still, they'd both left me. Just left me, hanging in the wind.

Sam seemed like maybe he understood my darkness, but wanted to lead me out of it. And I knew that's what I *needed.* I knew if I sat in front of Gerald and described these two men, he'd throw me bodily into Sam's arms, and call the cops on Cain.

I knew I needed a man like Sam who wanted what was good for me.

But Cain...

Cain was what *I* wanted.

That tiny, distant voice in the back of my skull *shrieked* that Cain and I would destroy each other... While the part of me that needed danger sobbed that Sam would end up watching, helpless, as *I* tipped over the edge...

I was so confused.

Both men made my heart beat faster. Both made me nervous, though for different reasons.

How could I possibly choose?

I knew I'd have to, because neither of them was going to share.

But when I got to my bedroom and threw my clothes in the hamper, still feeling strange and off-balance, and *horny,* as I slipped between the covers and slipped my hand between my legs, it hit me.

Hard.

My eyes flew open and I froze, mind racing…

Visions of Cain in pursuit… fighting… winning.

Everything I wanted.

Visions of Sam, carrying the pain and darkness because he empathized with me…

Everything I needed, but…

I took a long, slow breath and started to grieve a little bit. Because there was no choice.

Sam wasn't just going to lead me into light, he would *fight* the darkness in me—and I didn't think that was a battle either of us could win. So what would happen when he finally figured out that I was always going to be dark?

I knew *exactly* what would happen.

Cain and I were mutually assured destruction.

But Sam… I would just destroy *him.*

Which meant there was no choice. It had to be Cain.

But the risk…

The risk with Cain was that he'd leave completely. Decide I wasn't worth the risk. And then where would I be?

The panic that coursed through me at that thought was potent and terrifying… and left in its wake a sudden clarity.

Maybe that was point?

Maybe Sam had been asking the wrong questions all along. Maybe he'd been right that this was all intentional on God's part—to show me the way to the end?

Maybe God didn't bring me Sam to save me. Maybe he was just there to make it all clear. To point me down the path I'd been avoiding since the beginning with Cain.

Maybe I was just supposed to find the *right* way out. With Cain.

It had to be.

Something settled over me then and I thought of my computer.

I got out of bed naked, but I didn't feel cold as I walked down the hall to my office and turned on my computer. Just sad. Really sad.

And kind of relieved.

It was almost time.

44. In the Cage

SOUNDTRACK: *Shout* by Sleeping Wolf

~ BRIDGET ~

DeadGirlWalking: I'm not trying to entice you, Cain. But I have to tell you something. I changed my mind about changing my mind. I want you on the hunt. I want you coming for me. All the way. And if you won't do it, I'm finding someone else.

DeadGirlWalking: This isn't part of the game. I'm done.

I didn't even wait to see if he'd respond.
Then I pulled up the forum again and made a new post in the playground.

[DeadGirlWalking has made a Post!]
I want to fight for my life… and lose.

My notifications and DMs lit up in seconds and I smiled grimly at the screen. I knew most of those messages would just be the idiots and trolls, either wanting to goad me, or watch.

I closed the forum and almost shut the computer down—nothing would disappear for another twenty-four hours. But even though my DM thread with Cain hadn't lit up, I couldn't deny the prickling sense that he was watching.

Out of morbid curiosity, I went back to the post and started scrolling through the comments. There were already dozens.

I'll fill you up, then slit your throat, bitch.

-

OH NO, DON'T DO IT! YOUR LIFE IS WORTH SOMETHING!

-

God, another attention seeker. If you really wanted to die, you'd just do it without all the fanfare.

I rolled my eyes and was about to shut it down, but I'd already scrolled down when another comment caught my eye.

I already know how to make you come alive.
Link.

My heart began to slam against my ribs—my mind tripping back to the very first time Cain commented on my original post: *I know how to make you feel alive.*

It was him. It had to be.

But my pulse ratcheted even higher when I saw the two comments *beneath* Cain's.

DM me.
-
I understand. Check out my gallery: <u>Link.</u>

With shaking hands I quickly clicked into the two new profiles and saved the links, took screenshots of the messages, then DMed the first guy nothing but a question mark, and the second guy a single line telling him I was going to look into it and get back to him.

Then I went back to Cain's message.

I bit my lip, wondering whether he'd just repeated his earlier message to make a point, or if there was something deeper.

But when I clicked the link, it took me back to our DM thread.

How the hell had he done that?

SYSTEM NOTE: CHAT ENCRYPTED END-TO-END. ENSURE ALL ACCOUNTS ARE LOGGED OFF BEFORE DISCONNECTING.

DeadGirlWalking: Is this supposed to be funny?

I waited, heart pounding, but he never replied, and the message never said that he was typing.

I was groaning to myself for being hopeful and about to click out again when my computer pinged because the other guy had replied to my message. And the darkest part of me squeezed.

SYSTEM NOTE: CHAT ENCRYPTED END-TO-END. ENSURE ALL ACCOUNTS ARE LOGGED OFF BEFORE DISCONNECTING.

TheClowne: You for real?

DeadGirlWalking: Flesh and blood. And yes, I meant it.

TheClowne: What's your timeframe?

DeadGirlWalking: Before Christmas. But the sooner the better if we match. I have some questions.

TheClowne: I'm sure you do. But that's not how I play this game. Either you want help or you don't. If you do, I'll get there. If you don't, we're done here.

I frowned, uncertain whether to respond to that or not. I clicked through to the guy's profile to see if I could get a read on what kind of person he was, but it was entirely blank, except for the date he'd joined—several years ago—and his name, he'd left everything empty.
I chewed my lip, debating whether to respond.
But then the computer pinged again.

TheClowne: You didn't say you were working with Cain. I'm out.
[TheClowne has left the chat.]

What the fuck?!
Every piece of sadness, grief, and grim determination floating in my veins suddenly morphed into white-hot rage. I pounded the keyboard so hard my desk rattled.

SYSTEM NOTE: CHAT ENCRYPTED END-TO-END. ENSURE ALL ACCOUNTS ARE LOGGED OFF BEFORE DISCONNECTING.

DeadGirlWalking: What the fuck, Cain! You don't want me, but you won't let anyone else have me either? What the hell is wrong with you?!

SleepingBeast: We aren't finished.

DeadGirlWalking: I told you I was looking elsewhere if you bailed and you fucking bailed!

SleepingBeast: I said, we aren't finished.

DeadGirlWalking: You're toying with me. This is a game for you, but it's not for me. You can set all the rules you want, but I don't get any? That's bullshit, Cain. I'm done. I'm finished. I know what I want. Either you're in or you're out—and stay out of my fucking posts. I can talk to whoever the fuck I want!

SleepingBeast: You aren't listening, I said: We. Aren't. Finished.
I blinked and went still, breathing hard because I was *furious,* but a sudden wash of hope burned through me too.

DeadGirlWalking: Are you saying what I think you're saying?

SleepingBeast: I'm saying what I already said: Soon.

DeadGirlWalking: What is "soon"? Soon is bullshit. I've got a priest out here getting ready to give up God for me, and you can't even hunt?

SleepingBeast: You only told me you were back in the plan a few minutes ago. And for the record, that pussy would never give you what you want.

DeadGirlWalking: A) You never told me jack shit at any point, so who cares, and B) You don't know him, so you don't get an opinion.

SleepingBeast: I know enough.

DeadGirlWalking: Then you know that "pussy" has a dark side—and he'll actually answer phone calls and TALK TO ME. Who knows maybe I'll give up the darkness and become a preacher's wife.

SleepingBeast: I didn't think you were a liar. You and I both know you'd chew him up, spit him out, and be back in my pocket in days.

DeadGirlWalking: Being in your pocket has brought nothing. I thought we were connecting. I thought we had an agreement. Then you just ghosted.

SleepingBeast: You changed the rules.

DeadGirlWalking: And now I'm changing them back.

SleepingBeast: And maybe you've noticed that we're talking?

> I blinked.
> He was right. He was here. He was messaging again.
> Hope and thrill and fear and need all churned in my guts.

DeadGirlWalking: Whatever. I'm getting desperate. I can't just sit here waiting. It's driving me insane. Are you in? And are you in NOW? I need this. And I need it to be soon.

[SleepingBeast is typing…]

SleepingBeast: >>> We. Aren't. Finished. <<<

DeadGirlWalking: I'm done with the vague-posting. I told you at the beginning, if it's not you, it'll be someone else. If you're real, and you're in, come for me. Otherwise, stay out of it. Because I'm going to find someone.

SleepingBeast: Soon.

[SleepingBeast has left the chat.]

I slammed my fist on the desktop and screamed a curse at the screen. There were tears in my eyes.

My DMs were lighting up and the post notifications were increasing in front of my eyes, but all I could do was look at that line.

[SleepingBeast has left the chat.]

I wanted to reach through the screen and grab him by the throat and shake him until he returned the favor.

I wanted to fall into his arms and weep.

I wanted to fuck him silly and beg him to stay with me.

I wanted so many things and none of them seemed possible in that moment, and suddenly I was in a cage again. My breath got quick. Too quick.

My ribs were too small. My lungs wouldn't inflate properly.

Lights flashed on the edge of my vision as my head began to spin.

Suddenly woozy, vision blurred with tears, naked and shaking, I stumbled back to my room and dropped onto my bed. But dropping so fast, my head lurched and the world flipped. A wave of nausea rocked through me. I gripped the quilt on top of my bed because it felt like my bed was rising and falling, threatening to roll over.

And my heart was beating so fast it felt like a vibration in my chest.

Shit…

Shit.

I threw a hand out for my phone and realized I'd left it… somewhere.

Double shit.

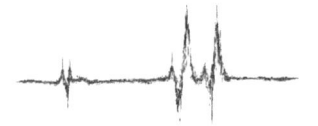

~ CAIN (Twenty minutes earlier) ~

Fucking pussy. Couldn't close the fucking deal—thank *God.*

If it weren't for the fact that I couldn't let anyone see me, I would have been pacing the street outside her place.

She kissed him.

She fucking kissed him.

And not like she was just looking for a quick hook-up.

She kissed him like she kissed me except… less sure. Like he scared her. And I knew that in her eyes, that was a good thing.

FUCK.

Was that what she wanted?

Gentle?!

It should be. I was smart enough to know that much. But I couldn't believe it. She was so much more than him. So much more color. So much more *fight* in her than that ball-less wonder.

He wanted her though. No one would miss that. And I couldn't blame him.

But that thought just took me back to how all this started and *fuck.* She went out with him. Dressed up and everything. Like a date. The question was, had she only done it because I'd been gone? Or did she really want someone like him?

But then I remembered those messages, and that post.

She was getting to the edge. She was reaching her limit. I'd been surprised when she didn't freak out and do something stupid after I disappeared, but that just meant all that crazy was winding up tighter and tighter.

Thank God I'd had the instinct to check the messages from my phone. I didn't usually take the risk, but knowing he'd left her and she'd been looking for me... I'd had a feeling.

I'd been pissed when I saw her threat in the DM—so pissed my fingers shook, and I accidentally tapped into her profile instead of the reply button, which was how I saw her post.

My heart *detonated* when I saw that.

FUCKING *FUCK*.

She didn't even give me *minutes?!* Had she already given up?

At least I'd been able to head off Clowne, that dude was *dark*. I'd seen some of his gore-porn. If I didn't avoid cops like the plague, I would have sent the images to the Police. I was pretty sure the guy was a bonafide serial killer.

Thank God he was territorial and recognized her as mine. Thank fucking Christ.

I couldn't keep talking to her right now, when I was so physically close. The risk was too high. I was buzzing. Losing control. Starting to justify shit in my mind that was going to get us *both* killed—or thrown in jail—and I couldn't let it happen.

Hunting her *had* to be planned. I had to be clear headed.

But what if she found another guy in-state tonight? What if...

My heart was beating so hard it thrummed in my skin. I hissed a curse at the dark window of my car, and the dark shadows around her house.

I was sleep deprived, and I *had* to work tomorrow. I had to leave her. Had to get out of here and wrestle back control. My trackers on her phone would alert me if she moved, but... But the thought of leaving her when she was so obviously on the verge of blowing up her own life...

FUCK.

It took minutes, but I got my breathing under control and muttered at myself that *I* wasn't the pussy, and I needed to work tomorrow. But I couldn't shake the feeling that something was desperately wrong.

And then, just as I was about to pull the car into the street—I still hadn't turned my lights on—I saw a car pass and realized it was the same one I'd seen glide past about fifteen minutes earlier. And this time it slowed right down outside her house.

Every instinct prickled and my mind went quiet as I went on the alert, watching.

It didn't speed up, just eased around the corner.

I waited. Were they looking for a house number in the dark? Or was someone stalking her?

Already?

I turned the car back off and sat in the silence, every sense heightened and perked for any—

There. On the lawn. A shadow pulling away from the hedge and *running across the lawn towards the back of the house where her bedroom was.*

I was out of the car and sprinting after the fucker before I could blink.

45. Almost Done

~ BRIDGET ~

I was still laying on the bed, naked, and doing my breathing exercises. My heart had slowed finally, but the tightness in my chest was making me nervous, which was counter-productive. I felt fragile and emotional and… I felt too much. That was the problem.

Inhale… exhale…

Live.

For now.

I'd been so consumed with my racing thoughts and racing heart, that I didn't even realize anything was going on until a shadow passed over my window. And the only reason I saw that was because it was an almost full moon. The hunched figure outside my house got silhouetted against my curtains for a second as they headed for the back.

I stopped breathing immediately as my heart roared painfully into top gear again.

Cain. It had to be. No one else had enough information. And the new guys probably weren't even local.

He'd come. He'd fucking come. He must have already been close. Thank *God.*

The relief slowed my heart a hair—but then I realized he was coming for me, which meant I was finally going to get to touch him, and that just turned my pulse into another tailspin that *hurt*.

I lay there, trying to breathe slowly and *quietly* so I could hear.

There was a click and a very small creak—the back door being popped.

I didn't have the security system on because I was home and moving around.

I smiled as I imagined if I'd had my phone. I would have turned it on and lay here unmoving until the sensors caught his movement in the hall and the alarms screeched to life. My neighbors would have the cops here in minutes.

I wondered how fast he would have moved *then*.

I hadn't put the security system sensors on the blueprints. I would have snorted, but my chest was aching and I was a little bit worried, so I kept breathing, ears perked, waiting for some indication about how deep he'd gotten into the house so far.

But there was nothing. He was silent as a cat.

Very impressive.

Then my bedroom door, which was only half open—not enough for those broad shoulders—began to slowly, silently slide open.

I watched it, my heart hammering harder and faster as I tried to imagine what his first word would be.

I almost missed the moment he peered in—it was dark in the room, and the moonlight behind the curtains only made the barest glow. I could see shapes, but no detail. And he was crouched low, barely higher than the doorknob as he crept in.

I almost said something, almost moved so he'd know I was watching him, but I was grinning, waiting to shock him, mentally preparing a defensive move for when he struck, deciding whether to try and roll him off the bed, or hurt him first—when the figure half straightened because he'd reached the carpet of the bedroom and it occurred to me that the shoulders weren't right.

Not quite broad enough.

A little too streamlined.

As he crept along the wall towards the side of the bed where I lay, I blinked, my heart pounding as he slowly straightened… and then something in his hand caught the light. Some kind of metal.

Cain didn't bring weapons.

Instinct launched me off the opposite side of the bed like my hair was on fire, grunting because I pushed myself so hard, then rolled to my feet with the bed between us, sucking in a breath to scream—and mentally cursing *myself* for not knowing where my phone was.

But there was no time for thought beyond that as the guy hissed, *"There you are,"* and my entire body tensed, my brain flashing a memory of Ronald outside *Vigori*, leering. *"And already waiting for me,"* he added lecherously.

"NO!" I screamed, throwing myself towards the door, praying I was quick enough and it was dark enough that he wouldn't make it to me before I reached the hallway. I had a panic room just off my office and if I could put enough space between us I could—

"RUN, BRIDGET!" Cain roared, tearing into the room, hands extended and clawed, going straight for Ronald and ignoring me completely.

"He's got a knife!" I screamed, twisting out of his path as the two of them launched at each other.

A thick hand landed on my waist and *threw* me out the door so hard I fell to my knees on the hard floor. But I didn't even feel it, just leaped back up, whipping around to watch the dark shadows come alive, grunting, snarling, smacking—and flashing.

I gasped, hands over my mouth when I saw that blade flash and heard the slap of flesh on flesh—but that shine was halted almost immediately and there was a moment when neither of them really moved as they wrestled for control—Ronald trying to slide that blade under Cain's ribs, and Cain gripping his wrist, snarling.

Something happened, the shadows of the two men melding, turning, then there was a thunk and a single flash as that blade tumbled to the floor, then one form flipped with a roar, crashing against the wall near my bathroom and suddenly everything was still.

One form, hunched, back and shoulders heaving, stood for a moment, hands extended, staring at the other, crumpled on the ground.

I plastered myself against the wall behind me for a second as I blinked and blinked and tried to breathe, but my vision was blurring and I couldn't figure out which one of them it was... until he straightened all the way and turned towards me.

Hooded.

Broad shoulders.

Body like a God, filling out a hoodie like—

"Cain?" I breathed.

He took two, halting steps then slapped the wall next to my bedroom door, flipping on the light and flooding my bedroom with light that silhouetted his form from where I stood in the hallway.

"You said this was real. That it wasn't a game," he snarled.

I couldn't breathe. "It's... it's not—"

"Is this what you do? You just taunt and tease and seduce until a guy can't resist anymore, then you make sure he gets hurt? Does that make you feel good, Bridget?!"

"No! I wasn't—"

"It's fucking *Sid Vicious!*"

"I know—I mean, I didn't know, but I realized when he spoke—"

Cain was prowling towards me, one finger stabbing towards me, then Ronald, as he ranted.

"You gave me only *minutes* warning that you were back in on this! What if I'd been one minute later, Bridget!"

"I didn't call him!"

"Bullshit! You played with his fucking mind and now he's—"

"NO! I didn't! That's a lie!" I screamed at him and realized my vision was blurred with tears as he stepped right up over me so I was locked between him and that wall. His body so big and shoulders so broad I couldn't see the room behind him, and the light only haloed his shape as he loomed over me, that mask still obscuring his features so I couldn't see his eyes.

"This is what you're toying with—is this what you want? You want all of us coming for you at once—killing each other off? Is that the game you're playing?!" he snarled.

"No! Cain—"

"One of these fuckers is going to get past me and you're going to fucking die if you keep this up."

"B-but… that's the whole point," I breathed.

"FUCK THAT. The end of this is my choice, Bridget. This is *my* game!"

My heart gave a painful clench and I slapped a hand to it, clutching my chest.

With a growl of fury, he grabbed for me, one hand at my throat, forcing my chin high, though he didn't actually cut off my air as he pinned me hard against the wall with that stone pillar of a body.

It was instinct to slap a hand to his chest, to try and brace, to keep my space, but he was too strong. With his other hand he just gripped my wrist and slammed it up against the wall, forcing my head back as he leaned down, his breath tearing in and out, fluttering against my cheek even through the mask.

"Are you trying to get *me* killed, Bridget?" he rasped. "Do you get off on that?"

"No," I whimpered, shaking my head hard, the tears finally spilling over my lashes and down my cheeks. I was mortified.

I needed to be stronger than this. But my tears were *relief,* because he was here. He was warm and strong and *here.*

"Thank you," I whispered. "I didn't move… I thought it was you… I was waiting for *you.*"

There was a moment he went still, that mask less than an inch from my face, our chins almost brushing and I knew he was searching my eyes, trying to figure out if I was lying.

My body thrummed with a confusing mix of fear and arousal.

His breath was heavy, rasping, and mine was getting heavier too. But my chest was pinching and those lights still flashed at the edges of my vision.

I was feeling more than a little unhinged—and tense with the awareness that Ronald was on the floor behind him.

"Did... did you kill him?"

Cain's breath rushed out of him, but he shook his head quickly. "Not yet," he said menacingly.

I swallowed, my throat rubbing against his palm because of the way he held me and wished I could see his eyes.

"Did he touch you?" he growled.

"N-no. He didn't have a chance. I'm... God, Cain, I'm so g-glad you're back," I managed to get the words out, though only barely. Because they made me vulnerable, and I was afraid he was still blaming me and would try to punish me by running. But he just tightened his grip on my jaw. His breathing got deeper and he looked down at where his body pressed against mine. I felt the low rumble in his chest against mine and almost laughed.

I was naked. And he was fully clothed. And I could feel him getting hard.

"It's time, Cain," I whispered. "I'm ready."

"The fuck you are," he muttered, still looking down, but then he released my wrist he'd had pinned against the wall and trailed that hand down my arm, against the side of my breast, then down my side, following the form of my waist and hip, then down...

I sucked in when he touched me.

He rumbled again, because I was already slick, and he entered me with two fingers immediately.

I bit my lip, but between his body and the way he held my throat, I couldn't move without physically fighting, struggling. And I didn't *want* him to let me go.

"Is this what you want?"

"Yes," I breathed.

He snarled. "This is *all* you want—"

"No!"

"Don't lie to me, Bridget."

"I'm-I'm not. There's... there's something about you, Cain. I want *you.*"

He went still for a moment, then pulled his hand away like my skin burned him.

He started to ease back, and I panicked.

"No! Cain!" I grabbed for him, but he fended me off and turned back to my bedroom, prowling back to Ronald's crumpled form on the floor—one arm in a strange position that made me a little sick. I thought Cain had dislocated his shoulder and...

And it didn't matter because Cain was pacing the floor of my bedroom, back and forth in front of Ronald.

"Bodies are evidence, Bridget. Difficult to hide."

"I know. I wasn't—I didn't know he was coming. I swear, Cain. I thought it was you!"

Back and forth, his huge body prowling like a lion's, his head shaking, but I could tell his gaze never left Ronald for long.

"This isn't a game—I'm not playing anymore," he growled.

"Me either. I swear. I wasn't—"

He stopped dead and whirled to face me, pointing one man-hand at the floor at his feet. "Last chance, Bridget. You say the safeword and I leave. I'll take this fucker with me. He won't bother you again and this is over. Say it, or this ends on the next hunt."

"Wasn't... wasn't that tonight?" I breathed.

"I told you—no one else chooses this for me—for us!" he snapped. "Make your choice, Bridget. Safe word. Or the last hunt?"

I licked my lips and said nothing, because now that he was here... I didn't want either of those things. That was the truth.

"Bridget," he snarled, a warning in his tone. "I'm not fucking playing."

"I'm not giving you the safe word. Ever," I whispered. "I mean it."

With a menacing growl, he came for me again, grabbing me, lifting me, slamming me up against that wall again, prying my thighs apart with his knee, then reaching for me, hiking me up with one hand to keep me high, and invading me with the other, using the pad of his thumb on my clit at the same time he finger fucked me and pleasure rocked through me.

I gasped and grabbed for his shoulders, my head thunking back against the wall as he leaned in, catching the bottom of the mask on my shoulder and nudging it up so he could open his mouth on my neck, and sucking *hard.* Marking me, I realized.

I curled one hand over his head, cursing that hood and that mask, desperate to touch his skin and see his face. I reached down with the other, trying to find him—his buckle, his hard length—but his body was in the way and he was too strong, and—

"One more, Bridget," he came off my neck and whispered hoarsely. "There's only one more—take what you need now, because the next time I find you, this ends."

"But… I need *you.*"

"You've got me… for now. Take it, Bridget. Take what you want."

Letting my head fall back against the wall, I kept my eyes on his mask, trying to find his gaze as I began rolling my hips, urging him on, seeking that release. He shuddered as my hip thrusts grew shorter and faster and I rode his hand, never looking away until my body was rising, rising toward the climax. But then, just as I reached that height, he groaned and let me go so unexpectedly, my arms flailed and I clawed hands into his shoulders, feeling like I was about to fall.

But he'd only let me slide down the wall, down his body, so my feet reached the floor, and now he was dropping to his knees in front of me.

"Cain, what—"

He tipped his head up, his face still obscured by that mask, his chest heaving. Then he slid one hand up the back of my leg, cupped it behind my knee and lifted it, hooking it over his shoulder.

"I need to taste you," he growled. "Close your eyes… Close your fucking eyes, Bridget," he hissed.

Then he dropped his chin, pushed that mask up to the top of his head like a shield from my eyes, and laid his mouth on me.

A high, whimpering cry broke in my throat as he licked me from my core to my clit and my hips bucked.

He gave a low chuckle, grabbed my ass with both hands and held me there, thumbs on my buttcheeks, his fingers curling between my thighs and holding me apart.

I was perched there, balanced on the ball of one foot, the other knee hooked over his shoulder and my body quivering with every pass of his tongue.

But the pleasure… the warm, slick feeling of him, the rumbling in his chest, his breath—and mine—echoing in the empty, still house.

I broke in seconds, crying his name, clutching his head, my body arching, bowing against the wall and pressing harder against that incredible tongue… until all strength left me.

My heart was hammering so hard I shook from head to toe. And I was weak.

So fucking weak for him.

He propped me up against the wall as I tried desperately to get my breath back, pulling his mask back down before he looked up at me.

And then, my feet were on the floor again, but his warm, steel strength was upright and pressing me into the wall, one hand cupping my face, his thumb on my cheek, his fingers at the back of my neck and he leaned down.

His lips would have brushed my ear, I thought, but instead that cold mask filtered his breath against my skin.

"Get ready, Bridget. There's only one more hunt."

"W-when?" I gasped.

"That's *my* choice." When I tensed, he gripped me harder and shook his head. "Man up, Bridget. You chose our agreement. I choose when. You get what you want. And so do I. That's how this works."

Then my skin—flushed and heated from my orgasm—went cold, because he let me go and whipped around, grabbing Ronald and throwing him over his shoulder, then stalking out of the bedroom, down the hall, and out the back door where they'd both entered.

And he didn't say another word.

46. Done with This

~ CAIN ~

I used my kit to tape Ronald's wrists together, tight behind his back—which would be excruciating on that shoulder when he woke up. Then I tossed him into the trunk of the car and drove him into the city, fighting the urge to just slit his throat the entire drive.

But that wasn't my game anymore.

I found the building I wanted, parked in a nearby alleyway praying that the towing company wouldn't be diligent tonight, then grabbed Ronald and threw him over my shoulder, walking straight into the security area at the front door.

The moment the door closed behind me and I was out of public eye, I relaxed a hair. But one of the guards looked like he was going to stop me, so I grabbed Ronald's hair and lifted his head so they'd see his face.

"Oh shit," the younger one said.

"You get Val," the older one told him, then looked at me with an assessing gaze when the kid darted inside. "It's been a while," he said in a low, warning tone.

"She'll let me in. You know she will."

He didn't respond right away, but his eyes dropped back to Ronald again and he shook his head. "This guy is more trouble than he's worth."

"Make sure Val understands that," I growled. "Because next time I run into him he's not going to need a hospital, he'll need a morgue."

The guy grunted, but then the kid leaned through the door and peered around, eyes wide. "She said come to her office."

I took a deep breath then followed him down that dark hallway, back into *Vigorí,* back into my fucked up past. And I was mentally cursing the entire time, because I'd sworn I'd never come back to this place.

The kid ushered me into a back entrance so I didn't have to carry Ronald through the lounge—Val obviously thought that would be bad marketing. Then he pushed open another door and stepped back, not preceding me into Val's office.

Still a newbie then.

Val was sitting at her desk with a drink. Her brows rose when I walked in with Ronald still over my shoulder, but dropped him onto the couch where she could see him. I didn't bother with greetings.

"He's fucking unhinged, Val. If you don't keep a collar on him, I will."

Her lips pursed. "Good to see you too. Yes, it *has* been a while. Seems like you've had an eventful night. Do you want to tell me why you're carrying one of my Doms in here like he's nothing but a meat-sack?"

Not giving away the ache in my shoulder and back from carrying that fucker, I stalked straight up to her desk and leaned on the other side of it.

I wouldn't touch Val, and she knew it. She knew that *I* knew she could push one button and there'd be half a dozen guys in here just as strong as me.

"I'm only going to say this once," I growled. "That's not a Dom. That's a fucking psycho looking for an in. Get rid of him, Val. Or I will."

She took a deep breath then looked past me to where he was slumped on the couch, still bound. His shoulder twisted and ugly.

"I'll take care of it," she said, her nose wrinkled like she'd agreed to put her hand in a bucket of shit.

"Thank you," I said, and turned on my heel, starting for the door, my hope rising when I got all the way there and a hand on the knob without her speaking up—but I should have known she was just waiting for her moment.

"Don't try and leave without catching up, Sam. It's good to see you. I didn't know you were working again."

I huffed a sigh, but turned back to face her again, shaking my head. "I'm not. I'm done with this shit. I told you that already."

Her eyes dropped to Ronald, then returned to my face and one brow rose.

I gave her a flat look. "I was helping a... friend."

Her eyes narrowed. "You're helping a friend... that *Ronald's* coming for?"

I didn't break the gaze, but I let her see the fury building in my chest. "You *knew* he was coming for her and didn't warn her?"

"I didn't *know,*" she corrected me. "But... I can figure it out."

I glared, uncertain whether to believe her or not—but she smiled like a fucking viper and flapped her hand. "I'll collar him, don't worry. He's small fry. I have leverage, and I'm not afraid to use it." Then she glanced down at Ronald and shook her head. "I'm sure God is very pleased with you for protecting your "friend." What's the quote? *Greater love hath no man, than that he lay down his life for his friends?"*

I swallowed hard. "I didn't know you read the Bible, Val. Impressive. But I'm pretty sure this isn't what He meant," I snarled, tipping my head towards Ronald.

Val tilted her head. "Does your *friend* know who you are?"

"No. And you won't tell her."

"No, I won't. But... I'm assuming you know who her father is?"

I went very still and let her see the warning in my eyes. Val rolled hers, but moved on.

"In any case," she sighed, "it appears that you've taken away one of my Doms before it was time for a switch. If you want to bring your whole *Holy Man* schtick here, I'll give you his den. Sid's been a pain in my ass since day one."

I shook my head. "I'm done with that shit. I told you—"

Valerie shrugged and waved me off. "Don't say no. Just in case. The offer is open. Keep it in mind. An option for your... very promising future. After all, God will forgive you, right?" she said with a biting smile.

I was quiet for a second. "I sure hope so," I muttered, then opened the door and left.

47. Breathing Down My Neck

SOUNDTRACK: *Of These Chains* by Red

~ BRIDGET ~

I slept in the next morning. And when I finally woke, it was to four texts and a voicemail from Sam, growing increasingly worried.

The very real tone of concern in his voice was touching, and for a moment I lay there in bed and thought about what it would be like to be with a man like that actually cared. And was careful. Protective. Capable of violence, but holding himself in restraint.

I got a picture in my mind, and for a second it warmed me.

Sam, standing at the front of the church, preaching. And me watching. Examining those fantastic arms, knowing the tattoos that his button down shirt was hiding.

Finding him after the service. Excusing him from a conversation with a pearl-clutcher, then pushing him into a back room and fucking his brains out because I'd been waiting to do it for hours.

On one level, it was thrilling. A little bit naughty. And the mental image of laying, sweaty and panting in Sam's arms, hidden from a very judgmental world… it felt safe.

But that was the problem.

The memory of the furious, adrenalized Cain stalking straight for me having just disarmed and busted up Ronald flashed in my head, and my entire body throbbed.

Of course, thoughts of Cain made me blink and remember the rest of what had passed between us last night. What he'd said. And what was going to happen.

Soon.

I swallowed and my heart jumped in my chest. It was happening. One more hunt—he would fuck me, finally. Then kill me.

And there was only one part of me that was sad about it. There was a lot more fear, but that was thrilling and…

My phone buzzed again. Another text.

SAM NOTPRIEST: Bridget, please let me know you're okay?

ME: I'm fine. Late night. Just woke up.

SAM NOTPRIEST: Are we okay? I didn't want to leave last night, but I needed to clear my head.

ME: We're good. I admire your self-control.

SAM NOTPRIEST: I had to leave because of the control I lack. But I want to make it up to you. Dinner? Take-out this time. My treat.

It was so cute that he tried so hard. I wasn't used to a guy trying when he wasn't pawing at me and expecting sex. The fact that he wanted me to be comfortable and wasn't planning to fuck me was a little disconcerting.

ME: Next week. Name your day. I'm flexible.

And I was. Because there was a very good chance I'd be dead by then.

Strange feelings I couldn't quite identify twisted up in my guts at that thought.

SAM: Sunday at 7 again. Is that close enough to next week for you?

I thought about it, and decided it was. If I got to Saturday, I could always make an excuse and put him off. Or maybe, go see him. See if I could break through that self-restraint he was working so hard to maintain.

But then it hit me… if Cain was hunting that night, Sam might get caught in the crossfire and try to protect me. I didn't want to be the reason he got hurt.

I'd just cancel it if we got that far.

ME: Sure.

I was slow to get moving that morning and found myself standing in the bedroom looking at that space where both guys had appeared last night—and the mark on the floor where Ronald had lain. Apparently he'd been bleeding, at least a little. It was just a smear, but seeing that did weird things to my insides and stole my appetite.

But then it occurred to me.

Shit.

I had to email Jeremy, because he was supposed to be meeting Ronald tomorrow, and if Cain had killed him…

Shit.

I hurried to the office and turned on the computer, trying to figure out how I could lead into this without giving Cain away.

My heartrate spiked through the roof.

My fingers were shaking as I typed in the password.

Sure enough, Jeremy had already emailed. But when I read the subject, my eyes widened.

FROM: Asshole (Jeremy Haines)
TO: Bridget
SUBJECT: Your psycho got himself fired
Val messaged me this morning. Turns out you were right about delusions of grandeur. This fucker got himself hospitalized and arrested last night. And she's shipping him

back to the East Coast. Turns out our friends over there were looking for him.
What did you do?

FROM: Bridget
TO: Asshole (Jeremy Haines)
SUBJECT: Re: Your psycho got himself fired
Nothing. I was an innocent bystander.

I had meant to be funny. It wasn't until the split second after I pressed send that I realized I was effectively telling Jeremy that I was involved and nonononononononononnooooooo.

I actually grabbed for the computer, like I could somehow stop the email sending. Then I cursed myself roundly.

What a stupid mistake!

I really was in a tailspin if I wasn't thinking through the things I sent to Jeremy. What the fuck?!

My stomach sank as I stared, wide-eyed, at the screen waiting for his response, because he was almost always in the office now and—

FROM: Asshole (Jeremy Haines)
TO: Bridget
SUBJECT: Re: Your psycho got himself fired
Where the fuck were you when this guy was getting himself on Val's shit list?
What aren't you telling me?

FROM: Bridget
TO: Asshole (Jeremy Haines)
SUBJECT: Re: Your psycho got himself fired
I was making a joke

FROM: Asshole (Jeremy Haines)
TO: Bridget

SUBJECT: Re: Your psycho got himself fired
Do you think I'm an idiot, B?

FROM: Bridget
TO: Asshole (Jeremy Haines)
SUBJECT: Re: Your psycho got himself fired
No.

FROM: Asshole (Jeremy Haines)
TO: Bridget
SUBJECT: Re: Your psycho got himself fired
Tell me what the hell happened last night?

Fuck fuck fuck fuck fuck!

My head was spinning. I didn't know what to tell him. I didn't know how close to the truth to get with him. I didn't want to lie outright—he had an uncanny ability to sniff that out. But I couldn't tell him—

FROM: Asshole (Jeremy Haines)
TO: Bridget
SUBJECT: Re: Your psycho got himself fired
That's it, B. We're meeting. We're doing this in person. I'm looking in your eyes while you tell this story, because I don't trust you anymore.

FROM: Bridget
TO: Asshole (Jeremy Haines)
SUBJECT: Re: Your psycho got himself fired
It's not like that.

FROM: Asshole (Jeremy Haines)
TO: Bridget
SUBJECT: Re: Your psycho got himself fired
So, you do think I'm an idiot. Well, joke's on you. I'm making sure that wingnut leaves the state tomorrow like he's supposed to, then when I know he's safely in the hands of our

377

friends on the other side of the country, you and I are talking face to face. We can do that at your place, or mine. But we're doing it. No more delays. No more excuses. No more bullshit. You're up to something, and you're going to tell me what it is.

FROM: Bridget
TO: Asshole (Jeremy Haines)
SUBJECT: Re: Your psycho got himself fired
Fine. Your place though. It's weird when you come here.

No way was I bringing him here, right under Cain's nose.

Which sent my head spinning in three different directions, because no matter where I went, it would be under Cain's nose. And he and Jeremy could not meet.

Shit. Shit!

Jeremy and I went back and forth two more times—time, place, and his insistence that I actually showed up—then I shut down my email and stared at the computer screen, my heart pounding.

This was bad.

This was very, very bad.

If Cain caught wind of Jeremy... hell, if Jeremy got a sniff of Cain.

Either way I was screwed—and not the way I wanted to be.

"Fuck fuck fuck fuck fuck," I muttered to myself as I opened the forum again and accessed my messages with Cain, but for the first time I wasn't thrilled, or hopeful. I was slow. Reluctant. Resigned. Because it became very clear, very quickly, that there was only one way out of this that avoided allllll the drama...

SYSTEM NOTE: CHAT ENCRYPTED END-TO-END. ENSURE ALL ACCOUNTS ARE LOGGED OFF BEFORE DISCONNECTING.

DeadGirlWalking: I'm not being dramatic. And I'm not trying to entice. Things are happening here and shit is getting real. I need you. I need you quickly. And I need you to end this. Please, Cain. If you don't hunt soon, I might get taken away and I can't stress enough how critical it is that you do *not* let that happen.

I pressed send and waited, my breath rushing out of me when that little green dot appeared next to his profile name. I was so relieved I almost cried.

SleepingBeast: Stop worrying. Our annoying little friend has been marginalized. He won't be coming for you again.

DeadGirlWalking: I know.

SleepingBeast: How do you know?

DeadGirlWalking: I know because you aren't the only one talking to other people. Look, there are other people in my life—nothing to do with you—that are dangerous. And I can't risk them finding out about you. But one of them is going to show back up in two days. Let's just say, he's very unimpressed with Ronald's conduct. And mine for getting involved with him. And now he's got a fire under his ass to "check on me."

SleepingBeast: Bridget, what the fuck is going on?

DeadGirlWalking: I can't tell you. But it doesn't involve you. I just hope you'll help me solve the problem. Because if you don't, the day after tomorrow, someone else is going to. Except, they won't fix it the way I want them to. I refuse to let anyone put me in an institution.

SleepingBeast: Why would anyone do that?

DeadGirlWalking: I'm sorry, have we met?

SleepingBeast: This isn't a joke, Bridget. You're changing the game. I don't change the game. No prep means things get dangerous. What are you doing?

DeadGirlWalking: I don't know how to answer that. I'm definitely not explaining all of this online. I need you. I need to see you.

I waited, biting my lip. But he didn't send anything, and he wasn't typing. With every passing second, my skin got tighter and it got harder to breathe.

DeadGirlWalking: Look, I'm not changing the rules, just setting a timeframe. I always told you I wanted this done quick. And I told you why. It's up to you. Here's the deal. I'm going to be home all day tomorrow. But if it gets dark and you aren't here, then I'm going to the park. Where we met the first time. If I make it to dawn without you, then… I guess you're saying no?

[SleepingBeast is typing a message…]

SleepingBeast: I don't like being told what to do.

DeadGirlWalking: Then don't do it. But I'm telling you the truth. You said "Soon." Tomorrow is soon. Any day after that will be too late. Please, Cain. I'm actually begging here. No shit.

SleepingBeast: Is this fucker going to kill you?

DeadGirlWalking: No. But he'll ruin my fucking life.

SleepingBeast: I need to think about this.

DeadGirlWalking: As long as you get your thinking done before midnight tomorrow, we're golden.

SleepingBeast: What the fuck, Bridget?! That isn't how this works!

DeadGirlWalking: If you decide to come and it's the final time, can I see your face? It's not like I'll be around after to turn you in. I wouldn't want to. But I want to see you. I want to know you, Cain. You're going to be the most important person in my life when I die. Can you please show me your face?

[SleepingBeast has left the chat.]

I gaped at the screen, but that little green dot blinked out and I was left sitting there, willing him to come back. Willing him to not just leave me hanging like that.

"No! Fuck!"

Was this it? Was he leaving me for real?

I pushed away from the screen, shaking my head. He couldn't.

He wouldn't.

Would he?

I popped out of the chair, pacing the room, glancing at the screen every time I turned, waiting to see if he'd come back.

And he didn't.

He fucking didn't.

Was this how he took control? Leaving me uncertain, right up to the end?

Or had he actually bowed out?

And how the fuck was I going to figure it out in time if he didn't show up tomorrow?

Fuck you, Cain.

Fucking fuck you.

48. Caged

~ BRIDGET ~

In the dream, I could feel him watching. Always somewhere behind me. Always just out of sight. And every time I turned my back he got closer. Until I was turning away from him on purpose, because it drew him nearer, faster.

Then he was there, breathing down the back of my neck, panting like he'd been running.

"I made it… I made it on time," he croaked in my ear, wrapping his arms around me from behind and clinging, leaning over me, covering me.

"On time for what?" I gasped, suddenly near tears, even though I didn't know why.

"You aren't dead yet."

"No," I said, but that reminded me why I was sad, and I had to swallow the lump in my throat. "Nope. Not dead. Not yet…" I trailed off lamely.

"Bridget—"

"Can we just… can you just… stay here with me for a little while?" I whispered.

He sighed heavily, his breath rushing across my cheek as he curled himself around me until the rest of the world disappeared, and all I could see was the safety in his shadow. And all I could feel was the steel warmth of him.

I clung to his arms that were wrapped around me, and a weird noise came out of my throat.

"Bridget, what—"

"Don't let go," I whispered through numb lips. "Please... don't let go."

"I won't, babe. I won't—I'm here. I promise, I'm here."

"But you won't stay."

"Yes, I will!"

I shook my head and he growled, tightening his grip at first, then whipping me around suddenly and staring into my eyes, his forehead furrowed, more lined than I'd ever seen it before.

I lifted a shaking hand to comb his thick hair back from those lines, and realized that I'd never done that before. Never touched his hair. Never buried my fingers in it. Never clawed at his scalp, or gasped his name.

So I did that—all those things. I grabbed for him with a little, broken whimper, pleading with my eyes that he wouldn't say anything, because we were almost out of time and I was scared, and he made me feel safe... so why...? Why couldn't we make this work?

"Bridget—"

Suddenly, something wrapped around my middle, clamping around me so hard I lost my breath, then started pulling me slowly out of his arms.

I gasped and grabbed for him, clawing—and he cursed and tried to grip me too, but I was being dragged backwards, away from him. And it was breaking my heart.

"Bridget! Please! Don't—"

"It's not me!" I sobbed. "It's not me! Hold on, Sam! Please! Don't let go!"

He opened his mouth, his eyes wide and terrified, hands clawing, every muscle rigid and flexed, like he was fighting something, trying to reach me.

I was the first to lose my grip, his sleeve tearing under my nails, then finally slipping out of my clenched fingers completely. But it was only a second before his man-hands were torn off my arms too.

He screamed my name like he'd been stabbed as I was jerked away and up—like I was being taken into the clouds.

He sucked away from me, his eyes wide, expression tormented, lips twisted into a scream of defiance, hands clawed and reaching.

"NO, BRIDGET. COME BACK!"

I woke up with a start, disoriented, crying, and suffocating.

I was sucking at the air, trying to get my lungs to inflate, blinking blinking blinking, until finally I was breathing.

My vision blurred in a new wave of tears, and I reached out to steady myself and realized I was on the couch, with the lights on.

Alone.

No Sam. No Cain. No Ronald. No one. Just me. Alone.

I dropped my face into my hands and sobbed.

Then I lifted my chin and screamed a curse at the ceiling because that looming weight was a symbol of the cage I lived in. And there was no fucking way out.

You couldn't escape a cage that was inside yourself.

You couldn't escape a horror that lived in your mind relentlessly.

You couldn't do anything.

I had tried facing my demons when I was younger. I had tried outrunning them. There were no paths left but to accept that this was the way life would always be.

I blinked away the tears, wiping my nose on my sleeve and let myself fall back, let the couch catch me, let my head sink back on the cushions.

I sighed heavily. I couldn't stop any of this. I was going to die. *Everyone* died.

The only thing I could choose was *what* killed me.

And when.

That was… if I'd been able to convince Cain to actually show up.

God, if only he'd been willing to change the rules. At least then, we could have run away together…

And that was when I saw it. The alternative.

And the black window looking out on my doom cracked open to let in the tiniest sliver of hope.

My heart *raced.* I licked my lips.

It would never work.

But what if it did?

If it didn't work, I was dead. Plain and simple. And… acceptable.

I'd always said I wouldn't ever just roll over and die. I wanted to go down fighting.

Well… maybe I'd lose this time. But I was gonna go out in one helluva bang.

Fireworks.

And I'd take my whole world down with me.

Then, finally, I felt calm.

Clearing my throat and wiping my eyes, I pushed to my feet and trotted into my office, to my computer, and opened my email with a weird sense of anticipation.

I didn't actually know if this was going to work.

But I was going to try.

TO: Asshole (Jeremy Haines)

SUBJECT: Change of Plan

J, we need to change the plan—but only a little bit…

49. Unsent

SOUNDTRACK: *Sound of Silence* by Lexxi Saal and NOCTURN.

~ BRIDGET ~

It was done. The wheels were in motion, and wouldn't stop now until this was over—one way, or another.

Nerves made my stomach trill, and that made me nauseous.

I thought of my dream and picked up my phone, tapping into my text messages to find a specific thread.

SAM NOTPRIEST

Even looking at his name made me swallow a pinch in my throat.

ME: If only I met you first, I wonder if this would have gone differently?

He replied almost immediately.

SAM NOTPRIEST: Bridget, what's going on? Are you safe?

ME: As safe as I will ever be. I was just thinking about you. I dreamed about you last night.

I wondered if I imagined that his lips pulled up in that adorable half-smile when he read that, or if that was some kind of prescient sight that God gave me because my heart might stop soon.

SAM NOTPRIEST: Oh? What kind of dream?
ME: It doesn't matter. I just wanted you to know that.
SAM NOTPRIEST: I can't tell if you're flirting or warning me. You're making me nervous.
ME: Don't be. This is me being my normal not-normal self.
SAM NOTPRIEST: Are we still on for Sunday? I'll come sooner if you want to.
ME: Said every man, always.
SAM NOTPRIEST: You just made me spit my coffee.
ME: Then my work here is done.
SAM NOTPRIEST: Bridget, seriously, what's going on?

I silenced my phone and slipped it into my pocket, because looking at his name was making me sad. I had a very busy day of pacing my house ahead, waiting to see if Cain was on the hunt. Wondering how my life would be different if I'd had a different dad.

I tried to imagine the world where my father had never existed.

Would I even be me?

Would I still have ended up here? Torn between Cain's claws and Jeremy's cage?

God, I'd love to put Cain in Jeremy's cage and see who'd win.

My heart said Cain was stronger, that he had more to fight for. But I knew Jeremy had been honed like a weapon. He couldn't be underestimated.

For a little while, I entertained myself with a parody of superheroes, imagining Jeremy and Cain as rival villains, duking it out to win the heart of the damsel in distress. Namely, me.

Except, it was kind of impossible to see myself just sitting by, watching that happen.

And Sam kept cropping up, intruding on my little fantasy. Because, even though I had turned off the ringer so my phone wasn't making any noise, it was getting heavier with every passing minute. And I knew… I knew he was trying to reach me. And I had to make sure he didn't. Because he was brave. And he was good. And if he had even an inkling of the shitshow that was about to descend on my life, he'd try to save me from it, and no doubt get himself killed in the process.

Sam would never play the hero in a villain story. He was the wise man. The loveable advisor and friend. The one who got killed in the third act so everyone cried, but could still cheer for the hero.

And I couldn't do that to him.

An image swam into focus in my mind. Sam standing in front of his car, leaning back on it, watching me, smiling a little and holding up that bag of food.

He was strong, and confident, and… uncertain of himself with me.

I hated that I did that to him.

I wondered if he knew that it was just because I was so damned uncertain of myself, I didn't know where to begin with anyone else.

That was why I belonged with Cain. Cain was just as broken as me. There was no uncertainty, because there were no boundaries.

Cain wouldn't ask me on a date. He'd break into my house and slip into my bed with no warning.

Cain wouldn't take me to a restaurant and pull out my chair. Cain would throw me over the hood of the car and fuck me from behind.

Sam thought that was a bad thing, but it wasn't.

Sam was too good to understand if I tried to explain this. He'd fixed his own life, so he'd think he could fix mine. He wouldn't accept that my monsters were finally catching up with me and there were too many of them for me to win.

I thought of Sam at that restaurant again, probably stretching his thin resources to pay for that meal, but doing it because he wanted to be a gentleman—because he was trying to make himself new. He *had* been dark—I could sense that in him. It was still there. But… muted.

Fading.

While my darkness just got bigger, and deeper.

It was good that I would stop showing up in his life. I would have destroyed him in the end. And I didn't want to. Surprisingly, I *liked* his light. I didn't want to drag him back down into the depths with me, like some horrific predator.

For once, I would do something *good* for someone else, and let Sam go.

I wouldn't answer that text.

I wouldn't confirm Sunday.

He'd never hear from me again. And even though it would suck, he'd get over it.

In a few months, he'd meet someone else. Someone lighter. And he'd be grateful that I let him go, like I was grateful that he'd shown up, because he'd given me a little bit of light in an otherwise dark world.

So, in my mind, I said goodbye to Sam. Then, I took my phone out and blocked his number, which wiped the message thread.

Then, in a burst of inspiration, cursing that I didn't have a cell phone number for Cain anymore, I darted back to my office and the computer and got into the forum. I quickly tapped out the message, praying he'd see it quickly, even though his profile wasn't showing online.

SYSTEM NOTE: CHAT ENCRYPTED END-TO-END. ENSURE ALL ACCOUNTS ARE LOGGED OFF BEFORE DISCONNECTING.

DeadGirlWalking: I have a story I want to tell you. About why I don't want to live through another Christmas. Maybe… maybe you could come for me and we could talk first? Then I'll run and you'll hunt and this will be over. One way or another, I need it to be over, Cain.

DeadGirlWalking: Something happened a long time ago and my heart and my head got love mixed up with darkness, and now I can't find love anywhere. Only the dark. But I need both. I'm not a mushroom. I'm a plant. I need light like I need air, and I haven't found light in a long time.

DeadGirlWalking: I feel like you're like me. I feel like we understand each other. That's why I wanted to change the plan. I had this crazy idea that maybe if we shared the shadows, the dark would get a little thinner. But the truth is, I'd rather be connected to you forever in the next life, than living in this hollow nothing without you. So… come. Come *talk* to me at my house and then we can figure it out from there.

I sat there, breathing too quick, eyes alight, my hands poised over the keyboard… but then I read it all back and it was just… just meandering gibberish. Just irrational verbal diarrhea.

Stupid.

He'd think I was just trying to manipulate him again.

And as I sat there, ready to crack my chest and open my ribcage to the world just to show him my heart… the darkness weighed down.

His online light never came back.

He didn't reply.

And I lost my nerve.

DeadGirlWalking unsent a message.
DeadGirlWalking unsent a message.
DeadGirlWalking unsent a message.

I turned off the computer and started to pace again. Waiting.

I wished I didn't feel so sad.

I wished the clock moved faster.

By the time the sun was starting to go down, my heart wasn't even beating hard anymore. I was just tired.

And Cain still wasn't here.

I had to accept that he might never come. He might have given up. And there was nothing I could do about it.

I could hear Sam's voice in my head, saying whatever came was God choosing for me. For a reason.

If that's true, God, I just want you to remember: I did the right thing. I kept Sam out of this.

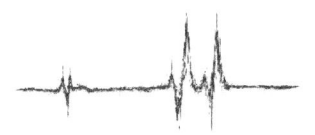

Around seven, as the sun began to dip and the shadows lengthened outside, my nerves came back a little. I walked back to my bedroom and pulled out the black athletic clothes Cain had told me to get for a hunt. I slipped my phone in the pocket on the side of the leggings, zipped the stretchy shirt all the way up to my chin, slipped on the black shoes with good, wide soles for traction and better ankle support.

I didn't take any weapons.

Most women never understood that when you were fighting a stronger foe, more often than not, they'd just take any weapon from you and use it against you.

I wasn't ignorant. It wouldn't happen to me.

I also didn't take food.

Or water.

What was the point?

As twilight descended, I got in the car and drove right to the park.

It was going to close at full dark.

I purposefully left my car in a very obvious spot, so no one could miss it. I ignored the shifting shadows under the trees that hid Cain's eyes. I was almost certain of it.

Or was that just my hope talking?

As I got out, the sky was turning bright orange and purple overhead. It gilded the trees in gold, and turned the grass lavender.

I sighed.

Was this the last sunset I'd ever see? If so, it was a pretty one.

Before I took the first step away from the car, I hesitated.

For a long breath, I seriously considered calling the whole thing off.

But no matter what angle I looked at this from, the end result was the same.

That's the thing with monsters... the only way to beat them is with a bigger monster. A truth my mother discovered to her own detriment.

I had always vowed I wasn't going to go out wailing in a puddle of my own blood and piss the way she had.

I shuddered and pushed the images from my mind.

Then I started down the trail into the forest.

And I never looked back. Because I had hope.

Either this was going my way, and I'd see Cain again. Or it wasn't, and it would all be over anyway...

50. Black as Night

SOUNDTRACK: *Rise* by Tommee Profitt

~ CAIN / SAM ~

I watched Bridget get out of the car and stop, staring up at the sky and my chest squeezed.

Her dark hair, black as night, gleamed and shot sparks of gold in the dying light. Her face was pale, but her cheeks were flushed and her lips pink.

I was staring—gaping, if I was honest with myself—my heart pumping and palms sweaty because we were *here*. In hours, possibly minutes, I'd finally show her my face and then it would be over.

Had she brought a weapon?

She was hardly a rule-follower, so I wouldn't put it past her. But I guessed that she wouldn't. She wanted to win by herself.

That was, if she wanted to win at all. I hadn't liked the desperate tone of her messages. Like she wasn't running towards me, but away from something else.

Some*one* else.

There was still so much I didn't know about her.

I ground my teeth and sank lower behind the bushes as she gave a little shudder, a ripple of unease that traveled through her body, then shook her head and started walking briskly towards the trees.

Every hair on my body stood up, and some other parts of me too. This was it. It was happening. My instincts kicked in and I started moving, following her, still scanning to make certain she hadn't been followed. But there were no signs as I followed slowly towards the trail that was closer to where she'd started. I'd known which path she'd take and wanted her ahead of me.

I smiled as I watched her look around for me, her face tight with tension. I scanned her beautiful body, wrapped in black tonight, which seemed fitting. I was glad she'd remembered.

Then she disappeared under the shadows of the trees, and the night seemed darker already.

The park would close in a few minutes. There were only a couple other cars here, and no sign of people. But I slunk through the bushes towards that trailhead, keeping myself out of sight just in case.

I liked that she had dressed in black and would be hard to see.

I hadn't brought my phone. I wouldn't use the trackers. I would make this an honest to God *hunt*.

When I made it to the trail I kept low, darting between the trees alongside the path as quickly as I could while still keeping my steps quiet. I kept my breathing low, through an open mouth, but my body was alight, my pulse thrumming in my head.

It was happening.

It was finally happening.

She was here. And this was going to end once and for all.

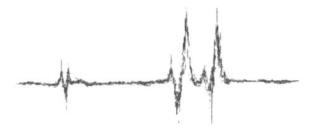

Twenty minutes later my heart was thrumming, and I smiled into the dark, but she still eluded me.

I was having to watch my breathing so I wouldn't give myself away. I knew I could move faster than her through this, and I knew the rough direction we were traveling. But I also knew she was clever and wouldn't just walk to that clearing and wait for me.

She was making me stalk her, and my body thrilled with it.

The mask was an annoyance in the dark—the moonlight was bright tonight, but didn't reach beneath the treetops.

Her request for me to remove it had made my heart thud in my chest.

She had no idea.

She was getting everything tonight. More than just my face.

Holy *shit*.

I paused in walking, listening hard, hitching up the small backpack I'd brought with a few items just in case. Including night vision goggles that would let me see, and could be set to heat sensor if I really couldn't find her.

But I wanted to find her without all that. I wanted this to last.

A little voice in the back of my head said I was dragging it out to keep from reaching that final confrontation, but I pushed it aside.

I'd thought when she said she didn't want to die that it was all over. That there was no more work for me to do. And under any other circumstances, it would have—

A twig snapped somewhere off to my right and I froze, smiling.

"There you are," I breathed, grinning into the dark before creeping off in that direction as quickly as I could without giving away my own location. "I'm coming, Bridget. I'm coming for you."

It was time to stop playing at the edges of this.

It was time to empty my mind, sink into my senses, and *hunt.*

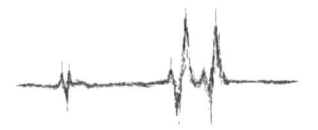

SOUNDTRACK: *Beast Within* by In This Moment

~ *BRIDGET* ~

I could feel him, watching.

My heart beat so hard I felt it in my fingertips. I'd started the night feeling sad and agitated, but as the darkness surrounded me and the night went quiet, I embraced this.

It was going to end either way. So why not give myself up to the hunt and enjoy it while I could?

I was smiling by the time I heard a boot scuff on a tree root.

I'd taken a wide arc through the trees in the rough direction of my clearing, but with the dark and my distraction, I wasn't entirely sure if it was still ahead, or I'd overshot it. Still, it didn't matter, because I could feel him getting closer. It made my breath shake and my skin prickle. It was terrifying and delicious, and I could hardly wait until he got his hands on me.

But since this was the last time, I wasn't going to make it easy for him to catch me.

I'd always said I would go out fighting, and I had every intention of doing exactly that. So, I kept my hands clenched to fists in preparation. I crept through the dark, sweating a little bit, but keeping my pace slow so that I could stay quiet and force him to find me.

There was a rustle in the bushes off to my right and I froze, heart pounding, breath coming faster and faster.

The explosion, when it came, was low to the ground—a snap and flutter of wings, quickly followed by a small shriek as an animal lost it's life.

My heartrate spiked, then dropped quickly when I realized it wasn't Cain, but a totally natural kind of predator.

I slumped, clutching my chest and shaking my head.

"Fucking anticlimax," I muttered under my breath, turning in the direction I *thought* the clearing was in—just as a shadow moved on the edge of my vision.

I went still again, not breathing at all, waiting, peering into the dark, every one of my senses heightened and alert.

And then the shadow of a tree separated from its brothers about twenty feet away, and I caught the shape of a large, hooded male body.

I bolted.

I wasn't even trying to be quiet—he was stronger and faster than me, but not as light on his feet. My only hope of staying out of his hands was to keep my path unpredictable.

I sprinted between trees, tripping over tree roots, my shins scraped by brambles.

Then I turned sharply on the back side of a large tree, praying he was close enough behind me to overshoot and have to double back when he realized I wasn't ahead of him anymore—and instead, ran into a steel bar halfway around the tree.

At least, that's how it felt.

Every ounce of air in my lungs whooshed out with an *oof* as that bar caught me right in the middle. My feet swung up, my arms shot forward as my momentum bent me almost in half over his arm.

He swept me up into his chest, clapping the other hand over my mouth and leaning into my ear.

"Hey, beautiful," he rasped in that gravelly, deep voice that made my blood shiver. "Lovely night for a hunt."

51. The Takedown

~ BRIDGET ~

Cain was so smug! I could hear the smile in his voice, and it warmed me. For a second I closed my eyes and just let my body sink back into him.

I felt him press his face into my hair, and he inhaled deeply.

Which was when I slammed one heel down right on the arch of his foot and threw my head back to try and break his nose.

He cursed—and so did I, because he'd worn the fucking mask—but his hold on me loosened enough that I could slip free.

At least, I started to.

Fucking Cain and his fucking cat-like reflexes. He recovered fast from the shock, his hand snapping out to clamp on my forearm so I was jerked back to face him as I tried to run.

And suddenly, we were dancing.

The only hold he had on me was that forearm. His fingers dug into my flesh painfully. I'd be bruised if I lived through this.

I tried to dart past him, to bend his arm at a weird angle and break his grip.

But Cain just gave a low, delighted chuckle, side stepped, and I was slingshotted to the forest floor as he used his superior weight to counterbalance and throw me down.

I tumbled, eating dirt, rolling, but clawing into the soft layer of rotting leaves and damp earth, pulling myself back to my feet, and running.

I aimed for the only clear path through the trees I could see—the silver light from the moon lighting up a gap that I thought was probably my clearing. If I could get there first, I could—

"Oh no you *don't—*"

It was like being tackled by a freight train.

My head snapped back at the same moment the oxygen whooshed out of my lungs.

I hung in the air for a moment, sucking in a fresh lungful for a scream.

But then I hit the ground so hard my teeth clacked, and it felt like a horse landed on top of me, flattening my body, so I was suddenly grateful for hollow earth under tree roots, and that cushion of leaves and pine needles.

Yet, once again, he'd pinned me to the ground. The most difficult position from which to fight, and the one from which I'd always struggled to grapple.

I planted both hands on the ground and tried to heave, but Cain just chuckled breathlessly, grabbing for one of my hands, trying to pry it around and behind my back—but his grip slipped and I saw my chance.

My elbow was bent up already. When his grip slipped, his balance shifted, and he leaned down for a split second.

I snapped that elbow back, right into his face and when he jerked away, I rolled him, scrambling to my feet. But I'd forgotten the fucking mask!

I hadn't actually hurt him, just made him flinch. So, even though I got my feet under me, they slid right back out when he roared and launched himself, grabbing for my legs and taking me to the ground again.

I screeched like a cat, clawing for him because he'd flipped me to my back this time. He crawled up and over me, growling, muttering, clawing his way up my body and grabbing for my hands.

We wrestled.

Teeth gritted, nails out, I fought. Struggled. My heart pounded in my skull so hard it hurt. Like my brain was expanding. I saw stars and barely registered over the thrumming in my ears that Cain was snarling.

"Bridget—*fuck!*"

"Coward!" I spat through my teeth as he got both hands gripping my wrists and pulled my hands high over my head, which immobilized my body because I had no leverage. "Couldn't even let me see your face *now?!*"

"Listen to me—"

"Couldn't risk yourself at all—you fucking pussy! I gave everything up for you! I was willing to fucking *live* for you—"

"What? But—"

"—and you can't even show your fucking face!"

"Bridget—" he snarled through his teeth, pulling himself up to straddle me, using his weight to keep my hips pinned to the ground, making my efforts to push up and away, futile. My heels scrabbled in the dirt, finding no purchase. And he leaned over me, shifting both my wrists to one of his hands, locking both of them in his strong fingers and pinning them over my head. *"Bridget, stop fucking fighting for one second before I hurt you!"*

"Why?! That's the whole point! If you won't even let me see—"

"I SAID, *STOP!*" he bellowed, squeezing my wrists so hard my hands tingled, leaning over me, panting, his chest heaving.

"Why? What are you going to do—kill me?!" I screeched. "Newsflash, Cain—"

He reached back to somewhere on his thigh and suddenly there was a flash of light—the moonlight gleaming on a straight blade longer than his hand.

The words died in my throat, and my heart screamed. I couldn't take my eyes off it as he flipped it in his grip like someone who was *very* familiar with handling a knife, and brought it up to press against my throat.

"Just… stop…" he said hoarsely.

My chest was heaving too, and my entire nervous system jangling with alarm. He was here. He had me. He was going to kill me and *not* fuck me? And he wouldn't even show me his face—

"Don't. Move," he snarled.

With that blade still pressed at my throat with one hand, he let go of my wrists and sat back slightly, leaning into the knife so I could feel the chill of its edge against my skin.

But just as I tensed, bracing for the pain—for the *end*—he reached up with that free hand, grasped the bottom of the mask and tore it up and off his face, throwing back his hood at the same time, then staring down at me, jaw tight and flexing, his stubbled cheeks shadowed in the moonlight, his eyes a little wild, hair mussed and sticking up because of how he'd forced the mask back.

And everything in my body—even my heart—went still.

Utterly still.

Quiet.

Unmoving.

I searched his eyes—those tormented, glinting eyes that were fierce with male aggression and… pleading?

"Sam?!" I breathed.

What the fuck?

What the *actual fuck?!*

52. Breach of Trust

SOUNDTRACK: *Slayer* by Bryce Savage

~ CAIN / SAM ~

I was panting so hard I had to swallow, try to gather my scattered thoughts, pull myself back from the edge because I wasn't here to kill her, but to convince her that she still wanted to live. Yet, I'd seen that moment when she closed her eyes and braced for me to plunge that knife into her.

Holy shit.

God, help me.

"Sam?!" she squeaked in a small voice, her eyes so wide they were white all the way around. Then she blinked and her brows pinched down over her nose. "What... the... *fuck?!*"

"I need you to listen, Bridget—"

"No way. No fucking way!"

"—this was always the plan, I was never going to—"

"You told me not to do this! You told me Cain was a monster! You said—"

"I AM!" I roared, plunging my free hand into her hair and pulling her head back, pressing that shaking blade harder against her skin, then hissing at myself because a drop of blood welled under it and I had to *fight* for control. "Please, Bridget... I need you to *listen."*

All my senses were thrumming, every inch of my skin on fire.

I swallowed hard and stared right into her eyes, terrified of what I was going to see there, pleading with her to understand, to see that I never planned *this*. She was *never* supposed to meet me as Sam. Only as Cain. She was *never* supposed to care for me—or me for her.

With a groan dripping in self-disgust, I threw the blade aside, away, deep into the bushes, cursing it and everything it stood for. Then I stared down at her and took her precious, shocked face in my hands, silently begging her to understand.

I'd done this all wrong. Right from the start. The fact that we'd gotten this far was all my fault. When she got so desperate, I was terrified she'd find someone else. So I'd agreed to come. But we could still salvage this, if only she'd—

I went still as her eyes welled and her chin trembled. "Fuck you, Sam. *Fuck you!* I thought you were the good one!"

"I am... fuck, Bridget. I am—can't you see? This is a battle I fight every day, and sometimes I win, and sometimes I lose. But I'm here and..."

"You've been lying to me!"

"No! No! Everything I said was true. All of it—it was real. I changed my life. *God* changed my life—"

"You said you were going to kill me!"

I grimaced and shook my head. "No, I... I never actually agreed to do that," I murmured, loosening my grip in her hair and shaking my head. "I let you think that when I talked about hunting you... But it was never... I was always going to try and convince you not to go that far. I always planned to disappear when you changed your mind—it's what I do! And I did... when you said you wanted to live, I walked away! But I couldn't let *you* go. And you didn't either and... it wasn't supposed to be this way, Bridget. I didn't know you'd come to the church—I wasn't even supposed to be there! But I can see now, it was meant to be. I'm telling you—"

"Oh shit," she hissed, and suddenly started struggling.

At first I tried to stop her. "No, please, let me tell you—"

"Get off me… *Get off me!*" she shrieked.

I shoved off her with a curse, stumbling back, but keeping my hands up as she rolled onto all fours, choking and coughing, sobbing, staring up at me with welling, devastated eyes.

"Bridget—"

"You have to go!" she sobbed. "You have to go… *right now!*"

"No. I know this is a shock, but—"

"No, Sam. You don't know. I didn't know it was you. You didn't tell me so *I didn't know!*"

I frowned, dropping to squat in front of her, trying to take her face. "I need to explain—"

"You can't. You don't understand—you have to *go!*" she shrieked, batting my hands away. "Go! Get out of here! Leave me *alone! Fucking leave!*" she screwed her eyes shut and screamed so hard her face shook. "DO IT! GO! NOW! GET OUT OF HERE—!"

"I'm not leaving you!" I barked back.

The sound of a cocked pistol rang through the dark like the gunshot it threatened.

Every sense jangled with alarm—I shoved to my feet, already stretching to run, but jerked to a halt immediately as several large, male forms inched out of the trees dressed in head-to-toe black with weapons gleaming in the moonlight and pointed directly at my chest.

I turned to see if they were also behind me, just in time to find one of them leveling a pistol at me and circling around to step between me and Bridget, who was still sitting in the dirt, her face now in her hands so I couldn't even see her eyes.

Our eyes met and his narrowed.

"I'm Special Agent Jeremy Haines with the Federal Bureau of Investigation," he said, tearing a velcro flap at the chest of his black ops suit with one hand while keeping the gun on me with the other. The flap dropped to reveal a badge and identification.

My heart sank to my toes, but I put my hands up, swallowing hard. "Agent, I know how this looks, but it's a fully consensual—"

"Sam Priestley, you're under arrest for violation of parole, and on suspicion of stalking as defined by Oregon statute 163.732, and attempted murder as per statute 163.115—"

"Wait, *what?!*"

"—You have the right to remain silent. Anything you say can and will be used against you in a court of law. You have the right to an attorney. If you cannot afford an attorney, one will be provided for you."

"This is bullshit!"

"Clasp your hands on top of your head and turn your back to me."

"Bridget! Tell him!"

"It wasn't supposed to be you," she croaked without looking at me. "I thought you were Cain… I thought *you* needed saving…"

The agent shifted to put himself between us so I couldn't see her properly, and he glared. "Hands up, Priestley. *Now!*"

I had no choice. Not if I wanted to live.

I threw my hands up and laced my fingers over my hair, everything within me screaming in protest. I had been here. I had changed my life. *I wasn't going back!*

My chest started to heave. I wasn't sure if I was going to vomit or scream.

"Bridget," I said through my teeth. "You have to *tell him—*"

"Trust me, he knows. But… your last name is Priestley?" she asked faintly… and then she started *giggling,* a strange, high, unhinged sound in this black night.

"Keep your hands on your head and turn your back to me, Mr. Priestley."

I bellowed my frustration and rage into the night, but did as he instructed. And the moment I turned, rough hands took hold of mine on my head and a sharp kick to the back of my knees forced me to drop to the ground. The men around us rushed in, guns still pointing at me, as I was planted face down in the dirt and my hands levered behind my back while I roared my protest.

The *click-click-click* of the handcuffs tightening on my wrists felt like a death knell. My heart began to jump and quiver in my chest. *I couldn't go back—*

"Bridget, tell them!"

"Tell us what, you creepy fuck? That you're a convicted felon carrying a weapon and pursuing a woman in the dark at night? Or that you've been following her for the past week?"

"I wasn't—she knew—"

Bridget's laughter cut off abruptly. "Week?" she asked breathlessly.

"Find that weapon he threw. Get his phone, and search the vehicle. Everything by the book. This one is slippery."

I turned my head, mashing my nose into the mud to do it, but finally I could see her, beyond the forest of legs surrounding me, still sitting, staring at me, wide-eyed, tears tracking down her cheeks.

Tears from laughter? Or tears of grief?

"I wasn't lying," I snarled through my teeth. "I wasn't fucking lying, Bridget!"

"I didn't know, Sam. I'm sorry… I really didn't know it was you. I would never have—"

"That's not the point—"

"This isn't your first rodeo, Mr. Priestley. My advice is to keep your fucking trap shut and stop incriminating yourself by attempting to manipulate my colleague."

Bridget's head snapped up, and she glared at Special Agent Jeremy Haines like he was a piece of shit. But then his words came home to me.

Colleague?

And that was when I realized. My jaw dropped. I grunted as a knee ground into my lower back, sending a jolt of pain up my spine.

"You're an *FBI Agent?*" I ground out.

"No," she breathed, then licked her lips quickly and her eyes dropped to the ground. "I just—they protect me and… and I help them."

"A fucking *narc?!*"

409

"That's colorful language for a Priest," Special Agent Haines commented dryly.

"Shut up!" Bridget and I both snapped at the same time.

Then her eyes cut straight to mine and it felt like she was begging me. But for what? I was clueless.

"I'm sorry, Sam," she breathed. "I wasn't lying. I wanted Cain—wanted you. But I thought he was like me and needed saving from himself... just like I do."

"Stop feeding the animals," the agent hissed at her, then I was being dragged up, my entire body weight being lifted by their grip on my arms craned behind my back. I bellowed in pain and scrambled to my feet.

Still standing between me and Bridget, Jeremy flicked the safety on his gun, then holstered it before reaching for the radio unit at his shoulder. "We have the suspect in custody, send in the medics for Bridget, and we need CSI," he said calmly into the black unit. Then he caught eyes with whoever was behind me and nodded.

And suddenly I was being *ushered* out of the forest at a rapid clip.

"Bridget," I started, uncertain what, exactly, I was going to say.

"Jeremy, please," she murmured to the agent. But he'd already stepped in front of her again as I was moving, glaring at me, a very unimpressed warning in his eyes, and Bridget behind him, her face hidden by his thighs.

"*I* wasn't lying, Bridget! I told you I wouldn't! Every fucking word was true—but I guess I was the fool, right?"

I thought I heard a little noise—a tiny hiccup of a sob. But I couldn't be sure. Because there were suddenly people rushing from every side, some of them with the black ops kit on, others in coats and... and I was being frog-marched out of the clearing.

I kept looking back over my shoulder to where Jeremy stood, glaring at me, hands clenched at his sides, blocking my view of her.

And then I hacked a single cough of a humorless laugh, because the way he was standing, chin down, eyes on me, feet planted...

Dear God.

It hit me that he was just one more fool who'd fallen for her broken bird vulnerability.

One more idiot who had decided he could protect her—from the world, and from herself.

"We're both victims of the same crime," I called back to him. "Do you realize that? She fooled us both!"

"Ca—I mean, Sam! *No!*" she protested.

But Jeremy turned to look at her on the ground behind him and shook his head, murmuring something I couldn't hear. But I saw his lips move.

Then the medics reached her, all of them dropping to kneel and start checking her out, and she was completely hidden from view.

But he wasn't. Not for a little while longer.

He watched me get marched away, his eyes locked on mine, and his upper lip curled away from his teeth.

"How many times did you fuck her?" I called back. "Huh?"

Jealousy, envy, and *rage* burned behind my ribs. As he passed out of sight I roared my frustration because I knew… I knew there was nothing I could do.

They had me. They were taking me back to a cage.

And it was all her fault.

53. Two Become One

SOUNDTRACK: *Let it Rain* by Kendra Dantes and Pei Pei Chung

~ BRIDGET ~

My head spun so badly, and I was so confused, nothing really registered until Jeremy's team got me back to the parking lot of the park and sat me down in the back of an ambulance they had kept waiting a couple blocks away until they had Cain…

Sam. Until they had *Sam*.

How the hell had this happened?

I kept running through those memories in my head of when he'd taken me down. Specifically, the moment he tore off that mask and looked down at me… and his fierce eyes were pleading, *begging* me to understand—

"You did good, Bridget. I gotta say, I thought you were backing out on us. But you came through." Jeremy stood in front of me in his black, special ops gear, feet shoulder width apart and his arms folded across his chest.

Even with his blonde hair that was just starting to gray, he looked like Captain fucking America. All he was missing was the stars and stripes.

"This is all wrong," I muttered through my teeth. "He's the wrong one. He wasn't the mark—and you didn't tell me you'd been following me."

"We weren't following you, we were following *him,*" Jeremy said sharply. "The convicted felon who appeared suddenly in your life right when you got squirrely? God, you really do think I'm an idiot."

"That's not—"

"I don't give a shit how you want to frame it in your head, Bridget. But that's *exactly* how it happened. When are you going to realize that I'm *not* going to let you kill yourself?"

I closed my mouth with a snap and fixed my eyes on the cement under his feet, frowning.

The truth was, *Cain* had appeared in my life right after that night in the bar. But Sam was… two weeks later? Three? I couldn't quite remember. So had Jeremy really only known about Sam for a week? Or was he hiding the fact that he'd known about Cain since I got drunk that night and started asking for someone to hunt me?

Then it hit me.

Holy shit, Sam was Cain. Had *Sam* killed Richard?

My blood went cold. "Jeremy?"

"What?"

"Did Sam have anything to do with Richard Fitch's death? My old chaplain? The other priest—er, preacher?"

Jeremy shook his head. "Not that we can tell. They were hours apart—confirmed—when Richard died. And the Coroner says it was definitely a heart attack. He'd been on medication for a decade."

Relief washed through me. Then I blinked as a car rolled past with the interior lights on and I caught the briefest glimpse of Sam in the back seat bracketed by a couple of agents, his jaw tight and eyes fixed straight ahead.

I looked at him, pleading for him to see me, to see how sorry I was, how this had never been what I wanted for him.

That I'd thought I was catching Cain so he'd have at least a chance of a future…

But, with the bright lights inside the car, Sam couldn't see me outside in the dark. My chest squeezed. And then went still.

As that car rolled out of the park—slowing only to show credentials and be passed through the cordon Jeremy had placed around it the moment Sam and I disappeared in the forest—everything in my body went quiet. Still.

Dead.

It was an effort to make myself inhale.

Cain was Sam. Sam was Cain.

How was it possible? I'd kissed both of them—how could I have missed… but my mind tracked back to those moments, so few and far between. Cain's desperate, clawing kiss, Sam's tenderness—even when he'd gotten desperate he'd held something back.

But which of them was the real *him?*

Did it even matter? They'd both been lying to me this whole time.

Why? Why would he agree to kill me as Cain, then try to talk me out of it as Sam? Sam had threatened to call the Police! It made no sense! Had this whole thing been a game? Was he somehow connected to my father?

Oh shit.

Oh, shit.

I looked up at Jeremy, who frowned deeper. "What is it?"

"You knew? That Sam was Cain—my stalker? You knew they were the same?"

"I knew you had this fucker following you around, and that for whatever reason, you kept going to see him too. Nice, hiding that little plan, by the way, B. If you think I'm ever trusting another word out of your mouth, you're fooling yourself."

"Cut the shit, Jeremy. Did you find any links between him and my dad? Did my father send him? Was this all just one more of his mind-fucks?" *Had I been wrong about Cain? Had I caught a true monster after all?*

Jeremy stared at me a second, his expression softening a hair.

Adrenaline shoved through my veins. "Tell me."

"Sam served his time in the same prison, some of it on the same floor. We don't have proof that they're associates. Yet. We're looking into it."

No. *No!*

My heel started hopping and Jeremy clocked it right away.

"Leave it alone," I said, biting my cuticle that kept catching.

"Bridget," Jeremy said in the tone he got when he was being *concerned.*

"I said, leave it."

He sighed. Neither of us spoke while the medics checked me over again, eventually complimenting me on how low my heart rate was.

"...under the circumstances, that's impressive."

"Cold as ice," I muttered, my heel still tapping on the steel step of the ambulance.

Jeremy was on the phone, but with his back to me, I couldn't hear what he was saying over the sound of all the people nearby, and the running engine of the ambulance.

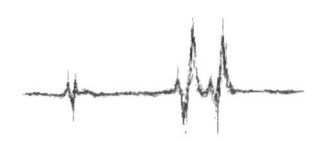

Two hours later we were at the office and he took me into one of the interview rooms that they used for "clients" who needed psychological assessment.

I'd been in those rooms more times than I could count. They were definitely more comfortable than the police interrogation rooms, but I still wasn't impressed.

As Jeremy and two of his colleagues offered me a seat on the thick couch, I dropped into it, crossing my legs and arms and staring at him sullenly like I was still sixteen—which was how old I was when we met.

I didn't realize I was rapidly tapping my heel until Jeremy took his own seat, glanced at my foot, then back up to my eyes.

"He's not even in this building, Bridget. Relax. You're going to be fine. We've got this."

No, they didn't. They didn't have it all. And neither did I.

I'd done a lot of fucked up shit in my lifetime, but this was the first time I was pretty sure that I screwed over one of the good guys.

God, I hoped it was the first time. And the last.

This wasn't what I'd been trying to do.

I shook off the dark thoughts as Jeremy started asking me questions that made it very obvious he'd known a lot more than he let on.

I was pissed.

At one point, when another agent asked me about Ronald breaking into my house, I glared at Jeremy. "You knew, and you didn't stop him?!"

"Val told us what happened, but I thought you *invited him*," Jeremy growled, looking just as pissed as I was. "That's when I started following Priestley and monitoring you more closely."

But I wasn't backing down. "You promised I could have my life back! You said after that psycho wanted to suck out my intestines that I could bring them to you when *I* felt like it. You said you wouldn't follow me anymore!"

"And I wouldn't have if you'd kept talking. But dear God, Bridget—talk about toeing the line. You called me in *yesterday.*"

My stomach twisted up and a wave of nausea washed through me.

I'd been an informant and asset to the FBI since I was twelve years old—the first time they had recorded me talking to my dad's associate on the phone. At fifteen they'd used me as bait for one of Dad's henchmen who suddenly showed up in town. And when I was twenty-two, I unwittingly fucked a guy from the mob and ended up getting embroiled in an active investigation.

Jeremy had been *thrilled.* He'd been my handler since I was sixteen.

But it turned out, when you threw together a reckless disregard for life, borderline antisocial personality disorder, and the freedom that came with all your actions being sanctioned by *law enforcement*, things could get hairy.

The FBI had always insisted on making me see doctors—the ones who tracked my heart monitors and the check-ups I got twice a year—as well as therapists and behavioral counselors, but I'd never trusted any of them. It was obvious most of them were only checking boxes to make the cash.

Jeremy got mad when I almost died—twice—while in the care of those people. Which was when he forced the Bureau's hand and made me start seeing Gerald instead.

Gerald was different. Better. But the rest of these people…

I huffed, shaking my head. Life was just one big love-fest around me. Selfless care oozing from every pore…

I ground my teeth as Jeremy launched into the *debrief* of this *operation* that I had known *nothing about.*

"…good news is that you delivered, Bridget. Headquarters were getting nervous, but this is going to remind everyone why we worked with you in the first place." He leaned forward, elbows on his knees, eyes piercing. "I'm proud of you."

I gave a one-shouldered shrug and blinked back tears because I'd been here before.

But this was the first time I'd ever cared.

It had always been a game before. Something I dared myself to do. Something to make life interesting. A thrill to walk the line and see just how close I could get to the Grim Reaper without actually being taken.

The guys I'd taken down before had deserved it. I'd had my fun, with protection to lean on, while doing the world a favor. It was a win-win.

But the last one had turned out to be a fucking *serial killer.* That had been scary, and something inside me never really recovered. After that, the whole *wanna die* thing wasn't a half-joke anymore.

The risk-taking wasn't just acting out. I had been tempting God.

When I went to the park tonight I'd already called Jeremy in, but I had told him I didn't know how it was going to go down. I'd known it was possible Cain would reach me first, and I'd die. And… there were times that felt like a relief.

I hadn't told Jeremy about Cain because right from the beginning it felt like Cain wasn't for the FBI. He was for *me.* Because ever since the serial killer, I had been toying with the idea of just going through it. Fantasized about it. Imagined Jeremy coming to pick up my latest predator and arriving just a fraction too late, so they'd kill me *before* he arrested them.

But this time… this time I had hoped he would stop Cain from becoming one of those monsters. Jeremy was supposed to keep him alive so I could get to know him outside of this masked, mysterious, insane hunt.

That was, if I could ever get him to forgive me.

But now?

Sam?

I'd walked away from Sam to save him from myself, and instead, I was going to be the one to bring him down when I didn't even want to!

God, I was such a fucking mess.

"...Our only real risk is that we're open to accusations of entrapment. Priestley has connections, and his lawyer is a shark. But don't worry, Bridget. We'll coach you through it. We'll go over all the transcripts and the reports before Court. Make sure you don't slip. But for now, don't answer questions without our lawyers present. Are we clear?"

We were. Except he was wrong.

I *had* been the one to put myself out there, to tempt him in. And if I'd known it was Sam I was getting, I never would have brought Jeremy in at all. Not even close.

Of course, it turned out Jeremy had brought himself in. I should have known, but *fuck*.

How had everything gone so wrong?

Then I reminded myself that I had been setting myself up for fun, trying to get around Jeremy. I'd thought I was so clever... Yet, I was too stupid to realize Cain and Sam were the same person.

What a fucking idiot.

My heart thudded slowly, like my blood was too thick.

"He's not what you think he is," I said quietly.

Jeremy, who'd been discussing "forward planning" with the other two guys, went quiet and turned to look at me.

"What did you say?" he asked carefully.

"I said... he's not what you think he is. He's not a killer. Not like—"

"A convicted voyeur, sexual assault *on a woman,* and he had a weapon, Bridget. Do not tell me you're somehow twisting that into *innocence?"*

"He threw the knife away. I didn't even ask him to."

"He'd probably gotten wind that we were there and was just trying to improve his case. He could still suffocate you with his bare hands, after all. He's a strong guy."

I glared at him, but he just glared back.

"Do not tell me you were actually convinced by all that spluttering and—"

"He used to be dark—which was when he was convicted. But he's changed. He's turned his life around. He's a *good guy."*

"He's a fucking felon with a record as long as your arm, and he was planning to *kill you,* Bridget. We pulled his kit—in the bag he carried into the forest, he had night vision goggles, another knife, zip ties, and some scarves I assume were to gag you. His car had duct tape, and—"

"And he had me at knifepoint and did nothing."

"Because we showed up!" Jeremy protested.

I just stared at him, my head spinning. Now that my heart had slowed down and I wasn't feeling nervous anymore, all I could do was think *back*. All the things Cain had said—was Sam right that he'd never actually said he would kill me? I had a strange notion that he was. And he'd bailed on me when I said I wanted to live. I'd thought it was because those were the rules of the game. But now…

"Has he been booked yet?" I asked quietly.

Jeremy shook his head. "We've got some questions for him before things get official."

I wanted to laugh in his face, but I swallowed it back. "I need to talk to him."

"Abso-fucking-lutely not."

"You said yourself we're going to lose this on entrapment—"

"No, I said his lawyer is going to try and say that. We'll fight it."

"But it's better if we don't have to. Let me talk to him. Let me get him to incriminate himself. He pursued me, Jeremy. He *knew.*" It was all bullshit of course, but I needed Jeremy to give me a chance to talk to Sam, so I could explain. Apologize. Plead for forgiveness.

…The way Cain got soft and started issuing careful instructions when I got winded the first time he took me down…

…the rage he held for Ronald and the way he'd carried me into the bathroom and stripped me so carefully… the aftercare… no wonder he never fucked me. Not once.

…that moment tonight when he had me caught and could have slit my throat, and he tossed the blade. It flashed as it turned over and over before disappearing into the bushes…

His eyes pleading with me… "I was always going to try and convince you not to go that far. I always planned to disappear when you changed your mind—it's what I do! And I did… when you said you wanted to live, I walked away! But I couldn't let you go. And you didn't either and… it wasn't supposed to be this way, Bridget. I didn't know you'd come to the church—I wasn't even supposed to be there! But I can see now, it was meant to be…"

"I'M NOT LEAVING YOU!"

"Bridget!"

I blinked out of the memory of Sam squatting in front of me, begging me to understand, to find Jeremy sitting in the chair across from me, leaning closer, his elbows on his knees, and his fingers twined, watching me warily.

"I'm not putting you back in his hands, Bridget," he said firmly. "I'm sorry. It's too risky."

I wanted to scream. "Are you fucking kidding me—you'll let me walk into the dark with a *serial* killer, but talking to a *good man* in a cell is too risky? That's bullshit!"

He pointed at me. "I've done *nothing* but run around after you since you were a kid. Protecting you from yourself as much as these assholes. And this whole arrangement was *your* idea, let's just remember that!"

"So let me talk to him and—"

"No," Jeremy snapped. "You're a loose cannon, Bridget. And it's getting worse. We're not doing any more pick ups until you've had some… treatment."

My blood ran cold. "Treatment? You just told me I did good! Now I'm getting punished for doing *exactly* what I said I would do?!"

"By the *bare fucking minimum.* The boss won't know the difference, so we're clean, thank God. But fuck, Bridget. I'm not an idiot. I know what you were doing. I'm just glad you made the right decision in the end."

I scoffed. "The *right* decision—to give you what you want."

"No, Bridget—to fucking live! You think I put up with any of this shit from my other informants? You think I monitor your dad's associates just for kicks? No, I do that to keep *you* safe. But you're getting more reckless, not less. I'm not going to stand by and watch you get yourself killed when I could have stopped it. We're done with this. No more. Not until a *doctor* tells me you can do this without… going dark."

"That is such bullshit."

"Yeah, B, such bullshit that I care about what happens to you," he muttered, picking up his files and phone, slapping them all together, then tucking the stack under his arm as he got out of his chair and started for the door. The other two followed him without a word.

I sighed, muttering curses under my breath as I got to my feet to follow them out, but my head was still spinning with theories on how to convince them to let me see Sam. However Jeremy reached the door and saw me coming and turned to face me.

"Not you, you're staying here," he said quietly, moving aside so the other two could get out.

"The fuck I am," I snapped, hurrying closer. "You are *not* caging me, Jeremy! I did my job!"

"And we need to make sure you didn't get even more unhinged in the process."

"What the—"

"You're going to stay here, have a cup of decaffeinated coffee, and a chat. If he says you can go home, you can go home. But until then—"

"What the fuck are you *talking* about?"

"Sit your ass down and breathe, Bridget. Just… fucking breathe for a few minutes," he muttered, then stalked out, shutting the door too hard behind him.

And I heard it latch and *click.* Which meant they'd locked me in.

"YOU FUCKING ASSHOLE!" I screamed at the door. I pounded on the door with a fist, screaming at him—throwing curses and rude gestures at the security cameras where I knew they'd be watching. *"FUCK YOU! FUCK ALL OF YOU!"*

I whirled from the door and started across the room, uncertain what I was going to do, but needing to move.

But then I heard the door click again and I whirled… to find Gerald stepping inside with a folder under his arm and a grim look on his face.

He closed the door—it clicked again, *dammit*—then looked at me, his expression sad.

My entire body deflated.

Fucking *Gerald?*

"Seriously?" I hissed.

"I'll talk to him, Bridget. I'll tell him that's not how to handle this kind of—"

"I'm not doing this with you now," I said, turning on my heel and storming back to the couch.

"Yes, you are," Gerald sighed. I could hear his footsteps following me, heavy and slow.

"No, I'm not."

I was pacing the floor between the coffee table and the couch as Gerald took the seat where Jeremy had been a moment before and put his file on the little side table next to it before sitting back and taking a deep breath, then freezing. Then sniffing a couple times, frowning deeply.

"This chair smells like bacon," he said, pretending to be confused.

Despite myself, I snorted. It had been a joke for a long time. Gerald knew I called Jeremy a pig. But then I straightened my face and glared at him.

"You aren't funny," I muttered.

He shrugged, watching me carefully. "I'm just being observant," he said as he opened the file next to him and pulled out a sheet of paper, then pulled a pen from his pocket and clicked it. "Let's get started. The sooner we do, the sooner I can get you out of here."

"I said, I'm not doing this with you right now," I snapped.

"And I reminded you that you have no choice. Come on, Bridget. You can't really believe they'll just let you run loose without an assessment after *that.*"

"I don't give a flying fuck what *they* want. This was never—"

"Bridget," he said quietly, a strange weight in his tone.

I stopped pacing and turned to look at him, folding my arms. "What?"

He sighed. "They won't let you out of here without my sign off. And *I* can't do that unless I'm certain you're stable enough to be alone without being a risk to yourself."

My jaw dropped "I'm not fucking suicidal! I just want to die—you said you understood the difference!"

"And I do."

"Then leave me the fuck alone!"

"Not until we talk about what happened tonight and… and we come up with a plan of action for what you do if you hit crisis. Because… I'm sorry, Bridget, but I'm not seeing a woman in control of her world and empowered by bringing down the bad guy. I'm seeing a woman on the edge, and I'm *terrified* of where this will take you if something doesn't change."

"You're always fucking terri—"

"Is that how you want to do this, Bridget? You want to make this one more fight we have to have?"

"I wouldn't be fighting if you and Mr. Pork Chop weren't holding me against my will!"

"You deal with Jeremy however you want, I'm not here for him. I'm here for you."

"Well, I am saying I'm fine and let me the fuck out of here."

"And what if they find out that the guy you fell for is connected to your father? What if he turns out to be a plant, Bridget? Are you going to be fine then?" he asked quietly.

Somewhere deep inside, the glass around my heart went fragile and brittle, and started to crack.

I went still. "You fucking *asshole,"* I muttered through numb lips.

Gerald shook his head and looked down at his paper sadly, but he didn't write anything. When he looked back up at me, his eyes were pained. "Bridget, I'm sorry," he said slowly.

"For what?"

"Because these pricks have never understood what you're going through. But I do."

"Bullsh—"

"I'm sorry that it feels like no matter who you trust, they always turn out to have ulterior motives."

I shook my head and cursed, but that glass around my heart shivered again.

"…Sam served some of his time in the same prison. We don't have proof that they're associates yet. We're looking into it…"

"There are thousands of men in that prison—" I started, knowing how pathetic I sounded. But Gerald wasn't done.

"I'm sorry that it seems like no matter how hard you try, you always get deceived by the people you care about."

I flinched.

"I'm not deceiving you, Bridget. But I think Sam was."

Sam's eyes, pleading. "…Everything I said was true. All of it—it was real. I changed my life. God changed my life—"

"Stop," I whispered.

Gerald shook his head, but his expression dropped to misery. "Sweetheart, I am so *deeply* sorry that Cain—or Sam, or whichever one is his real name—might not turn out to be who you thought he was."

I hissed a curse and recoiled from that statement, fought it in my mind.

He never fucked me. Not once. Not even when I gave him permission. Not even when I begged!

I was going to talk to Sam. I would find a way to *make* him answer my questions if it was literally the last thing I did. Because apparently, while I'd been busy falling in love with two different men, they were the same guy. So that meant either both of them loved me… or neither of them did.

And then I realized… I'd brought the law down on a man who was a convicted felon, a Primal Dom, and a preacher who'd turned his life around.

If I'd been any one of those, I would never have forgiven me. Let alone all three.

I did this.

It was me.

That thin wall around my heart caved, the glass shattering and sending shards of glass plunging into my heart so it spasmed and shrieked with pain.

But this time it didn't stop.

The pain started in my heart, but radiated out. I clutched at my chest.

Gerald watched me, his brows pinching down. "Bridget, what—"

I sucked in a breath and clutched at my chest, and suddenly he came alive.

"Oh, shit, Bridget—is it your heart?!"

I couldn't talk. I tried. But the pain was so bad… I stumbled forward, throwing my arms up, towards him, trying to grab his shirt, but my hands wouldn't work properly.

Murmuring reassurance and muttering curses, Gerald caught me and quickly ushered me to the couch, laying me down, and screaming for help as he checked my pulse and—

Pain. Nothing but pain—and a hole in my chest that started sucking the light from my field of vision.

It was an odd sensation… kind of like sinking away from reality. As if I could see and hear what was happening outside my body, but it didn't touch me.

Somewhere, deep inside, I was vaguely aware that Gerald was bent over me, his face painted in fear and determination, and there were pounding feet and lots of voices.

But then the room got dimmer and those lights flashed on the edges of my vision—except, in a perfect, circular halo this time. All the way around. Not just in the corners.

And as I sank further from Gerald's quick, efficient movements and instructions, I started to laugh.

Because what fucking irony that on the very same night I found a reason to live, my body would finally betray me?

And they said God didn't have a sense of humor.

54. Can You Hear Me?

SOUNDTRACK: *Shout* by Sleeping Wolf

~ BRIDGET ~

ME: Sam, I almost died.
ME: I had what they're calling a *cardiac event.*
ME: I really want to talk to you.
ME: I hate you.
ME: I also think I love you.
ME: Who are you?
ME: Have we met?
ME: I wish you were here.

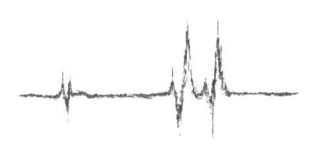

It was almost a week before they let me out of the hospital. I'd felt fine after the first two days, but the doctors kept insisting I needed "monitoring." They gave me back my phone, but not my car keys.

I suspected Jeremy's hand in that. Or maybe Gerald since he said he wasn't going to sleep from the moment they discharged me.

But I did everything they asked me to. Took every pill, ate every bite, and answered every question with a tone as close to helpful as I could manage. And eventually they had to admit that I was fine.

Well, I was as fine as I had ever been.

Jeremy had already said that he'd give me a ride home from the hospital when they discharged me. But I might have chatted with a nurse who'd heard rumors about me and shared earlier in the week that she'd suffered in former toxic relationships. I *might* have implied that Jeremy was an abusive ex-boyfriend, and gotten her help to get out of the hospital before he showed up the morning I was discharged.

She even helped me rent a car so I didn't have to drive mine because they had the keys, and I knew they'd have trackers on it.

When I got home I was wearing hospital sticky-socks, because no one knew what had happened to my shoes. But at least they'd found the rest of my clothes.

And it turned out they'd returned my car to my garage. Which meant they'd also been inside my house.

I parked the rental out on the street.

The first thing I did when I walked in the door was cry. In the shower.

Then, with red eyes and wearing my pajamas, I ventured into my office. And even though nothing had changed, and I couldn't find anything that had been moved, somehow I knew... Jeremy had sent a team here.

So my car had trackers. And my computer had either been replicated, or was now infested with some kind of mirroring software.

They'd see everything I did.

So, I did what they expected and checked into the dark web, answered messages from Nate. Checked Cain's profile. And even opened my email, though I ignored the one from Jeremy, because pissing him off was a little tiny thread of joy in the middle of an entire existence of… numbness.

For a second, I considered going back to *Vigori*, just to see if I could drum up some enthusiasm for *something.* But no… When I thought about getting railed by some random Dom my heart rate barely went up.

God, I was dead inside.

I went to bed, and I actually slept…

…and when I woke up the next morning I didn't want to move. I didn't want to get out of bed. I didn't want to talk to anyone, or see, or be seen. My blood felt sluggish and cool. I had no energy, and no motivation.

I picked up my phone because it was habit, but the only notification was a text from Gerald, and I didn't have the energy to read it.

It occurred to me in that moment that if I just lay in this bed and never left it… no one would notice. At least, not for a really long time.

And that thought scared me.

And the first thing I wanted to do was call Sam.

I started to shake and knew I needed to distract myself or this was going to get really dark, so I opened YouTube, looking for something to get my mind off everything… to find the local news channel video, front and center on my homepage.

DARK PRIEST OUT ON BAIL, FORMER PARISHIONER UNEASY.

I couldn't click the video fast enough and cursed as an ad played first, then finally the story, introduced by the local news anchor who looked like his hair was made of wax.

"Locals are uneasy today as District Court Justice Marklin in Salem confirmed that Samuel Priestley, dubbed the *Dark Priest,* was released on bail two days ago after several character references that the judge himself described as *very earnest,* were supplied by highly regarded witnesses that included another judge.

"Parishioners at the Church of Christ in Dayne, where Priestley was recently filling in after the death of the previous pastor, had mixed reactions to the news."

The image hard cut to an older woman with white hair looking worried, speaking to a nodding journalist holding a microphone in front of her face.

I couldn't even take in the words, because all I could hear was my own breathing and the thoughts screaming in my head.

Fucking *bail?*

Sam was out?!

Sam was *free?*

And he wasn't replying to my messages?

What the fuck was happening?

I threw back the covers and dressed so fast I almost toppled over before I got my yoga pants pulled all the way up.

"Jeremy," I whispered as I ran out to the rental car, my heart pounding in my chest. "What the fuck are you doing?"

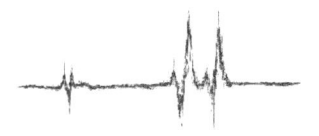

I got to Sam's house in forty-five minutes, with my heart rate just over ninety beats per minute.

The car tires squealed as I tore up his driveway and slammed on the brakes, throwing the car door open and running to the front door, pounding on it like a mad woman.

"Sam?! Sam, I know you're out! I know you're free! Open the door!"

But there was nothing. My heart didn't slow though. I caught a whiff—the tiniest scent of Cain and my entire bloodstream lit up.

I tore around the house towards that back lawn surrounded by the untended gardens and old trees—and slid to a halt when I found Sam standing stock-still on the old, cracked patio, his eyes wide, and his expression wary.

My heart *swelled.* And then froze.

I opened my mouth and...

"You knew him," I accused without preamble. "You knew my father."

Sam's eyes narrowed, but he shook his head. "Not like that," he said in Cain's voice.

"You're lying."

His lip tightened in rage. "I am *not* the liar here."

He tensed, obviously prepared to march me out of there, but I could finally take a deep breath.

I believed him.

My heart *sang.*

"Sam—" I rushed forward, but he was already backing up, his hands held up, palms towards me.

"You can't be here, Bridget. They have a restraining order against me—"

"I don't give a flying *fuck* about a restraining order—why aren't you answering my texts?"

He stopped backing up, but his shock turned to rage. "Because you *set me up!* I blocked your number! You can't seriously think—"

I took the two or three steps left between us and threw myself into his chest, wrapping my legs around his waist and my arms around his neck and planted a kiss on his mouth.

He turned his head away, grimacing, his forehead creased to lines. He tried to push me off, but I didn't miss that he was still careful not to hurt me.

"Stop. Bridget, you have to stop."

"No!"

"I'm not supposed to be within a hundred feet of you!"

"I don't care."

"Well, I do!" he snapped, prying my arms and legs off of him, forcing me to stand in front of him, and putting a hand up in front of me when I took another step closer. "I don't know what game you're playing, but I'm *not.* I'm not touching you, I'm not kissing you, and I'm not going to let you destroy my life—*again.*"

"I'm not trying to destroy your life, you idiot! I'm trying to talk to you! Because I get it!"

"Get what?!"

"I get it! Cain! Sam! The two of you… you're one person. Not normal. Definitely not normal—I get it!"

His head was turned slightly away from me, and his brows pinched. There was a moment when his eyes softened and he swallowed, but then his whole face shuttered, and he shook his head and backed away again.

"No, no, you need to get out of here. They've already got me on breach of parole. If they listen to you, I'm going back to prison, and I'm not coming back out. I can't do it, Bridget. I just can't!"

"You won't have to."

"Why? Are you going to get yourself killed before the trial? I guess at least then they'd know that this was on *you!*" he spat—and I heard tones of Cain's growl in the gravel of his voice again.

My heart danced. I knew I shouldn't be smiling, but I was.

"No! But that's the point! I don't want to testify against you. I don't… you aren't… you weren't what I was hunting for, Sam. But you're everything I need."

He blinked at me, staring, then shook his head slowly. "You're out of your mind. Is this another sting? You're wearing a wire, aren't you? You're going to—"

"No!" Even though I was smiling, it was true I was getting a little desperate. He didn't trust me because I brought the FBI to his door. I understood that. But I needed him to trust me. I needed him to tell me the truth. Then I had a burst of inspiration.

I pulled out my phone with shaking hands, turned it around and set it to video, before starting to record.

"My name is Bridget. My original legal last name was Reynolds, but I go by several different last names now. My father was Gordon Reynolds. And I am a criminal," I said, confidently.

Sam's eyes bulged and my heart thumped, and I smiled wider.

"I was looking for guys on the dark web, and when I encountered Sam Priestley, he was the only one who tried to convince me *not* to get myself killed. He was the only one who tried to help me instead of egging me on. I went after him because I'm deeply attracted to him, and wanted to make him break his vow to God and fuck me silly. He still hasn't done that, but I'm not giving up."

"Bridget—" he sighed, dropping his face in his hands, but I kept going.

"I know that Sam Priestley isn't a murderer. And he isn't even a criminal anymore. I pulled him into this whole stupid plan. The man is innocent. And… and I'm in love with him."

Sam went very still, his entire body frozen. His head jerked up and his eyes locked on mine.

Suddenly terrified, I dropped my phone to my side and looked at him, my heart dancing double-time now because I was scared shitless that I'd really fucked this up, and he was just going to call the cops and get me out of here.

"Did you… why did you say that?"

"Because I don't lie, either. Not when it's important," I said quietly, then swallowed hard when the tension on his face disappeared and he scoffed.

"Now I know you're lying–"

"No, Sam. I didn't. Everything I told you was the truth."

"Well, you left a *whole fucking lot out!*" he bellowed, then cut himself off, rubbing his face with his hand and muttering to himself.

"I mean, I'm not the only one…" I pointed out, but I was wincing. When he just looked at me flatly without responding, I lifted up the phone again. "Look, just tell your lawyers to ask for my phone files for the trial. You have the weapon to destroy me now. Even if I delete it, *trust me,* the feds can dig it up. But I won't delete it."

"Why… why would you do that?"

"I just told you—"

"No, Bridget. *Why would you?* Is this just another self-sabotage? Is this a game?"

Tears were starting to pinch the backs of my eyes. "No, Sam! This is the opposite of that!"

"Then what—"

"You said it the very first time. The very first line."

"Said *what?*"

I swallowed hard and prayed he'd remember. "You said you knew how to make me feel alive. And you were right."

His entire body slumped, and his eyes went dark. "That was Cain. Cain is a part of me that's not healthy, Bridget. I've been trying to use that monster for good, but—"

"No, Sam. Please. Listen to me."

He looked down at me warily.

I cleared my throat. "You might have meant it as Cain, but… but it's true for *all* of you. You're perfect. I *knew* Cain was what I wanted, but he scared me too. And then you came along. And you were everything I *needed.* But I didn't think you were strong enough. I thought I'd destroy you."

Sam raked a hand through his hair, the lines on his face growing deeper. "I hate to break it to you, Bridget, but you already—"

"Please! Don't! I came here to tell you, I don't want to testify against you. I don't want you in jail, or prison. I don't want them to breach your parole. I don't want *any* of this."

"But you're the one who called the FBI!"

"No, I didn't. Not until the very last minute and that was when… that was when I thought it was *just* Cain and I thought… I thought maybe we could get him help and… and maybe there would be a future where… where we could be together…" I said lamely, hearing the emptiness of that crazed hope as the words passed my lips.

"We? You mean you and Cain?"

I nodded.

Sam gaped at me. "Are you actually *insane?* You thought putting me in prison would make me *trust* you?!"

"No! No, I just… I knew if you killed me there was *no* future—"

"I was *never going to kill you!* I was trying to get you to see that there were things worth *living for!*" he roared.

I wanted to cry. "But I didn't know that! I *needed* you!" I said, my voice cracking so I had to take a second, take a breath, close my eyes, get myself under control. When I got myself together and opened my eyes, Sam was staring at me, searching my watery gaze, his eyes flickering between a fierce blaze, and a confused pleading.

I swallowed hard and made myself speak calmly. "I thought I was losing you," I said hoarsely. "And that made me desperate. If you were going to be out of my life I wanted to be gone too. So, I thought… I thought if I got Jeremy to catch you there was at least a *chance*. Maybe they'd lose the case. Maybe I could find a way to help you and then you'd listen… or… I don't know," I sighed, shaking my head. "All I know is, the second I heard you were out I came. I had to see you. I need you, Sam–or Cain. I need *both* of you. And you… you don't need your lawyer's help, Sam. You need *me.*"

A low, tormented noise vibrated in his chest. "You can't say stuff like that—"

"I can when it's true."

His forehead crinkled, and he swayed towards me, but then he shook his head and took another step back. "No, no. This is a trap. They've set you up because—"

"No one knows I'm here, Sam. I didn't bring my car. And this phone is a dummy. I'm not wearing a wire. I'll show you." I started unbuttoning my shirt to show him, but his eyes went wide and he rushed forward, grabbing my hands to stop me. But even when I did, he didn't let go.

He stood over me, his eyes shadowed and fearful… and fierce.

"If you don't testify, they'll subpoena you," he whispered. "And you'll go to jail if you refuse. You can't refuse."

"I don't care. I'm in love with you and… you're what I need. I'm *alive* with you, Sam. I've never been alive before. *Please.*"

He searched my gaze, his handsome face pinched and wary. But then he lifted one hand to my jaw, cupping my face slowly, his eyes still flickering back and forth between mine like he didn't think he could believe what he was seeing.

He was leaning closer, stepping in, and I leaned in too, up on my toes, sliding hands up his chest to his shoulders, reaching for the back of his neck as he leaned down—but then he froze.

His nose just inches from mine, he froze.

"Is this real?" he whispered.

I nodded, smiling happily. "It's real—"

He groaned, *"God help me,"* and took my mouth with a ferocity that set me backwards. Mouth open, tongue delving, fingers clawing at me, a ragged groan in his chest, Sam *kissed me.*

And he kissed me like fucking *Cain.*

Ecstatic, I threw my arms around his neck and pulled him closer, almost biting the tip of his tongue off with my enthusiasm. But he just growled and splayed a hand between my shoulder blades, pulling me closer and tilting his head—

"Shit!"

He tore away from me, staggering backwards, clawing both hands into his hair and shaking his head. "We can't. We can't—even if we could, we can't. I can't let you take the fall for—"

"I don't care!"

"Well, I do!" he roared. "Don't you get it, Bridget? The only reason I hunt anymore is to try and *intervene.* Being the one who a broken woman can trust not to take things too far—you aren't the only one out there, you know! But now? There's no winning here—if you take the fall, I go free, but you're in jail. And if I give myself up, you'll be alone—God, this is such a mess! You put us in such a mess!"

"But—"

"There's no fucking buts! Just go home! Leave! Do what they tell you to do! I'll get my lawyer to try and find a technicality to get me off. I am *not* going back to prison. I didn't earn that this time! But... I'm also not letting you throw your life away to save mine."

"But it's okay for you to throw away yours?" I asked carefully. "Because you know what they'll do, Sam. Unless

I fail them on purpose, they'll find a way. All Jeremy sees is your past. But I know that's not you anymore. I *know* that. You can't give yourself up to save me, either!"

He frowned. "I didn't say I was going to—" He cut off and turned his head, his eyes slowly widening. "Oh my God."

"What?"

His eyes darted left and right like he was looking for a way through something. He turned further from me, but distracted, like he was so deep in his thoughts he hadn't realized he was moving. *"Would it work, though?"*

"What? Sam, what are you—"

He whipped back around to face me. "Are you real, Bridget? Is this for real?"

"Yes!"

"I'm not playing a game—I'm not just… I need to know if you mean all of this."

I nodded, barely daring to hope. "I came here for you, Sam. I've been dead inside since that night. I promise—no games. No lies. I'm not leaving anything out… I mean it."

He blew out a breath. "Then… do you trust me?"

I blinked, but nodded. "I do, Sam. I… I know you'd never hurt me—not even as Cain. I want… I want out of this… for both of us. We can run together and—"

He took the steps to close the space between us at pace, and I smiled because I thought he was going to kiss me again, but instead he grabbed my elbow and started marching me back towards the end of the house.

"If you're real, and you trust me, you go home. You say nothing about this to *anyone.* I'll contact you tonight. Be ready."

"But—"

"No buts, Bridget. We can't risk it. Just go. *Go!"*

He pushed me ahead of him as we were about to reach the end of the house and be visible to those in the street, but I caught myself and turned back to him before I was out in the open.

"Bridget, please—"

I took his face in my hands and pulled him down, kissing him, deep and soft and slow.

He sucked in a breath, then one arm snaked around my waist and pulled me closer. He tipped his head to deepen the kiss further and I sighed into his mouth.

Moments later, he plunged a hand in my hair, pulled my head back, and rasped. "You have to go *now*. I will see you tonight."

Then he gave me one short, desperate kiss and shoved me out past the house, turning on his heel as he sprinted back to the house.

55. Home of the Free

SOUNDTRACK: *Go to Hell* by Letdown

~ BRIDGET ~

I was pacing my living room floor, back and forth, back and forth, well into the night. When it was almost midnight, I began to tremble.

Had he tricked me? Had he just been getting me out of there? Had I been right the first time, that Cain was *actually* a monster?

What was I going to do? I'd taken that video and—

"You're really here alone?"

I gasped and whipped around to find him standing in the small entryway from the back door, staring at me.

It was such an intense moment, and such a *mindfuck.*

From the soles of his shoes, to his throat, he was Cain–dark, stretchy clothing that covered his arms, gloves, the bulk of his muscles hugged by stretch cotton and the smell of night. But his face…

He'd thrown his hood back and wasn't wearing a mask. And he was Sam.

He was fucking *Sam.*

"God, you scared the shit out of me!" I breathed, rubbing my arms because I was goose bumped all over, every hair on my body standing tall.

I was alive.

But he didn't move towards me. Just stood there, staring with a strange, feral intensity.

"Sam, what's going on?"

His throat bobbed. "I had to... do some stuff. Preparations."

"Preparations for what?"

He swallowed again and my breath got shorter.

"I love you too, Bridget. I do. It's so crazy. I... I can't quite explain how it happened—"

"Don't worry, I get it."

"—but I want you to know it's real. And I think... I think I have a solution for us... if you'll agree."

I smiled and a strange warm feeling fizzed in my chest.

Happiness.

I swallowed hard. "What is it?"

He stepped forward, slowly positioning himself within arm's reach, but still not touching me. "I did some research and..."

"And?"

He cleared his throat. "Bridget, no American citizen can be forced to testify against their spouse. If... if I'm your husband, they can't make you do it."

My eyes flew wide as he lowered himself to one knee and pulled a ring box out of his pocket, flipping it open in front of me.

"Bridget..." he murmured breathlessly. "Will... will you marry me...?"

EPILOGUE

~ *SAM* ~

The whole drive to Las Vegas was a mind-fuck.

We took her rental car because it was the least likely to be identified as ours.

Fifteen hours of driving and I didn't feel drowsy at all.

We talked. And *talked*.

Bridget held my hand over the console.

She *smiled*.

My head kept spinning between screaming at me that this couldn't be real, she couldn't really want me—both sides of me—and this had to be some kind of trap... then washing in relief and pure joy because Bridget was *happy*.

She was happy, and it was because of me.

I didn't know how this had happened. I knew it was crazy what we were doing. But I couldn't drive fast enough. Still, I had to stay *close* to the speed limit because we couldn't afford to be pulled over, especially once we crossed out of state.

I was breaching parole again. But it was worth it.

We made it to the Las Vegas Strip just as the sun was going down and the sky was turning purple and pink. Just as all those neon lights began to really glow against the deepening dark.

Bridget had spent the last hour on the phone arranging a hotel room and a chapel.

We were really doing this.

God, is this real?

An hour later, I stood in a white room, with two strange men in suits—one who was a celebrant, and the other who was a butler, or something. I couldn't quite figure out what his title was, but he was helping Bridget get everything she asked for.

I made sure they gave her a veil. I didn't give two shits that she was wearing dark jeans and a hoodie—and she apparently didn't care that I was dressed the same.

We stood in front of those men and we vowed our lives to each other. I held her hand and stared into her eyes and all the problems, all the questions, all the obstacles that were going to try to push us apart just fell away when she spoke.

The celebrant gave us a chance to say what was on our hearts, and her words made me shake.

"Sam, I… I know this is crazy. And I know I'm crazy. But I'm also crazy for you. All of you. You're the only person I've ever met who seemed to understand me. Really understand me. And want the same things I want. I… I know I'm going to let you down, but I don't want to. I want to be with you every day. I want to stand up for you. I want… I just want *you,*" she breathed.

My heart skipped a beat at her big eyes, so wide and fixed on me, like she was a little bit shocked, and a little bit scared, and a little bit awed.

I had to clear my throat before I could speak. I was already holding her hands, but I tugged her a little closer so I was standing over her, looking down. I wanted to kiss her already, but I knew I needed to do this first.

"I've never met someone who saw me… all of me," I said hoarsely, squeezing her hands. "From the first second I saw you, you've never been out of my mind. I'm… stunned to be standing here with you. But so grateful too, Bridget.

This is what I want. *You* are what I've always wanted. Someone who shares every part of me, every day."

"I will," she breathed. "I promise, Sam. I will."

"Me too," I rasped.

I was swaying towards her, drawn in, unable to resist, but the celebrant chuckled.

"Not long now—just bear with me for a moment so we can make this legal…"

I didn't even hear the vows, but I knew what they were.

For better or for worse.
For richer or for poorer.
In sickness and in health.
As long as we both live.

And my entire being sighed with relief when she responded, *"I do."*

I didn't wait for the announcement, I took her face in both hands, pulled her in and took her mouth with every ounce of the desperation and urgency I was feeling. Because I needed her to be *mine.* I needed to brand her. And I knew she felt the same way, because her arms wrapped around me and her fingers dug into my back and she plastered herself to me from knee to chest…

One. We were one.

Or about to be anyway.

Finally.

I would have taken her right then and there, but the celebrant cleared his throat and after a few more kiss-drunk moments, we broke apart. He smiled apologetically and muttered that we needed to sign the contract.

My hands were shaking, but I gripped her with one hand while I signed with the other, and she did the same. Then they witnessed for us, gave us our certificate, and we were moving again, both jogging through the halls, Bridget laughing and smiling, running out to the car—where she drove because she'd already booked the hotel and knew where we were going.

I could barely think straight. Kept clawing hands through my hair and shaking my head because I could barely believe this was real.

I didn't think I'd ever been happier—or more terrified.

The drive to the hotel was short—and fast because Bridget drove like she was testing for Formula One. The tires gave a short squeal when she stopped in the parking lot, but then suddenly… nothing.

She was sitting, staring at the bushes in the garden at the base of the hotel, her hands gripping the steering wheel so hard her knuckles were white.

I blinked and reached for her leg. "Bridget, what's—"

"Is this real, Sam?" she breathed, then licked her lips and turned to look at me, her eyes wide. "Was all of that real?"

I nodded slowly. "It was for me. Was it real for you?"

She nodded too. "That's why I'm so scared."

I took a deep breath. "Me too. But I don't want to go back."

"Neither do I. I just…"

She stared at me and for the first time ever, it seemed like she just opened herself up—no badass indifference, no sarcastic brutality, no airy, reckless endangerment or dismissal.

She stared at me like a child afraid, and a woman in crisis. "I don't know if I know how to do this," she whispered.

And I knew *exactly* what she meant. I knew, because when I'd first found God, it was exactly what I'd said to Him.

"I get it," I whispered back. "But that's the whole point, Bridget. *You* don't have to do this. *We* do. And now… now I just want to be with you, and enjoy you, and make memories. The rest… the rest we'll figure out *together."*

Her eyes welled a little, but she blinked it away. "Do you promise, Sam?"

"Babe, I just vowed my life to you. I'll give you whatever promise you want."

She gave a quick little nod, but she hadn't let go of the steering wheel and she turned away, looking straight out of the car and at the side of the hotel.

I scrambled, remembering when I'd felt so lost and so adrift… What had helped me?

I needed to help her get grounded.

I needed to give her something *good* to focus on.

So, smiling and squeezing her thigh, I whispered, "Do you want to know what I want to do right now?"

She turned quickly. "What?"

I leaned across the console so my shoulder brushed hers and our faces were only inches apart.

"I want to get you alone, and naked. I want to see every inch of you without any risk of being interrupted, or pulled away," I said hoarsely—and honestly. I let my hand play up the inside of her thigh and her hands tightened even more on the steering wheel. "I want to stroke that soft, soft skin on the inside of your thigh. I want to be skin to skin with you. I want to feel you get wet for me. I want to watch you come again and again and again—and then when it's over, I want to do it again. Bridget… I've waited. I've waited *so long.* Now I want *everything* with y—"

She sucked in a breath and kind of leaped at me over the console, clambering into my lap, kissing me open mouthed and desperate, straddling me, clawing hands into my hair.

Then, just when I thought maybe we were going to do all that *right here,* she pulled back suddenly and met my eyes, her chest heaving with her panting breath.

"Me too," she gasped. "All of that. And anything else too, Sam—whatever you want. I'm game. Just… *yes.*"

I swallowed, gripping her ass because I was keeping her hard against me. My voice, when I spoke, was a deep gravel and her eyes twinkled.

"So… you need to get out of this car *right now,* and go find out what room we're in and text it to me. I need to dodge the cameras as much as I can."

She nodded quickly, biting her lip—which made me groan and kiss her again, and that kept her in the car for another couple minutes until I grabbed the door handle and practically threw her out of the vehicle, my breath panting.

"Go. Now."

She laughed as she stumbled out of the car—then teased me by leaning back in, over my aching, straining lap to grab her little purse and phone from the console, dragging her hand—the one with the ring on it—over my cock as she straightened. Little tease laughed again when I growled.

When she was gone, trotting across the parking lot towards the main entrance, I sat back in the seat and focused, breathing, *praying* that I could relax enough to walk into the hotel without pitching a tent. I tried to distract myself by watching Bridget smiling at the receptionist, talking animatedly, and leaning her elbow on the tall desk so that the little diamond on her finger sparkled.

It wasn't much, but I'd used what savings I had to get her a real ring.

Seeing her smile was like air after being underwater. She *sparkled.* Then and there I made a resolution to make sure she smiled every single day.

Help me get this right, I prayed. *She's perfect for me. Thank you. Now… don't let me fuck this up.*

Then, a couple minutes later she was taking a little wallet from the woman, shaking her head, and smiling even broader, before she stepped away from the desk and started towards the back of the lobby, hunched over her phone.

BEAUTIFUL: Room 7805. There's no external stairs that high, but there's a bank of elevators on the first floor, just inside the exterior door. I'll leave it propped open for you, but get there fast because they usually have alarms if they're open more than a minute or two.

ME: Got it.

I jumped out of the car, grabbed our bags from the back and slung them both over one shoulder, gripping them with one hand as I started towards that exterior entrance. I took the stairs two at a time until I found the door she'd propped open—but Bridget herself was nowhere to be seen.

I smiled, but kept my hood up and my chin down as I got into the hallway, letting the door close behind me, and pushing the button for an elevator, impatiently.

I didn't look up, kept my head down and looked at my phone so the cameras wouldn't catch me, and darted out into the hallway on the seventh floor looking for the signs—and instead seeing Bridget, almost at the other end of the floor, walking quickly with her back to me, and her head down like she was looking at her phone.

Instinctively I slipped behind one of the pillars that extended out of the wall alongside each doorway—and my instincts prickled.

I smiled and leaned out just far enough to get one eye out and see where she was. She was just turning from looking for me, but still walking briskly.

Then I felt my phone buzz in my pocket. Slipping back behind the pillar again, I checked it quickly and smiled.

BEAUTIFUL: Where are you? You can't get into the room without a keycard.

I was about to answer, but then I had an idea.
Peering out again to see where she was, I caught her turning a corner at the other end of the floor and had to slip back behind the pillar quickly so she wouldn't see me.

ME: I'm coming.

I waited a few more seconds, checked that the hall was empty, then trotted the length of the hallway, keeping to the wall so the pillars obscured my position from anyone looking around the corner.

BEAUTIFUL: Oh, to be a man and for it to be so simple.

I snorted.

ME: New rule. Next time we're going anywhere, you don't tell me and I have to find you.
BEAUTIFUL: Great in theory, but with ten floors, it might have taken you a while. I would like to have at least one orgasm before the sun comes up.

Fair point.
I reached the intersection of hallways at the end and peered around—but now it was my line of sight that was obscured by the pillars. But there were only two doors on each side, so very few options. I smiled, and sent her one word.

ME: Soon.

Still uncertain whether she was in the hallway behind a pillar, or had gone into the room and was waiting for me to knock, I crept forward, peering around the first pillar, and mentally cursing when she wasn't there—which meant our door had to be the second one on this side, because I could see the other two from this angle and the numbers were even.

My heart was hammering, my body tightening again in anticipation. But just as I made it to the next pillar, I heard the elevators on the main floor ding.

Cursing, I whipped around the pillar, relieved to see that it was our room, and knocked quietly.

There was no sound for a moment and I shifted the bags on my shoulder, my breath becoming shallow as I imagined her inside—

There was a clunk, and the door swung open and Bridget, *my wife,* stood there in the doorway. Beaming at me.

And naked as the day she was born.

I stopped dead, staring, taking in the sight of her. Adrenaline coursing through my veins as I scanned her gorgeous body all the way up from her toes. I was fully erect immediately—and stunned.

"Hey…" she said quietly… and a little shyly?

I locked eyes with her immediately. I was panting.

"Do you need food or water… a bathroom… anything?" I growled at her, still standing just outside the door.

Her brows went up. "Right now? No. Why, are you hungr—"

She shrieked laughing as I launched myself at her, throwing the bags aside and leaning down to pick her up and throw her over my shoulder, kicking the door closed behind me and slapping her ass as I carried her deeper into the room… and stopped dead.

It wasn't a room. It was a fucking *suite.* A big one.

It had an entryway, because there was a kitchen on the other side of the wall, a long island, then an even longer, wider dining area that ran under the huge windows—they started a couple feet up from the floor and ran all the way to the ceiling, with windowsills so deep Bridget would be able to curl up with a pillow and a book.

"Bridget—" I started hesitantly as the room opened up to my right and then I could see that those windows ran the length of the living room that was large enough for a recliner, a sectional couch, a drink bar, and the door into the separate bedroom, that I couldn't see, but knew had to be just as luxurious as the rest of this place.

"Don't worry, I've got it covered," she said, still giggling, her stomach jumping against my shoulder in a way that made my cock twitch.

"But—"

"I figured we wouldn't be getting out much and… if you're worried about it, you can repay me in services rendered," she said slyly, her voice vibrating against my back.

I took another couple steps into the room, swallowing, because this place was massive and beautiful.

Then she clapped her hand on my back a couple times. "Husband? *God* that seems weird to say, but anyway… Are you going to freak out about this? It's the closest thing I could do to a honeymoon on such short notice."

"No, no, of course not…" I rumbled, leaning down to put her back on her feet, and straightening because I needed to look at her again.

Her face was a little red from hanging upside down over my back, but she tipped her chin up to catch my eyes, smiling, though I could see the uncertainty in her gaze.

I cupped her face with one hand and held her waist with the other, glancing over her back at the stunning room behind her then back down to her shining eyes.

"God bless whoever designed this hotel," I said, low and husky, stroking her cheek.

She arched one brow. "Oh? Why?"

I grinned at her. "Because those window sills are deep enough to sit in… or bend you over."

Her eyes widened and her smile turned saucy. "You should see the shower."

"I'm going to see every inch of this place," I vowed to her, pulling her right up to her toes because I was about to kiss her. "But first, a new rule."

She tipped her head. "You and your rules—"

"No clothes the moment we cross that doorway—ever. For as long as we're here," I growled.

Her smile broadened as I leaned down to kiss her, but then she grabbed my face in her hands and pushed me back.

"Bridget! What—" My voice was muffled against her palm, but she shoved me back and waggled a finger at me.

"The Dom has to play by his own rules. Don't worry, I'll help."

Then she reached for the hem of my hoodie and started pushing it up my torso, wrestling because she was so much shorter than me—and because the button-fly on my jeans didn't want to release. Too much pressure behind it.

But finally, finally, breathless and laughing, I was naked too and she grabbed me immediately, pulling me down into a kiss. I appeased her, but kept leaning down, sliding hands down her back to cup her ass, then pick her up and carry her into the bedroom.

She wrapped her legs around my waist and opened her mouth on my neck, sending a wash of need down my spine as I hurried through the suite with her. I was panting by the time I got her in the bedroom, then wrenched her off and threw her onto the huge, king sized bed.

She shrieked and laughed when she bounced, pushing up to sit. The laughter died on her tongue when our eyes locked, but her smile got wider as she began to back away.

I was crawling onto the bed, prowling towards her. When she tried to evade me, I shot a hand out to grab her ankle and yanked her towards me so fast her head bounced on the bed and she shrieked again.

Her laughter echoed around the vaulted ceiling as I crawled over her, using my weight to press her into the thick bed as I covered her. I couldn't resist kissing my way up her body, teasing her nipples with my teeth until she gasped, then pulling myself up to take her open, smiling mouth.

Plunging my hands into her hair, I tilted her head and delved her mouth with my tongue boldly.

She wasn't smiling anymore. She had already hooked one knee over my hip and was writhing underneath me, rubbing herself against me in time with the kiss, her hands clawing up my back leaving me shuddering as she arched her back and tried to pull me *into* her.

Planting one hand over her shoulder to brace, I reared over her, mouth open, and rocked my hips to draw myself against her slick heat.

Her mouth dropped open and she grabbed my ass with both hands, pulling me against her.

"Don't tease me, Sam," she gasped. "I've waited too long."

I almost choked on my own lust. "You think *you've* waited?" I growled, leaning down and grabbing a fistful of her hair, pulling her head back and nipping at her chin. "Between prison and God, I've practically regrown my virginity."

She snorted, but her jaw dropped when I flexed my hips and held, arching her against the grip I had on her hair. It felt so good I shuddered, and her breath stopped, so I did it again.

"Sam... please."

"I like you begging for me."

"Please!"

Our bodies were already slick, she was gripping me, arching against me, *asking* for me, and I almost lost control. But there was a moment when it all came home to me.

She was here.

She knew me... *all of me.*

And she wanted me.

She wanted me with a fire I could see in her eyes.

It was... humbling. And so arousing, for a second I was genuinely afraid I'd explode the moment I entered her.

So I rocked against her one more time, holding the pressure, then releasing her hair to cup her face and hold myself over her—and I didn't move.

I was panting, so my breath rushed in and out, but so did hers.

"Sam, I said *don't* tease me!"

"I'm not, I'm just... taking it in," I said, my voice gruff with need.

She blinked and her face softened. "Taking in what?"

"You. The miracle that you're here. That you want me. *All* of me."

Her eyes widened and she let go of my ass to trail her fingertips up my back, then along my sides, then around to cup my jaw in both hands, staring at me as if she was awed.

"Sam... you remember you're the *good* guy here, right?" she said, and there was a flash of a shadow as she searched my eyes—a hollow fear in her that made my stomach pang and made me want to fight demons for her.

"This isn't about good or bad, babe," I murmured to her, swallowing as I positioned myself, ready to take her. "This is about *right.* And you are so... so *right* for me."

She nodded. "I am." Her eyes shone and she bit her lip.

"Are you ready?" I murmured, sliding my free hand under her nape, to cup her head and hold her.

She went very still, and there was a flash of panic in my chest—was she having second thoughts.

But then her throat bobbed and…

"I've been ready for you my whole life," she whispered.

"Oh, *God,* Bridget!" I groaned, then took her mouth and plunged into her, taking her in a single, claiming stroke.

Her mouth opened under mine, our twin breaths roaring, mingling. Her head dropped back, and I cradled it as I took her again and she whimpered. Then again, breaking a cry from her throat. Then again.

And again.

And again.

My body quivered with need, every muscle rigid, teeth gritted for control as she met me stroke for stroke and the pleasure coursed through my veins like a drug, my skin tingling, prickling, every hair standing in ovation to the perfect pleasure she clawed from me. As if when her hand clapped to my back, she didn't just reach for my skin, but inside me—diving into my soul and dragging out into the light the parts of me that had been buried for so long in shame, and uncertainty.

It was beautiful. *She* was beautiful.

And so fucking hot, I was going to explode.

"Bridget—"

"I'm almost… keep going… *Sam!*"

I threw back my head and let the guttural roar come, since I was still holding back the rest of me, but I was losing my grip. Arching my back, I planted both hands over her shoulders, bracing her against my wrists as I picked up the pace and felt my body spiraling up and up and up…

I was going to come.

"Bridget… *Fuck!*"

"Sam, don't stop!"

We barely parted before I was plunging into her again, and she rode me, her ankles hooked behind my back, her mouth open—then her eyes widened and began to roll back in her head.

"Sam... Sam... *SAM—*" She cried my name with abandon, her face alight with joy.

Actual joy.

My wife *loved me.*

She wanted me just as desperately as I wanted her—and the monster in me, the creature that had never been satisfied, roared with delight.

"Mine!" I rasped. "Bridget... *you're mine!*"

Her back bowed and her nails dug into my back as her body clenched around me.

My leash snapped.

Still bracing on one hand, I slid the other under the hollow of her arched back and pulled her against me, pounding into her, jaw slack and growling her name, feasting on the sight of her breasts bouncing as she rode the wave of an orgasm that went on, and on, and *on.*

And then I crested that wave with her, the sheer ecstasy detonating at the base of my spine and spiraling out—pleasure, bliss, and fire filling my veins and leaving me shaking and roaring, fisting the quilt under her and shuddering... until I collapsed over her, covering her, cupping my hands over her head and burying my face in her neck, letting my hot breath rush against her skin as my body twitched and jerked in the aftershocks of pleasure.

She grabbed for me, clinging desperately, pulling me against her, in an embrace as frantic as our lovemaking, and just as needy.

"Sam..." she whimpered. "Sam, that was..."

She turned her head, tipping it back to meet my gaze and I made myself focus, my body still trembling, because there was something in her eyes...

Fear?

I blinked. "Bridget, what—did I hurt you?!"

"No! No, I..." her eyes welled with unshed tears and she shook her head, then her eyes screwed shut and her chin crumpled and she buried her face in the crook of my shoulder. "No, I'm just… so *happy,"* she whispered. "And so scared they're going to take you from me."

"Hey, hey—"

I pulled her in, rolling off her only enough that I wouldn't suffocate her, and could wrap my arms around her.

She clung to me, arms and legs wrapped around me, her breathing quick and labored against my neck.

"Bridget… Bridget, look at me," I whispered.

But she shook her head and just held on.

With a heavy sigh, I dropped my chin to kiss her shoulder.

"I love you," I breathed against her neck. "I don't give two shits what anyone else thinks. Or what they try to do to us. God made you for me. You're mine."

"But—" she pulled her head back, her eyes red and shining with tears. But I shook my head.

"No buts, Bridget. You're my *wife.* You're mine forever now. And I will burn down any motherfucker who tries to say otherwise."

THE END

Acknowledgements

Jesus, firstly and forever, thank you for saving me from my own darkness. Thank you for loving me even when I fail. And for showing me what unconditional love really means. Thank you that I always have a safe place to fall. Without you I would have no gifts, and wouldn't even be here. I owe everything to you, and I'll always remain grateful.

Alan, thank you for being the kind of husband that romance books are written about. You dismiss me when I tell you that you're still hot—and that you're #husbandgoals. But trust me. It's real. I couldn't do all of this without your example, and without your support. Thank you for trusting my judgment, and putting our money where my mouth is. I'm praying God blesses *you* for being an amazing, loving, and strong husband and father.

Harry, thank you for laughing with me, and for only judging me for my sexual content a little bit (lol.) I pray when you find your wife she loves you with all the passion and gratitude that you deserve—and that you do the same for her. Now… I guess I can't tell you not to read this stuff anymore. But insert a "mom look" here. I mean, there's permissable, and there's what's *good* for you… You choose. *Wink*

A very special thank you to the Beta Development Reader crew who came with me on REAMstories.com/authoraimee (otherwise known as the #Suspatrol) who have helped me throughout the writing process, both with feedback, and cheering along. Your eyes and hearts have been a *huge* asset to me. I'm so grateful that you're taking this journey with me! (If you'd like to join my advance reader group, you can find it on reamstories.com/authoraimee)

As always, I also have to thank every single one of Author Aimee's Reader Tribe (find us on Facebook!) the most hilarious and loving group of women on the internet! I tell you in every book that you made my dreams come true because it's *true.* You literally make every day a joy, every book a triumph, and every #AuthorFail a funny-rather-than-embarrassing moment. I'll never stop thanking God for you.

Thank you, finally, to *you* for taking the time and investment to be here. Without *you* I couldn't do what I do. I hope you'll seek me out on social media and say hello (you can find all my links on linktree.com/authoraimee) I've been wishing to have you in my life since I was seven years old. So, thank you.

You all changed my life. I will never not be grateful.

Aimee

Other Romances by the Author

Aimee Lynn is a bestselling and award-winning serial romance writer and has several books available right now on Amazon, and various reading apps!

Available on Amazon

Prey for You (Hide & Seek series Book 2)
The King has Fallen (spicy romantasy)
Slave to the Wolf King (dark shifter romance)
The Virgin Hunter (new adult shifter romance)
Beast of Baal (spicy romantasy, *coming 2025*)

Available and complete on your favorite reading apps:

Only on Webnovel
The Anima Series
Falling for the King of Beasts
Taming the Queen of Beasts
Rise of the Dark Alpha (spin off)
Mated to the Warrior Beast

Only on MyFavReads
(Pen name: Aimee Lynn-Lane):
Heart of Fire
The Guardian Alpha

Only on Dreame (Pen name: Aimee Lane)
His Stolen Luna
Also available as audiobook on DreameFM

AND MORE!
Find them all on:
Linktree.com/authoraimee

Printed in Great Britain
by Amazon